AF427463

THE GLASS FROG

J. Brandon Lowry

J. Brandon Lowry
Visit my website at jbrandonlowry.wordpress.com
Printed in the United States of America
First Printing: March, 2022
Trailerback Books
ISBN: 979-8-9864912-0-2

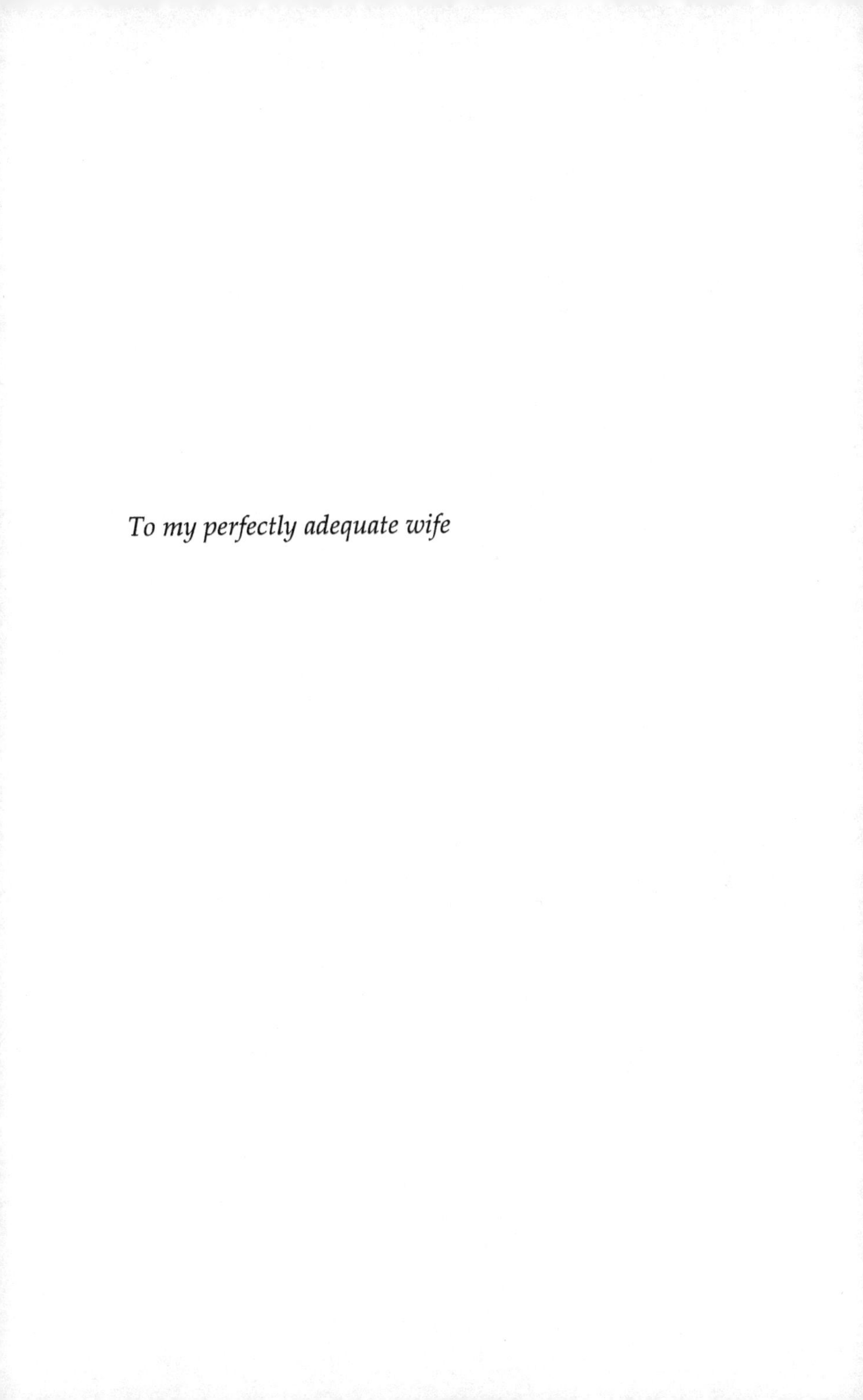

To my perfectly adequate wife

Every Who is shaped by a Where.

In this case, the Where is a tiny coastal village named Seaside. From the beach there is a constant, breathy shhh-ahhh *sound as the waves flow first in, then out, each exhalation coating the simple, whitewashed buildings with a fine, salty mist. Through the village center runs the Queen's Road, a winding ribbon that traces the curving shoreline of the island nation to which Seaside belongs. Grassy, rolling hills surround the village to the north, so that when viewed from above, it appears as a single pearl on a string nestled on a bed of seagrass.*

Seaside was given its unimaginative name by its unimaginative people. In fact, hostility toward creativity and change is a central feature of the Seasider mentality, a proud tradition handed down from generation to generation. They value simplicity, practicality, and—above all—uniformity. For this reason, it has been decreed that every building in the village must adhere to the same basic plan: squarish shape, white walls, dark roof. This arrangement makes it obvious which villagers are lax in their home maintenance, and are therefore not to be trusted. The same principle applies to matters of appearance, behavior, and topics of conversation. Unsurprisingly, the most popular topic of conversation is the failure of others to conform.

Despite its dull name and general sameness, Seaside is actually quite quaint. The village is organized around a central square, where the farmers sell their produce, the fishermen hawk their fish, and the busybodies swap stories. The square is one of only two paved surfaces in Seaside. The other is the Queen's Road, and both are cobbled in stone. The villagers don't mind the lack of paving all that much, as this story takes place in a world that has not yet discovered the commonplace miracles of our technological utopia. In this world, electricity comes from the sky, long-distance communication is delivered by hand, and maps of the world bear images of terrible monsters.

Most of the villagers are happy with the way things are. Most, but not all. There are those who wonder where the road ends and where it begins, those who are curious about the world Out There and the people in it. They are the ones who dare to imagine that life can be different. Better, perhaps. On rare occasions, one of these intrepid individuals actually musters up the courage to leave.

Those who do are never heard from again.

With the matter of Where set aside, it is time to meet our Who—Sophie Farrier, a kind-hearted and imaginative young girl who fits into Seaside about as well as a whale fits into a rowboat, and has been just as uncomfortably shaped. She waits for us on a tall and gently sloping rise known as One Tree Hill. Astute readers will know the reason why . . .

An Unnecessary Guest

The Girl on the Hill

THE EPONYMOUS TREE WAS A GRAND OLD OAK, with thick, gnarled roots and heavy branches that sprawled out in all directions. Sophie lounged comfortably on a tuft of grass beneath that expansive canopy, reading a book. At a glance, she gave the impression of being permanently disheveled. Her clothes were simple, plain, and mostly free of holes. Mostly. Her long, mousey hair kept falling into her face as she read, only to be automatically tucked behind her ear once again. So completely absorbed was she in the fantastic tale that was unfolding on the page that she barely noticed her hair's obstinacy. It was a story about a far-flung kingdom beset by evil; a beautiful princess in terrible peril; a malevolent witch with a host of hideous, monstrous familiars and a lust for vengeance; and the brave, stalwart knight hacking and slashing and stabbing his way through them all. Her eyes rapidly scanned the pages in a mad rush to get to the end.

Only three pages left.

Two more.

One.

With the final words read, Sophie took a deep breath, slammed the cover closed, and tossed the book aside.

"Rubbish."

Sophie pulled a sheet of paper from her knapsack, a list. She scratched *Sir Bridgard and the Woods Witch* at the bottom. It was the thirty-seventh entry on her list, joining such classics as *The Knight of Eryrie by the Sea*, *Roddy Tottenham's Fantastic Misadventures*, and *The Vengeance of the Merling King*. At the top were written the words CHILDISH NONSENSE.

"They're all the same," she complained aloud. This was a normal thing for Sophie. There weren't many other children her age in Seaside, and so far as she knew none of the others even owned a book, so she had no one to share her hobby with. No matter; the oak was a great listener. "Once again, the hero returns without a scratch to sweep the swooning princess off her feet. For once I wish the ending would be different, somehow. New. Unexpected." She continued to ramble, sharing her literary critiques with her oaky friend. If, coincidentally, she happened to be putting off her daily chores by continuing the conversation, well . . . that was a matter of circumstance.

One Tree Hill was a risky place for Sophie to be, on account of the view. The southern slope faced the village, with the beach and the ocean just beyond, all plainly visible from the summit. Common knowledge held that such a marvelous view could lead to dangerous pastimes, such as daydreaming, woolgathering, mooning, and other forms of general ideation. There was no telling what sort of things might occur to a person while sitting beneath that tree.

But there was another risk to being up there, one that only those villagers who had ventured Out There could have warned her against—the call of the hills. They spoke with the voice of the wind, whispering her name every time the breeze caressed the brushy stalks of field grass, and spinning fanciful yarns about the adventures awaiting the brave. That soft, soughing voice never failed to draw her eyes to the endless, verdant sea. In those moments, she'd wonder if a place that looked so peaceful could really be so bad.

These combined hazards ensured that Sophie's trips to One Tree Hill were unaccompanied and undisturbed. Safely insulated from the prying, judgmental eyes of adults, she could read and discuss her books in peace—which suited her just fine. The place had become hers, and hers alone.

On this morning, though, the hills were silent. She let her gaze linger outward to watch the waves wash over the beach. They were low and calm and not at all like the frothy breakers that had erupted from the sea the night before. A sudden and terrible storm had come barreling ashore, the kind accompanied by massive dark clouds, heavy torrential rains, and great peals of thunder. Now, it was as if the storm had never existed at all. Such a horrifically beautiful day, and she was meant to spend it doing other people's laundry. Resigned to her fate, Sophie collected her things, brushed herself off, and began the trip home.

It was only once she'd stood that she noticed the brilliant light flashing up at her from the beach. Golden hued and twinkling, it looked as though a star had fallen from the sky. She wondered if perhaps it had been jostled loose by the storm. Beguiling as it was, Sophie ignored it and moved on, for she had more pressing things on her mind. There was no way she could have recognized that light for the beacon that it was, nor could she have foreseen the path that its bearer would set her upon.

The Bright Side

THE DAY AFTER A STORM is the best time to harvest kelp. Kelp farming, for the unaware, is the act of gathering dead kelp that has washed ashore, hauling it onto land, and drying it out for various industrial uses. Dead kelp, for the unaware, smells an awful lot like rotting sulfurous diarrhea and feels like the skin of a slug that has had its guts squeezed out. Successful kelp farmers, therefore, have a knack for looking on the bright side of things.

In the same way that a butterfly's wing stirs the mighty hurricane into life, so it was that the bright side of a thing brought the winds of change to Seaside by blinding a moderately successful kelp farmer that day. His name was Mert.

Mert had just stooped over a particularly rich glom when a gleaming, golden flash caught his eye. He glanced up, looked around, and seeing nothing out of the ordinary, shrugged and dug his bare fingers into the moldering, mucousy mound at his feet. The flash came again, this time accompanied by the gentle *shhh* of an incoming wave. *Ahhh* said the wave, and the light stung Mert's eyes for a third time. Frustrated and glad of the excuse to get his face away from the horrendous slime pile, he stood and stared at the shoreline.

Mert was motionless for a full minute, waiting for the momentary bursts of reflected sunlight. An internal struggle was taking place. Having been born and raised in Seaside, and—it must be said—being of a somewhat simple nature, Mert's powers of imagination were shamefully impotent. He'd never seen anything so shiny on the beach before. It was clear he should investigate, but he simply couldn't imagine what the source could be. Surely, it couldn't be anything interesting enough to justify leaving his kelp behind. Or could it?

It was a real conundrum.

His inactivity caught the attention of his wife and fellow kelp farmer, Frances. "Mert," she said. "'Chu doing?"

"Uh?"

"I asked whatchu was doing."

Mert pointed. "There's a thing."

"A thing?" She put her hands on her hips and frowned. "What sort of thing?"

"Dunno."

"Then why you starin' at it?"

Mert's gnarled face contorted, contemplating. "Was thinking 'bout going over there."

"Well I don't much like the sound of that." Frances came from a long line of proud, practical people who really knew how to keep their noses to the kelp. Mert, on the other hand, had a great-great-granduncle who had disappeared after wandering Out There. This marred family history had caused quite a lot of tension over the years. "Why d'you want to go and ruin our perfectly adequate day? We've got all these fresh gloms lyin' about and a nice spot of sunshine to boot. What more could you want?"

Mert secretly harbored all sorts of wants. Long experience had taught him that this question was rhetorical in nature.

Shhh. Ahhh. Flicker-flash.

It's hard to explain why Mert did what he did next. It may have been the sunshine, or his rambler's roots, or the weight of all those hidden desires. Perhaps he was simply tired of being told what to do. Whatever the reason, Mert hitched up his britches and said, "I'm going over there." And then he did.

The source of the glinting lay half-buried in a loose mat of kelp. It was a medallion, a thin, circular wafer of onyx surrounded by a rim of gold. Arcane symbols were engraved along its circumference. It bore an inlaid rosette formed from triangular gemstones, each point radiating outward from a pearl embedded in the center. An attached chain disappeared into the ropy, rotting glom. Leaning over to admire it, Mert was shocked.

No, really. As he reached out to touch the medallion, a tiny bolt of lightning leapt out and singed his fingertips. Instinctively, Mert shoved his insulted digits into his mouth, completely forgetting their sulfurous, slimy slug coating. He collapsed to the sand, retching. Moments later, an exasperated Frances stood over her husband, who was busy admiring the puddle of warm breakfast between his palms. Feeling that Mert had not been sufficiently punished for giving in to his curiosity, Frances said, "Serves you right."

As if in agreement, the kelp groaned.

Mert and Frances had seen a lot during their time as kelp farmers, but not once had either of them encountered a glom that groaned. It was simply too much. "Come *along*," said Frances, desperate to get Mert up and away from this new oddity, lest his curiosity take hold of him again. Frances had been haranguing him for decades; she knew what a slow learner he could be.

But it was too late. A fist pushed up to the surface with a thick, slopping noise. It held tight to the medallion's chain. The glom groaned again, and Mert's imagination leapt into overdrive. This time, however, he was untouched by indecision. For once, he knew exactly what to do. He began clearing the kelp off of the fist's owner, and after a moment's deliberation, Mert and Frances hauled out the unconscious stranger and began a trek that would end at the only place that made any sense.

A Trip to the Pub

Of Seaside's two pubs, Walden's was by far the more popular. The food and drink were bland. The service, passable. The atmosphere, subdued. Only two things tarnished its otherwise sterling reputation. The first was the large picture window along the pub's rear wall, which provided a spectacular, unimpeded view of the ocean, and was widely regarded as a terrible business decision. Its installation had caused quite a stir. Nominally, it was for the enjoyment of his guests. Secretly, though, Walden just wanted something nice to look at while he was working.

The pub's other infamous feature was its location on the edge of town. This was viewed as some inconvenience by the pub's stuffier patrons, which gave them plenty to complain about on the walk over. This feeling of being slightly inconvenienced nourished their sense of self-importance and superiority. Said customers generally felt that they were doing Walden a favor by the time they actually arrived. Not one of them recognized the man's sheer tactical brilliance.

The door to Walden's crashed open, disgruntling the lunching patrons within. Two animated silhouettes shuffled and shoved their way through the portal, carrying the limp third member of their disruptive trio like a life-sized marionette. They also carried a powerful stench that completely ruined an otherwise unremarkable meal. Eventually, the kelp farmers cleared the obstacle and dragged their slack companion inside, laying him out on an unoccupied table.

A loose circle formed around Mert and Frances and their strange, unconscious counterpart. And to them, he *was* strange. Neither his skin tone nor the angles of his face were known in Seaside. His long hair extended well past his shoulders, black with a shock of white. He wore a white shirt with frilled cuffs and collar, now stained, and over this a vest of midnight blue, upon which unfamiliar shapes, swirls, and lines had been embroidered in gold. Similar sigils had been graven in his skin in black ink. His chest rose and fell slowly, body loose and relaxed as if he were merely taking an afternoon nap, all except for his right hand, which still clutched the medallion's golden chain.

Walden pushed politely through the crowd, his face knotted in confusion and concern. "Mert? Frances? What's all this?"

"Found a man on the beach," Mert replied.

"Well, why have you brought him—"

"*Ahem!*" A man's voice spoke from across the room. It was very familiar to everyone, inspiring sensations of anticipatory dread. His approaching footsteps were accompanied by the clomp of a heavy cane on the floorboards. The curtain of curious patrons parted before the owner of that voice. "I will ask the questions here, if you don't mind."

Horace Halderman looked like a boar standing on its hind legs. A portly gentleman, he wore a dark jacket and trousers, and walked with a cane simply because he liked the way it felt. His eyes were small and close together, his nose round and upturned, his cheeks jowly and plump. Further, his four front teeth on the bottom were missing, which made the neighboring canines look a bit like tusks. Horace was the shortest person in the pub, yet he still managed to look down on everyone. His voice was similarly lofty, the voice of a man used to getting his way, because he always *did* get his way. He couldn't imagine it otherwise.

Horace strode forward to regard the interminable interlopers. "Now then," he said, clearing his throat and folding his hands atop his cane. "Mert? Frances? What's all this?"

"Found a man on the beach."

"I can see *that*," said Horace, his tone turning the final word into a knife. "Why have you brought him *here*?"

"Pub was closest," said Mert. "He's heavy."

"I see. And did it never occur to you that other people might be at this establishment? That perhaps those other people might be enjoying a perfectly adequate lunch?" Walden's heart beamed with pride. The phrase "perfectly adequate" was the highest compliment a Seasider could give.

"Knew there would be people," Mert muttered.

"Is it possible," Horace continued, "that two *kelp farmers* such as yourselves have had your nostrils so completely and utterly ravaged by the vileness of your occupation that you failed to account for your putrid, fetid, positively noxious scent? Hm?"

"Alright, Horace, I think he's had enough," said Walden. "Mert, where did he come from?"

"Dunno. Saw that in the kelp," said Mert, pointing at the dangling medallion. "It's shiny."

"I told him not to go over there," said Frances. "But oh no, he just had to follow in Great-Great-Granduncle Ferd's footsteps and investigate!"

"Thought we should help him."

"Well there's your problem," said Horace. "You *thought*."

"What's done is done," said Walden, seeking to put an end to Mert's verbal thrashing.

"Quite." Horace fixed Mert with one final, sharp glare. "Right then, let's have a look at this fellow." He proceeded to circumnavigate the stranger, poking and prodding, each new discovery leaving him more unsettled than the last.

He frowned gravely as he traced the patterns of golden silk embroidery . . .

. . . eyed with suspicion the shock of white hair . . .

. . . audibly huffed at the man's tattoos!

The murmuring crowd leaned in closer with each repulsed reaction. Slowly, carefully, Horace lifted the lacing of one frilled cuff, turning his head away as one expecting to see something nasty beneath. The offensive marks extended further up the man's arm! Horace grimaced. The crowd gasped.

And then Horace reached the medallion.

"Hello there," he said with an odd, gentle purr. He knelt to watch the talisman gently twist and turn as it hung in space.

"Wouldn't touch that," said Mert. "Lose your lunch if you do."

"Nonsense!" said Horace. "It's meant to be touched. Just look at it." Horace understood very little about the world beyond Seaside, but he was a positive scholar when it came to matters of wealth. Not even the dim light of the pub could dull the medallion's golden shine. Full of ignorant confidence, he lovingly reached for it. White-hot electricity surged through the air and knocked Horace flat on his back. He sat up, dumbfounded, a black circle of charred flesh smoking steadily betwixt his brows.

"Told you," said Mert, with a touch of satisfaction.

Walden took the opportunity to reassert himself. "Mert, you can't leave him here. It's not good for business, you see. You should take him to Doctor Murphy's."

"That's all the way up the hill," Mert protested. "He's heavy."

"Alright then, your cottage is nearby. Why not take him there?"

"Oh no, not in my house!" said Frances. "He's distracted us from our kelp for too long already. I'll not have him filling my Mert's head with any more *ideas*. Nope, not happening, not ever."

"Well he has to go somewhere," said Walden, meaning somewhere *else*. The assembled crowd clearly agreed. They began muttering suggestions as to just where that somewhere else should be.

"You should drag him out by the Queen's Road."

"Lay 'im out to dry with your kelp, Mert."

"Or leave him behind One Tree Hill!"

Horace's imperious voice cut through the babble. "We should give him back to the waves."

The room went silent.

"Back to the waves?" said Mert. "You mean to the beach?"

"I meant what I said." Horace climbed to his feet, resettling his jacket and mustering his dignity. "To the waves."

"Surely you can't be serious," said Walden.

"Surely I am. Look at what he's done to us already! Me burnt, Mert without his breakfast, and the whole lot of us arguing. I say he's a nuisance. An ugly, stinking, dangerous, *Unnecessary* nuisance."

This was a very serious injunction. Visitors to Seaside came in two categories: Necessary and Unnecessary. Necessaries either delivered things to the village or took them away to be delivered elsewhere. These folk were grudgingly tolerated because they performed a vital function for the village. Unnecessaries, on the other hand, were those who arrived unannounced and with no purpose. They tended not to hang around very long.

Horace's pronouncement was met with murmurs from the crowd.

"Tell me, if he causes this much trouble while asleep, how much worse when he *wakes*?"

The murmurs grew.

"It is too risky to let him stay any longer than he already has, much too risky. Mert, Frances, take him to the dock. We'll stick him in a boat, row him out to sea, and return him from whence he came." Walden opened his mouth to protest but was cut off by the spectators' chorus of approval. The smug satisfaction on Horace's face convinced him to keep quiet. After all, he had a business to run. "To the waves!" Horace said again, and this time the crowd took up the chant.

"To the waves! To the waves! To the waves!"

An Unlikely Hero

THROUGHOUT ALL OF THIS, one person had remained seated by the window, calmly sipping his pint and enjoying the view. As a rule, he kept out of village affairs. He was a young man, not yet twenty years old, but close, with ruffled and unkempt brown hair that was almost black. His clothes and demeanor exuded an air of near-poverty. Grievous sorrow never left his eyes.

As the chanting grew louder and more insistent, it became clear that he, along with everyone else in the room, was about to become a murderer. He had no interest in being a murderer. This act of contemptible cowardice had to be stopped. Damon Farrier drained his drink, got to his feet . . .

. . . and then he began to applaud.

This was not normal applause, the rapid, excited kind that follows a good show. No, this was slow and loud and brimming with derision. Heads turned. The chant faded as Damon approached. "Well done," he said to them, raising his voice to be heard. "Bravo. What an impressive act of imagination. You've all taken this unconscious stranger and turned him into a rabid, slavering beast. I wouldn't have thought you lot capable of such a feat, but here we are."

"This does not concern you, boy," said Horace. "Go on back to your window and your seascapes and your drink. How many pints have you had this morning, eh?"

Damon ignored the jab. "You're wrong, Horace. I find this very concerning, all of you should! This man may be a stranger, but he is still a man. He needs our help. Yet you would have us throw his life away for the imagined crime of being an inconvenience. No, I won't let you do it. I won't allow it."

The crowd fell silent. Horace's face burned red. "Inconvenience . . . *won't allow* . . ."

"Every single one of you has been in need at one time or another," Damon continued, letting Horace flounder. "Mert, Frances, you had some difficult years during the Great Kelp Drought, didn't you? But rather than let you starve, you were extended a generous line of credit down at Codwallader's. Isn't that right?"

"Yup," Mert agreed.

"I'll have you know we paid back every bit that was owed," said Frances, looking indignant.

"I'm certain you did," said Damon. "What about you, Walden? Remember when that storm ripped half the roof off of this place? Terribly inconvenient. But we didn't just sit back and watch you struggle. No, the whole village came out to help clean up and rebuild."

"And to help empty every surviving cask of ale," Walden put in, drawing hesitant chuckles from the crowd.

"That we did. We all know I've had my own troubles over the years—"

"Yes, you certainly have," said Horace, composing himself. "And you've received your fair share of this village's generosity, as well. More than your share, some might say, given how that generosity has been repaid." He arched his eyebrow and fixed his haughty glare on the young man, a move that had wilted many an upstart. Damon met his gaze, unmoved. "My boy, if anyone in this room should be on my side of this, it should be you. Or have you forgotten what happened the last time an Unnecessary was allowed to remain in Seaside?"

A shocked gasp went up from the room. Heads were hung in embarrassed silence, feet restlessly shuffled. A few stout souls had the strength of character to shoot disapproving looks at Horace, but he was too busy looking simultaneously up and down at the young man, waiting for some response.

"I remember," he said quietly. "I also remember you losing a number of teeth."

Horace pointed his cane menacingly. "Why you insolent, *impudent —*"

But Damon was already on the move. He crossed the room and tucked his hands beneath the stranger's armpits. "Mert, get his feet."

Mert winced at the sound of his name, but did as he was told. The two of them hoisted the stranger off the table and toward the door. "Where we goin'?" he asked timidly.

"Anywhere but here."

One Family, Two Homes

Just as Damon and Mert were stepping out into the sunshine, Sophie was letting herself in to the masterpiece of calculated modesty that was her Aunt Elle's house. As a Seasider, born and raised, Aunt Elle's sensibilities would never allow her to admit her aspirations of wealth and status to anyone. Instead, she let her house speak on her behalf. Everything had been chosen for maximum practicality, from the plain wooden floors to the unadorned white walls, to the simple, functional furniture that was comfortable for no more than ten minutes at a stretch. There was not one, single decorative item, nothing to catch the eye or leave an impression or stand out in any way. Decorations had no purpose according to Aunt Elle, and in her mind, there was no higher offense. Stepping in to Aunt Elle's house was like walking into nowhere at all.

Arms overflowing with laundry fresh from the line, Sophie carefully maneuvered through the kitchen and into the dining room, where she unceremoniously dumped it on the table. Aunt Elle would have been scandalized to see it so used, a fact that brought a self-satisfied smirk to Sophie's face. Then her hands went to work, moving with an automatic precision that can only be earned by countless hours of repetition. She transformed the single large pile into several neat, deliverable stacks, humming idly as she did so. This also would have set her aunt's teeth on edge had she been home to witness it. But Sophie was alone, so she did exactly as she pleased.

The folding complete, Sophie's first stop was her cousin's bedroom. Though plainly styled, Petunia's room was far better appointed than Sophie's own. She had both a dresser and a wardrobe for her clothes, a spacious bed for sleeping, and a vanity for her vanity. Sophie opened the wardrobe and was met with Petunia's collection of pastel-colored dresses. According to Aunt Elle, a woman's goal should be to catch the eye of any potential suitor without being offensively ostentatious. The dresses, therefore, were simple, dignified, and almost flattering, which her aunt considered perfectly reasonable for a girl of fourteen. A box of matching hair ribbons sat above them on a shelf. Sophie hung the clean clothes carefully, making everything look uniform and even and straight, organizing them all by color and making sure that each matching ribbon was present and accounted for. If anything was just slightly out of place—or even if it wasn't and Petunia was simply bored—Aunt Elle would surely hear about it.

Sophie harbored no envy for her cousin's collection of dresses or any of her other stuff, with one exception—the writing desk. It sat all alone beneath the window, ignored and largely untouched, used for little more than catching dust. Sophie felt bad for it. Sometimes, when she was alone in the house, Sophie would sneak in and sit at it for a while, staring out into space while imaginary worlds and imaginary people popped into existence behind her eyelids. That's when she'd hear the drawer start to rattle and shift in its frame, as though the pens, ink, and paper were trying to escape their confines and join her out in the light. And, truth be told, she did liberate these writerly prisoners from time to time, offering them safe haven with the rest of her meager possessions. But she already took a scolding every time Aunt Elle caught her with a book in her hand. If she'd ever been caught writing—and writing *fiction* at that—well, there was no telling what her aunt would do. And so, the imaginary people and places stayed bottled up inside her brain, disappearing back from whence they'd been summoned, unwritten and unrealized.

Her next stop was the master bedroom, which belonged to Aunt Elle and her husband Roger. It was essentially a scaled up version of Petunia's room. The wardrobe was a bit larger, and so were the dresser and the bed. As for Aunt Elle's vanity, it took up an entire wall and most of the floorspace. Being in there made Sophie uncomfortable, for reasons she didn't totally understand. It wasn't merely the sensation of being watched; it often felt as if Aunt Elle was standing just over her shoulder and scrutinizing not only what she did, but who she was. Strangely, though, this feeling also worked the other way around. Being alone with her aunt and uncle's things made her feel as though she were spying on certain private activities that were better left unexplored. She hurriedly stashed their clothes and moved quickly on.

Her final two stops took her back out into the daylight and across the yard to the barn. The heavy, sliding door opened onto an open area flanked by workbenches, above which hung tools on pegs and hooks. Beyond that were four stalls for Uncle Roger's horses, two on either side of a narrow aisle.

Above all of this was a loft, which was Sophie's destination. Half the width of the building and nearly as long, it had at one time been used to store hay. Now it was an apartment of sorts. There was a living area with a hanging lantern, a braided rug, and a single wooden chair. Cheap, thin walls framed in two small bedrooms. Neither one had a proper ceiling, so when the horses were brought in for the night, all of their sounds—and their smells—permeated the air unimpeded. Sophie and Damon shared this spare loft apartment. It was the only home she had ever known.

She tossed Damon's shirts onto his bed, then went to her room and pulled open her dresser's top drawer. It was stuffed with rough, tatty house-dresses, each one identical to the last. They were plain, undignified, and flattening. No little box of ribbons for her, though the piece of twine she sometimes tied up her hair with did match quite nicely. Like Petunia, Sophie was also fourteen, but unlike her cousin there was very little chance of her catching anybody's eye, potential suitor or otherwise. Which was just fine with her. There were no suitors in the village that suited her anyway.

Well, there might have been one . . .

No sooner had her mind begun to conjure that special someone when she heard voices approaching from outside. Two of them. They sounded strained and sweaty. She was about to go out and investigate when one of them said something that hit her ear funny, a sentence that, without context, sounded significantly darker than it otherwise might have.

And the speaker sounded a lot like her brother.

Relieved of Duty

Damon and Mert were having quite the time of it.

They suffered mainly from a lack of coordination, which is key to successfully moving any cumbersome object as a team, but especially to moving a floppy, bendy body. Damon had chosen to curl his hands beneath the stranger's armpits and walk backward. With each step, the man's limp arms flapped like the wings of a lazy baby bird. Mert, meanwhile, had one calf securely tucked under his left arm, and a faltering grip on the opposite ankle. Though moving forward, he was utterly incapable of keeping to a straight line, forcing Damon to repeatedly correct their course while also watching the road over his shoulder for any dips, bumps, or debris. No easy task after a couple of pints. Each correction slowed him down, leaving Mert to come on at speed and fold the man in half, only to slow down until he was stretched back out again. Without meaning to, their weaving, lurching, contracting, and stretching made an excellent imitation of an enormous, drunken inchworm.

In this manner they had scooched themselves through the center of town and all the way out to Aunt Elle's house, where a handful of goats watched their labored approach with total disinterest from behind a white picket fence. An immaculate white picket fence. Flawless, one might say. It was the sort of fence that could earn its owner a handful of cool compliments and a lot of heated jealousy — which was exactly what Aunt Elle had intended. The human inchworm maneuvered through the gate (which opened and closed without the barest hint of a squeak) and made for the barn. They'd barely come through the big outer door when Damon spoke the words that had convinced Sophie to remain hidden in the loft.

"Hang him, he's heavy! Let's toss him over here!"

They made their way to a shady spot near one of Uncle Roger's workbenches and relieved themselves of their burden. It should be noted that no actual tossing of the stranger was done, though the landing was a bit rougher than either of them had intended. Damon shook out his cramped hands while Mert bent double, gasping for breath.

He needs some sort of bed, Damon thought. He looked around the barn for some sort of solution. The loft was out, unless the man woke up and climbed the stairs himself. And there was no way Aunt Elle would tolerate his presence in her house; of that, Damon was completely, absolutely, positively certain. That left the barn's floor as the only option, which meant throwing together some sort of mattress. There was plenty of hay they could use for stuffing. What he really needed was a great big sheet of canvas . . .

Damon's gaze landed on the little door at the far end of the barn. Half the width of a regular door and without a frame, the splintered wood had faded to the same grey color as the surrounding wall, making it hardly visible in the darkened space. A great amount of effort had been expended trying to make that door disappear completely from his mind. He hesitated, trying to come up with a better solution, and failing.

Just be quick about it. Can't let her see.

"Come on," Damon said to Mert, "let's get him up one more time. I've got an idea."

They hauled the unconscious man further into the barn, coming to rest beside the neglected, disused door. A rusty squeal assaulted their ears as Damon wrenched it open. Inside was a collection of storage containers—boxes and trunks and crates and more, all covered over with a thick canvas sheet that bore a heavy coating of dust. Damon asked Mert to gather some straw, then busied himself in removing the canvas and clearing space in the aisle. They piled up the straw and stretched the canvas over it, then carefully placed the unconscious man on top. The job complete, the two of them stood back and watched the stranger at rest.

"Now what?" asked Mert.

"I don't know. To be honest, I wasn't thinking that far ahead. I just wanted to get him out of that pub and away from Horace." Damon ran a sticky, kelpy hand through his sweaty hair and sighed. "If I'm lucky, he'll wake up soon and go on his way. If not, I'll have to send for Dr. Murphy."

"Mm. Fine, fine," Mert said, nodding absently.

"What's on your mind?"

Mert looked at the young man uncertainly. "Sure you want to take him in? I mean, after what happened—"

"Yes, Mert, I'm sure." Damon clapped the kelp farmer on the shoulder. "Thank you for your help today. I'm sure he thanks you, as well. You did the right thing bringing him to

Walden's, don't let anyone tell you otherwise. Especially not that bloated gasbag Horace."

"Gasbag," said Mert, tasting the word, rolling it around on his tongue. A guilty little grin appeared on Mert's face. As it happened, he knew a thing or two about gasbags, since kelp is held afloat in the ocean by specialized, gas-filled leaves. Dead kelp releases this gas, contributing to its peculiar stench. Mert liked this word in relation to Horace Halderman. He liked it quite a lot. "Gasbag," he said again, more confidently this time.

Damon smiled. "Why don't you run on home, now, Mert. No doubt the missus would like to have a word with you."

It suddenly occurred to Mert that there might be more to be done for the stranger. A lot more. "Sure you don't need anything? Could get the doctor for you, if you like."

"Mert, I hereby relieve you of any further acts of heroism." They shook hands, and Mert went on his way, tittering and muttering his new favorite word under his breath. Then Damon turned to regard the stranger asleep on the makeshift mattress, one fist lying on his chest and grasping the magical medallion's chain. *What the hell have I gotten myself into now?*

"Damon?"

He flinched at the sound of Sophie's hesitant voice. He turned, and there she was, coming down the stairs with a puzzled, concerned look on her face. "What are you doing?" she asked. "And why was Mert here?"

Heart pounding, Damon turned and shoved the door closed, eliciting another horrid, rusty shriek. Then, as calmly as he could, he beckoned her closer. "Sophie, we have a guest."

Making Introductions

Sophie stared at the man as Damon told her the whole story — Mert's discovery, the brouhaha at the pub, his showdown with Horace, and the decision to bring the stranger here. She barely registered any of it. Her mind raced, calling up images of the heroes from her books and the distant lands they inhabited. Noble knights and rugged rogues and calculating captains flashed behind her eyes. Of course, all of those characters were made up, part of the CHILDISH NONSENSE she was too old to believe in anymore. Or so she had thought. Now, being face to face with someone who looked as though he had jumped right off the page, she was forced to reconsider that position.

"There wasn't anywhere else to put him," Damon said, "so here he is." He drew her attention to the medallion on its chain. "Now, I know I don't need to tell you this, because you're not the snooping type, and you wouldn't go disturbing our guest's things while he's sleeping, would you?"

"Of course not," Sophie said, fully aware of the trap being laid for her.

"But in case you *do* choose to be a sneaky snoop," he went on, "you are under no circumstances to touch that thing. I don't know what it's for, but I know what it does. I watched it blast Horace and put him right on his rump roast." Damon raised his eyebrows theatrically. "With lightning."

"*Lightning?*"

"Uh huh. It jumped right out of that pearl and struck the old porker right between the eyes. Left a little charred spot and everything."

"You're lying."

"Smelled just like bacon."

"Gross, Damon!" She laughed as she said it.

"Come on, we should let him rest." Damon led his sister back toward the barn's main door.

"How long will he be here?"

"Hard to say. I kept expecting him to wake up the whole time we were moving him. He must be really sick." Damon's face hardened. "I should go get Murphy."

"What? No! You can't."

"Why not?"

"Because he'll want to take him away."

"So? He needs help, real help, more than what either of us can do. Besides, Aunt Elle's going to pitch a fit, a serious one." Sophie opened her mouth to argue more, but Damon held up a finger, cutting her off. "I'm already going to have to fight her on this. Don't make me fight you, too."

"Fine," Sophie agreed sullenly. "But you be quick about it, Damon Farrier."

"Back in a flash, little butterfly." He rumpled her hair, and she shot him a reproachful look, pretending to dislike the nickname. Then he trotted out into the sunshine and across the yard and through the gate to go track down the village doctor.

As soon as he was out of sight, Sophie ran across the barn to stare at the stranger some more.

Curiosity pulled her gaze in a hundred different directions at once. Here was living proof that the world was far larger than anyone in Seaside had ever dared to imagine. His very appearance told a story, from the style of his boots to the cut of his hair, the marks on his arms, the outlandish clothing, and most of all the dangerously alluring medallion. The man was a book full of empty pages, a story mute. It was maddening. She wished desperately for him to wake, wanted to yell and scream, to poke and to prod, to shake the stranger and slap him until he opened his eyes and surrendered all of his secrets.

Tentatively, she leaned in closer to study the alien angles of his face: the width of his eyes, the height of his cheekbones, the set of his jaw. A close-cropped beard grew over his muzzle, accentuating the area and giving him a cat-like appearance. He was older than Damon, certainly an adult, but with only the faintest lines marking his features. Sophie marveled at the white streak in his hair, and the bizarre sigils graven in ink on his forearms and hands. She wondered at their meaning, and how they got there, and if everyone had them where he came from.

Most of all, she wanted to know about the medallion. With its golden rim, glittering jewels, and black disk of onyx, it seemed to glow of its own accord, reflecting every stray beam of light that happened to chance upon it. "Lightning," Sophie whispered. She held up a hand and pretended to shoot bolts of godfire from her fingertips, then quickly gave it up, embarrassed.

Eventually, it occurred to her that it was odd to watch someone sleep, especially when that someone was not only a stranger, but a guest. The logical solution was to introduce herself. "Hello," she said. "My name's Sophie."

The act of speaking to an unconscious person was slightly less embarrassing than pretending to cast magical lightning bolts. But only slightly.

"This is my home," she went on, hoping the sound of her voice might rouse him. "I mean, it's not really mine, my aunt and uncle own it, but this is where I live, and so does my brother. His name's Damon. He takes care of me, and I guess now we're going to take care of you. What's your name? Where's your home? Do you have someone to take care of, or does someone take care of you?"

The stranger did not reply.

This isn't going to work.

Then inspiration struck. She raced across the floor, thundered up the stairs, and charged into Damon's bedroom. A stout, wooden trunk sat at the foot of his bed. She unfastened the hasps, threw open the lid, and dug through the stash of books stored within. Then she did all of it in reverse, ending at the stranger's side with a book in hand. It was called *Alec Ventureforth and the Dastardly Devil of Demonia*. "My brother reads to me when I'm sick," she said, puffing and out of breath. "So I thought maybe I would read to you. If you don't mind." She grabbed a nearby crate, dragged it beside the sleeping stranger, then sat and opened the book to the first page. "Once upon a time . . ."

Doctor Murphy

Sᴏᴘʜɪᴇ ᴡᴀs ʜᴀʟғᴡᴀʏ ᴛʜʀᴏᴜɢʜ the third chapter when she heard the steady *clip-clop* of hoofbeats from outside. Panic gripped her. Damon hadn't exactly told her to keep away from the stranger, but it had been heavily implied. *It'll be fine*, she thought. *It's not like I'm doing anything wrong.* Still, she decided the most prudent course was one of plausible deniability. She rose and went out to meet the doctor's carriage as it rolled up outside the barn. Doctor Murphy sat in the driver's seat, reins in hand, while Damon sat beside him holding on to a black, leather bag. The vehicle came to a stop, and the two men descended.

"Hi, Doctor Murphy," Sophie called out in her sweetest, most innocent, I-definitely-have-nothing-to-hide voice. A look of suspicion immediately clouded Damon's features.

"Hello, Miss Farrier," said the doctor, waving politely as he hurried briskly past her and into the barn. Damon was hot on his heels. Sophie turned and followed them, struggling to keep pace but determined not to be left out of whatever came next. "Your brother has been telling me quite the tale. I must say if this fellow is half as interesting as he's been made out to be . . . oh my." Murphy came to a halt that was so sudden he nearly caused a pile-up in the aisle. "I must confess," he said slowly, "I believed you to be exaggerating a bit, Mr. Farrier. My apologies."

"No need, doctor. I wouldn't have believed me, either."

Doctor Murphy stood motionless a moment longer. One hand scratched the top of his head through his tangled bird's nest of stringy hair. Consternation, concentration, and concern worked in concert to tug down the corners of his bushy handle-bar mustache. "Perplexing," he muttered, his hand coming to rest flat-palmed against the balding dome of his skull. He made to sit on the crate beside the sleeping stranger, then paused to remove *Alec Ventureforth*. With eyebrows raised, he handed it to Damon, who in turn handed it to Sophie with a less-than-friendly look in his eyes. "Seems our guest took up a new hobby while I was away," Damon said, speaking out the side of his mouth.

Sophie flushed, her guilty guts all a-twist. "Sorry."

His chastising gaze stayed on her just long enough to get his point across, then softened again. "Any idea what's wrong with him?" he asked the doctor.

"It could be any number of maladies," Murphy mused, sounding distracted. "I shall know more once my examination is complete. You said he washed up on the beach?"

"That's right."

"Well, that accounts for the smell, at least." He took the bag from Damon, set it between his feet, and opened it. Sophie goggled at the collection of tools, implements, and gadgets peeking out through the top. She could almost hear a chorus of little metallic voices vying for his attention. "Me next! Me next!"

they cried, eager to be useful. It was a wonder Murphy could concentrate with all that racket. In rapid succession they were pulled out, used, put back. "What about that one?" she asked, pointing to a device that looked like a tiny hammer.

"Mmm, nothing wrong with his reflexes . . ."

She pointed to a neglected wooden handle next. "How about that one?"

Unbeknownst to Sophie, the handle was attached to a saw. Murphy lifted an eyebrow, then pulled it from the bag and showed it to her. "A bit early to be considering amputation, don't you think?" He smiled as her eyes went wide. "Whatever the answer is, I don't think it lies in this bag." He went back to absently scraping his bald spot. "Curious. Apart from the fact that he won't wake, he's perfectly healthy. All that can be done is to observe and wait, which I believe will best be accomplished at the clinic. Damon, would you help me move him into the carriage?"

Once again the unconscious stranger was hoisted and hauled like a limp sack. However, the job was considerably easier this time around thanks to Doctor Murphy's expert guidance. Sophie looked on with her shoulders slumped, disappointment plain. "Are you sure you have to take him away?"

"I am certain," said the doctor. "Patients in his condition can take a sudden turn for the worst. Better for him to be at the clinic, where either Albert or myself can intervene if necessary. Of course, I don't expect that to happen. He'll most likely come out of it soon enough. Then we can send him on his way, and everything will return to normal."

Doctor Murphy had no way of knowing, but this was exactly the wrong thing to say. For Sophie, Normal was a world defined by the narrow limits of their small village and the small-minded people who lived there, where the adults discouraged reading and daydreaming and exploring, where she was treated differently because of what had happened to her parents, where she had to sleep in an old hayloft in her aunt's barn, where her brother struggled to find work between bouts of drunkenness. Normal had not been good for either of them. The appearance of this exotic stranger was new and exciting and definitely not Normal. She meant to cling to every second of it.

"Besides," he continued, "this will be good for Albert, a proper introduction to long-term care and the four B's: broth, bath, bedsores, and bedpans. Bedsores are no laughing matter, believe you me." He gave Sophie a knowing nod, as if in mutual appreciation of the terrible scourge of bedsores. Sophie returned the nod solemnly. She had no idea what a bedsore was. "If you truly wish to help," he continued, "there is one thing you can do. People in such conditions often recover faster in the presence of friends and family. Perhaps one or both of you could visit from time to time."

Sophie brightened. "Really?"

"Certainly. You would be doing a favor to him, and to me."

The orphans thanked the doctor as he climbed back up into the driver's seat. Sophie watched from the door until the carriage disappeared down the lane, her mysterious new friend leaving her life as suddenly as he'd entered it.

Visitors, Imagined and Real

WITH BOTH THE MORNING and the mysterious stranger gone, there was nothing left for the orphans to do but get on with their respective days. For Damon, this meant going out into the village in search of odd jobs that might need doing. Sophie, meanwhile, decided it would be best to take some time to process. It wasn't every day that a stranger from afar washed ashore in the village. Besides, how was she supposed to concentrate on washing stupid dishes or sweeping stupid floors or dusting stupid shelves after seeing a real-life, *bona fide* adventurer? In her own house, no less! She would simply be too distracted to do any of those jobs well. Then she'd be forced to do them all over again, only this time with an irate aunt standing over her shoulder. Really, Sophie was saving time by procrastinating now. She climbed the stairs, crossed to her bedroom, and tossed herself onto her bed with a heavy *whumpf!*

Staring up at the rafters, Sophie let her mind wander. Dust motes danced in the shafts of sunlight high above. She imagined the world growing and growing as she became smaller and smaller, and smaller still, until she was small enough to fit on the head of a pin. Such an enormous world was daunting, intimidating, but was also free of rules and restrictions and responsibilities. Anything was possible in such a world, even hopping on a mote of dust and simply floating away. A gentle wind would lift her up and out of the loft and beyond the confines of Aunt Elle's perfect picket fence. Coasting on the breeze, she would dance on the tips of the swaying stalks of field grass and befriend all the little creatures who lived there. She would climb the craggy bark of her friend the oak tree and soar from the highest branch, flying above the forests said to grow north of Seaside, or explore the vast halls of Queen Avantia's palace, or visit worlds more stunning and alien than anything ever imagined by any writer who ever lived. If Sophie could ride on a mote of dust, she would do as she pleased.

If Sophie could ride on a mote of dust, she'd float in through the window of Doctor Murphy's clinic to spend more time with the mysterious hero from Out There.

That he *was* a hero was a given. He met most of the criteria, after all. Sophie ran through her mental checklist: he stood out from those around him; he possessed special powers; he had arrived under conspicuous circumstances; and he had survived imminent danger. The only item missing was whether or not innocent lives depended on his success. And really, that was merely a technicality, more a measure of his employment status than anything else.

Maybe he's a brave knight, she thought, sitting up to gaze out her little window. Many of her books—or rather, Damon's books—were about knights. They were always on the hunt for injustice, protecting the simple folk from bandits or rival kings or monsters, meeting evil head-on in epic battle. She imagined the stranger walking around in the yard below, dressed in a flashy suit of armor. It hung loose on his spare frame, the ill-fitting steel jangling with each step. Then she gave him a group of bandits to fight. The fantasy ended with him lying fetal in the grass while the bandits kicked and pounded at his metal shell. *No, definitely not a knight.*

She combed her memory for clues. He had washed up on shore, so he must have been out on the ocean. Sophie imagined him as a swarthy swashbuckler, standing on the prow of a great sailing ship and surveying the horizon with a brass spyglass, salt spray splashing up all around. Suddenly there was a great crash, a hollow boom, rumbling planks underfoot. Pirates had opened fire on the ship . . . and they were being boarded! The mysterious hero drew his cutlass and bounded deftly around the deck, swinging at the marauders. Then his mouth opened to let fly a witty quip, a keen taunt to keep his enemies demoralized and off-balance. Nothing came out. Sophie's fantasy dissolved as she realized she had no idea what the stranger's voice sounded like. Besides, his face was too calm and peaceful to be the sort of person who went around fighting all the time, and in any case there were no pirates in the waters near Seaside. Merlings, maybe, if the fisher-folk were to be believed. But definitely no pirates.

Perhaps he was a reluctant hero, a kind-hearted soul who had never wanted to go on an adventure to begin with but had been swept up in something much larger than himself. She saw him out in the yard, working, wearing the same stained brown and beige that she and Damon wore. It looked more ridiculous than the suit of armor had, what with his two-tone hair and tattoos and magical jeweled medallion . . .

"Lightning," she whispered. That was it. He was a wizard.

Had to be. Of course, all the wizards in her books were old and grey, and the stranger was neither. He didn't wear a robe, either, or carry a staff, though it was possible he'd lost it in the ocean. Sophie frowned. Wizards weren't exactly known for being friendly, and they often cared much more about secret, esoteric knowledge than other people. It was entirely possible he wouldn't want to have anything to do with her when he woke up. This possibility did not sit well with Sophie—not at all.

Then a voice called from outside.

"Hey Sophie, you in there?"

It was a boy's voice, high and hesitant, with the faintest traces of an emerging lower timbre. She knew that voice. It belonged to Robbie Codwallader. Sophie flushed.

For many years, they had been the best of friends. Every day Robbie would make the walk out to Aunt Elle's house, and then stand in the doorway to the barn and call up to her in the loft. The two of them would run around and play, jumping into the haystack, sometimes going into town to run around the square or even all the way down to the beach to make castles in the sand. And then one day, shortly after his ninth birthday, he simply stopped showing up. Concerned, Sophie had gone to his house to see what was the matter. Robbie's mother had met Sophie at the door and informed her that Robbie would be her playmate no longer. He was too old to be seen playing with girls, and in any case they needed his help at the family grocery. Sophie had been grasping for words when the door shut in her face.

"Sophie? Hello?"

Five years had passed since then, and they'd had about as

many conversations. None had begun with him calling into the loft. Sophie hopped up off the bed and hurried downstairs.

Robbie was standing just inside the wide main door by the time she reached the ground, in the same spot where he used to meet her. He was taller than she remembered. His face was plain, his eyes kind, and when he smiled, his left cheek dimpled. A strange feeling gripped her around the middle as their eyes met, a tingling, tightening sensation that made her a little lightheaded. Robbie's face did a convincing impression of a tomato as he looked quickly away.

And then stupid Richie Spindler opened his stupid mouth and ruined everything.

"Pig's ears! Is this where you live?"

Richie Spindler was one of Robbie's new friends, the others being Chet Walker, Barrett Garamond, and Nigel Atkins. They were all older than Robbie and picked on him mercilessly, but Richie was the worst of the lot. True to his surname, he was stick thin and tall, with broad, froggy lips and bulging eyes beneath his unsightly mop of black hair. For some reason the other girls thought he was supremely handsome. Sophie found his looks to be a suitable substitute for ipecac. The other boys weren't much better, in either looks or temperament. Why Robbie went around with them she couldn't understand. The four of them came in out of the sun, looking around excitedly, as if they'd never been in a barn before. Robbie had the good grace to look embarrassed, mouthing the word "sorry" at her. "Right then," Richie said, "where's the freak?"

"What freak?" Sophie asked.

"The Unnecessary. The smelly one with the funny clothes and black marks all over him."

"And the killer necklace," Nigel said excitedly. "I heard it stopped ol' Horace's heart dead."

"Don't be stupid," said Richie, punching Nigel in the shoulder for his idiocy. "It was Halderman told us 'bout 'im in the first place. He's going 'round whinging to everybody who'll listen."

"I didn't say it stopped permanent," said Nigel, rubbing his wounded arm.

"Can we see him, Sophie?" Robbie asked, stepping in front of the others. "Just a quick look, then we'll be on our way."

"He isn't here."

"You're lying," said Richie. "That idiot kelp farmer said he was here. Said your brother took him out the pub and made him carry the ugly weirdo to your barn or house or whatever this is. Why you trying to hide him, anyway?"

"Probably wants him to be her boyfriend," said Barrett.

"Only a freak would want to be her boyfriend," said Chet, eliciting laughter from all but Robbie.

"He's not a freak," Sophie said, indignant. "And I'm not lying. He *was* here, but then Doctor Murphy came and took him away." The boys let out a collective groan of disappointment.

"Now look here," Richie said imperiously, "I didn't walk all this way for nothing. I came to see the freak from the beach, and I mean to see him. We're not stupid. You're obviously hiding him somewhere, and we're going to find him."

He made to go further into the barn, but Sophie stepped in front of him with her arms crossed. "I told you he's not here."

"Get out of my way."

"Hey, Richie, maybe we should just go to Doc—"

"You shut your mouth, Rob." Richie spoke without turning around. "We're going in there, and no little horse-smelling barn swallow is going to stop us. Come on, boys." He pushed Sophie aside as easily as if he were shooing a fly. She stumbled and came to a leaning stop against a support post. Then Robbie was there, helping her regain her balance as the other boys marched past. "I'm so sorry, Sophie, I didn't know—"

"Don't touch me!" Sophie said, pushing him away. The two of them stood in awkward silence as the older boys searched the barn, throwing open every door and cupboard they could find, tossing hay and horse tackle and tools everywhere, even going up into the loft to ransack the bedrooms, all the while chanting, "Find the freak!"

Thankfully, they worked quickly.

Richie looked miffed as he led his pack back downstairs. "Good job, Rob. Should've known this would be a waste of time." He left the barn without bothering to even look at Sophie, followed closely by his fellows. They were already halfway across the yard by the time Robbie mustered up the courage to speak again. "I really am sorry," he muttered, then turned and ran to catch up with the others.

Aunt Elle

FOR A MOMENT, THERE WAS NOTHING Sophie could do but stare in shock at the huge mess the boys had kicked up. It looked as though a storm had been let loose in the barn, scattering everything that wasn't lashed down. She rubbed her elbow as she surveyed the scene; it had been bumped when Richie pushed her, and the pain was starting to set in. Hot, angry tears threatened to spill over her cheeks. She resolved to keep them at bay, and set to work erasing the evidence of their invasion. If only she could erase Richie Spindler and his stupid friends.

She was nearly finished sweeping together the errant hay when she noticed the door at the end of the aisle was hanging partway open. The sight struck her as supremely odd. She had never once opened that door in her whole life, not that she could recall, anyway. Nor had anyone else, for that matter. In fact, the camouflaged half-door had occupied so little of her mind that she was left wondering if it had always been there. She approached slowly, broom raised as though there might be something dangerous inside. The only light in the room came from the between the barn's exterior slats, dimly illuminating the tiered, blocky shapes within. Another step forward. Now the shadows resolved into individual boxes, trunks, and crates, all stacked up and shoved back against the walls. Sophie marveled at their number, curious at what might be inside.

She pulled the door open and flinched as the hinges screamed. It was well-known that Aunt Elle detested squeaky hinges and had made it her personal mission in life to eradicate them from Seaside—even from homes that weren't hers. That such an egregious oversight was sitting right under her aunt's nose was both astounding and delicious. Sophie gathered up the canvas from where it had been kicked aside, emptied the rest of the straw out, and shoved it back into the storage room before swinging the door firmly closed.

While Sophie busied herself setting the loft to rights, her next visitor made her way up the lane toward the house. An older woman, she had apple cheeks, green eyes, and curly dark hair cut to exactly twenty-seven and three-quarter inches in length. She wore a bottle-fly blue dress with black lace trim, and a wide-brimmed hat that had a white feather tucked into the band. Her quick little steps set her bustle bouncing and jostled the jaunty feather. Beside her walked a fourteen year-old girl in pastel green with a matching ribbon in her hair. They came through the gate together, then separated as the older woman stopped to swing the door open and closed a few times, hoping to ferret out some minuscule imperfection. Satisfied, she bustled across the yard and into the barn. She came to a stop at the bottom of the loft staircase, looking upward, delicate hands resting firmly upon her hips, handsome face set, and one eyebrow raised archly.

"*A-hem!*"

Sophie appeared at the banister with a book in hand. Aunt

Elle's already stiff posture somehow stiffened even more at the sight of it. "Come down here, please." Sophie obediently descended to stand before her silently churning aunt, the novel held sheepishly behind her back.

"I heard the most unbelievable story at the flower market today," said Aunt Elle. "I heard it again at the bakery. Then at the butchers', the fruitery, and all over Codwallader's Grocery. Do you know to which story I am referring?"

"No." Sophie was fairly certain she was lying.

"Curious." Aunt Elle didn't seem to be curious. In fact, she seemed quite certain of herself. "So you know nothing about the unconscious man found on the beach today? Or how your unthinking brute of a brother assaulted poor Horace Halderman when he was only trying to protect the good people of this village? You haven't heard a word about Damon bringing a dangerous, foul-smelling, ugly Unnecessary under my roof without my permission?"

"Damon didn't assault anybody," Sophie said, her frustration rising. "Mr. Halderman wanted to throw the stranger back in the ocean. Damon saved his life. And he's not ugly or dangerous. He's just different."

"So it is true." Aunt Elle's lips puckered tightly. "After all I've done for the two of you, this is how you repay me! Well, where is he? Where are you hiding him?"

"Doc Murphy came and took him away."

"*Doctor* Murphy. Have some respect for your elders, young lady." She fixed Sophie with the same look she'd given the gate hinges. "Well. For the best, really. There's no telling when the foreign weirdo might wake up, if he ever does. We could have been stuck looking after him for days. Weeks. Months, even. What a burden that would have been." Her eyes grew far away as she spoke, her tone reflective. "I couldn't have let him stay out here in the barn, that's for certain. Too much responsibility for the likes of you. No, he simply would have had to come into the house. Which presents its own problems. And of course there would be the curious to consider, coming up from the village, wanting to come inside and have a look around and stay for tea . . ." Sophie watched her aunt as the words leaked from her lips, saw her mind busily calculating, every disingenuous denial betraying her own disappointment at the stranger's disappearance. In that moment Sophie understood what the doctor had really done for the stranger by moving him. Damon may have saved his life, but Murphy had kept him from becoming a token in the ever-shifting game of oneupsmanship that dominated Seaside's social life. ". . . and anyway, we *do* have space for him, in that little front room down on the first floor, right next to the lane-facing windows. But it would have been such a bother to reorganize that space."

"Such a bother," Sophie snarkily agreed.

The remark snapped Aunt Elle out of her reverie. "Yes, a real bother, just like your indolent brother. What a fine mess he's created. I'll have to bake poor Horace a trio of cakes by way of apology, and Damon will do even more than that, I'll see to it. Where is he, anyway?"

"I don't know. Out looking for work I expect."

"Well when will he be back?"

"I don't know."

"Perhaps you might know a thing or two if you didn't spend so much time with your nose in those awful books." Aunt Elle reached out and took a lock of Sophie's hair in hand, appraising it. "Honestly, Sophie, I don't understand what you get out of those silly, made-up stories. You could do so much more with your life. Something practical. Sensible. Ladylike." She let the hair go, twiddling her fingers as if she'd just touched something nasty. "Don't you think it's time you started at least trying to make yourself presentable? You are nearly of marriageable age. People talk, you know."

Sophie knew all too well the ways that people talked. It was the main reason she wasn't a fan of people.

"Several young men in the village are on the brink of surrendering their bachelorhood," she continued. "Michael Spindler's eldest, for example." Flaxley, Richie's older brother, was nearly ten years Sophie's senior and a known tomcat about town. He looked even more like a stretched toad than Richie. Suggestions of this kind only reinforced Sophie's conviction that her aunt hated her. "And of course it's well past time Walden took a wife. Word is he's taken a shine to my Petunia, but a barkeep's wife is no fit life for such a delicate flower. No, only a fine young man like Sterling Halderman is good enough for her."

Upon hearing the name Sterling Halderman, Sophie's mind sketched a picture of her "delicate flower" of a cousin walking hand-in-hand with the rotund, bristly, upright swine of a human being that was the fruit of Horace's pickled loins. He took Petunia's hand, lowering his face as if to press his lips to it in a gentleman's kiss, and instead snuffling his snout up her arm like a hog rooting for truffles. Next came Petunia surrounded by piglets in her aunt's living room, a whole litter of them, squealing and grunting and prodding her for milk, while Aunt Elle fawned over them from her seat in the corner.

Sophie felt laughter building, her stomach muscles contracting, the corners of her mouth lifting, and she knew she shouldn't laugh in front of Aunt Elle but that made it even funnier and before she could clap her hands over her mouth a pair of short, barking laughs escaped from her mouth. Her wide eyes regarded her aunt with a mixture of shock and embarrassment.

Aunt Elle was not amused.

"Honestly, why do I even bother?" she huffed, bustling out of the barn as quickly as her short little steps would carry her.

Polite Dinner Conversation

Dinner time, and still no sign of Damon. Sophie came inside and took her customary place at the dining room table. Aunt Elle and Petunia were already there, gabbling on about the day's gossip and picking apart every little detail. The evening meal was already on the table—boiled chicken with steamed vegetables, mashed potatoes, and day-old rolls. Aunt Elle's cooking was something of a miracle; somehow, she managed to sap the flavor from everything, including the salt.

Uncle Roger ducked in through the doorway. He had to. He was the tallest man in Seaside, a full head taller than his nearest competitor, though it must be said he possessed a bit of an unfair advantage thanks to his impossibly angular skull, which sloped up to a pronounced ridge and gave him an extra few inches. The calciferous crest presided over protruding brow ridges, high cheekbones, and a lantern jaw. Both hands and feet were far too large for his lanky long limbs. He spoke slowly and seldom. "Evening, my lovelies," he said, coming around to kiss them all on the forehead, even Sophie. He took his seat at the head of the table and began filling his plate, signaling that the meal had begun.

"Oh Roger," said Aunt Elle, "it's been the most scandalous day, simply earth-shattering. Have you heard?" Uncle Roger shook his prodigious head, and she was off to the races, the words once again stampeding around the same well-worn track. Sophie barely listened, focusing instead on getting her fill before Petunia snatched up all the best bits. She did notice, however, that Aunt Elle managed to give herself the starring role in every one of her stories, even the ones she hadn't been present for. It was an odd trick she had mastered. Sophie didn't particularly care for it.

She'd been talking for fifteen minutes straight when Damon arrived. "Well well well, look who finally decided to show up for family meal time," Aunt Elle said by way of greeting. Damon didn't respond, didn't even look at her. He simply took his seat beside Sophie and picked through what was left. There was whiskey on his breath. "What do you have to say for yourself, young man?"

"Say for myself?"

"Oh don't play the fool with me! You know very well what you did. Why else would you disappear for several hours but for your shame?"

"I'm not ashamed," Damon said around a mouthful of roll. "If anyone should be ashamed it should be Horace and everyone else in that pub who didn't have the guts to stand up to the bloated old porker." Aunt Elle and Petunia gasped in unison. "And I didn't disappear. I was working."

"Helping Walden empty his casks hardly counts as work," Petunia said tartly.

"I made one quick stop on the way home, that's all. Had a feeling I wasn't going to be met with a hero's welcome." Damon dug in his pocket and then slapped a handful of coins onto the table. Sophie stared at them, amazed. In one day Damon had made more than he usually did in a week. "Would you like me to count out your share now?"

"Take those disgusting things off my table," said Aunt Elle, flapping a dismissive hand at them. "And you should feel shame for treating this place like some common inn or poorhouse. I should have been consulted first. Damon, that Unnecessary is dangerous! Not even conscious and he assaulted two men. Poor old Horace is scarred for life, did you know? Who's to say what a man like that is capable of. It's simply unimaginable. When you brought him here, you threatened not only the safety of this family, but our reputation as well."

"There it is," Damon shot back, "that's what you really care about, now isn't it? Your precious reputation. Wouldn't want to be seen taking in a stranger, lest anyone think you generous, compassionate, or kind."

"You hold your tongue," said Aunt Elle. "Everyone knows how much I've done for you and your sister, at great personal cost, no less. I've fed and clothed and housed you both since the unfortunate unpleasantness with your parents. I have tried again and again to weave you into the fabric of this community, and yet you refuse to integrate. I have been generous, compassionate, and kind to you both, for what good it's done me."

Damon regarded her, his eyes smoldering, weighing whether or not to let his next arrow fly.

"I only did what Father would have wanted."

Aunt Elle's lower lip began to tremble. "Don't you dare bring my brother into this. You don't know what he would have wanted, considering the circumstances." Uncle Roger took her demure hand in his giant one and fixed Damon with a stern look. "I should like for you to leave now," said Aunt Elle, directing her gaze somewhere up on the wall.

"Gladly." Damon pushed back from the table, grabbed another roll, dunked it in the gravy boat, then stuffed it in his mouth as he stormed out.

Saving it Up for a Rainy Day

Damon was sitting in their rickety rocking chair when Sophie climbed up into the loft. His hands gripped the arms tightly as he rocked back and forth beneath the hanging lantern. She sat beside him on the braided fabric rug, leaning back on her palms, feet kicked out in front. For long moments neither of them spoke. Down below, Uncle Roger's horses stamped and champed and whickered away.

Finally, Sophie broke the silence. "Where did you get all that money?"

"I told you, from working."

"But you never make that much money in one day."

Damon sighed and ran his hands over his face, pulling the skin tight for a moment before letting go. "Today's not a normal day. Everybody wanted something done, even Old Lady Magpie."

"Really? What did she want?"

"Same thing as all the rest—my story. First she offers me a couple coppers to move some boxes from her shed into the house, then follows me around and asks a thousand questions while I'm doing it. Soon as I'm done, she changes her mind and wants them back in the shed. Seems everyone in Seaside suddenly forgot how to sweep floors, trim wicks, and fill baths."

"At least they paid you."

"It's not what I want," said Damon, standing. "I need a real job, li'l butterfly, one that's gonna get us out of here and into a proper house. I need a workshop, someplace where I can do business. We deserve better than this."

On this point Sophie was in complete agreement. The little loft had its charms, but it was sweltering hot in the summer, freezing cold in the winter, and always smelled of horse dung. As the siblings had grown older and developed needs for privacy, it had become more and more difficult for the two of them to share the space comfortably. Life in the loft was better than being homeless, but only just.

As to Damon's talk of business, this sprang from the one major contribution Aunt Elle had made to their future, and that was securing a farrier's apprenticeship for Damon. Currently, there was only one farrier in Seaside, a man named Gregory Tacklesmith. He was a very disciplined and no-nonsense individual who approached his craft with an understated gusto. He was strikingly handsome, lived in a sensible square house, had a fantastic relationship with his family and the villagers in general, and was a teetotaler besides. In short, Gregory Tacklesmith was everything that Damon Farrier was not. Yet somehow Aunt Elle had cajoled him into teaching his craft to Damon, which was indeed quite thoughtful of her. Unfortunately, without a workshop, his skills were next to useless. Aunt Elle had denied Damon's requests to build a workshop on her property, and even worse, laughed in his face when he'd asked for a loan. So now he was reduced to doing odd jobs around town, scraping together what coin he could in the hope of gaining independence for himself and his sister.

"We'll get there someday, Damon, I know we will. Hey, I know what will cheer you up." She rose and went to their special hiding spot, a loose board at the back of the loft. She pulled it from the wall to reveal a heavy glass jar sitting on a joist. It was a little over two-thirds full with coins, mostly copper, with the occasional bit of silver floating within. She removed the jar and carried it over to her brother. Damon took the coins from his pocket and poured them in, savoring the steady *clink* as they cascaded down on the others within. By the time he was finished the jar was three-quarters full. Once they reached the brim, Damon would take their money to the bank and put it in the account they shared. They'd made six such trips so far, and Damon reckoned they'd need at least six more before he could afford a little patch of land. With some property to his name, he'd be able to ask the bank for a loan instead of Aunt Elle, and they would finally be free. "See, it's nearly full!" she said cheerily.

"Thrilling."

"Come on, don't be a sulkabout." Sophie resumed her seat on the floor, and Damon joined her, somewhat calmed. "At least Aunt Elle isn't trying to marry you to Mr. Hinkley."

"Mister Hink—*Walden?*" Damon shook his head as if trying to clear water from his ears. "You're too young to marry anyone, let alone Walden. He's twenty years your senior, at least! What could she possibly be thinking?"

"I'm fourteen years old, nearly marriageable!" she protested. Not that she had any actual interest in marriage. She just didn't like it when her brother treated her like a child.

"Besides, I thought you liked Walden. You certainly spend enough time with him. He's a respectable business owner, you know. If I were his wife, I could convince him to give you the loan you need."

"Absolutely not," said Damon. "It's my job to look out for you, I'll get us out of this mess."

"But why can't I help? I can sweep floors, trim wicks, and fill baths better than you can. If we were both making money, we could get out of here sooner."

"We've talked about this," he said, getting agitated again. "It's my responsibility. I'll take care of it."

Sophie gave him a reproachful look, then decided to drop it. "Well, Walden is certainly a better choice than the other person she mentioned."

"Do I want to know?"

"Flaxley Spindler."

Their eyes met. An elemental understanding passed between them that said more than mere words could capture. A slow chortle built on both sides of that gaze, every facial twitch feeding the other's growing laughter, until finally the hilarity was too great and they each collapsed on the floor, hysterical, reveling in the joy of having their worries and ills temporarily put to rest.

Eventually, their momentum ran down, leaving the two of them lying on the frayed rug, gut-sore and smiling.

"Is it true?" Sophie asked.

"What?"

"What you said about father. Would he have done what you did?"

"Sophie . . ."

"I know you don't like to talk about them, but I need you tell me. Were they like Aunt Elle and Horace Halderman and all the others? It's okay if they were. I just want to know. Please?"

Damon took her hand, giving it a little squeeze. "If it was him in that pub instead of me, he would have stood up to Horace. I know it."

"How do you know it?"

"I do, that's all."

"And what about Mom?"

Damon sat up. "She would have made up a bed and let him stay as long as he needed. They were good people, Sophie. Too good for Seaside." He stood, hoisting the jar of coins, then helped her up. "Come on, li'l butterfly, it's been a long day. Off to bed." He kissed her on the forehead, as he did every night, then went to replace the coins in their hiding spot. She went to her room, undressed, and climbed into bed, where she lay awake long after the lantern had been put out and Damon's snoring had begun, her mind abuzz with questions that refused to be still.

At The Clinic

Sophie paid a visit to Doctor Murphy's bright and early the following morning. Doubling as the village medical clinic, his house was a tall, two-storied affair, with a brick stoop and a patch of carefully manicured lawn sheltered behind a stately wrought iron fence. She pulled open the gate and ran excitedly up the steps to knock on the door, waiting with her thumbs tucked under the straps of her knapsack.

A grumbling voice came from the other side. It grew in both volume and intensity as it neared. To the voice was added the metallic percussion of turning locks. Then the door was yanked open and the grumbler growled, "Yes?"

"Good morning!"

"What's so good about it?" The grumbler was Albert, the doctor's assistant. He stood blocking the doorway with his arms crossed over his chest. One hand was wrapped in a white bandage. A young man, Albert had short, coarse brown hair and dull brown eyes that peeked out rattily from behind his wire-framed glasses. Albert was not from Seaside, but because of his medical expertise, was tolerated as a Necessary. He returned the villagers' begrudging tolerance in kind. His distaste for Seaside was no secret, and he spoke of his home city of High Vandermeer at every opportunity. He was only in Seaside because the Royal Society of Healers had placed him under Dr. Murphy's expert tutelage in the hopes that it might improve his bedside manner. So far, the experiment had failed. "You don't look ill or injured."

"I'm not," Sophie replied. "I came to see the stranger."

Albert sighed heavily, pushing his glasses up his nose with a finger. "*Ingenue*, I told your friends yesterday that no one is allowed in without a genuine medical necessity. This is a house of healing, not a sideshow for every curious passerby to stick their head into. Didn't anyone ever tell you such novelty seeking is indecent? Now off with you, I've a busy morning ahead."

"But Dr. Murphy said I can visit anytime I want!"

"Oh did he now?" Albert asked mockingly. "You may not know this, young lady, but I am a graduate of the Royal College of Sophisticated Learnings. Your childish deceptions are futile. Now shoo, before I snatch you by the ear and drag you howling back to your mother!"

"I don't *have* a mother," Sophie shot back, putting her hands on her hips. "I do have a brother, though. He's the one who saved the stranger from Horace, and when Doctor Murphy came to our house he told me I could come and visit while you attend to the four B's."

"The four B's, did you say?" Albert's brow furrowed. His tongue poked the inside of his cheek as he considered. "Right then, what are they?"

"What are what?"

"The four B's. You say you spoke to the good doctor about our patient. Prove it. What are the four B's?"

"Um." This was a wrinkle Sophie hadn't foreseen. She wracked her brain, trying to draw the words from her memory. "Uh . . . oh! Bath! And also . . . bedsores. They're no laughing matter," she added, giving Albert the same stern, knowing nod Murphy had used the day before.

On either side of the human face is a muscle called the buccinator. It has several different functions, one of which is smiling. When Sophie did her best impression of Albert's mentor, a long atrophied series of ganglia in his brain fired weakly, causing the buccinator muscles on his right side to lift the corner of his mouth very slightly in what can only be described as non-consensual amusement. Of course, this impulse was quickly overridden and his face regained its usual dour shape. "Fine. I'll let you in. But get in my way and it's out with you, understand?"

"Yes, sir."

The ground floor of the house was divided by a central foyer, with two adjoining rooms to a side. Albert led her in and turned left, entering the examination room. There were charts and models all around, and in the center was a specially designed reclining chair for patients. A door set into the far wall led into the recovery suite, a guest room of sorts that was reserved for patients. With his hand on the knob, Albert knocked twice, waited, then opened the door slowly when there was no response.

The stranger lay asleep in the room's single bed with his head propped up by a pair of flat pillows. His face was impassive, peaceful. The shock of white in his unbound, onyx hair nearly disappeared against the pristine bedclothes. On the nightstand sat a neatly folded pile of clothes. His bare, tattooed arms lay atop the covers, one perfectly relaxed, the other tightly grasping the chain of the menacing, magical medallion.

"You may sit in that chair," Albert said, pointing, "but do not touch anything else. Not the patient, not his belongings, and certainly not that blasted piece of jewelry." He watched as she shrugged off her pack and obediently took her seat by the bed, and then, after one more warning glare, turned and left.

"Hello again. It's me, Sophie. From yesterday." She spoke quietly so that Albert wouldn't overhear. Unsure of what to do next, she watched the slow rise and fall of his chest, then let her eyes wander around the room, passing over the impressively bland, blank walls before stopping briefly at the window that overlooked the lane. Finally, her gaze came to rest on the man's collection of outlandish clothes. The shirt had been bleached as white as the bedsheets, the lacy frills of its cuffs and collar tucked neatly away. Then came the marvelous vest, with its iridescent midnight blue silk and golden embroidery. Next to the vest and shirt, his pants were positively bor—

Pants!

Sophie's eyes widened at the sudden realization that the man was naked beneath the covers. Not just shirtless. Pantsless, too. Her alarm gave way to a vague curiosity that had no clear object. She traced the bold lines of the man's tattoos with her eyes, from fingertips to shoulder to the top of his exposed chest, where both he and they disappeared under the blanket. His vague outline was etched in shadow on the pure white linen. For reasons that weren't immediately clear, she suddenly became very self-conscious. "You smell a lot better today," she offered, grasping for some way to break the tension. And it was true; both he and his clothing smelled lightly of soap, with not a hint of the nasty kelp stench left behind.

This was not going at all as she had expected.

"I brought some things for you," she said, hoping to change the mood a bit. Sophie began emptying her knapsack and setting the items on the nightstand. In case he was hungry, there was a pair of apples, a wedge of cheese, and a heel of bread, and also a paring knife for cutting slices of each. Next came a canteen filled with water. Last, she removed three books and stacked them beside his clothes. The one on top was *Alec Ventureforth*. She had meant to leave them for him to read on his own, but it was becoming increasingly clear that he wasn't going to wake up any time soon. With nothing else to do, she grabbed the book from the top of the stack and opened it. "I read on a bit from where we stopped yesterday, but don't worry, I'll catch you up."

For the next hour Sophie read aloud to the sleeping stranger. Her voice was careful and halting, bereft of the lyrical music she was used to hearing in her mind, and she stopped often to work through tricky passages or to explain certain story details that the stranger had missed. Gradually, she began to get the rhythm and flow of the language. The words rolled off her tongue as her confidence grew, and she even put on different voices for the characters, though in truth they all sounded a lot alike.

Eventually Dr. Murphy peeked his head in. Sophie closed the book quickly, embarrassed. "Sorry," she said quietly.

"There is no need to apologize," said the doctor, smiling his kindly older man's smile. He came fully into the room with his black bag in hand. "I'm sure he appreciates the company."

"Can he hear me?" Sophie asked.

"There is no way to know for certain until he wakes up. If he ever does. I went digging through the CC last night—"

"See see?"

"The *Compendium Comprehensium*, a multi-volume catalogue of medical maladies produced by the Royal Society. It is a reference manual for physicians. May I?" he asked, gesturing toward the chair. Sophie hopped up and the two switched places, with the girl standing bedside and the doctor seated with his bag at his feet. He continued, "I was looking for conditions that cause persistent sleep and potential cures. Unfortunately, it seems medical philosophy has not progressed far in understanding such conditions. All we can do is keep attending to the four B's, and wait. However, Albert and I are convinced that his mind is still active, though dormant, and simply waiting for the right conditions to arise to spring forth into consciousness once again. Do you see the way his right hand clutches tight to that golden chain?" Sophie nodded; it was impossible to miss. "That medallion must be incredibly precious to him, so precious that his unconscious mind has forced his hand to clamp down with unyielding force. Albert attempted to pry his fingers loose last evening, an attempt that will not be repeated." The doctor arched one bushy eyebrow, the hint of a chuckle playing about the corners of his mouth. "He is overreacting a bit, if you ask me. Hardly a mark on him. But I digress. Whether our friend can hear you or not, it certainly won't do him any harm to have a friendly visitor."

"So I'm not getting in the way?"

"Not at all, Miss Farrier. Who put that idea—oh, of course." Murphy shook his head slowly. "Pay no mind to Albert. There is a little extra gruff in his grumble today. There were a lot of nosy neighbors stopping by yesterday, including a group of young men who were quite demanding and exceedingly rude. But you are not like them. You are doing a very fine thing for our patient. I know it, and deep down I think Albert does as well." Sophie smiled, not sure what to say. "Now, it is time for our patient's morning examination. Would you like to stay and help?"

Sophie's mouth dropped in surprise. "Can I?"

"Certainly." He pulled a notebook from his bag and handed it to Sophie. Murphy performed his series of arcane tests while she recorded the results for him, writing down numbers on lines and having no idea what any of it meant. The examination ended with another extended bout of puzzled head scratching. "All perfectly normal."

"What will you do now?"

"As I said, there is not much to be done. I have begun drafting a letter to the Royal Society asking for guidance, but by the time I receive a response he will have either woken on his own or passed on." Her eyes widened at his casual suggestion that the stranger might die. "I am certain it won't come to that," he added quickly. Then he thanked her for her help, making it clear that she was being politely dismissed. She grabbed her pack, leaving her gifts behind, all except for *Alec Ventureforth*, which she found she was starting to really enjoy. Albert fixed her with a sour look on her way to the door. Unperturbed, Sophie scowled right back, then scampered out to face the limitless possibilities of a new day.

What Is, Was, and Could Be

Ripples on the Water

LIFE CHANGED FOR THE ORPHANS in the days that followed. Sophie spent her mornings at the clinic. They usually began the same way, with her sitting at the stranger's bedside and telling him about the previous day's events, all while watching the foot traffic on the lane and making comments about those walking past. She also took great pleasure in categorizing the snooping methods of the villagers as they tried to surreptitiously spy on the sleeping man. The "peek and look away" was quite popular, right up there with the "casual side-eye" and its less frequent variant, the "casual side-eye with raised eyebrow". Of course, some were more brazen than others. Several times she caught Robbie's friends lifting themselves using the iron fence and craning their necks to get a good look. Robbie himself never appeared. Invariably, these visits ended with Sophie reading aloud to her new friend.

Meanwhile, Damon enjoyed a marked uptick in the amount of work coming his way. Word of his stand against Horace had spread like wildfire, and the moths were swarming to its light, eager to get the tale from the source. Of course, they couldn't simply ask him to tell it; that would be too transparent to be polite, and in any case it wasn't wise to be seen with the likes of Damon Farrier in a social setting. So they contrived clever excuses. Most, like Old Lady Magpie, assigned him simple tasks that could be performed while making small talk; if the incident at the pub happened to come up, well, who could be blamed? But some of the villagers offered him proper work. Not true employment, exactly, but the kind of jobs that required multiple days to complete and paid significantly more than he was used to. These offers tended to come from people who'd had disagreements with Horace Halderman in the past.

Aunt Elle, as the adopted parent of the young man who'd caused such a stir, had managed to turn the whole affair to her advantage. To those who sided with Damon, she claimed to be the source of his courage and strong moral fiber; to those who sided with Horace, she was scandalized more than anybody, unable to fathom how the young man she'd worked so hard to raise could be so uncouth. Her social calendar grew busier than ever. Petunia accompanied her mother to these engagements, not only so that she could learn how to navigate the choppy waters of village politics firsthand, but also to be shown off to the prospective suitors Aunt Elle had picked out for her.

All this meant that Sophie increasingly found herself returning home to an empty house . . .

Hidden Treasures

ON A BORED AND RESTLESS AFTERNOON, Sophie decided to investigate the old storage room. It had been stuck in her mind ever since the stranger's arrival. Try as she might, she still hadn't been able to think of a time when anyone had ever even mentioned it, let alone gone inside. That in itself was out of the ordinary. Yet it was the sight of all those trunks and crates and boxes that was truly disturbing. Aunt Elle was a notorious spendthrift and detested waste. Strange, then, that so much space should be devoted to storing useless junk.

The room looked much the same as it had on that fateful day, with the sheet of canvas balled up on the floor where she'd left it and the containers stacked up along the walls. No one stood out from any other. They were so nondescript, so faceless, so dull that it took her a full minute to decide if she even wanted to open one, because surely whatever was inside would be just as boring. Having nothing better to do, she knelt before the nearest trunk and popped open the lid.

Sophie's heart caught in her throat. Buried under a few layers of soft padding was an object of such ordinary purpose and simple beauty that she scarcely believed it was real—a decorative dinner plate. The rim was a brilliant cobalt blue and molded with concentric ridges like miniature waves frozen in time. A sandy island was painted on its center, with a patch of green grass and animals playing in the water.

Sophie had never seen anything like it.

There were others beneath it, and she pulled out the entire stack, examining them all one by one. Each bore a unique beach scene. The existence of something so different, so novel, so imaginative touched her in a way that took her completely by surprise. Sophie hugged a plate to her chest and began to cry.

Once her joyous tears had dried, her curiosity ran rampant. She wondered where her aunt had found the plates, and why they were hidden away in the barn, and why she'd bought them in the first place. It was hard to imagine Aunt Elle as the younger, bolder person she must have been, instead of the stuck up, miserly shrew that Sophie had grown up with. Not even an imaginative young lady like Sophie could picture a version of her aunt that enjoyed, well, *anything*. Where had that Aunt Elle gone, and why?

Sophie dug through the storage for another hour. She found dish sets, flatware, assorted cooking implements, and other kitchen gadgets. Each was lifted out reverently as Sophie tried to imagine the space each one must have occupied in the distant past. Taken together, they added up to a colorful, inviting kitchen that inspired its occupants to create deliciously imaginative meals that went far beyond perfectly adequate. Surrounded by those colorful bits and bobs, Sophie mourned for the kitchen that was and wished that it could be once again.

Then she found the watercolors.

Sophie pulled out the neat stack of paintings and leafed

through them. They depicted landscape scenes of all sorts. One showed a busy marketplace, with its rows of covered wooden stalls arranged within the confines of a busy city square. Another showed a small carriage stopped by the side of the road in a dense forest, with a tent and campfire off to one side in the grass, and a pair of horses drinking from a nearby stream. There was a red bridge spanning a river, a grassy meadow and pond, and a distant, misty mountaintop. Sophie flipped through them all, then came to a sudden stop, gasping. The anonymous artist had captured the view from the top of One Tree Hill. It was unmistakable. She had seen that view so many times that she knew right where the painter had been sitting. Yet Seaside looked different somehow. Better. The painted version was warm, friendly, positively inviting, the kind of place someone would visit and never leave again.

But that wasn't the only difference. Something about the painting was very slightly off, as if none of the angles added up right. Sophie searched and searched for the point of difference, to no avail. It was maddening, like having a popcorn hull stuck between her teeth and no way to get it out. Thankfully, there was an easy solution. Sophie hurriedly packed it all away, doing her best to remember what had been where and how it had all fit together, saving out the watercolor of Seaside and one of the blue beach plates. These went into her knapsack, which she slung onto her back as she sped out of the barn.

Sophie's energetic strides carried her all the way to the top of One Tree Hill. She greeted the oak with a sunny smile, then shrugged off her pack, removed the watercolor, and then found the place where the artist had once worked such creative alchemy. Her eyes moved back and forth between the two Seasides. What lie in the distance was spare and grim and forbidding, while the painted version was vibrant, vital, and vivacious. The ocean looked inviting, the fields bountiful, the houses less stilted. Sophie wanted to live in *that* village. If it had ever existed.

"I don't suppose you remember who did this?" she asked the tree. The only response she received was the gentle soughing of the breeze playing amongst its branches.

She was about to put it away when she finally noticed it, the unnamed point of difference, the crucial detail that had remained hidden like a faint star that can only be seen from the corner of the eye.

The artist had included an extra building in Seaside.

Shopping For Information

CODWALLADER'S GROCERY WAS ONE of the largest and most prominent businesses in Seaside. Conveniently located in the square, its unremarkable selection catered to its patrons' uncomplicated tastes. Sophie rarely visited, mostly because Aunt Elle did all the household shopping, which gave her an excuse to bump bodices with the other village busybodies. This arrangement also reduced Sophie's chances of running into Robbie Codwallader in public, a situation she generally tried to avoid. Unless, of course, she had a perfectly adequate reason not to.

The store was busy when Sophie arrived, meaning that there were three other customers already inside. They stood in a neat little queue before the counter. Robbie's father marked down each order on a little piece of slate, which was then handed to Robbie, who hustled up and down the short aisles to retrieve each item and bundle them together into neat, easy-to-carry packages. This left the customers with little to do but stand around and chat—another reason why Codwallader's was held in such high esteem.

Sophie crept in, hoping she and her knapsack would go

unnoticed. Robbie was speeding around the store with his arms full, totally engaged in his task, moving with an unconscious grace and confidence that she'd never seen in him before. He knew right where everything was, tracing neat, efficient paths across the floor and collecting multiple items on each trip. Sophie stopped to watch him, impressed. In that moment she saw the potential in Robbie Codwallader, saw the man he could be instead of the boy she knew, and that funny lightness touched her stomach again. Whatever anger she may have felt towards him for the incident with stupid Richie Spindler evaporated. If it had ever really been there at all.

"Sophie Farrier?"

The voice caught Sophie by surprise. She jumped a bit, snapping back to reality. Abigail Atkins was beaming at her with a look of bemused shock. The surrounding chatter died away as all eyes came to rest on her . . . including those of Johnathan Codwallader, Robbie's father. He regarded her as he would a venomous snake. Then Abigail enveloped Sophie in a smothering hug and cried, "Oh you poor dear!"

Abigail's reaction bears some explaining. At an early age, it became clear to Sophie that relations between grown-ups and orphans were governed by a different set of rules than those for non-orphaned children. Adults froze up momentarily whenever they saw her, eyes blank, as if listening to some secret internal warning. Then came the Look. It was an expression of careful calculation that betrayed the weighing of every word and phrase and destroyed any chance at genuine conversation. The Look was inescapable. Sophie hated it.

To make matters worse, not everyone had the same orphan rules. Most people fell into one of three categories. The first and most common were the Nervous. They would shuffle from foot to foot and say "um" a lot and look down or up or anywhere but at her. Annoying, but tolerable. Then there were the Huggers, who specialized in awkward, overbearing, uninvited hugs that were too tight and too long and too often accompanied by well-meaning platitudes that made Sophie feel worse instead of better. And then there were the Disdainful. These were miserable old sots like Horace Halderman who found her continued existence an affront to decency and a mark on Seaside's whitewashed facade. Sophie had no idea why they hated her so, but at least they were honest.

Mrs. Atkins was a notorious Hugger.

"How are you, my dear?" she asked Sophie, holding her by both shoulders and pulling a sad face as though she were about to cry. "I haven't seen you in ages. Look how tall you are!"

Sophie had no idea how to respond to such a mindless observation, so she didn't. She glanced over Mrs. Atkins's shoulder instead. Robbie was standing at the counter. He glanced at her questioningly before going back to his work. Finally, she said, "I'm doing fine."

"Is that so?" Now a new look stole into her eyes, one that was familiar but difficult to place. "You know, my Nigel said he saw you out and about the other day."

"Did he?" Sophie wondered if her stupid son had also told her how he and his stupid friends had stormed her home.

"As a matter of fact, he did. He said he saw you . . ." She pretended to think it over. Sophie knew she was pretending because Mrs. Atkins was a poor actress. So were the others standing in line. They were pretending not to listen in on their conversation. Suddenly Sophie remembered where she'd seen that mischievous glint before—in Aunt Elle's scheming eyes. "That's right, he saw you coming out of Dr. Murphy's clinic. You did say you're feeling well?"

"Next," announced Mr. Codwallader.

"I only ask," Mrs. Atkins continued, "because it would be odd for someone well to spend so much time at the clinic. Unless, of course, there was another perfectly adequate reason to be there. I really can't imagine what reason that might be, though." She raised her eyebrows expectantly.

". . . a pound of bacon, a dozen eggs, two pounds of flour, a half dozen ears of corn . . ."

"Sorry, I have to go," Sophie said, breaking Mrs. Atkins's grip and speeding down an aisle. At the end she turned and came partway up another, stopping beside the bags of flour. Then she took off her pack, opened it, and waited.

Soon enough Robbie came down the aisle with an armload of corn and a carton of eggs balanced on top. Their eyes met. His feet collided. The boy spun around and staggered backwards toward her, managing to maintain both his balance and his grip on the wobbly stack of goods, but only just. Slowly, he turned in place, eyes wide, cheeks pale. "Sophie. W-w-what are you doing here?"

"I came to see you. I need your help with something."

"Uh, I'm kinda busy at the moment . . ."

Sophie ignored him and pulled the plate from her bag. "You remember that day you came up to my house?"

"Yeah. I'm really sorry about Richie. He's not always like that."

"Yes he is too," she said, shooting him a look that said he should be ashamed for lying to her. "When those idiots tore apart the barn they opened a door at the back that's full of boxes and stuff. I went digging through them today and I found this." She held her prize out to him, watching eagerly for his reaction, waiting for him to drop everything in shock and fall to his knees and marvel at the miracle of imaginative artistry before him, to clutch it tightly as she had, to shed tears of joy at the limitless possibilities such a specimen heralded.

Robbie shrugged. "Neat."

Sophie huffed and tried again. "Aunt Elle had this. *Aunt Elle*. Don't you think that's strange?"

"I guess so."

Clearly, Robbie did not understand the enormity of the situation. She decided to cut to the chase. "I want to know where she got it."

"Then why don't you ask her?"

There were many reasons why this would not happen. If Sophie had taken the time to articulate them, it might have gone like this: "Well, Robbie, if I tell her I found this beautiful spectacle then she will know I went snooping through her things. Also, the Aunt Elle I know would never spend her money on something so colorful and imaginative. She might be so ashamed at seeing it again that she'll break down in tears or go into a fit of rage. Finally, I don't particularly trust her to tell me the truth, or understand my interest, or to even care about my basic needs, so I'm not comfortable talking to her about anything, least of all the origin of this extraordinary piece of art that's been lying buried in the barn like a forgotten skeleton."

But that was a lot to get out all at once, so instead she said, "Because!"

It was just as effective.

"Robbie." Mr. Codwallader's disapproving countenance loomed behind the counter.

"Sophie, I gotta go."

"Wait wait wait! I just want to know if your dad sold it to her. Aunt Elle buys practically everything here, so I thought maybe he would know where it came from."

"Then why don't you ask him?"

"Ugh, Robbie!"

"Okay, okay, I'll ask him. But later. I really have to get back to work." He turned, then came halfway back. "Um, Sophie? Can you put one of those sacks of flour in my left hand?" He wiggled his fingers to show which one he meant. With a huff, Sophie grabbed one off the shelf and placed it in his waiting hand. Then he was off, hurrying up the aisle to deal with the next order. Sophie put the plate back in her bag and left.

Another Odd Reaction

Sophie was in bed reading when Damon came home that evening. He poked his head into Sophie's room with a goofy, groggy grin on his face and said, "Whatcha doin', li'l butterfly?"

She smiled up at him. "Nothing. Reading. How was your day?"

"Was alright." He gave her a great big smile that might have fooled someone else. "Gotta get to bed. I have a feeling tomorrow's gonna be another busy one."

"Wanna put the coins in the jar?" she asked. "It should be almost full by now."

"S'alright," he slurred, waving for her to stay put. "I'll do it in the morning. G'night."

"Wait! Lemme show you something." He leaned in the doorway while she dug through her knapsack, watching with a bemused smirk as she struggled to remove the blue beach plate from the bag's narrow opening. She finally wrenched it free and held it up for inspection. "It's beautiful, isn't it?"

Damon's drunken good humor disappeared, his sleepy, sappy demeanor replaced by an expression she didn't quite recognize, one that squinched up the corners of his eyes and tightened his jaw. She offered him the plate for closer inspection. He made no move to touch it. Empty eyes stared coldly at the object in her hands, as though it were something dangerous. A black widow, perhaps, or a shining, silver knife. The seconds dragged long. Finally, his eyes lifted to meet hers, and when he spoke, his voice was serious and strained. "Where did you find that?"

"In the storage room." Her voice was hesitant, cautious, gradually normalizing as she rambled. "I got bored today so I decided to dig around a little bit. There's all kinds of fun little things hidden away in there, but these plates were the best. I found a whole bunch of them sitting in a box, which is a real shame because they're too pretty to just leave buried like that. Who would've thought Aunt Elle would have something so pretty—"

"You need to put that back," Damon said quietly.

"Why? No one ever goes in there, she won't even notice."

"Sophie," he said, more forcefully than before. "Put the plate back where you found it and don't go down there anymore. Okay? Promise me you won't go back in the storage ever again."

"But why? I'm not going to break anything, and even if I did—"

"*Promise me*, Sophie. Please." Her brother's eyes burned.

"Okay, fine," she whined. "I'll put it back first thing in the morning." She knew there was no point arguing with him, not in his current state. Better to wait until tomorrow, when he would be more reasonable and could fully appreciate her newest treasure. She shot him a sour look.

"Put the plate back," he said before disappearing into the little hallway that separated their rooms. She heard the strained creak of his bed frame and knew that his snores would soon follow.

What was that all about? she wondered, suddenly glad she hadn't mentioned the watercolors. She climbed back into bed with the plate in hand and admired the beachy island floating on the sea of blue. Two cartoon frogs played in the waves, standing on their hind legs like humans do and wearing human bathing suits. It was clear to her from the way they looked at each other that they were in love. It was also clear that, no matter what Damon said, there was no way she could simply tuck it back away and pretend like it didn't exist. Sophie set the plate gently on the nightstand and went back to her book, but only for a little while, for she was quickly overtaken by the somnolent waves of sleep.

A Partner in Crime

Sophie had meant to make good on her promise. Truly, she did. But some things simply aren't meant to be.

The following morning saw her kneeling on the floor of the storage room, surrounded by colorful nicknacks. She was busy freeing their companions from their long confinement when she heard Robbie calling to her. She rose and stuck her head out the door. He stood just beyond the open barn door, hands tucked behind his back, looking expectantly up toward the loft. "Over here!" she said, waving, before disappearing into the storage room once again.

Robbie entered as she was unwrapping a decorative birdhouse with a bright red roof. Ladybugs and bees were painted on its walls in bold colors. A second birdhouse sat on a trunk nearby, identical but for its blue roof. Sophie set the red one beside it to make a pair. She imagined them hanging from the roof of Aunt Elle's house, with tiny birds flitting back and forth between them, chirping and twittering contentedly. "What are you doing?"

"Just having a look around." She rose and turned from the display. Her voice brimming with hope, she asked, "Did you ask your dad about my plate?"

"Yeah." Robbie directed his gaze somewhere between her shoes.

"And?"

"He scolded me for wasting time at work. Then he said I'm not supposed to talk to you anymore. It's not your fault," he added hastily. "It's your brother. Damon really upset Mr. Halderman. He's a big customer, Sophie, and my dad doesn't want to make him mad."

Horace. Of course. "Well, *Mr. Halderman* is a stupid fat pig, and so is your dad."

"Sophie . . ."

"Did he tell you about my plate or not?"

"He said he'd never heard of such a thing. Wherever your aunt bought it, she didn't get it at our store."

Sophie slumped. "Thanks," she said without enthusiasm. "Don't you have some corn to fetch or something?"

"Not really. I told my dad Richie asked me to go fishing with him."

"*Ugh!* So it's okay to run around with a stupid, gross jerk like Richie but not me?"

"My dad gets his fish from Mr. Spindler, and he gives us a good discount. They're friends." Robbie shrugged. "So, what's in that one?" he asked, pointing.

Sophie eyed him, unsure if she should stay angry or not. In the end, she decided it wasn't Robbie's fault that his family and friends were awful. "Kitchen stuff," she said. "I already went through all of those ones. This one's next. Help me with it?" They hauled a trunk into the open central space and undid the clasps.

The two halves parted to reveal a bunch of clothes. One

side held a tangle of men's shirts and trousers, the same dull grey, green, and brown that made up the wardrobe of every man in Seaside. Sophie ignored them completely, captivated by the brilliant, bold rainbow that spilled from the other half of the trunk, which held a collection of neatly folded sundresses. She pulled one out and held it up, marveling at its fiery orange color and shapely cut. "It's gorgeous!" she said, turning it this way and that. "Don't you think it's gorgeous, Robbie?"

"Yeah," he said, mustering up as much fake enthusiasm as he could. He held up a second dress, this one a brilliant sunshine yellow. "This one's really pretty."

"You think so?"

"Uh huh. Don't you?"

Sophie took it from the boy, holding it at arm's length and tilting her head from side to side. "There's no way Aunt Elle would wear a dress like this. I don't think she *could* wear it. It's far too small."

"Maybe that's why they're in a box," Robbie offered. "My mom has a bunch of old clothes that she never wears anymore. She says she's too fat for them, though my dad always says she's exaggerating."

"Maybe." She was unconvinced. It wasn't a matter of her aunt's girth; it was her height. *It might fit me, though.* "Wait here," she said, taking the dress and leaving Robbie alone in the storage room. "I'll be right back."

Sophie climbed the stairs and went to her bedroom. She began to undress, pulling off her drab, undyed cotton blouse and heavy brown skirt. Robbie's face flashed in her mind and she felt that electricity again, realizing that he was no more than twenty feet from where she now stood, separated by a few thin planks of wood. What if he snuck up the stairs and tried to peek at her while she was changing? Sophie thought she might not mind all that much. She undid the buttons on the back of the dress, stepped in, and tugged it gently into place. It felt snug, but in a good way, as though it were lifting her up. She wished she had a mirror so she could see what she looked like before presenting herself. She took a deep breath before going back out.

Robbie was poking around amongst the nicknacks when she returned. "Well?" she said. "What do you think?"

The boy turned. His jaw fell open.

"Uh, wow! You look, I mean, you . . . *the dress*, the dress looks . . ."

Now it was Sophie's turn to look away, the hopeful smile slipping from her face, arms crossing protectively over her chest. "It's okay. You can say it. I'm ugly."

"No! No, Sophie, I've never seen you look so pretty." He came forward with his arms outstretched, then quickly dropped them, remembering the last time he'd tried to console her. "You're not ugly, Sophie. I never thought so. But, in that dress, it's like you're a totally different person."

Eyes lifted, searching for hints of untruth. "You mean it?"

"I do. I would say you should wear that dress all the time, but then the other boys . . . and, well . . ."

Sophie rushed him, drawn forward by the crackling lightning running through her veins. She craned her neck up, closed her eyes, and let her puckered, tingling lips lead the charge.

Robbie was shocked.

No, really. As the tender flesh of her lips came within an inch of his, the static electricity that had built up from playing around in all that dust discharged and zapped him right in the face. He recoiled, and the two of them looked at each other, mortified.

"I, I just," Sophie stammered, her eyes wide as dinner plates. "Thank you. No one's ever called me pretty before."

Robbie's face went redder than a sunburn. "I meant it."

They stared at each other for long moments, unsure of what to do next. Robbie finally broke the silence. "Come on, let's see what else is in these boxes."

They spent the afternoon digging around in the storage room together, their conversation coming in fits and spurts, neither of them addressing the near kiss. Eventually Robbie said he had to go before he got in trouble, and Sophie playfully scolded him for not helping her clean up. She watched him walk away and wondered when he would come back. He turned back to wave one final time and nearly tripped over his own feet, drawing good-natured laughter from the smitten girl, who resigned herself to putting her newfound treasures back in their chests before her grumpy older brother came home.

A Totally Different Person

Sophie lay awake long after lights out, visions of Robbie Codwallader playing through her mind on a loop: the hopeful, expectant look on his face as he waited for her in the barn door; his reaction to her in the yellow dress; and most of all, the startling, shocking almost-kiss they had shared. One side of her thought she had made a mistake and scared him off by being too forward. The other was convinced her mistake was in not trying again.

Frustrated and full of nervous energy, she slipped out of bed and opened the bottom drawer of her dresser, where she was met with ocean blue, sunshine yellow, and an idealized vista of Seaside. Where had they come from, these captivating relics from her aunt's past? They hadn't just appeared from nowhere. Sophie ran her fingers over the dress. Someone had made this. They had offered the wearer a selection of fabrics, taken her measurements, and carefully stitched it together to create this flattering, flashy garment. It was hard to imagine anyone in Seaside asking for such a dress, let alone making it. Her eyes landed on the watercolor, tracing the shape of the mysterious extra building she had discovered. *Maybe things were different back then.* It sounded nice, but she didn't quite dare to believe it.

Sophie pulled the dress from the drawer and stood, admiring it, remembering how good it had felt to wear. It had been a nearly perfect fit. Like it was made for her. She wondered what it would be like to walk through the square with it on, radiant as the sun fallen to earth, to watch the Unimaginatives of Seaside recoil in scandalized shock, to finally be seen, to be a spectacle, unforgettable.

. . . it's like you're a totally different person . . .

Robbie's words stuck in her mind like cottonwood fluff on a bramble. "Different person," she muttered. A perfectly square house full of plain, boring stuff and plain, boring people. Boxes packed with energy and life. Hidden. Forgotten. Clothing that was too small for her aunt, and not because of her weight. *Different person, a totally different person, someone my size, someone who refused to stay hidden, someone with an imagination, a different person, a totally different person who . . .*

Tears stung Sophie's eyes as she realized whose things she'd been playing around in. It was them, the two people who had cast an unavoidable shadow over her whole life without ever being present. A strange mixture of elation and anger washed over her. She was overjoyed at the chance to finally learn more about her parents, even in an oblique, tangential way. She was furious that her aunt would hide them away for all these years and never say a word. There was nothing to do but hug the dress to her body as she sobbed, rocking it back and forth, squeezing desperately in an attempt to extract her mother's lost love from the fabric itself.

A loud snort ricocheted off the roof like a shot.

Damon!

She rose, impelled by a sudden urge to wake him up and tell him of her discovery, but stopped before she'd taken a single step. Some silent instinct held her still. He had always been so sensitive when it came to the subject of their parents, so stubborn, so spiky, and Sophie knew it was because he was so deeply pained by their loss. She wanted him to feel as she did, to experience the joy at being reunited after so long apart. But he could also be unpredictable. His anger at Aunt Elle might simmer over and push him to say something so mean and rotten that it got them both kicked out for good. No, this had to be broached in just the right way. Sophie put her mother's things back in the dresser and then crawled back into bed. Though her eyes were open, they saw little, for she had become lost in her imagination, devising the perfect way to tell her big brother the good news.

Afternoon Surprise

Sᴏᴘʜɪᴇ ᴄᴜᴛ ѕʜᴏʀᴛ ʜᴇʀ ᴍᴏʀɴɪɴɢ visit to the clinic, rushed straight home and barged into the storage room. She tore free the canvas sheet and threw open the containers at her feet. The items within were quite ordinary, which is to say they were the same sorts of things that everyone keeps around the house, yet each was imbued with their essence, whispering to Sophie across the gulf of years in a language understood only by her heart. She gave herself a moment simply to listen. These were the scattered pieces that remained of her parents' lives, and like a jigsaw puzzle, she would reassemble them to create a picture of what had once been. Damon was going home.

It was a bold plan, built on simple reasoning. Damon had never really stopped mourning the loss of their parents; therefore, if she could make him feel as if they had truly returned, if only for a moment, he might feel some level of peace, which would temper his inevitable anger at their aunt. At the very least he would be happy to have so many things to remember them by. If she was lucky, he might even begin to fill in some of the missing pieces for her. He had been working so hard to try and save her. This was her chance to do the same for him.

Sophie ran into her first obstacle almost immediately. The room itself was not very big, and most of the space was occupied by the containers themselves. She would have to carefully choose what to display and leave the rest where it was.

This proved a harder task than one might imagine. It was far too easy to become distracted and get carried away by her imagination. A teacup transported her to a dining room of the mind, where Sophie sat across from her mother and put jam on scones and talked about whatever it was that daughters discussed with their mothers over tea. A box of nicknacks left her wandering the aisles of some impossible, faraway marketplace, carrying a basket while her mother and father picked through the displays and bartered with the shop owners. Later, she stood beside her father in an imaginary hallway with a handful of nails, while he used the hammer she'd uncovered to put up a shelf to hold their latest purchases. In the end, Sophie decided to let her imagination lead the way. If something she found inspired one of these happy daydreams, it joined the display, along with her prized beach plate, the watercolor, and the yellow sundress.

Then she came across a collection of figurines, an entire village of little people and animals frozen in time. Most were made of wood, but there were others done in more precious materials, as well. Among them was a pair of finely made glass frogs. One was stately and stout, a deep green color with brown eyes, its face serious and stern. She held it to the meager light and examined its gleaming surface. The glass was perfectly smooth, without a single scrape, scratch, or pit. If not for that glimmering sheen, she might have mistaken it for the real thing. Sophie set it down and picked up the other, which lay broken in three pieces. It was considerably more slender than the first, its skin a bright yellow-green, with a single red stripe down the spine and ocean blue eyes. Sophie could swear it was smiling at her. She set the pieces down beside its mate, pushed them back together, and held them in place. "You two are quite the pair," she said aloud. Something tugged at her mind as she spoke, an entombed memory announcing its existence and nothing more, like a hollow thump that resonated through the layers of lost time, felt rather than heard. "Have we met before?" Sophie asked, tilting her head, puzzled. "I'll bet you came dearly. They must have kept you out somewhere special, right where everyone could see." She decided she would do the same. Sophie cleared a space in the center of the room and set them up next to each other on the highest crate, using bits of stuffing to buttress the broken pieces of the slender, green frog and hold them in place.

She'd been at it for nearly three hours when Damon came home.

Wrapped up in her reverie and not expecting her brother until well after dark, Sophie did not hear his footsteps at all, nor did she mark the shifting passage of his silhouette as he crossed the floor of the barn to stand outside the storage room door. He watched her work, silent, stricken. Still, she did not notice him. If it had been otherwise, she would not have been shocked by the sudden fury in his voice.

"Sophie."

Her heart leapt into her throat. Damon stood trembling outside the door, eyes ablaze, jaw locked tight. Balled fists stuck straight down at his sides. His mouth opened, and in that moment Sophie was sure he was going to scream at her, to berate her, to call her names and break her down, never mind that her brother had never done anything like that before, had never even raised his voice to her, because her brother was no longer with her, it was rage personified wearing Damon's skin, and she was trapped. "Damon. What are you doing here?"

He held up a hand. There was something in it. Something metal. His eyes roamed around the room as he spoke, taking in her meticulously crafted display. "Bought a lock," he said. "For this door. I told you not to come in here."

"But look. I-It's them." His face contorted when she said it, an expression caught somewhere between curiosity and agony. She'd been rehearsing this moment in her mind, practicing what to say and how to say it, all of her justifications arranged in neat rows like soldiers on a battlefield. That voice and that expression wiped them out like artillery fire. What was left was a nervous, jumbled rush. "All of it, all of this stuff, they've been right here this whole time! Aunt Elle had them hidden away from us and I wanted to tell you last night when I figured it out but I thought maybe if I made it like it used to be that it would . . . that you'd be happy and . . ." A wave of emotion washed her words away and carried them silently from her brimming eyes.

In a voice that struggled with itself for control, he said, "You can't be in here, Sophie."

"*But why?* Because of Aunt Elle? I don't care if she finds out. It's not even her stuff! It belongs to you and me. Look at this," she said, snatching up the watercolor and shoving it in front of his face. "One of them did this. They were here!"

"I know, Sophie." His voice wavered. "I was there when Mom painted it. So were you, riding around in her belly. I was there. Don't you understand? *I remember.*"

A deep, jagged crack shot through Sophie's tender, young heart.

"You knew. You knew and you didn't tell me." Her grip tightened unconsciously, crumpling the painting. Her voice rose as she spoke, hands gesturing wildly, the paper crackling and whipping through the air as her own anger rushed to the surface. "How could you do this to me, Damon? You, Aunt Elle, this whole stupid boring village, you all got to have your time with them and I didn't and now I'm not even allowed to ask questions or anything and it isn't fair, Damon, they died and ruined my whole life and *it isn't fair!*" The painting ripped. Not clean through, but enough to rend the sea.

"Get. *OUT.*"

Sophie screamed and threw the paper at him, an inarticulate outburst of uncontrolled rage. Then she barged past him, stamping across the barn's dirt floor, seething breath growling through gritted teeth. She marched across the yard, flung open the gate, and ran.

Telling Stories

SOPHIE HID FROM THE WORLD amongst the branches of her friend the oak tree. Silently she stared out at the horizon, watching the sky as it traversed the spectrum of color from one end to the other. She marked the passage of time by the fading of the last bar of neon orange light from the horizon and the gradual appearance of the stars, only turning for home once the chilly ocean winds became unbearable.

She was halfway across the yard when a voice called out to her. "Sophie! Come here, please!" She cringed. Aunt Elle was standing on the front stair and beckoning with a lacy handkerchief. If there was one person Sophie wanted to see less than her brother, it was her aunt. She considered simply making a run for it, but decided against it, knowing that Aunt Elle would simply follow her up into the loft with even more ammunition for her scolding.

"Come in, dear, come in," said Aunt Elle, giving her a quick, awkward squeeze that almost counted as a hug. Something was wrong with her voice. It sounded pleasant. "You've been up on that hill again, I see. You must be terribly cold. And hungry." She put an arm around Sophie's shoulders and pulled her into the foyer. "I dislike it when you miss dinner. It makes me worry, you know."

"I'm sorry, Aunt Elle."

"It's quite alright, dear," said Aunt Elle, picking debris from Sophie's hair. "Why don't you come join me inside?"

Another ominous sign.

Uncle Roger was seated in the parlor, shifting uncomfortably while he struggled to refill his pipe. It looked like a child's toy in his enormous hands. "Roger, dear, would you mind letting us have the room for a bit. I need to have a chat with Sophie. Girl talk. You understand."

He was not normally the sort of man to move quickly, but at the mention of "girl talk", Uncle Roger snatched up his things and fair bounded from the room in two strides of his lengthy, lanky legs.

"Please, have a seat, dear," said Aunt Elle, motioning toward the now empty chair before taking her own. A side table separated the two of them; on it was the damaged watercolor of Seaside. Someone had tried to flatten it out, but it still bore creases from being crumpled. A slash of white ripped through the clear blue sky where it had been torn. Aunt Elle picked it up and examined it, her eyes scanning rapidly over its surface. "I haven't seen painting like this for a long time," she said. "Not since . . . well, your mother used to make these silly things. She certainly had an eye for the outlandish. Only natural, I suppose."

"Why do you say that?" Sophie asked.

"Because she was an outlander."

Sophie was gobsmacked, not least because of the off-handed way the remark had been delivered. Of course, now that it had been said out loud it was obvious. A flood of questions surged into Sophie's mind, each one fighting so fiercely to be asked first that none had the chance to escape. She was still deciding where to begin when Uncle Roger came back in and handed her a plate. On it was a slice of bread that was deformed and squashed, topped with uneven smears of hard butter and little blobs of raspberry preserves. The presentation spoke to Uncle Roger's complete lack of utility in the kitchen. Sophie had never seen him make food for anyone, not even himself. Something serious had happened while she was away. She was sure of it. "Thank you," Sophie said and took a bite. The bread was a bit hard but otherwise palatable. He smiled down at her from his impossible height, pleased at his handiwork, then disappeared again.

"Go on, dear," said Aunt Elle. "You must be positively famished." Sophie took another bite. Oddly constructed though it was, the treat did make her feel slightly better, the bursts of sweetness pricking up her spirits. "I understand you and Damon had a bit of a spat this afternoon."

"Yeah. Aunt Elle, I—"

She held up a hand for silence. "That is between the two of you. I do not wish to be involved. However, I will say that I support his decision to keep this and all other fanciful faffery separated from our daily affairs. What you do in the loft is your decision, but I won't have it in my home. Is that clear?"

"Yes, ma'am." The implication of her aunt's words sunk in. A glimmer of hope shone in Sophie's eyes as she asked, "Does this mean I can move their things into my room?"

"The matter is for you and Damon to decide. Personally, I would rather that you did not. Such impracticality is damaging to the development of a young lady's mind. But this is not what

I wish to speak to you about." She set the watercolor aside and settled herself primly. "I understand that you have been inviting boys over while no one else is here."

"What? Aunt Elle, I never—"

"You may keep your lies, young lady."

"But I'm not lying!"

"Oh you poor, lost child," Aunt Elle said, shaking her head sadly. "It's as if you simply can't help yourself. I must admit, I've grown used to dishonesty from you and Damon. One of the difficulties of raising orphans, I suppose. But this is very serious business and I simply cannot look the other way." Sophie opened her mouth to speak, but her aunt kept right on going. "Don't try to deny it. Abigail Atkins told me that she saw you working your charms on Johnathan's boy. Right there, in the store, in front of everyone! Robbie was spotted coming to and from our home the following day. I would not have believed it, but then Johnathan himself told me that he caught his son lying about his whereabouts."

"I must say I'm surprised at you. After all, you've never shown much interest in love or romance, not like my Petunia, who is blossoming into a lovely young woman. But that is neither here nor there." Aunt Elle sat forward, took Sophie's hand in both of hers, and sighed dramatically. "I suppose I'm partly to blame. I mentioned Flaxley to you as a potential match and already you're trying to make him jealous. Clever girl. But now you've led poor Robbie down a dangerous path, sneaking away from work and lying about it. What will people say when they hear how you've seduced him?"

"I never . . . I didn't . . ."

"Oh, whatever are we going to do with you, you poor,

broken child?" Her eyes grew somber. "I do try to remember all that you've been through, but really, these deceptions must come to an end. Now, I am willing to look past these recent transgressions, but only if you will do something for me in return."

"But I didn't do anything!"

"That's quite enough of that." Aunt Elle's voice took on an edge. "My patience has its limits. Are you going to help me or not?"

"Help you with what?"

"Well." She hesitated, choosing her words carefully. "There is much curiosity in the village surrounding the mysterious man who washed up on our shore. No one has been able to learn a single thing about him. No one except for Doctor Murphy and his wretched assistant, that is."

Sophie saw right where this was going. Her aunt's story about Damon and Horace had run its course. If she was going to maintain her newfound popularity, she needed a new one. The initial friendliness, the accusations, the guilt, they were all a set-up to get her to this moment. "I don't know anything more about him than you do, Aunt Elle."

"But that just isn't true, dear," she said, squeezing Sophie's hands. "That dreadful Albert changes the sheets occasionally and bathes him, and Murphy himself examines him daily, but you're the only one who spends any length of time with the Unnecessary. Surely you must have gleaned *something*. Just one or two little morsels of gossip to share."

Sophie's brow furrowed. "How do you know how often the doctors visit?"

"I have my ways."

Sophie tried to figure a way out of this without getting in any trouble. Good girl that she was, she kept coming back to the truth. "Really, Aunt Elle, I don't know anything."

"Try, dear." She squeezed Sophie's hand painfully. "Your mother always had a good imagination. I'm sure you can come up with something. I hope you can, for your sake. It would certainly be a shame if word got around about your habit of lying. If there's one thing a man won't stand for, it's a woman who lies."

A dull throb ached in the corners of Sophie's eyes. Her vision blurred. She wanted to cast away Aunt Elle's clamping hand, to tell her that she didn't care one whit for the opinions of Seaside's small-minded men, to lay before her all of her failings as a god-mother and a guardian and a human being, to scream it all in her face and barge out the door and slam it forever closed.

I would love to tell you that Sophie did all of those things.

"Um," she said, choking back her tears. "His tattoos are quite interesting . . ."

Aunt Elle smiled.

It's In The Horses

Sitting on her bed with her knees hugged to her chest, Sophie stared out at the night from her darkened bedroom. Clouds floated across the sky, ghostly inverse silhouettes over a pin-pricked field of black. Languidly they lingered, moving, but only just, their passage marked dimly in relation to the lone oak in the distance. The wind spoke to her with its many voices and sought to drive her out. It moaned wraith-like through the eaves. It whipped up the noxious and inescapable scent of horse dung. It caressed the distant stalks of field grass and carried their whispered invitations to wander, to explore, to feel the tickle of their brushy tips along her tracing fingers, to leave behind Seaside and all of its inhabitants, to strike out on her own and take her chances Out There. This last voice was the cruelest of all, for she knew in her heart that this was her life.

From below came the sound of feet mounting the stairs. Damon. She turned from the door and lay down and pulled the covers over her head. Her body stiffened as his footfalls reached the landing. The living room. The hall. They stopped outside her open door. The smell of alcohol drifted into the room. *Go away.*

"Sophie?"

His voice conjured a confusing mix of emotions. She was happy he was home safe, angry that he had hidden so much from her, wounded over her betrayed trust, afraid that he would resume his assault, wary to confide in him about her "chat" with Aunt Elle, anxious over how he would react when she did tell him. But above all else she was too exhausted and worn down and tired of feeling.

I don't want to be here anymore.

"You're a bad faker. You're too stiff." His voice was labored, mushy. "It's late, isn't it? Isn't it late? You should be asleep. Asleep and sleepin' li'l butterfly dreams."

Sophie threw back the covers and rolled over to face him. "Go to bed, Damon."

"Yeah," he agreed, not looking at her, not moving. His eyes stared intently at the bare floorboards, focused but empty, as though his gaze had been snagged on a nail. Freed from their usual limits by thorough inebriation, the muscles of his face contorted in an expression of worry that was almost comic in its dramatic intensity. "I didn't mean to make you fly away, li'l butterfly. It's—" Damon pushed off from the wall and overbalanced. In an impressive display of drunkard's grace, he did a half-pirouette, one foot raised in the air while his hands waved for balance. Then he landed hard on his ass beside Sophie's bed, making a little *whumph* sound as he touched down. "There. Better." His glazed eyes rolled up to find hers. "I didn't mean to make you fly away."

"Well you did."

"I know. I did a bad thing. But you don't understand. It's not the same for you as it is for you. For *me*. You didn't lo—*uuurrp*." He looked at her sheepishly as she sat up, waving a hand before her face. "Sorry. I'm sorry, Sophie."

I'm sorry. Those words were not at all satisfying, not after what he'd done. But he was moments away from passing out and she was simply too drained to press the point any further. Not tonight. She ran a hand through his hair and said, "I'm sorry, too."

"What?" He clumsily shook a finger at her. "No. *No*. You're not sorry. You're *not*. I was the one who . . ." He sighed heavily, and the rest of his thought blew away with his breath. Damon rested his head against her knee and closed his eyes.

"Damon?"

"Yeah?" Almost asleep.

"Why did mom paint an extra house in the village?"

"Didn't. She was really good. Did it right. She was there, and dad was there, and the house was there, and the frog man . . ."

"Who?"

"'Morrow, li'l bu'erfly. Come and see. It's in the horses." And then he said no more.

Sophie retrieved his pillow and blanket from his room and made him comfortable on the floor. Then she climbed back into bed, trying to shut out the choir of cruel evening voices as she pondered the mystery of the frog man and wondered what could possibly be in the horses.

The Incalculable Speed of Gossip

Doctor Murphy himself opened the door when she arrived at the clinic the following morning. He wasn't exactly scowling as he greeted her, but his usual good nature was absent. "Ms. Farrier," he said, his voice grave. "I should like to have a word with you. Please, come inside."

Her heart, battered and bruised, sank further.

Albert stood in the foyer with his arms crossed as she entered. He was definitely scowling. "We shall speak in the examination room," said the doctor. "Albert, would you make some tea for the three of us?" His assistant, not one to pass up an opportunity for a good scowl, enjoyed his moment a bit longer, then left to do as bid. Murphy escorted Sophie into the exam room and had her take a seat in the patient's chair. Once they were settled, he spoke. "Young lady, I learned some very interesting things as I was taking my breakfast at Walden's Pub this morning, some very interesting things, indeed. Did you know, for instance, that the man sleeping in the next room has those strange markings on every inch of his skin?"

Sophie's head sagged. Aunt Elle. It was incredible how quickly gossip spread and morphed and grew in the village.

She'd said only that his tattoos went all the way up his arms and onto his chest. It seemed her aunt had more of an imagination than she let on.

"Did you also know," he continued, "that they dance and move when he dreams? Or that his medallion fires sparks at random intervals and threatens to burn this clinic down? Already I've had two concerned citizens at my doorstep asking if it's wise to keep such a hazard in Seaside's only medical facility. After a bit of investigation, I discovered that all of these stories have the same source—your aunt." He emphasized his point by raising his eyebrows at her.

"I never said any of those things to her, I swear."

"Am I to understand you told her nothing of your time in this clinic?"

Sophie remained silent.

"As I thought." Albert entered with the tea and served, his smug scowl full of self-satisfaction as he handed Sophie her cup. She took a sip. It was surprisingly delicious. Albert may have been bitter, but he liked his tea sweet. "I am not surprised to hear that Elle has involved herself in the spread of these gross exaggerations," said Doctor Murphy. "But I am surprised at your behavior. I offered you access to my patient because I believed you cared for him. Part of caring for someone is protecting their privacy. Whatever one says to a doctor must be kept in the utmost confidence. It is a cardinal rule of medical practice. How would you feel if the whole village knew your private business and talked about it publicly?"

Sophie knew exactly what that felt like. She knew it very well. "Not very good."

"Not good at all. Now, it occurs to me that you are not,

in fact, a doctor, though I believe you have the presence of mind to become one should you so choose." Behind Murphy, Albert's face contorted as though he were trying not to laugh. "Regardless, I expect you to keep what you see and hear in this place a secret if you are to continue your visits."

Albert jerked as if he'd been prodded in the backside. "Doctor, we agreed—"

"Hush, Albert," said Murphy, raising a hand to cut him off. "No more telling stories, Ms. Farrier, not even to your aunt. Is that clear?"

Sophie looked up hopefully. "Does this mean I can stay?"

"Only if you give me your word."

"Yes! I won't say a word about the stran—*the patient* to anyone ever again, not even to Aunt Elle." *Especially not Aunt Elle.*

"Well then, that's settled." Murphy sipped at his tea and stood. "If you will excuse me, I have some correspondence to attend to, and I believe you have some reading to do. Albert, bring the rest of this wonderful drink up to my apartments, would you?" He gave Sophie a friendly pat on the shoulder as he left.

Albert measured her from behind his sour, surly face. "My eye will be on you," he said, gathering up the dishes.

"You'd better hurry upstairs, or else the doctor's tea will get cold," Sophie said tartly.

"Now listen here you little whelp, I am a graduate of the Royal College of Sophisticated Learnings, and you will—"

A sound from the other room cut him off.

Not the foyer. The observation room.

It sounded like a voice.

Sophie and Albert were staring at each other, unsure of

how to proceed, when the voice spoke again. Albert swallowed hard, then set down the tea in a hurry.

"The patient is awake."

Awake At Last

Sophie and Albert stood stone still beside the observation room door, each with an ear pressed to the wood. Indistinct noises came from the other side. Creak and rattle of the bed frame. Rustle of bedclothes. Incoherent muttering.

"Go and fetch Murphy," Albert whispered.

"Why do I have to fetch him?" she whispered back. "You're his assistant."

"Little girl, I am an *adult* and I am telling you—"

The voice again, louder now. Neither of them were going anywhere. Slowly, Albert put his hand on the doorknob, grasping it with anxious strength. With the other he rapped on the door.

The observation room went silent.

"Hello in there," said Albert. His voice was calm and nearly confident. "We are coming in now."

No answer.

"Go on, open it!"

Albert's eyes grew defiant, but he turned the knob anyway, driven by curiosity and his duty to the patient. Their hearts raced in anticipation of an angry, obliterating blast of magic. When nothing happened, he pushed the door open fully.

Sophie crept in behind Albert, peeking over his shoulder at the formidable figure sitting cross-legged in the bed. Dark, powerful eyes tracked them as they slunk into the room. His back was arrow straight, body taut, each hand grasping one bent and blanketed knee. The medallion dangled from his neck and rested on his bare chest, which was indeed covered in the same lines and sigils as his arms. While he slept, his shock of white hair had been a mere curiosity; now, the contrast lent him an aspect of wild unpredictability. The light of consciousness had transformed Sophie's helpless, harmless friend into what he truly was—a stranger. A sickening thought arose in her mind:

What if Horace was right?

The man spoke. His tone was calm and serious, his words incomprehensible. Sophie and Albert looked first at each other, then back at him, confused. He spoke again. His second attempt was as jagged and bizarre as the first.

"What's wrong with him?" Sophie asked.

"Be quiet," Albert hissed. He approached the stranger with tender caution, as he would a growling dog. "We mean you no harm," he said slowly. "My name is Albert."

The stranger only stared.

"Albert. Go on, you can say it. *Al*-bert."

"He doesn't know what you're saying."

"*That is obvious.*"

The stranger became impatient and searched the room. Sighting his neatly stacked clothes, he lifted out the midnight blue vest and felt at the pockets. A deep crease lodged itself between his furrowed brows. His eyes blazed. He spoke once more, his voice captive thunder.

Comprehension lit Albert's face. He made what he hoped was a calming gesture and said, "Stay here." To Sophie he added, "Don't let him leave."

And then he was gone.

The air in the room grew very still. Her eyes flicked up to meet the stranger's, then away, landing and alighting like a bee among flowers. Finally, she worked up the courage to say something. "Hello."

Silence.

"It's nice to finally meet you. I'm Sophie."

Silence.

"I'm the one who's been telling you about Seaside and the people who live here." She reached into her knapsack and pulled out *Alec Ventureforth.* "And I've been reading you this." The stranger's gaze softened somewhat. He glanced at the nightstand again, where the other books she'd left him still sat, along with remnants of the daily treats she had brought for reading time. He spoke again, and this time his tone was a touch kinder, gentler. Sophie shrugged apologetically. "I'm sorry, I don't understand."

Hurried footsteps without, and then the doctor and his assistant came in, Murphy holding his black bag, Albert carrying a small wooden box. "Good morning, I'm Doctor Murphy." His voice was calm and pleasant, with no hint of hesitance or fear. "I am the chief medical practitioner for the village of Seaside. You are probably a bit confused as to why your belongings have been removed from your person. It was necessary to wash both you and your clothes upon your arrival.

Dead kelp is a rather nasty and persistent smell, you see. We took the liberty of removing your possessions from your pockets prior to washing, but you will find them in this box, all present and accounted for."

Albert stepped forward with the box held out at arm's length. Mistrust lingered on the stranger's face as he took the outstretched offering. Then he opened the lid, saw what was inside, and visibly relaxed. He dumped its contents on the blanket and began taking stock of what was left to him. There were all manner of strange looking trinkets: pendants and baubles and plumbs, crude carven figurines, bracelets, rings, necklaces, a handful of square metal disks, a pipe and pouch, and a notebook. He selected a simple leather choker from the pile, put it around his neck, then continued his search.

Finally, he found what he'd been looking for—an unlabeled tin that was no larger than a deck of cards. The observers leaned closer as he opened the lid. There was dirt inside, packed and hard like mud that has been left to dry in the sun. The stranger dug in it gently. Then, curling his finger, he scooped out the limp corpse of a worm, small and pink and droopy, no more than an inch long. He laid it reverently inside the metal lid. A second soon joined the first. There was nearly a third, but then one end of it lifted and moved about as though sniffing the air. A look of satisfaction fell over the man's face.

Then he did something peculiar.

Inclining his head so that it was parallel with the floor, he dangled the worm over his ear. Alarmed, Albert made to stop him, but Murphy stilled him with a hand. "First, we observe. We will intervene only if necessary." To Sophie he said, "Look away, Ms. Farrier. You don't need to see this."

He may as well have told the tide not to come in. She watched, transfixed, as the twisting, searching worm sniffed and sniffed, then pointed itself toward the waiting, open hole. It slithered from the man's grasp. Sophie's mind leapt into overdrive. She was in the stranger's body, was sitting on the bed herself, her stomach turned by the autonomous slimy squirm in her ear canal, heard the papery whispers as the worm dragged itself along her eardrum, an incoherent demon's voice bent on her insanity.

"It is worse than I imagined," Doctor Murphy said. "The prolonged period of unconsciousness must have damaged the brain."

"Nonsense," said the stranger.

"You can talk!" Sophie exclaimed, then clamped her hands over her mouth, embarrassed.

"Certainly, I can." The stranger snapped the tin closed and tucked it into one of the vest's many pockets. Then he took hold of the heavy bejeweled medallion dangling from his neck, the one that carried the power of lightning. He spoke. Innumerable points of golden light flowed from the pearl embedded in the center of the disk. They swirled and spun before settling into a hemispherical cloud over the medallion's surface, arranged at random intervals to each other, as though he held the night sky in the palm of his hand. Wordless, he stared at the glittering display. Then the miniature stars disappeared. "What lies that direction?" he asked, pointing toward the blank wall.

"Only the village," Murphy answered. "And beyond that, the sea."

"The sea." His jaw clenched tight. "I need a ship."

"That's as may be," said the doctor, "but I fear you are in

no shape for travel, my friend. You have been asleep for quite some time. Your muscles may have atrophied, and it is common to experience a distorted equilibrium. I must insist you remain here for observation, for a time, at least."

"I cannot afford to wait."

"There are ships at port in High Vandermeer," Albert offered.

"Fairport is far closer," said Murphy. "But surely you can wait one day . . ."

The stranger threw aside the bedclothes and stood. Sophie averted her eyes as the man dressed, embarrassed. "You have my gratitude for restoring me to health, but I have rested long enough. I must be on my way. Lives hang in the balance."

Sophie gasped. *Lives hang in the balance!* The final qualification had been met. Just as she had suspected all along, he was a hero. There was no doubting it now.

Murphy spoke as the man refilled his vest pockets. "Then permit me a few moments of your time for one final examination. We can prepare you a meal, then my assistant Albert will ready the carriage and speed you on your way. You won't be able to help anyone if you collapse again."

"I appreciate your concern, but I must leave immediately. You have my thanks." He inclined his head gravely, then brushed past and strode brusquely from the room, leaving them all in stunned silence.

A Strange Tale

Sophie burst out into the midday sun with her bag hastily slung over one shoulder. It jumped and bumped against her as she ran to catch up. The stranger disappeared around a corner, heading toward the square. She put on a burst of speed. Moments later, she was resettling her bag and looking up at him expectantly as she matched his steady pace. Silent, his stolid gaze remained fixed straight ahead.

Villagers materialized on the empty lane as they passed. They leaned out of windows or stepped out on their stoops. Others went door to door, urgently alerting their neighbors. The entire village had been desperate to learn more about the bizarre Unnecessary who had caused them all so much trouble. Now they were getting their chance, though at a good safe distance. This suited the onlookers just fine. They pointed and shrugged and scratched their heads as the unlikely pair walked by.

Turmoil roiled Sophie's belly. This was her chance, too. If she wanted answers to the seemingly endless questions that had nagged at her from the moment she'd laid eyes on him, she needed to get him talking. Now. That knowledge only made it harder for her to speak. He had no time to waste on a silly girl from some nowhere village that he would never see again, her mind whispered. As far as he was concerned, she didn't even exist.

Then what does it matter? asked a small, insistent voice inside her. *Go on, say something, anything!*

Finally plucking up her courage, Sophie pulled the cork from her mouth and let the words flow freely. She introduced herself for the third time and told him the story of how he'd got there, of how Mert had found him and Damon had saved him, of how she'd been visiting him every day and waiting for him to wake up, of how everyone in Seaside was curious to know who he was and where he'd come from and where he was going. Not once did he open his mouth to reply, but if he had, Sophie's buffeting torrent of nervous speech would have rendered him silent. "And now you know everything," she finished, smiling up at him. "What's your name?"

He glanced at her sideways, their eyes meeting for the briefest of moments—his dark and hard set, hers bright and hopeful. Seconds passed. It seemed he had no more to say to her awake than asleep. Dismay set her tummy churning even worse than before. She had overwhelmed him by dumping so much information on him all at once. *I should have kept my mouth shut,* she thought. *I should have just kept walking and said nothing and then maybe he would've opened up on his own and—*

"I cannot say."

"Oh." A tiny flicker of hope reignited itself. It wasn't much of a response, but it was something. "You're going to Fairport, though, right? To get on a ship?"

"Correct."

Sophie smiled.

"Why do you need to get on a ship? Where are you trying to go?"

"I cannot say."

"Why not? Is somebody after you? That's it, isn't it! That's why you can't tell me your name or anything, because then whoever's chasing you would know you were here and where to find you. Right?"

"I cannot say."

"Can you at least tell me where you came from?"

Another brief, silent glance.

"You can't say?"

"I cannot," he agreed.

Another corner, and they reached the square. Little knots of chatting Seasiders unraveled as their conversations died *en masse*. Front doors popped open as shopkeepers and homeowners streamed outside. Sophie spotted Robbie among the growing throng. His jaw hung open as he stared at the stranger, while his father openly glared with his arms crossed, head shaking in disapproval. He was far from the only one. Sophie wondered who disgusted them more: him for being so brazenly outlandish, or her for choosing to walk alongside him. Aunt Elle and Petunia were notably absent, for they had gone up the hill to Horace's house for a social call. Damon was more than likely holed up across town at Walden's. Sophie wasn't sure if she should be grateful for her family's absence, or disappointed.

Then she was reminded of another outsider who'd had a flashy wardrobe—her mother. Aunt Elle was fond of saying, "You can learn everything there is to know about someone from the way they keep themselves." If that was true, then her mother must have been as strong and proud and unashamed as the man beside her. Her mind flashed back to the day she'd worn her mother's brilliant yellow dress and how uplifting it had been. Despite the combined weight of all those glaring eyes, Sophie raised her head a bit higher. *Let them look.*

They reached the place where the Queen's Road intersected the square, where one could either go east or west, toward Fairport or away. Sophie herself wasn't entirely sure which way was correct, yet the stranger made his choice with the confidence of one who has walked the exact same path hundreds of times before. "How did you know which way to go?" Sophie asked him.

His brow furrowed. "Do you not recognize me for what I am, child?"

"I'm not a child. My aunt says I'm old enough to marry." *Nearly.*

"Age matters little. I have known men who were children, and children who were men." Their eyes met, and though his face remained stolid, there was a slight hint of light in them. "I am a Navigator."

As if that explained everything.

"So . . . what is a Navigator? What do Navigators do? Are there a lot of them or are you the only one? And where do Navigators come from?"

There came the briefest of sudden outbreaths from the Navigator, a short, quick huff, like laughter quickly quelled. "You know not what you ask. Such knowledge has been guarded jealously since the foundation of my order."

"But why? Why can't you tell me?"

The Navigator stopped and turned to face her fully. He loomed over Sophie, pinning her in place with his gaze. She was frozen, exposed, as though he were rummaging through the storage room of her mind and examining the contents one by one. Seaside faded. Time stopped. There was nothing else; his eyes had become the sea and earth and sky. The sensation was frightening, but only in the way that all new things are frightening at first, for there was no fear of him in her heart.

And then it was over. His feet resumed their motion, and Sophie followed.

"Long ago," said the Navigator, "Maravel the Lost was the Empress of Theruvia. She was a direct descendant of Theruvon, the first emperor, from a line unbroken for untold generations. The Theruvians craved war. They were conquerors, and each of Maravel's predecessors had used their might to expand the empire's borders. But the entire known world had been assumed by the time Maravel came to power. There were no foes left to vanquish, no territory left to take. It was an unprecedented moment. Maravel ascended with no purpose, no direction, no goal, for there was not one person alive who did not bow to her will."

"At first, Maravel felt free. City-wide festivals were thrown in her honor, with parades and exhibitions and massive feasts. The finest examples of the world's greatest creative minds were on display for her pleasure. Yet she soon grew restless. Bored. Maravel called upon her advisors and demanded a cure for her malaise. Ten counsellors, ten solutions, not one lasting success. The advisors were imprisoned for their failure, and her listlessness grew."

Sophie and the Navigator reached the docks. As he spoke, she glanced down their length to see the Spindlers at work. Richie and his older brother Flaxley were busy hauling in a net full of shiny, flopping fish, while their father stood by lighting his pipe. Richie looked up and saw them. Sophie stuck out her tongue at him and pulled a face, but he didn't even notice, for he was too busy staring at her companion. So distracted was he that he released his side of the net and spilled half the fish back into the boat. His gawping reverie was broken by a swift slap to the back of the head. Then the three of them were arguing animatedly as fish flipped over the boat's sides and back into the water. *Serves you right*, thought Sophie before turning her attention back to the story.

"In an attempt to regain his freedom and Maravel's trust, one of her advisors made a suggestion most foul. 'Seek out a Navigator,' he said, 'for they have but one purpose—to know the way.' He whispered to her of secret magics and enticed her to subjugate my order to her will, for if she were to succeed, no Theruvian ruler would ever be lost again."

"But a place can not be conquered if it can not be found. The Navigators have long understood this truth. In time, Maravel understood it as well. Her explorers combed every inch of the massive empire. Through snowy forests and dry deserts they trekked. They rode over grassy plains and hacked through the undergrowth of humid jungles. They paddled across placid mountain lakes and sailed upon tumultuous, stormy seas. All for naught. Years of fruitless searching left Maravel despondent and frustrated."

The home of Old Lady Magpie came into view. Hers was the last house in the village; from there, the Queen's Road followed the bend of the coast, climbing upward and disappearing over a small rise, where Seaside ended and Out There began. Sophie felt an odd tugging sensation that made her next step fractionally harder to take, as if there were a rubber band attached to her back that was just beginning to pull taut.

"One day, the captain of Maravel's city guard brought

her some urgent news. A Navigator had arrived at the gates. The empress ordered him brought to the palace. She treated the Navigator as an honored guest and sought to win his friendship. She plied him with the finest food and drink, and gifted him with private apartments inside the palace. The grand festivals of her early years were re-created in the Navigator's honor. By her order, he was never far from Maravel's side. Time and again she broached the subject of his homeland, hoping to gain some clue to use to her advantage. The Navigator told her nothing. Polite inquiries became frustrated demands. She tried to seduce him with riches and power, and when that failed, with her body. Bribery, blackmail, trickery, torture, Maravel attempted every conceivable method of coercion, but no information could be wrested from the Navigator's lips. So all-consuming was her desire that she failed to see the slow rot that had taken hold of her empire."

The road rose before them. They began to climb.

"In one final desperate attempt to succeed, Maravel visited the Navigator in his dungeon cell. He was beaten, bruised, starved, and scarred, but it was the empress who was broken. She cursed the circumstances of her life and her lack of purpose. She wailed over her failures as a ruler. She bemoaned the loss of gold spent on fruitless exploration. She raged over his silence, her ruin, and for the continued decay of her empire. Her vitriol spent, Maravel fell silent. It was then that the Navigator chose to speak. 'All are responsible for the path they choose.' He was executed the following day."

The Navigator went silent.

Sophie looked back over her shoulder and found she

was halfway up the hill. She came to a stop. "And then what happened?" she asked eagerly.

The Navigator turned, halting. "Maravel was not the final ruler of Theruvia, but the empire's collapse began under her reign, and eventually its name faded into memory. There is not a single living Theruvian today."

"What? You can't end a story like that!"

"Why not?"

"Because . . ." she trailed off, trying to come up with a good answer. "Because you can't!"

The barest hint of a smile lifted the corners of the Navigator's lips. "That is a childish answer for one who claims not to be a child. History holds the lessons of humanity's successes and failures, its triumphs and tragedies. Both hold important lessons for us all."

"Then I don't think I like history," Sophie pouted.

"That is a shame." The Navigator resumed his climb. "Think on it, child," he said over his shoulder. "See if your mind does not change."

Sophie lifted her foot. Hesitated. Put it back down. The gold embroidery of the Navigator's vest faded into the dark silk as the distance between them grew. The lines of his body became indistinct. He rose, and rose, and then began to shrink as a line of cobblestones climbed his backside, heels disappearing first, followed by calves, knees, torso. She watched helplessly, waiting for him to turn back, to beckon her onward, to give her permission to take that next step and snap her connection with Seaside forever. Then the Navigator's two-toned hair vanished, leaving her puzzled and alone and wondering what came next.

Where One Thing Ends . . .

The rest of the day passed in a morose haze.

Sophie drifted back home, sticking to side roads and cutting through fields, moping all the way. She moped as she pushed open the gate to Aunt Elle's property. She moped across the yard to the barn. She moped up the stairs and into the loft and into her room, where she unceremoniously dropped her knapsack onto the floor and then flumped face-first into bed. She lay with her nose pressed to the mattress and breathed through the rough fabric for what felt like a very long time.

Eventually she got bored of being bored and decided to do her chores. Each was performed with a complete lack of alacrity. There was no daydreaming, no woolgathering, no mooning, not one single solitary flight of fancy, just the automatic carrying out of mundane tasks fueled by a barely functioning self-preservation instinct bent on avoiding any more trouble.

Her robotic housework was interrupted by the return of Aunt Elle and Petunia. The two of them stood before her, talking excitedly and demanding all the details of her day, genuinely interested in Sophie for the first time in her life. Her answers were short, many of them consisting of only a single syllable.

It could be presumed that she was behaving this way out of some righteous form of teenaged spite. But it wasn't so. She simply didn't have the energy to care. The two gossip hounds quickly grew frustrated and resumed their usual smarmy disregard. Sophie moped away somewhere else and left them flabbergasted.

Blink, and she found herself standing outside the storage room. Her hand reached out, touched the latch, then fell away. Not even the prospect of exploring the hidden legacy within could cast off her malaise. It only brought back memories of her fight with Damon, of words spoken and unspoken, of his drunken nonsense ramblings. For a moment she was tempted to wonder where he was. Then she remembered she didn't care. Caring interfered with her moping.

Dinner came and went with no sign of Damon. Food appeared on her plate, which was odd because she wasn't hungry in the least. Meanwhile, Aunt Elle and Petunia gabbled on and on and on and *on*, while Uncle Roger listened and nodded patiently and cleaned his plate twice. Sophie joined him in his silence, if not his appetite. She excused herself and went to the loft to hide.

And to mope.

Sitting in bed, surrounded by the soft yellow glow of a lit lantern, she listened to the patter of evening rain and read her book. In truth, she was reading only in the most technical sense. Her eyes scanned the pages and interpreted the symbols as words, but her mind was closed off to their meaning. The author's words simply deflected off some mental barrier like flies against a window pane. She tossed the book aside with the sort of dramatic flair that is the sole property of teenage girls.

Why didn't I take the next step?

The question had been lodged in her mind all day like a rock in a shoe—the longer she'd ignored it, the more uncomfortable it had become. She knew the answer had something to do with that strange tugging sensation she'd felt on reaching the edge of town, that feeling of being drawn back toward Seaside. At the time it had felt as real as the wind in her hair, the stone beneath her feet, the heft of her knapsack, yet as soon as she'd turned for home it had disappeared. Where had it come from? Why should she be drawn to this place? She had no friends, no money, no job. Her parents were dead and everyone treated her like she was damaged. The boy she liked wasn't allowed to talk to her. Her aunt made her live in a barn. There was nothing for her in Seaside. Nothing at all.

Except for Damon.

Mope as she might, she still cared about him. That only made things worse. She had trusted him, completely, unconditionally, and in return he had lied to her. Not once. Not a handful of times. Every day of her entire life. Damon could have taken her into the storage room any time he wanted. They could have gone through the boxes together, with him telling stories about what they were like and where they had come from and who they had been. He could have shared their love with her. But he hadn't. Damon had betrayed her trust. She might have helped him with his grief, but he had deprived her of that opportunity, just as he'd kept her from finding work and helping them get free of the loft. And now, he had deprived her of the opportunity to leave this little nowhere village where she had no future. All because she still loved him. Bitter resentment pried at the crack in her already broken heart.

All are responsible for the path they choose.

The truth of the Navigator's words hit her like a slap across the face. Yes, Damon had chosen to keep his secrets. Just as she had chosen to follow him blindly, had chosen not to find her own work when he told her not to, had chosen to look to him as some storybook hero instead of what he truly was—a person. And people were fallible, sometimes disastrously so.

She could wait for her savior no longer. Her belief in him had gone dry, was no more alive than those little pink worms the Navigator had plucked from the dirt. There was no sense waiting for a day that would never come. To do otherwise would be CHILDISH NONSENSE.

It was time for Sophie to choose her own path.

. . . Another Begins

DAMON HAD MEANT TO make good on his word. Truly, he had. But some things simply aren't meant to be.

The barn was fully dark by the time he stumbled in. He'd stayed at Walden's longer than intended on account of the rain and had left as soon as it let up, but by then his head was swimming far more than was pleasant, making it difficult to navigate the wet, muddy lanes of Seaside. Twice he'd stopped to retch in the bushes. Damon wobbled his way into the barn and came to rest against the post at the bottom of the stairs. Save for the heavy breathing of horses and the occasional swish of a tail, all was silent. Clutching the post, Damon listed from side to side, eyelids drooping briefly before snapping sharply open again. *Time to get this over with.*

He climbed the stairs and peeked his head into Sophie's room. She was curled up snug under her blankets, her body rising and falling with every dreaming breath. It made him smile to see her so at peace. They had a lot to talk about. None of it would be easy. That was the very reason Damon had spent most of the day working up the courage to tell her the truth, every single word of it, the good and the bad alike. He wondered if his little sister would ever sleep so peacefully afterward. He certainly never had. *One more night,* thought Damon. *She deserves it. I'll tell her first thing in the morning. I promise.*

"Love you, li'l butterfly," he whispered before stumbling to his room, where he sank into blessedly dreamless oblivion.

*   *   *

There was one thing Damon could absolutely be counted on to do—snore like a ripsaw.

Sophie waited until his raucous breathing began, then threw back the covers and sat up. Her knapsack lay beside her in bed, bulging and heavy, the top cinched up tight. She was wearing her mother's bright yellow sundress. It was hardly a fitting choice for sleep, but she had no intention of sleeping, not that night. She stood and shrugged on her jacket, then hoisted her pack and settled it on her shoulders. There was only one thing left to do. She pulled a letter from her nightstand drawer and left it sitting on top where Damon was sure to see it.

Then it was time to go. She chose each step carefully, knowing which boards squeaked and which ones didn't. One by one she crept down the stairs. When her head came level with the floor of the loft, she stopped and took one last look down the hallway toward where Damon slept.

"I love you, too, big brother."

*   *   *

A crescent moon hung in the midnight sky. Its borrowed brilliance seemed to shine on her and her alone, a spotlight for the unseen eyes that surely observed from all sides, hidden in nocturnal shadow and recording her every movement for some terrible future reckoning. Her every footfall was impossibly amplified so that the grass crackled and crunched underfoot with a clamorous racket. The chilly night air urged Sophie to change course and seek refuge in her warm bed. Even time itself worked against her. She well knew that it took no more than two minutes to cross the yard and reach the gate, but under the lunar disk, the journey lasted hours, days, an entire lifetime. With each step the gate slipped farther and farther away, taunting her, whispering what she had long feared was the truth—she would never be free of this place.

Of course, this was all in Sophie's imagination. In reality she reached the gate in one minute and thirty-eight seconds, and was observed only by a solitary goat, which lost interest in her almost immediately. She praised Aunt Elle's particular brand of persnicketiness as she unlatched the gate and pushed it open. The sound of its opening was less than a whisper on the wind. A fat, fluffy cloud floated across the moon, and as the light faded, so did the sensation of being watched. The dirt and gravel crunched at their normal volume, the air wasn't quite so nippy, and time resumed its steady flow.

Sophie followed the lane away from town. Up ahead, it turned south and joined up with the Queen's Road, but rather than follow the curve she cut straight ahead through the moist, springy soil of the field. Crickets chirped all around. Sophie wondered why they only came out at night, and what it was they talked about, and if maybe they weren't deaf since they had to talk so loud.

Her old friend the oak waited up ahead. Standing tall and

silhouetted against the starry sky, it was even more majestic in the moonlight than during the day. Pinpricks of light peeked from between its gnarled branches. "Good evening," she said as she reached the top of the hill, running her hand along its knotty bark. "Beautiful night, isn't it?" It wouldn't be so for long. Out to sea, clouds hung heavy over the horizon. Lightning rippled and arced from the iron grey clouds, illuminating the seething waters and revealing the frothing turbulence below. With any luck, she would be gone long before it reached Seaside.

The wind rustled the branches of her ligneous friend, their breathy susurration giving the oak tree a voice. It was time to move on. "Yeah, you're right," she said, patting its bark. "Thank you for always listening. I'm going to miss you." Then she turned her back on Seaside and descended One Tree Hill, this time moving in a new direction, one she'd never taken, and each step carried her farther from home than she'd ever been before. Despite the heft of her pack, they came light and easy, unburdened by any backward pull.

Sophie had done it. She was Out There. She was free at last.

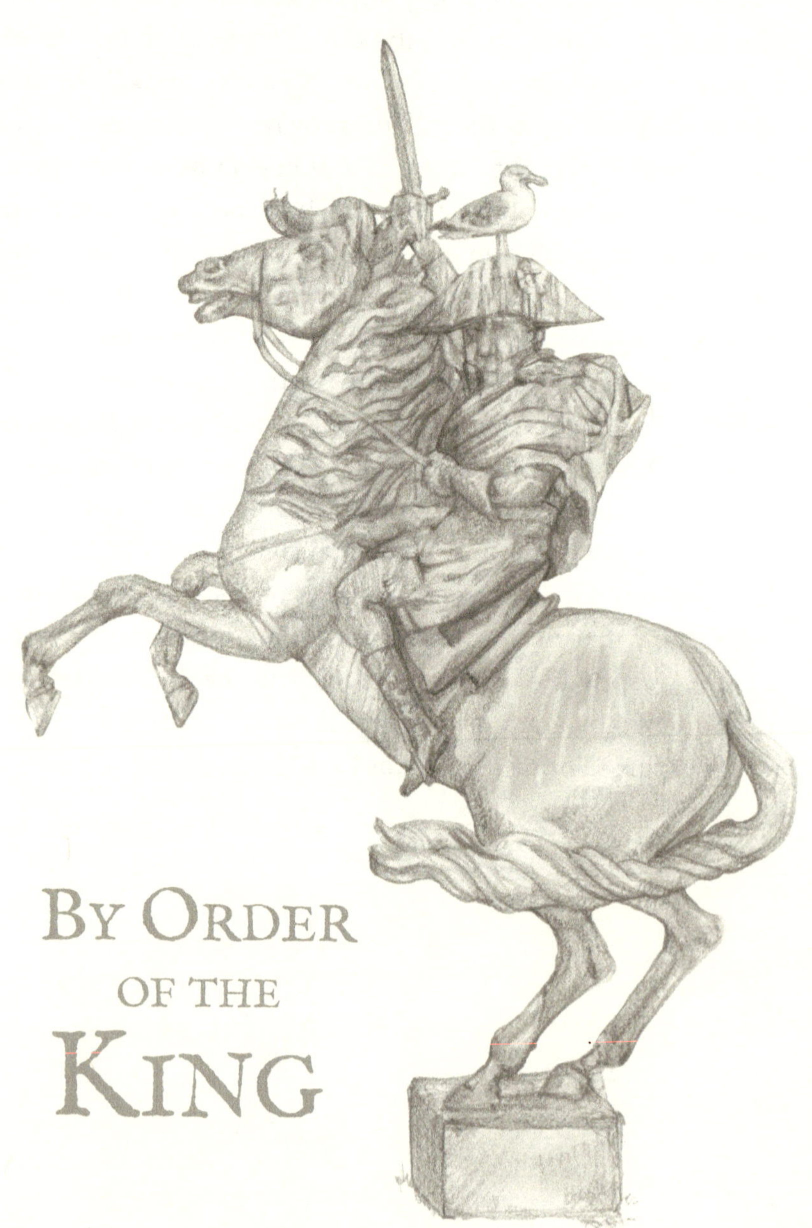

By Order of the King

Further Occupational Hazards of Farming Kelp

THE STORM ARRIVED THE FOLLOWING MORNING. Thick, heavy raindrops pelted the sand of the beach, creating a legion of shifting, miniature craters in the sand. Two stooped figures in oil-soaked leathers wandered along the shore, collecting the hefty gloms of kelp hurled landward by the crashing waves. Tromping through the wet sand and rain with his arms full of damp, ropy kelp, Mert wore a vacant smile. He was not really on the beach, you see. He was experiencing the potential joys of a new profession—sheep farming.

"Mert!"

It all started the day of the Navigator's arrival. Frances had always been a world-class haranguer, but she'd attained new levels of badgery when Mert returned home that afternoon. She'd taken to assaulting his venturesome spirit and lethargic work ethic with a sharpness of tongue that would make a razor blush. Then Mert's mind had done a funny thing. For the briefest of moments, he had imagined himself on the beach, standing in the sunshine and breathing in the salty sea air. Alone.

Mert's powers of imagination were not very potent at

first. He wondered what life would be like with a different occupation. A shell collector, perhaps, or a purveyor of interesting sands. But repetition is the source of all mastery, and Frances made sure he got plenty of practice. One morning, Mert achieved a major breakthrough when he asked himself, "What if I didn't scavenge from the beach anymore?" A whole new world of possibilities opened up before him. Mert had been busy exploring them ever since.

"Oy! 'ave your eyes gone the way of your useless mind? You walked right past two perfectly good gloms!"

Mert's imaginary farm wasn't particularly fancy, but he found himself returning quite often. Frances would fix bacon and eggs for breakfast, then he would go out and move the herd from one place to another, which in Mert's mind constituted the totality of sheep husbandry. He even had a favorite sheep, an especially fluffy ewe named Becky. She would walk at his heel as he herded the rest of the flock, feeding her bits of carrot that he carried in a pouch on his belt and lovingly patting her on the head. Around midday they would curl up under a shade tree for an afternoon nap. Becky would lay down first, then Mert, resting his head against her like a pillow, and the two of them—

"*MERT!!!*"

He snapped his head up, rudely jerked back to the sodden, stormy beach. Frances, meanwhile, looked like a neglected kettle. It was a wonder she hadn't begun to shriek. "Eh?" he asked casually.

"You great galumphing loaf! What you doing, having a leisurely stroll? We been out 'ere in this rain for two hours now and you've hardly collected a thing. I swear, sometimes I think there's naught twixt your ears but wool!"

Frances had no idea how right she was.

"Why you grinnin' like that?"

This was a dangerous question. He couldn't very well tell her about his new life on the sheep farm. However, his powers of confabulation had already been stretched to their limits, so lying was out of the question. Mert's mouth moved inarticulate, soundless. He was drowning from inaction. And then, like a fresh glom of juicy kelp washing ashore, his memory tossed him a line. It was one Frances had used many times before. "Rain or shine, the kelp is fine."

Frances was gobsmacked. Her face flushed red and then right on to purple. Veins throbbed in her neck, her head trembled with rage, and Mert knew he shouldn't laugh, but he could see steam coming from her ears and there was nothing he could do to stop it. His embattled wife sucked air deep into her lungs in preparation for one final, cataclysmic verbal volley. *"YOU—"*

The sky exploded overhead, obliterating her tirade. Fingers of lightning cast the beach in brilliant hues of violet-white. The very horizon was erased as rain pounded from the ebon clouds above. A single huge bolt reached down and touched the sea just beyond the rocky shore, then another, and another, striking the same spot over and over again, and in that spot a great churning whirlpool began to form. Mert and Frances stared, awestruck, their argument canceled by the spectacular display of nature's might.

"Think we should go!" Mert shouted over the tumult. Seawater flooded the beach like the coming of the tide impossibly accelerated. Soon they were struggling through knee-high water to reach a nearby rock. Mert boosted his wife up, then quickly followed. The astonished kelp farmers

huddled together on their stony isle, nervously waiting to see if the water would rise any higher.

Meanwhile, the whirlpool's black funnel grew wider and deeper. Figures like men on horseback rose from below, riding along the swirling wall of water as if climbing a narrow trail along a cliff's edge. A dozen riders, arranged in a short column and led by two standard bearers, pounded toward the shore. They galloped past the rocky break, over the sand bar, and finally onto the flooded beach. One of the riders gestured menacingly toward the terrified kelp farmers. The column turned and trotted their way.

Mert was having serious doubts about his choice of profession.

His burgeoning imagination had failed to prepare him for this. The men on horseback weren't men at all, but crustaceous creatures in the shape of men. Instead of skin, they had a sickly green carapace that was mottled and covered in knobs, bumps, and spines. One of their two arms ended in an enormous, meaty pincer. Where eyes should have been, two bulbous black orbs sat atop short, stubby stalks, and instead of a proper nose, there were only two narrow slits. A thin, dark line like an inverted smile hinted at the presence of a mouth. Their mounts were made entirely of seawater. Bits of sand and debris floated within their aqueous bodies; a pair of flittering silver fish chased each other about the belly of one such beast. Only one thing about the horrific invaders made any sense to Mert, and that was the horse tackle. It had been fashioned from kelp and driftwood, and to Mert's practiced eye, it had been assembled by someone who was quite the kelpsmith.

One of the standard bearers trotted ahead, the horse moving over the water as if it were solid ground. The creature's mouth slit opened to reveal rows of needle sharp teeth. "Humans," it said, "consider yourself blessed." Its voice was high pitched and grainy, as if speaking through a throat full of sand. "On this day you will stand before the Master of the Maritime, Overlord of the Ocean, Supreme Ruler of the Nine Seas. Go, sodden wretches, go and gather all your kind, for you have been summoned for an audience with the Merling King."

Keeping Promises

DAMON FARRIER WOKE ALL AT ONCE. His head was painless and clear, though it had no right to be. He sat up, full of energy, his mouth a little sticky and dry, but otherwise no worse for the wear. Some water with breakfast and he'd be right as rain. He counted it as a small blessing, for he knew that he could put off his conversation with Sophie no longer. Better to face what lay ahead with clarity and focus. He planned out the day as he rose and dressed. They would eat in the dining room together, then the two of them would go out to the storage and he would explain where it had all come from and why it had remained hidden for so long. Then he would ask for her forgiveness. *She'll understand,* he reassured himself. *She has to.*

Damon knocked on the wall outside her door and said, "Hey, you awake?" When there was no answer, he stuck his head in and saw nothing but empty, rumpled bedclothes. Disappointing, but not unusual.

What was unusual was the sight of Petunia at the wash basin. She was up to her elbows in soapy water and dirty dishes, wearing a pastel pink dress and a look of petulant disgust. Plates went into the basin covered in bits of dried egg and bacon grease; they came out in much the same condition, only wet. In other words, Petunia was as proficient at washing up as Uncle Roger was at making toast.

"What are you doing?" Damon asked.

"What does it look like I'm doing?" Petunia shot back angrily. "Your airy-fairy sister has run off somewhere and left me to do her housework."

"Wait, what do you mean, 'run off somewhere'?"

"I mean she isn't here. She didn't come down for breakfast, she didn't do any of her chores, and now mother is making me do them when it isn't my job. Oh just look at my dress. It's ruined! Sophie's going to pay for this, I swear."

"Uh huh." While Petunia continued to fume, Damon got into the bread box, cut himself a slice, and scavenged a few bacon bits from an unwashed plate. "Do you know where she went?"

"*The moon.*"

Damon took his leave. He munched on his meager breakfast while searching for Aunt Elle. She was in her bedroom, seated at her vanity and working on her hair. He rapped lightly on the door, and she looked up at him through the mirror. "Damon. I see you've decided to add to my misery by scattering crumbs about the house. What do you want?"

"I'm looking for Sophie. Have you seen her?"

"No, I have not. Nor do I care to." She swiveled around to face him. "Honestly, I do not know what has gotten into that girl lately. First she starts sneaking around with that Codwallader boy—"

"What?"

"—next she's picking fights with you and ignoring her duties around the house. And don't get me started on the shameful spectacle she made of herself yesterday. I can't tell you how thankful I am that I wasn't there to see it myself. I might have fainted. Damon, I am this close to securing a match between Petunia and Sterling Halderman. I won't have your ragamuffin sister ruin it with her silly obsessions and flagrant disregard for the family name." She paused thoughtfully. "Or you, for that matter. Have you apologized to Horace yet?"

"No, I haven't. And I won't."

She shook her head. "You're impossible. Can't you see that this isn't about you?"

"But it is! Horace has spread the word that he won't do business with anyone who's seen with me. I haven't worked in over a week!"

"A situation easily remedied by a simple public apology," Aunt Elle pleaded. "Horace gets what he wants, you can go back to work, I get my match for Petunia, and everyone is happy."

"Never."

Her eyes narrowed. "You are as stubborn as your father. It never did him any good, either."

"I'll reckon with my own mistakes."

"You certainly will." She turned back to the mirror and her hair. "When you find Sophie, tell her I wish to speak with her. This behavior cannot continue."

"Yeah. Sure." Damon brushed the crumbs from his hands and onto her clean floor as he walked away.

Sneaking around with that Codwallader boy. Damon didn't like the sound of that. Not that he had anything against Robbie. He seemed nice enough, despite his family and friends. It was the idea of Sophie having a relationship at all, and especially a secret one, that he didn't like. Another thing for them to discuss. Still, he was glad that he knew. It was clear he would have to go into town to find Sophie, and now he would make the grocery his first stop. After going back to the barn and putting on his rain gear, that was.

Damon had just reentered the barn when the summoning bell began to toll. That was when the seeds of worry truly took root. Frozen, he spared a glance toward One Tree Hill in the vain hope that he would see his sister fleeing the rain. No such luck. He cursed himself for not waking up earlier, for not catching Sophie before she left, for not having the courage to face her sooner.

Damon threw on his slicker and boots, steeling himself for the long, wet walk to the square.

The Arrival of the Merling King

THERE ARE TWO FEATURES of Seaside's square that have not yet been described. The first is a bronze statue on a concrete pedestal. It depicts a lithe, handsome man in military dress on a rearing stallion, sword raised heroically, his penetrating gaze directed forward to pierce the armored hearts of his unseen foes. The man on the horse was meant to be Duke Truculo, Lord and Master of the Westerlands, of which Seaside was a part. It had been bestowed upon the village as a gift, not only *by* the duke, but *for* the duke. To call the likeness "flattering" would be an understatement bordering on falsehood. And yet, no one in Seaside had dared to question the artist's integrity . . . or to refuse Duke Truculo's generosity. On the day of its unveiling, he had said to them, "Good people, if ever you are in need, look upon my image and let it fill you with confidence. Know in your hearts that you can always rally to my side, for I shall surely rally to yours!"

To ensure that they would indeed rally to his side, he had also installed the square's other previously unremarked upon feature—a heavy, bronze bell. Its purpose was to summon the villagers prior to the duke's arrival so that he would receive the adulation and fanfare that he so rightly deserved. The hollow, metallic *tong* sound induced feelings of resignation and dread throughout the village, heralding a period of grudging toleration that could last for hours, sometimes days. Of Seaside's Necessary visitors, Duke Truculo had been deemed the least necessary of all.

The villagers were understandably slow to respond to that morning's summons.

Their reluctance was compounded by the sight of Frances tugging on the bell rope while Mert jumped up and down in the middle of the square, waving his arms frantically and shouting at the top of his lungs. The first few ventured into the pounding rain to see what all the fuss was about. Seeing them, more followed, then still more, until finally the whole village was standing in the square beneath a flock of sodden umbrellas, grumbling and miserable and not at all sure why they were there.

Damon and his family were among the last to join the unhappy congregation. He pushed his way through the crowd, calling out for his sister. The sprouting seeds of worry sent their searching roots burrowing through his stomach and chest. Only one thing mattered in that moment—ensuring Sophie's safety.

"Damon? What seems to be the matter?"

Dr. Murphy frowned at him from beneath a big black umbrella. Albert stood beside him, scowling and looking very out of sorts. "I'm looking for Sophie," Damon said to them. "Have you seen her?"

"No, not since yesterday. She chased out of the clinic after our patient—*former* patient—and I haven't seen her since. I had hoped that her interest in our profession might extend beyond a mere curiosity for the exotic. It seems my hopes were misplaced." Albert scoffed and smugly smirked. It withered under Damon's angry glare. "I am certain you will find her," said Murphy. "More than likely she is huddled up with her friends somewhere, as bewildered as the rest of us."

Once again the doctor had missed the mark, for Damon knew exactly how many friends Sophie had. He was about to say something to that effect when a burst of blaring, discordant notes rang out over the village and stilled all conversation. Confusion built upon itself as the rain came to a sudden halt. The villagers gasped in unison. A circular aperture opened in the clouds overhead to reveal the clear blue sky above, while all around a swirling, churning mass of dark mist enveloped Seaside like an impenetrable wall. The reaching vines in Damon's gut grew thorns and gave him a nasty twist. He raised up on his toes to locate the source of those eerie notes.

The crowd parted as the creatures from the beach rode into the square. Those in front bore hoisted banners, their poles made of gnarled, grey driftwood, their pennants no more than strands of sickly green seaweed. As one, they pushed the humans back and secured a wide lane. The creatures regarded the villagers from atop their nightmare mounts with their bulbous black eyes. Then each standard bearer lifted a great conch shell to its mouth slit and gave another deafening, hellish blast.

A shocked cry went up from the crowd as two enormous lobsters scuttled into the square. Each was the size of a draft horse. Their segmented, exoskeletal legs scrabbled madly across the cobbles, coming onward with the sound of hundreds of hobnails clattering on stone. Between them they pulled an ornate chariot made of coral and seashells. It was occupied by another of the crustaceous man-creatures, this one much taller than the others, broader, with an extra pair of arms extending from its midsection. It was with these extra hands that it guided the terrifying beasts of burden, leaving its one remaining humanoid hand free to steady itself with a golden trident. On its head was a crown, opalescent, like the sheen of abalone shells. Each of its nine points was tipped with a pearl the size of a child's fist. A heavy seaweed cape flapped behind him.

The Merling King had arrived in Seaside.

The Pronouncement

THE MERLING KING DISMOUNTED and came to stand beside the duke's statue. Each step was accompanied by a metallic *chink* as his trident connected with the cobblestones. His dragging cape left a slather of thick seafoam in his wake. "Kneel before the Merling King," commanded his standard bearer. The villagers grudgingly obeyed.

"Who amongst you will speak on your behalf?"

The crowd murmured, uncertain. Then Horace Halderman found his feet, holding his head up with as much dignity as he could muster. "I will."

"Approach."

Horace strode forward to stand before the giant maritime monarch. He then proceeded to cycle through a series of movements and gestures that had withered many a man, woman, and child. First, he haughtily adjusted his jacket. Then he furrowed his brow, now marred by a circular burn scar. He angled his head disdainfully. And, as a final touch, he put one hand on his hip and pointed his cane as he spoke. "Now see here!" he began. "This is a terrible inconvenience you've imposed upon us all, a terrible inconvenience indeed!

I should like to know the meaning of this tomfoolery. By what right do you . . ."

Casually, the Merling King reached up his great and powerful claw, put it around the neck of Duke Truculo's bronze stallion, and squeezed. The metal parted with a sickening squeal. There was a horrific hollow *clang!* as the head tumbled to rest at Horace's feet. He shut up. Fast.

"I have been cheated." The Merling King's voice was deep and grainy, uneven, like sand and stones in a rolling drum. "My forces battered and destroyed one of your seafaring ships, as is my right. Fifty-nine souls fed my minions. One survivor came ashore. Here. I have come to claim what is rightfully mine. You, village chieftain, will bring the survivor to me. Now."

"Ch-ch-chieftain?" Horace stammered. "I, uh, I don't know that I can call myself by that particular title. I am simply an, oh, let us say, respected upstanding member of the community, and not really—"

"Silence. It is not wise to test my patience. I want the Navigator."

"He isn't here!" Horace blurted. "He *was* here, yes, that is true, b-b-but—"

Doctor Murphy stood. "If I might interject?"

"Speak quickly."

"I am the village doctor. The man you seek was my patient. Up until yesterday, that is, when he woke from a long slumber and took his leave of us. I understand many of these humble folk personally witnessed this departure." At this there was a grumble of agreement. "We do not know his whereabouts, but he made plain to me his intention to return to the sea."

"Ah, there you have it," said Horace, clearly relieved.

"When he boards his next ship, you can simply sink that one and apprehend him at your leisure and forget all about—"

"No."

"No?"

"Your intervention saved him. I hold you responsible for returning him to me."

"Well, that hardly seems fair!" cried Horace. The villagers voiced their agreement.

The Merling King thrust the butt of his trident upon the ground. Lightning arced down from the sky and danced upon his weapon's triad of points before dispersing into the aether, silencing the crowd. "I shall return at the rising of the next full moon. You will hand over the Navigator, or I will summon the ocean and wash your village into the sea. Your homes will be as driftwood. Your flesh will feed the creatures of my dominion, great and small. Your bones will sink to the sea floor, to be ground by the eternal waves until naught is left but flecks of sand. This is the vow I make to you. Do not disappoint me."

Lost and Found

THE VILLAGERS CONTINUED TO KNEEL as the Merling King and his menacing minions withdrew. They neither stood nor spoke, scarcely dared even to breathe. Not until the clouds had stopped churning and the rain had returned did they break their stillness.

And when it broke, there was madness.

Damon was among the first to rise. "Sophie?" he called, his voice drowned by so many others speaking at once. He pushed through the confused, commiserating villagers, fighting his way to Codwallader's Grocery, where a circle had formed around Johnathan. He was assuring everyone in earshot that they were going to be alright. Robbie was among them. Damon grabbed him by the shoulder and spun him around. With urgency in his voice as he said, "Where's Sophie?"

"I-I-"

"Have you seen her today?"

"Of course he hasn't," said Johnathan, pulling his son away protectively. "He knows better than to associate with Unnecessary filth like you. Now move along."

"Please, I just need to —"

"I said move along."

Damon turned away, bewildered, dazed. He hadn't gone more than a few steps when he heard the murmuring.

"That's the one . . ."

"He should be ashamed . . ."

". . . run out of town, I say . . ."

No longer did he need to push to get through. The others removed themselves eagerly from his path. They actively recoiled, shielding their faces as though he were afflicted with some contagion. Damon tried to ignore them, to concentrate on his search for Sophie, his head turning, always turning, looking for some hopeful sign and meeting nothing but suspicion and anger, potent fertilizer for the wicked flowers of fear blooming inside. "What?" he said to the cowering villagers. "What? Why are you all looking at me like that? What do you want from me!"

"Don't you realize that this is all your fault?"

Horace Halderman stepped out from the crowd. His son Sterling stood behind him with a protective arm around Petunia's shoulder. Aunt Elle was with them, too, arms crossed, stilettos for eyes.

"I told you," said Horace, pointing with one gnarled trotter. An angry grimace revealed his missing teeth. "We should have given that hideous Unnecessary back to the waves when we had the chance. But no. You had to intervene! You had to take your shot at me while I was vulnerable, and now the one person who can free us from this horror is roaming around Out There while terrifying sea beasts threaten our perfectly adequate village!"

"That's ridiculous," Damon said sharply. "You didn't know it was going to come to this. No one did."

"Our bones ground to sand, Damon!" cried Aunt Elle.

"That's what he said. They're going to eat us and spit out our bones and it's all just so . . . *unimaginable!*"

"There, there, dear," said Horace, taking her hand and giving it a reassuring pat. "I will fix this. You'll see."

"How?" she wailed. The question was echoed by the encircling crowd.

"Well it's quite simple," said Horace, addressing them all. "I shall send to Duke Truculo for aid. He has promised to protect us in times of need. It's time he followed through!"

"What good will that do?" asked Damon. "You saw those things. Even if the duke's men could defeat them in battle, they can't hold back the sea."

"No, but they can find the foul outlander who brought this fate upon us and deliver him here before the next full moon. When the sea king returns, we will hand him over, *as we should have done before.*"

Damon shook his head, disgusted and incredulous. "Still trying to have your way, is that it? You petty, greedy—"

"You hold your tongue!" Aunt Elle fumed. "We are going home right now, right this *very instant.*" She took hold of Damon's arm and tugged at him, and though he could easily have brushed her aside, he let himself be led, sparing a single baleful look back at Horace. Damon vowed that no matter what happened, he would never let Horace Halderman send the stranger to his death. Never.

*   *   *

Damon climbed up to the loft, exhausted. He'd tried to ignore the growing, sickening tightness in his chest, but the twining, thirsty vines that had taken hold of his heart fed on hope, drinking it down drop by drop by drop, until the last of it was drained and he could no longer deny the truth. Standing in their darkened living space, he took his face in his hands and released a deep, shuddering breath.

Sophie was gone.

He staggered to her door, as he had done so often, only this time drunk with grief. The room looked exactly as it had that morning. He'd believed he would find her in the dining room then, having breakfast. Now he wondered if she'd eaten at all. Or slept. Damon entered and slumped down on her bed. Her knapsack was gone. So was her jacket. Her disappearance was planned. He lifted her pillow, fluffed it idly, then put it back.

"Where have you flown to, li'l butterfly?"

Then his eyes found the little white envelope on the bedside table. His name was scratched on it in Sophie's halting, unpracticed script. He tore it open and removed the letter inside. Tears streamed silently down his face as he read:

Dear Damon,

I am leaving Seaside. Not forever, just for a little while. I'm sorry I didn't tell you first, but you would have said no and made me promise to stay, and I didn't want to break another promise to you. And I'm not going to tell you where I'm going, either, because then you'll follow me and make me come back. I'm nearly an adult and I can't keep letting other people make my decisions for me.

You don't need to worry about me. I brought plenty of food and water and my jacket. I also took the jar of money. I'm sure you can get plenty more since you've had so many new jobs lately.

I think you should know that I am still mad at you. You lied to me. You hid mom and dad from me. For a really long time! I know it hurts you to talk about them, but couldn't you have at least tried, for me? It wasn't nice, what you did, and it wasn't fair, either. But you should also know I didn't leave because of you. All are responsible for the path they choose. This one is mine.

I still love you, Big Brother, and I will come back. I promise.

-Sophie

Forgotten Footsteps

Clear Skies Ahead

The sky was still shedding the last of its nightly shades as Sophie munched on an apple for breakfast. Rolling hills stood like frozen waves of earth, the crest of each highlighted by the sun as it peeked over the rim of the horizon. Wildflowers of every color grew sprinkled amongst the emerald blades of grass. She imagined them yawning and stretching as they woke, their faces lifted toward the blazing disc in the sky. Unseen birds raised their voices in praise of the coming day. They flitted through the air, wings flapping in furious bursts of activity, changing direction with impossible speed as they hunted for insects. Field mice rustled the grass as they scurried along their well-worn footpaths. From time to time one would pop out onto the road, look around in confusion, then disappear once again. Sophie took her final bite and then left the apple's core at one of these tiny trailheads. It would make for a nice treat, she thought. Smiling, she carried on, delighting in the feeling of cool, moist air against her skin.

Sophie had never experienced a more wondrous morning.

The dawn brought with it a strange sensation of duality. The fields and the hills, the birds, bugs, and other critters, the angle of the rising sun and the colors in the lightening sky above, each individual element was familiar. It was their composition that was different. Some giant had come along and rearranged her world without adding anything new. Not even One Tree Hill was immune. Over and over again she'd seen lone sentinels standing proudly atop their hills against the blue dome of the sky. If there was one thing she'd least expected to find Out There, it was more of the same.

What she had expected was for everything to *feel* different. How exactly she wasn't sure, but the villagers spoke of the outside world in such ominous tones that it didn't seem possible to simply walk around unscathed. The first hour of her journey had been marked by apprehension. Each step risked unleashing some mysterious malady. A sensation of drowning, perhaps, or a choking cloud of smoke. But those feelings hadn't come. Nor had she been kidnapped by bandits, eaten by wolves, or swallowed up by a sinkhole. All she felt was free.

Thunder rumbled from behind. She stopped and looked back the way she'd come. Heavy, dark clouds hung low in the sky. Over Seaside, she knew. They were no longer her concern. Sophie resettled her pack, put a smile on her face, and set off in search of what lay beneath the clear skies ahead.

The Innkeepers

It was mid-afternoon when Sophie reached the inn at the crossroads. The sight of it filled her with that same sense of dissonant familiarity. At first glance it could have been any building in Seaside—a squat, boxy rectangle with white walls and a brown shingled roof. Yet Sophie had been so inured to a life of uniformity that the differences leapt out in sharp relief. For starters, there were two chimneys, one at each end. Such a duplication of exhaust handling would be enough to create quite the scandal on its own, but the support beams had also been left visible, creating a neat pattern of dark brown triangles that would have been deemed a health hazard due to the ensuing rash of apoplectic fits. Then there was the overall state of the place. The paint was faded and cracked and chipped, the shutters hung lazily askew, and the property's rail fence was gapped and leaned at odd angles. A signpost stood by the roadside. The sign itself was missing. Sophie could only imagine the disgust, outrage, and unbridled superiority Aunt Elle would muster upon seeing such a place.

It was love at first sight.

There was one other reason the inn felt familiar. She had

seen it before. Sophie shrugged off her knapsack and opened it. Carefully pressed between a pair of books were her mother's watercolors. A moment of digging, and then she was looking at the inn's identical twin, a sibling made of pigment on paper instead of wood, plaster, and stone. There was a stable and a fire pit in the painting, neither of which Sophie could see from where she stood. There were also people painted there, sitting in the sunshine at long picnic tables with mugs in their hands and smiles on their faces. It looked warm and inviting and not nearly so shabby as the real thing. With the watercolor in hand and her pack on her back, Sophie approached the inn, maneuvering around to find her mother's former vantage point. The stable and the fire pit and the long tables all came into view, and they, too, had fallen into the same state of neglected disarray. Sophie pulled in a deep breath and closed her eyes, trying her very hardest to feel her mother's presence, if only for a brief moment. Then she crossed the little yard and pushed open the inn's heavy front door.

Sophie Farrier was no stranger to horrible smells. Much of her life had been spent in the updraft of wet horse apples and their associated gaseous emissions. She'd sat beside the kelp-encrusted Navigator in the confines of the barn and barely wrinkled her nose. All of this should impress upon you the unbridled power of the moist funk that assaulted poor Sophie as she stepped through the door of the inn. She plugged her nose and pressed on.

The sticky floorboards crackled beneath her with every cautious step. To her left was a bar. Two tap handles stuck up behind it. Against the wall was a shelf of dusty, unused glasses. A door stood open at the bar's far end, revealing counters and sinks and stacked serving dishes. To her right was a large common room with tables and chairs haphazardly scattered. All were empty. There was a large set of double doors on the back wall. Each held a pane of greasy, grimy glass, through which she could barely discern the outdoor space. "Hello?" she called out, her voice nasal and choked off from her pinched nostrils. "Is anyone here?"

Pots and pans clattered against each other in the kitchen. A hoarse woman's voice called out, "One moment!" More rustling and shuffling. Metal crashing to the wooden floor. "Shitpile!" the voice muttered, and Sophie blushed. Then the owner of the voice revealed herself, a hefty woman with a rough, pitted complexion wearing a heavily stained apron over a dark house dress. A kitchen towel dangled from one shoulder. She wiped at her beaded brow with it, slung it back into place, then waddled over behind the bar. "Take a look at you," she said, her tone gruff, almost accusatory. Her words carried an unfamiliar, lazy accent. "Holding your nose like that. Yer like to insult the owner of this establishment, which ya happen to be looking at. Not the best way to start things off, is it?" Sophie, not wanting to be rude, reluctantly released the grip on her nose. "Don't worry, the smell will leave ya soon enough. Now, what can I do for ya, girl?"

I'm not a girl, Sophie nearly said, then changed her mind. The sooner she could get out of here, the better. "I just need to know how to get to Fairport."

"Fairport." The woman leaned on the bar, hard eyes narrowed. "Obviously y'haven't come from Fairport, then, else ya'd know yer way home, and since nobody ever comes from that way—" she pointed east, in the very direction Sophie *had* come from "—ya must be from up north. Dress like that, I'm guessing yer an Islington girl. Am I right?"

"No, ma'am."

"Aw don't start in with that 'ma'am' stuff now! You call me Cass. It used to be Cassie, but that was back when I was your size."

"Ha!"

A man sat up sharply from behind one of the tables, his hair sticking up at odd angles as though he'd been asleep. Groggily he rose, stumbled over to the bar and leaned against it. He turned his grin on Sophie. Beady blue eyes regarded her from over a long, narrow nose and protruding buck teeth. One eye looked straight ahead, while the other was aimed somewhere over her right shoulder. He looked like a deranged rat that hadn't eaten in weeks. "Don't lie to the poor girl," he said, "you were never her size."

"Go on, Feeney, say that again," said Cass, putting a hand jauntily on her hip. "I'll crack yer head with my skillet and knock your eyes back straight."

Feeney cocked a thumb at the big woman and said, "She's the one who put 'em this way to begin with." Cass slapped his shoulder twice with her towel, and he jumped and played like it hurt. Sophie relaxed a bit, the beginnings of a smile forming on her face.

"So, not from Islington, eh?" said Cass. "Channing's Breen, then, is it?"

"No."

"Well I'm sure ya haven't come all the way from High Vandermeer, not without a horse and carriage y'haven't."

"Who says I don't have a horse and carriage?"

"I do, that's who." Cass pulled a glass from the shelf behind the bar and polished it thoroughly inside and out, using the same towel she'd used to wipe her face. "If ya did have," she continued, working the ale tap, "yer driver would be in here asking the questions, if he didn't already know the way. And, ya wouldn't a bothered to bring yer whole life in on yer back." Cass set the ale on the bar, sloshing a little over the side. Feeney eyed it greedily. "Here, sit, have a drink, sunshine girl. Yer not the first runner we've had in here, far from it."

"Um . . . I don't drink that stuff."

"Ohhhh," Feeney intoned, shaking his head solemnly. "I see how 'tis. Reminds you of what you're trying to leave behind. That's a shame, 'tis, a right shame. S'alright, you just push that glass right over here—"

"Get yer greedy mitts off it," said Cass, snatching up the beer and taking a big swig. "No husband o' mine's going to be a worthless, drunk layabout."

"I knew it!" Feeney jumped up and did a little jig. "I knew if I just kept a-wishin' and a-hopin' and a-drinkin', you'd finally come to your senses and grant me that divorce. You hear that, lass? Feeney's a free man!"

"Yer free to get your bony arse into the kitchen and see to that stew."

Feeney stopped dancing. His head and shoulders drooped melodramatically, and he stomped his way into the back. "Yes, mum," he muttered, winking at Sophie as he went. She giggled.

"And clean up that mess while yer back there, ya shifty grifter!" Cass turned back to Sophie, her expression softening. "Go on, take that pack off. Sit. Let's have us a little chat, woman to woman as it were." Sophie did as asked, climbing up on one of the unsteady barstools. "Who is it yer running from? Yer dad? Brothers? Uncle? Ya can tell me, s'alright now."

"It's not like that," Sophie said. "I just got tired of Seaside and left."

"*Seaside?* Well, now I understand! That place is about as exciting as a wet cow flop." Sophie giggled again. "How d'ya stand it, everything being the same all the time?"

Sophie shrugged. "I couldn't, I guess."

"I suppose yer right. So why's a bright sunshine girl from a wet cow flop town going to Fairport, eh?"

"I'm looking for somebody. He's my mentor," Sophie added, not knowing she had meant to until the words were out.

Cass pointed to the watercolor in Sophie's hand. "And he's teaching ya to do that, is he?"

Sophie looked down quickly, having forgotten it was there. "Oh. Uh . . . yes. I'm going to Fairport to learn to be an artist, and this is what he's going to teach me. He's an artist." She hadn't meant to lie to the innkeeper, but now that it was out, it seemed the prudent thing to do. Easier this way. Cleaner. She tried to sound casual as she said, "Actually, you may have seen him yourself. He's also traveling to Fairport."

The woman's ruddy face lit up. "That solves it! Feeney and I just barely saw the back of him as he wandered up the road this evening past. Strange looking fella, yer mentor. We spent the better part of the evening arguing over who he was. An artist! I should have known."

Sophie's heart raced. "And you're sure he was going . . ."

"That way," Cass said, pointing, "same as you'll be."

A weight fell from Sophie's shoulders. She could finally get out of this smelly place with its strange owners. She was about to thank Cass for her help when the woman said, "Now then, let's see if ya've got any talent. Give it here." Sophie hesitated, then handed it over. "My word, ya've done the inn! Certainly taken some creative license here, haven't ya? Been ages since our fine establishment came at all close to this. Feeney! Come and see what the girl's done."

"What is it, mum?" he said, coming out of the back with his sleeves rolled up, his hands sodden and soapy and red from scrubbing pots. "Treachery? Piracy? *Murder?*" He winked at Sophie slyly.

"Little miss sunshine here's an artist. Look at this. Done us a real kindness, she has."

"She certainly has," said Feeney, marveling at the artwork. "You did this today?"

"Well, no," Sophie admitted. "I didn't do it at all. My mother did. I found it hidden away with a bunch of her old things. She must have stopped here when she moved to Seaside."

"*Moved to Seaside*? Now why would anyone want to do that?"

"I don't know."

"Must have been some time ago," said Feeney, squinting at the painting. "Fire pit's been falling apart for near on ten years now. And look at that, Cass, the stable's full. We haven't had that many people in at once in donkey's years."

"I don't suppose either of you remember her," Sophie asked, certain she knew the answer.

"What does she look like?" asked Cass. "My memory needs a bit of help now and again."

"I don't know," Sophie said quietly, steeling herself for the look, the one she hated so much, the one that took over every adult's face when they realized she was an orphan.

It never came.

"I see." Cass shrugged and handed the watercolor back. "I'm afraid I can't help you with that."

"Thanks anyway." Sophie climbed off the stool and put the painting back in her bag. "And thanks for the directions."

"Yer not leaving already, are ya?" The innkeeper looked slightly offended.

"I really should get going if I'm going to reach Fairport by dark."

Cass chuckled, bemused. "Do they not have maps in Seaside? Unless you walk faster than a horse can gallop, you'll not make that distance today. There is another guesthouse up the road a piece, but not for miles and miles. You'll not reach it by sundown, either. Why don't you stay here, sunshine girl? There's plenty of stew for all of us, and I'll put some bread in the oven so we'll have something nice and crusty to mop up the gravy with. And there's no shortage of beds. Ya'll have yer pick."

There were plenty of reasons for Sophie to insist on leaving. The smell, for instance, or the general disrepair, or the fact that she was worried about losing track of the Navigator. But her exhaustion had caught up to her now that she'd stopped moving. An ache had settled into her feet and legs, bone deep. Then there was the prospect of a hot meal to consider. However, the scale was tipped by the weight of her mother's ghost. Even if Cass and Feeney couldn't remember her, she had wanted to remember this place. The painting proved it. "How much for a room?" Sophie asked.

Cass stuck her hand on her hip again and said, "How much have ya got?"

"Um." Sophie hefted out the jarful of coins and set it on the counter. "Is this enough?"

"Oh you dear, sweet child," said Cass, finishing her drink at a gulp. "Yer not ready for Fairport, not by a long shot. Here's yer first lesson: never reveal how much money ya've got. Especially if yer walking around with that." Cass poured herself another ale, and one for Feeney, too, and the two of them spent the next few hours teaching Sophie the innkeeper's trade. They taught her the various cheats and swindles she was likely to come across and what prices were reasonable for which services. They taught her how to tell a real coin from a fake, and did her the favor of exchanging her small coins for larger ones. When dinnertime rolled around, they ate outside, the hot stew steaming in the cool evening air. Cass and Feeney cracked jokes at each other's expense. Sophie couldn't help but laugh along. By the time the sun went down, she couldn't remember why she'd been in such a hurry to leave. Sophie offered the innkeepers a fair wage for their hospitality, and they promptly refused, insisting it was worth more to know that they'd sent her on her way fully prepared. That night, she drifted off to sleep in an unfamiliar room, with unfamiliar smells, on an unfamiliar mattress, and an unfamiliar smile on her face.

A Traveling Companion

There was a new scent in the air when Sophie descended the following morning, one that reignited the growling, gurgling hunger in her ravenous teenaged belly—salty, smoky bacon. She poked her head into the kitchen and said, "Good morning!"

"Morning," said Cass, flashing a smile from overtop her great cast iron skillet. "How is our sunshine girl this morning? Hungry?"

"I could eat."

"Good, because this is nearly ready. Go on out and have a seat, sweetheart."

Sophie went out and sat where they'd taken their supper the night before. Her eyes wandered as she waited. The grass was sparse, coarse, bedraggled. Spiky weeds grew here and there in patches. Ashes and charred debris filled the neglected fire pit, and crumbled bricks lay forgotten at its side where it had partially collapsed. As for the stable, what stall doors remained hung askew, held on by warped and rusted hinges. There was more bare wood than paint. Sophie had delighted to see it so rundown at first, thinking only of the novelty of it and the fits it would have caused Aunt Elle. Now it stung her heart. Cass and Feeney were good people, she'd decided. They deserved a better home than this. She wished she could see it as her mother had seen it. Her gaze passed over the scraggly lawn again, and now it was covered in a lush, emerald carpet, the kind that invited bare feet to run and play. Afterward she'd rest her feet on the toasty red bricks and warm her dewy toes by the crackling fire. A whole team of horses stomped and champed contentedly in the stables while their owners were inside sharing a joke and a drink. That's how this place was meant to be, she decided, comforting and full of life. She wondered why it had stopped being that sort of place, if it ever had been at all.

"Ah, here ya are," said Cass, stepping through the double doors with a pair of plates in hand, each piled high and steaming hot. There were fried eggs, bacon, sausages, grilled tomato slices, baked beans, and two pieces of bread fried in bacon grease. It was far more food than Aunt Elle had ever offered her, and certainly more than she could eat in one sitting. She would still try, though; it was only polite. "Go on, stop starin' and dig in," said Cass, enthusiastically following her own advice.

"Where's Feeney?" Sophie asked. "No breakfast for him?"

"Wouldn't ya know it, that lazy loafer forgot to stock some of my essentials. I tell ya, most days he wouldn't lift so much as his empty head if I didn't force him. Anyway, I sent him to the neighbor to see about hiring a horse so he can correct this little oversight of his. He'll eat when he returns, if he's earned it!"

The food was irresistibly good; Sophie ate until she was miserable. Feeney arrived halfway through, sat down with his own plate, and proceeded to tear through the meal as though it were his last. Satiated and stuffed, they all sat back from the table, holding their bellies and secretly wishing for one more bite.

"I suppose you'll be wanting to hit the road before long,"

Feeney said to Sophie. "Long miles, only so much light in a day, all that."

"Yeah," she agreed, without much relish. "I'm not going to move very fast after that breakfast, though."

"See what you've done?" Feeney said to his wife. "Your kindness has hindered our guest."

"I'll hinder you, permanently."

Feeney ignored the jab. "It just so happens," he went on, "that I'm heading in your same direction today. And I'm certain that if that old nag tied up out front can haul a cart full of groceries, she can haul you up the road a piece. What do you say, would you like a ride?"

"Really? I don't want to be any bother."

"Not at all! I'm already going that way, and besides, it gets awful lonely out on the road all by yourself. It's no trouble, really."

Sophie didn't know what to say. This was a level of altruism she had never experienced, certainly not from people who had only yesterday been strangers. She wasn't quite sure how to process it. "You mean it?"

"I do."

"I'll go get my things!"

Not long after, Sophie learned that Cass was a Hugger. "Ya keep yer head about ya now, miss sunshine girl," she said, enveloping Sophie's tiny, bony body with her big, soft one.

Sophie's squished voice replied, "I will."

The woman gave her a smacking kiss on the cheek, then let her go. Feeney, who had just finished hitching his cart to the horse he'd borrowed, helped her climb up onto the weatherbeaten plank seat, and then joined her, taking the reins in hand. "Ya see she gets where she's goin' in one piece," Cass said to him, "else you won't be!"

"Ah, that's the lovely lass I married." Feeney's buck-toothed smile appeared as he pulled a battered flat cap down over his stringy hair. He hied at the horse and they were off, Sophie once again on the move toward Fairport and, she hoped, the Navigator.

The True Name of Waldendorf's Woods

As the morning and the miles gradually disappeared, so too did Sophie's sense of familiarity with the countryside. The hills were fewer, their slopes more gentle, making them suitable for cultivation. Sophie traced the neat, evenly-spaced rows where crops grew in the rich, tilled earth. Farmhouses dotted the land like lonely islands of civilization. There were a lot more people on this side of the crossroads, either toiling in the fields or else traveling in either direction along the great, stony track. Feeney was quick with a friendly wave and a shouted hello, which was nearly always returned. Seeing it all made Sophie wish she actually was learning to paint so that she could capture each scene permanently and revisit them later.

Unfortunately, the ride itself was less than comfortable. The cart was simply made, consisting of two wooden wheels on a single axle attached to a flat bed, which was enclosed on three sides by low panels. A pair of boards sat atop the panels to create a seat for driver and passenger. There were no cushions. There were, however, lots of bumps, jitters, and jumps as the contraption rumbled and clattered over the paving stones. The constant jostling forced Sophie to hold on tight. It was not the most relaxing way to travel, but it was both faster and much easier than walking.

Feeney did his best to make the journey more pleasant. He was talkative, loved jokes, and he had a surprisingly good singing voice. It was high and clear and even in tone, and not a single note was misplaced. Tapped feet and slapped thighs added a touch of percussion to his tunes, and he taught Sophie to count out simple beats so she could join him. His songs often ended with a freewheeling whistling solo. The music helped the time pass quickly, and Sophie began to feel optimistic about actually catching up to the Navigator before he set sail and disappeared for good.

Noon had come and gone when Feeney pulled the cart over beside a stream for some lunch. Cass had supplied them with bacon sandwiches, and Sophie gave Feeney one of her apples. They sat on the grassy bank and listened to the water trickle peacefully. A wide strip of dark green lined the horizon, stretching out as far as the eye could see. "What is that?" Sophie asked, pointing.

"That is the forest," answered Feeney, "though that particular word is no fit name for a place of such mystery, wonder, and power. Neither is Waldendorf's Wood, the name given to it by our illustrious lard and muster, Duke Alfred Truculo. No matter what the mapmakers say, everyone 'round here knows its true name. That, my dear, is Granelith's Weald."

"Oh."

"Oh?" Feeney looked at her sideways, incredulous. "Have you not heard that name before?"

"No."

"*No?*" He leaped dramatically to his feet and threw his cap on the ground. "It's a travesty I tell you, a tragedy, *no*, an injustice! How are you supposed to survive in the world with such a faulty education, hm? I blame those a-*dolts* who run things in Seaside. Rather keep their heads buried and complain about the stale, sandy air than stand up and breathe. Aggravates me to my core, I tell you." He bent and snatched up his cap, brushed it off, and settled it on his head once again. "Fine, fine," he said, sitting, "I suppose it's up to ol' Feeney to teach you your own history."

"Many years ago, in generations long since past, a prince came to Granelith's Weald. His name was Prince Harold Geier, and he was heir to the throne of Sklar, a vast, mountainous region to the north. Understand, there was no single king or queen in those days, but instead many small fiefdoms that fought for control of what territory they could lay their hands on. This was known as Varennen, 'The Far Lands'. On the very spot where Duke Truculo's palace now stands there used to be a much smaller castle. It was the seat of power for the King of Varennen, and his home. Prince Harold's father had proposed a marriage between his son and the king's daughter, so the king, wanting to take the measure of the young man, invited Harold for a visit."

"Prince Harold fancied himself quite the hunter. He was keen to explore Varennen in search of game, seeking to collect trophies and provide meat for a celebratory feast, and thereby demonstrate his ability to provide for the lovely young princess. The king granted his permission for a hunt on the condition that Harold stay out of Granelith's Weald. The prince was curious about this stipulation and a little aggrieved, but knew better than to question the king, so he agreed and set out on his venture."

"Now, Prince Harold did not appreciate being told what to do. He saw the command as a test of his loyalty, and a way for the king to keep all the best game for himself. But, as is the case with most men in positions of power, the prince was loyal to himself above anyone else. He preferred to hunt alone, so the king and his men were far away and unlikely to find him out of bounds. 'Even if I am caught,' thought the prince, 'it will be seen as a mark of my manhood, proof that I can make my own decisions, and am a born leader.' And so he entered Granelith's Weald with his bow and his arrows and his sharp hunting knives, searching for prey."

"Had our headstrong young prince taken a moment to think, he might have wondered exactly who this Granelith person was and why the forest bore that name. Granelith, you see, is the Queen of the Wood Nymphs. Do you ken what a wood nymph is?"

"No," said Sophie.

"I thought not. Wood nymphs tend to the trees and plants and all manner of living things in the forest. Some say they are beautiful women that cavort naked in the glades. Others make them out as terrifying creatures, with long, ugly faces and pitted bark for skins. Still others say they disguise themselves to look human, and that the only way to tell a nymph is by carefully watching their eyes, for their irises are made of wood and can neither grow nor shrink. But don't you pay any mind to those tall tales. Any sensible person knows that spirits such as nymphs are invisible, and make themselves known only in subtle ways.

One true thing about nymphs is that they are jealous creatures, and don't much like sharing their dominion with humanity, though they will tolerate those with good hearts who mean no harm to the creatures that live under their care."

"I'll bet they hated Prince Harold, then," said Sophie.

"Not at first. Even wood nymphs understand the need to hunt, for they also tend to bears, wolves, striders, and all manner of predators. Certain types of prey, however, are off limits. The beasts of the forest know these well, and stay far away. But, as I said, the nymphs speak to us in subtle ways, and humans are notoriously bad listeners. Especially rich pretty princes like our young Harold."

"Riding alone through the forest, he caught sight of the rarest and most magnificent beast in all the land—a white stag. Its hide was as beautiful and pure as untrodden snow. Its antlers were as wide across as a man is tall, and tipped with twelve points that glittered like diamonds. 'That is a prize fit for a king,' thought Prince Harold. With a dextrous, silent hand, he unslung his bow and drew back an arrow. But just as he was about to let loose, his horse nickered, alerting the beast and sending it flying off into the trees. The prince gave chase."

"The stag was blindingly fast. Over hill and dale it ran, through glen and glade, too, but it was panicked, for it enjoyed the nymphs' protection and had never known mortal peril. In its haste, it ran out into an open meadow. There was nowhere for it to hide when Prince Harold burst forth from the trees. He shot the stag from horseback and pierced that beauty's heart clean through."

"Unbeknownst to the prince, he had pierced Granelith's heart as well, for the white stag was her most beloved ward.

She came upon the prince as he was gutting the animal. The Queen of the Wood Nymphs wept to see that snowy hide sullied by so much crimson. Tears fell from her eyes, and a snowdrop bloomed where each one landed, living memories of the slain majestic wonder. Sorrow transformed to fury. The busy prince failed to notice the ring of trees and brush growing up around him, twigs and branches and boughs reaching out to one another to make a cage. He realized his peril far too late. There was nowhere to run. Granelith summoned her fearsome wrath and cursed the foolish prince. Black feathers sprouted from his skin. His handsome face became wrinkled, mottled, and discolored. A hard grey beak replaced his mouth and nose. The prince's hands, his dextrous hunter's hands, withered and shrank as his arms became wings, and his feet became gnarled talons. 'You have taken my heart's greatest treasure,' Granelith said to him, for now that Harold was a bird he could understand her plainly. 'And so I shall take yours. You will hunt no longer. Your fate is to look on as the bears, wolves, striders, and all manner of predators pursue their pleasure, and take no part. No, their leavings are for you, the cold dead remnants that crawl with flies and reek with decay. Your prize will be carrion and rot. This is my vengeance, Prince Harold Geier, interloper and slayer of my beloved.' The prince tried to apologize, but could make only a harsh hissing sound, for his transformation into a vulture was complete. He flew up into the air, leaving behind his bow and his arrows and his sharp hunting knives, resigned to his scavenger's fate."

"And that, my dear, is where the forest gets its name from, and why it is not to be entered into lightly."

Sophie sat listening to the stream for long moments,

considering how to respond. "Feeney, is that a true story, or did you make it up?"

"Of course it's true!" he said, a little defensive. "It's history. Tradition. Would I lie to you?"

"Do you swear it?"

"Every word of Prince Harold's tale is the absolute truth. I swear it on my own life. But you don't have to take my word for it. We'll be in Granelith's Weald soon enough. You pay close attention then, see if you don't feel the eyes of the wood nymphs, watching, waiting, judging whether you be friend or foe. And they're not the only spirits you're like to encounter, nosiree. One look at a greedy gnome, playful pixie, or flighty faerie and you'll change your doubtful tone right quick." Feeney wagged a finger at her. "Just you keep your eyes open. See if I'm not right."

Swallowed Whole

Tʜᴇ ᴅᴀʀᴋ ꜱᴛʀɪᴘ ᴏɴ ᴛʜᴇ ʜᴏʀɪᴢᴏɴ steadily grew as the day wore on. Details emerged while the horse's hooves kept time, *clip-clop-clip-clop*, a living metronome ticking away the seconds until they reached the ominous wood with its hidden spirits and its secret names. The single, thick band of indeterminate color became two, an impenetrable layer of forest green laid atop a porous foundation of brown and grey. Individual trunks solidified and took form, all similar, each unique. Sophie marveled at the vast stretch of innumerable trees. Anything could be hiding in there, anything at all.

Clip-clop-clip-clop.

The Queen's Road ran recklessly straight into that gigantic mass and disappeared into a hollow tunnel formed by the reaching branches of deciduous trees. It waited for them, that tunnel, waited to swallow them up, *clip-clop-clip-clop*, a giant's gaping maw, impatient, a portal into unending darkness that they were willingly approaching, *clip-clop-clip-clop*, they were nearly there, and Sophie wanted to tell Feeney to turn back, to beg him to call a halt and return her to the inn, but the hooves kept up their steady beat instead, *clip-clop-clip-clop.*

Then they were inside.

The temperature dropped as the sun disappeared behind the canopy above. Sophie shivered. Earthy spices scented the air, heavy and still and moist, the giant's held breath. She looked back and watched as the bright circle of daylight shrank, faded, disappeared. The maw had closed.

"You keep your eyes open now, girlie," Feeney said ominously, drawing her attention to what lay ahead instead of behind. She watched for movement amongst the trees. At first, nothing. The only sounds were those of shod hooves and cart wheels on stone. Then came a high pitched *chit-chit-chit* and a sudden burst of activity as two squirrels leapt to the forest floor, one pursued by the other. They bounced across the carpet of dead leaves, kicking them into the air with their tiny feet, then leapt onto another tree and climbed spiraling upward before coming to a simultaneous stop, their bushy tails held aloft as they chittered at each other once more. Sophie smiled. They weren't frightening in the least. She admired their reddish-brown fur and pointy ears and felt silly for having been so worked up. The pair sped off again, disappearing into the distance.

With each passing moment the forest felt less and less hostile. The grass of the fields had given way to bare earth littered with leaves, twigs, and loose bits of bark. Lichen and moss decorated the tall, twining trunks. Mushrooms clung eagerly to the decaying wood of fallen trees and sprouted up from the damp soil beneath. Despite the overriding gloom, there was color here, too, bright splashes of it from the rare flowers that sprouted up out of the humus, or else from the berry bushes that dotted the roadside, red and purple and blue. Birds fluttered and twittered about in the branches above.

Great waves of windswept susurration rustled the unending canopy, opening and closing a thousand tiny holes like the twinkling of daylight stars, a reminder that the sun was only hidden, not gone. Heavy, broad leaves spiraled and spun gently through the air as they floated down to the forest floor. A sense of calm washed over Sophie, and suddenly the idea of invisible forest spirits didn't seem so far-fetched. The nymphs made themselves known in subtle ways, Feeney had said; maybe this newfound peace was a message of acceptance and welcome. Maybe. Or maybe she was just getting used to being someplace new. Either way, Sophie relished the feeling as they moved deeper into the forest.

An Unexpected Detour

Twilight came early beneath the forest's dark canopy. Sophie pulled her jacket tight against the growing cold. "Hmmm," said Feeney. "I had hoped to get us to the other side before sundown. But, no worry. I've got friends in Ayer's Glen who can put us up for the night. It does take us out of the way some, but it's better than being caught out here in the dead of night. What do you say, d'you mind a little detour?" Sophie said that she didn't. Eventually they came to a fork in the road and turned off toward the hamlet of Ayer's Glen.

Sophie heard the river long before she saw it. The steady *ssshhhh* of moving water reflected off the surrounding trees and was amplified by it. Sophie looked upriver as they crossed the bridge and saw that the water ran through a leafy tunnel similar to the one enclosing the Queen's Road. Along the far bank were the homes of Ayer's Glen, boxy log cabins with billowing chimneys. Woodsmoke drifted on the lazy breeze. "It's just up here," said Feeney. "Not much farther now." On reaching the far side of the bridge, he slowed the horse and turned off onto a narrow dirt track. They drove all the way to the end.

The cabin looked like a slowly collapsing cake. Its thatched roof sagged in the middle, and the walls leaned inward on each other, with one side propped up somewhat by rows and rows of stacked firewood. The rough-hewn timbers fit together so poorly that firelight peeked through them. Sophie wondered if it had been done on purpose, because these little peepholes were the closest thing to windows it had. She began to have serious doubts about their chosen accommodations.

Feeney, on the other hand, was ecstatic. He leapt from the cart, ran to the door, cupped his hands around his mouth and began to sing. *"By the light of a summer's eve I see your eyes a-shining briiiiight-lyyyyy . . ."*

An excited squeal came from inside the shack, and three small children burst out into the yard. "Uncle Feeney!" they shouted, swarming him, hugging him about the legs and waist, jumping up and down, and making the sort of boisterous racket that belongs to the very young. Feeney's face beamed as he took first one tiny hand and then another, and soon they were all dancing in a circle as he sang. Sophie, having climbed down from the cart, stood back to watch. Never before had she seen an adult play so gleefully and with such complete abandon. It was painfully bitter and refreshingly sweet.

Then a vision of a young man appeared from inside, and Sophie forgot all about the lost opportunities imposed by her orphanhood, the sorrow and scorn of other adults, her unpopularity and loneliness, her joy at having discovered her mother's artistic talents and prodigious imagination, the warmth of being accepted by the wood nymphs, her quest to find the Navigator, her disappointing brother, her awful aunt, her maybe-boyfriend, her own name, and even how to breathe.

Sophie stared. Not for one second did it make her feel self-conscious, for her consciousness had been temporarily suspended. He smiled, and the entire world was made of gleaming white teeth and curling lips. He was tall, muscular but lithe, with a complexion that suggested outdoor labor. "Uncle Feeney," he said happily, clapping the man on the shoulder. The resonant tenor of his voice reached some instinctual place she hadn't known existed. She was paralyzed, shell-shocked by the sudden discovery that such boys existed in the world.

"Berent!" Feeney exclaimed, holding the young man at arms' length and inspecting him. "Still growing, eh? You'll be taller than me before long, and off to build a cabin of your own!"

"Now don't you go filling his head with ideas." A shaggy bear peeked its head out of the doorway, or so it seemed, until Sophie located the man's face buried within the tangled, bushy mass of brown hair. Narrow, dark eyes squinted out into the gloom, fixing Feeney with a stern look. "He's got enough of your damn fool stories floating around in there as it is," he growled. "Well? What are you waiting for, you animated string bean, a written invitation?"

"Bless me," said Feeney, feigning shock, "did you finally learn to write?"

"Oh-ho, you smarmy—"

Feeney held up a finger. "The pleasantries will have to wait a moment. Allow me to introduce my traveling companion." He gestured, and all heads swung in Sophie's direction.

Her eyes caught Berent's. He smiled. Again. This time at her. Two twin pools of bottomless, beckoning blue threatened to swallow her whole, and unlike Robbie, he did not look away.

"No need to be shy now. Come on over and say hello." Feeney waved to catch her attention. "Sophie?"

She finally snapped back to life. "Oh. Um, hello." Her hands clutched nervously at each other as she approached. "It's nice to meet you."

"Oh, brother," the shaggy man grumbled, shaking his head. "Alright, everyone in. Introductions are better made with a hot drink, am I right? Come on, come on." He ducked backward through the door as Feeney herded the little ones inside. Berent went in next. His father stopped him with a hand on the shoulder and a meaningful, warning look. Sophie lingered in the doorway, still uncertain about the leaning, airy cabin, until the big bear-man gestured expansively and said, "Welcome to our home."

A New Member of the Family

It was cramped inside the cabin. That was the first thing Sophie noticed after stepping inside. The only open space belonged to the shared living area, which took up the front half of the cabin and was centered around a low stone hearth. The rear half held what passed for a kitchen on one side, and a single large bed on the other. A loft hung over both; it was so close to the ceiling that only the youngest child could possibly have stood beneath it. The sight of the loft stung, briefly, until she pushed aside her thoughts of home.

The second thing she noticed were the four simple chairs arrayed before the fire. Seated nearest to it was a slight, trim woman, who was busy darning a sock. Her face was handsome and warm. Sophie liked her immediately. Beside her sat a young woman of about Sophie's age. She was also doing needlework, and conspicuously refused to acknowledge their guests, putting Sophie in mind of the petulant Petunia. "Loren," chided the woman by the fire, "if I've said it once I've said it a thousand times, you've got to stop feeding the strays. You'll never be rid of them otherwise." She winked at Feeney and smiled.

"I've missed you too, Melina." He bent to give the woman a friendly kiss on the cheek. "What's the matter, Berlin, too old to give your Uncle Feeney a hug?"

"No," she said, eyeing him coolly. "I just find my sewing more interesting." The rest of the family issued a collective *ooooh*.

"Don't be rude," Loren said, wagging an enormous, meaty finger at his daughter before resuming his seat. "Our guests will be wanting a hot cup of spruce tea, as will your mother and I."

"Me too," said Berent. He offered his chair to Sophie, who accepted it graciously.

"You can fix your own damn tea," said Berlin, her glare as sharp as the needle she laid aside. She busied herself with the kettle while the others settled in. Berent sat on the floor beside his mother, across from Sophie, where their eyes couldn't help but find each other. Meanwhile, the three little ones crowded together at Feeney's feet, clamoring for attention while he caught up with the adults. "Then yesterday, this one walks through our door with her lost doe eyes asking which way to Fairport. Cass and I talked it over, decided it wasn't right for her to travel so far all on her own, and now here we are."

"Wait a minute," said Sophie, "Cass told me you were buying supplies for the inn."

"W-e-e-e-llll . . ." said Feeney, looking sheepish. "Might be we exaggerated our needs just a bit. I couldn't let you wander through Granelith's Weald all by yourself, now, could I?"

Loren shook his shaggy head and let out an exasperated moan. "Whatever crazy things this man has told you, forget them. Been spouting that old drivel for as long as I've known him. There's no such thing as wood nymphs."

"There are so!" said Feeney. "I feels 'em every time I set foot in those woods."

"It's the back of your mind you feel," Loren insisted. "I've spent every day of my forty-eight years in these woods. I've hunted stags, been stalked by striders, and cut down more trees than I can count—"

"And how high is that, exactly?"

"—and never, not one time have I ever seen anything more supernatural than a fart no one will admit to." The little ones laughed and started saying "fart" over and over again, puffing up their cheeks and blowing loud raspberries until Melina shushed them all.

"Alright then, Mr. No-one-knows-more-than-I," said Feeney, "how d'you explain all those folks suddenly going missing? Hm?"

"I never said there wasn't danger here. The river is perilous deep and so cold it'll steal your breath. People drown. There are caves with no end, venomous snakes, man-eaters, poisonous mushrooms, and a hundred other ways to die if you don't keep your wits about you. It's an unfortunate fact of life in the forest."

"But twenty in half a year?" Feeney pressed.

"Some years are worse than others. That's all. And I'll tell you what else—half o'them who've disappeared aren't dead. They just run off somewhere without telling anybody." At these words, Sophie felt another brief jab of guilt. "But I'm certain of this—not one of them has been spirited away by vengeful wood nymphs."

"The spirits of the forest don't reveal themselves to doubters."

"And they *only* appear to empty headed ninnies."

"Boys," Melina intoned, still working at her stitching.

"Fine, fine," said Loren, throwing up his hands. "Never changed your mind before, don't expect I will tonight." The conversation lulled as Berlin passed out mugs of hot tea. Warmth radiated out from the carved wooden cup and into Sophie's hands. After Berlin had resumed her seat, Loren said, "So, why's a young lady like yourself going to the big city all alone?"

"I'm looking for someone," Sophie said. "My mentor."

"She's going to be an artist, like her mother," Feeney put in. "If she's got half her mother's talent, she'll be a master one day, see if she won't. Go on, now, show them what you showed me."

Once again all eyes were on Sophie. She was paralyzed by the sudden attention. Without knowing it, Feeney had asked her to share something intimately private with a room full of strangers. Still, they had invited her into their home without reservation. It felt wrong not to return their openness in kind. Sophie dug into her backpack and retrieved the stack of watercolors. "Have a look," she said, handing the stack to Loren.

The big man held them out at arm's length, squinting his eyes and angling them against the firelight to see them clearly. "Is that your place?"

"It is," said Feeney, beaming with pride.

"I'll be damned." There was real awe in his voice. "It's just as I remember it, back 'fore all these little scamps mysteriously appeared. Look, Melina." He held it up for his wife's inspection. "She captured it perfect, didn't she?"

"She certainly did," Melina said, smiling.

The little ones began to complain. "I wanna see!"

"Me too!"

"I wanna see the pitcher."

Loren passed it to Berent, who held onto it while the little ones got their turn. The older boy looked at Sophie over top of the paper, his eyes serious. "Beautiful."

Her cheeks tingled furiously as she blushed.

One by one the paintings were handed around in a circle, each garnering approval from the family. With every kind word Sophie felt more at ease. Even haughty Berlin seemed genuinely impressed, though she did her best to hide it. After they had all been passed around, Sophie tucked them away once again, feeling both proud and relieved.

After that Loren declared it was time for the children to go to bed, which they vociferously refused to do until Uncle Feeney had sung them a song. Then he retrieved a bottle of elm brandy, a distilled liquor made using his family's secret recipe. Loren poured for them all himself. "To friends old and new," he intoned, raising his cup. The others followed suit and drank. Sophie's lips and tongue burned from the amber, aromatic liquid, her nostrils suffused with its heady fragrance. Her face puckered and she coughed, which made the others laugh, but in a way that made her feel included and not apart. Her chest warmed and her head swam in a not entirely unpleasant way. In a flash she understood Damon's fiendish affinity for alcohol. *It tastes awful, though.*

At some point Berlin came to sit beside Sophie and the two of them got to chatting. It was awkward at first, but the elm brandy quickly dissolved whatever barriers may have existed between them and they became fast friends. They found they had plenty in common, commiserating over small-town life and how stifling it could be, even though Ayer's Glen and Seaside were worlds apart. Berlin was particularly aggrieved over the dearth of cute boys nearby. She spoke longingly of Fairport and its boundless supply of young men who were healthy, wealthy, and well-educated, and told Sophie how lucky she was to be going there. As her new friend spoke, Sophie's gaze drifted back to Berent, who watched with his serious, penetrating eyes. She wondered what he saw looking back: the poor, lost, pitiable orphan that she was, or the confident young artist brimming with untapped potential. "Ugh, gross," said Berlin, catching her in one of these surreptitious eye-locks. "He's pretty, but he's dumb as a stump. I'm tired, let's go to bed." She stood and announced their departure, then took Sophie by the hand and led her to the ladder that would take them up into the loft.

"I'm going to turn in, too," said Berent, rising to follow.

"Not so fast," said Loren. "You're sleeping by the fire tonight. Down here."

The girls climbed the ladder, and as they did, they heard the hurried scurry of three small children, who definitely hadn't been sitting at the edge and listening to the conversation below. Berlin led her to a pile of furs and blankets at the back of the loft that they would be sharing. Bundled up together under the thatched roof, the two new friends joined their lives together with whispers and giggles until long after the lights had been put out and everyone else in the crowded house was asleep. They only stopped when Loren growled up at them in exasperation. Maybe not even then.

Light in the Darkness

MORNING CAME MUCH TOO SOON.

Melina was up first, getting the stove lit for breakfast. Her stirrings woke the little ones, who woke everyone else with their noisy exit from the loft and subsequent pestering of Feeney. After their meal, arrangements were made to get Sophie into the city, as Feeney had promised to return the borrowed horse that day. She accepted the offer gratefully, and with a touch of disappointment, since Berent would not be the one to see her to Fairport.

The whole lot of them went outside to say their goodbyes, with the little ones doing their best to winkle one more song from their favorite uncle. After that came the hugs and the promises to stay in touch. Berent came around with the family draft horse, an enormous hazelnut beast with a black mane and matching feathering around its hooves. Sophie stroked its nose while the young man held onto its bridle. Fingers grazed fingers. Their eyes kissed, but not their lips, for Loren interrupted and the moment was lost.

He hoisted Melina up into the saddle before offering Sophie

his massive paw. "He won't get you there fast," Loren said of the horse, "but you'll arrive all the same."

"Don't you worry about us," said Melina, leaning over to stroke his beard. "We can take care of ourselves."

"I know." He slapped the animal on the rump, and they were off.

"You look after yourself, Miss Sophie," Feeney called after them as they trotted away. "Don't forget us when you're rich and famous!"

"Never!" she called back, smiling and waving goodbye.

They had barely begun to shrink and fade when the pain of longing struck. Hers was a life lived in shadow, a truth she only understood now that she'd basked in the warm sunlight of familial love. How brief it had been, that glimpse, blindingly bright and surprising in its intensity, illuminating every hidden crack and fissure in her damaged heart, and now only memories remained, vague afterimages in familiar shapes, the ghosts of what had been and should have been and never were. The pain reignited her anger at Damon. Her disappointment. Her frustration. Yet these were alloyed with guilt, guilt for the fact that she was missing the warmth of strangers, guilt that she had never felt the same for anyone in Seaside.

Melina spoke. Sophie clung to her words as one drowning, lest her tempest of emotion pull her under. "He's a good man, that Feeney. Got some funny ideas in his head, certainly, but a heart of gold, one he'd give away in an instant to anyone that needed it. Cass is much the same, though she doesn't like to show it. A shame we don't see the two of them more often."

Sophie didn't know how to respond, but wanted to keep

her talking, desperate for the distraction. "Why don't you see them anymore?" she asked, trying to keep her voice even.

"Oh, it wasn't any one thing in particular," Melina mused. "Life goes on. Things change. As the family grew, it got harder and harder to make the journey. Not that I'd let my family step foot in that place now. Last time it was dark and dingy, everything sticky, even the air. I trust you witnessed the same?" Sophie agreed she had. "Honestly, I don't know how Cass lets them live in such squalor. It's terrible. That picture you've got with you, that's how I remember the inn, clean and light and alive, and it was all thanks to them two. They worked so hard to make every single person feel welcome. Cass put on these great big feasts that drew people from all around. Feeney would bounce from table to table while she was cooking, filling every glass and putting smiles on faces, and when the eating was done he'd play his fiddle and sing. You should have seen them dancing in that hall. Even Cass would kick her feet up if the mood took her. Those were different days, better days."

"It sounds really special," Sophie said, sniffling. "Why did they stop?"

"As I said, things change. People change. It takes a lot of time and effort to do what they did. Eventually, they simply lost the desire to keep going."

"But they were happy. They made other people happy. How can that change?"

"Well," Melina said slowly, measuring her next words. "I've never asked them directly, but I have my suspicions. Surely you've noticed how they bicker. Always back and forth, forth and back with them. Some things *don't* change. Back then it was always about children. How many they were going to have, whether they wanted boys or girls, what names to choose. The sort of matters that get settled very quickly once the children actually arrive. But those matters never were settled, if you take my meaning. Over the years, first one and then the other stopped bringing it up. Messes were left uncleaned, repairs undone, songs unsung. Fewer guests came to stay, so there were fewer reasons to keep trying. Desire is like a flame, you see, and just as a flame needs air to breathe, desire needs hope. Deprive someone of hope, and their desire dwindles down to embers, or goes out entirely. That's why they took such a shine to you, I'd wager. They saw the hope in your eyes. It reminded them of that flame that used to burn within them both."

Melina's words were sharp and shocking as a lash. Sophie was an orphan, a child without parents; she had never considered that there could be parents without children. That's what Cass and Feeney were, absurd as it seemed. They had taken her in and cared for her not simply because they were good people, but because she was their glimpse at a life that could have been, their light in the darkness. It was the same reason Feeney doted on Loren and Melina's kids. *Yer not the first runner we've had.*

"It's a real shame about the inn," Sophie said quietly.

"Yes it is. It is, indeed."

The Frog Man

Cruel Sunshine

Damon stood at the base of One Tree Hill. His parents had brought him here often as a child. It loomed like a mountain in his memory, for so it had seemed to one so small and unsteady. His mother had been his guide. They'd walked hand-in-hand and counted their steps as they summited the peak. Once, he'd ridden his father's shoulders to the top. Damon had spread his arms like wings and pretended to be a bird as his father ran around the hillside. It had been magical, gravity-defying, to glide all the way to the top and then swoop around and dive back toward the bottom.

He had made the trek only once after they were gone. He'd been taller then, stronger, and could see the hill for its true size. That climb had nearly killed him.

The sun was brighter than it had any right to be. Sophie was gone, chasing after some wizard that he himself had rescued from certain death, and not one person in Seaside seemed to care. No one offered their condolences or told him that it would be okay. No one would dare to look at him anymore, save for his own family, and that experience was unpleasant at best. Aunt Elle had even had the audacity to blame him for Sophie's disappearance. Damon had been enraged, not because she was wrong, but because she was right. Sophie had said as much herself. There was nothing left for him but to go to the one place he was sure to feel her and finally have the talk that had been put off for far too long. That such a wretched day could be so beautiful was simply cruel.

Damon began to climb.

Halfway up, he lifted his gaze and found the place where she liked to sit. He imagined her there, leaning against the sturdy trunk, waiting for him. Something was wrong with her face. It wasn't until he reached the top that he saw what it was—she had no mouth. The vision stopped him dead, his breath withheld. Her accusing eyes bored into him. They tracked his approach as he came to sit beside her in the shade of the monolithic oak.

Long moments passed in silence while he gathered his courage. He trained his gaze out toward the village, empty, unseeing. Her eyes never left his face. "I'm sorry," he said to the specter of his lost sister. "I let you down. I lied. I told you I was looking out for you. Us. I think I even believed it sometimes. But really I was only looking out for me. I know that now. It's too late to ask for forgiveness, but I thought maybe, if I could explain, you would at least understand."

He stretched out a hand as if to show her something. In it was the watercolor of the village, only in his imagination it was undamaged, neither torn nor crumpled. "That was our home," he said, pointing. "Nothing special on the outside, but the inside was bright and colorful. Fun. Mom hated the way it looked just like every other house in the village. She was always trying to talk Dad into painting it or decorating it somehow, to make it different, unique. 'That's not how we do things in

Seaside,' he'd say. So she made up for it by making the interior her own. I still remember walking into Aunt Elle's house for the first time and being shocked at how dull and boring it was. Is."

"It was like that with everything," he went on. "Those plates you like so much, she made them when the selection at Codwallader's let her down. The kitchen was her own personal laboratory where she experimented with food. There was always something baking or sizzling or bubbling away. She even convinced Dad to be creative. He tried, anyway. Those figurines you saw, he made most of them, and she painted them. He didn't exactly boast about his hobby, but he never hid it, either. Even then I could tell other people didn't like her style. She never cared. She always did things her way. I guess you and I both got some of that. Don't know if that's a good thing or not."

Damon's voice hitched. He stopped to take a breath, get control. If he couldn't say it now, he'd never be able to say it in person. If he ever saw her again. Balled fists pressed into his eyes. A hard swallow to force the sorrow down. "Okay," he said, blinking back the tears, and told his sister about the day they lost everything.

A Pair of Frogs

THE MERCHANT DROVE HIS CARAVAN into the village. He wore an outlandish suit, forest green plaid shot through with pinstripes of red and yellow. A bright red pocket square stood out like a bull's eye on his chest. Curls of carroty, copper hair peeked out from beneath the brim of a black top hat. He wore a bushy mustache that was carefully groomed and waxed into a pleasing handlebar shape. A portly man, his nose was bulbous, cheeks plump. The caravan was impressive for both its size and its graceful construction. It too was red, the exact same shade as the merchant's pocket square. Bright gold letters stood out from a field of black, bearing the caravan's name—Marley's Marvelous Traveling Glass Menagerie.

Marley had an infectious smile, and he knew it. It was his chief selling tool. He was also keenly aware of the skeptical looks directed his way by the villagers of Seaside. Aware, but undaunted. His beaming smile was turned on one and all. "Come and see!" he called to them. His melodramatic voice was as finely honed as any duelist's blade. "Come and see! Yes, you, and you, ev'rybody! Come and see the Menagerie! Every animal you could ever hope to see! Some defy imagination, yes-sir-ee! It only costs a penny or three, plenty there for all to see! So come on, what are you waiting for? To the square with *you, to the square with me, to the square to see the Menagerie!" A troop of excited children formed behind his caravan, following along and smiling and parroting his calls to "Come and see".*

Robert Farrier and his wife, Erinella, were among those who witnessed Marley's arrival. Robert carried his two-year old daughter Sophie on his hip, while Erinella walked hand-in-hand with her seven-year old son, Damon. The family stopped to watch the passing spectacle. The boy's face lit eagerly. "Can we go see, Dad, can we?"

Robert would have preferred not to. He was a Seaside man, born and bred, and though he had adapted to his beloved wife's colorful ways, such audacious public displays made him uncomfortable. However, he knew Erinella well, and had understood that he would be paying the traveling merchant as soon as he'd spotted the man's outrageous conveyance. "Your mother and I are going. Seems only right for you to come, too."

"Yes!"

Robert turned to his daughter. "What do you say, little butterfly, want to go see what all the fuss is about?"

"Yee-ahh!" squealed little Sophie, a mostly toothless smile animating her adorable, tiny face.

"Go on ahead," Erinella said to her boy, "we'll be right there." Freed from parental constraints, Damon gleefully joined the chase, his feet pounding on the pavement as he sprinted away.

In the square, children were gathered at the base of a ramp that led up into the caravan. A large panel in its side stood propped open like a bird's wing. Glass baubles hung suspended from two mobiles, glittering in the sunlight and chasing each other in circles, propelled by the breeze. Marley stood inside, directing the flow of traffic. One by one, the children walked up the ramp and tossed their coins into Marley's upturned hat before disappearing through a heavy black curtain.

"Hello! Hello!" Marley cried as the Farriers approached. "It's a fine day for some afternoon revelry, a fine day, indeed." The man turned his smile on the family and received theirs in kind. His green eyes glinted mischievously. "I'm assuming one of these children belongs to you."

"I do," said Damon, holding up his hand.

"Marvelous, marvelous! A fine lad he must be, to claim his parents enthusiastically." Marley winked at the Farriers. "Now, I know what you're thinking. 'A glass menagerie's fine for children and simpletons, but what grown man or woman with a modicum of self-respect would throw away hard-earned money to look at some inert hunks of molten sand?' And if this were any other glass menagerie, you'd be right. That's because other purveyors of such curiosities rely on unremarkable methods of molding and manipulating masses of glasses to make their mundane, misshapen models. Not so Marley the Magnificent! Many and more of these pieces are true-to-life treasures, carefully constructed in lands near and far by grandmasters of vitreology, using techniques unknown to the common glassblowers who ply their trade on this island. After many years of arduous study, I learned something of their mysterious techniques and have since bent my will to filling in the missing pieces of my collection. You, sir, you seem like you have an eye for craftsmanship. Have a look at these bees, if you please. I'm certain you'll sees that Marley's is the best of menageries!"

Robert stepped closer and saw that the baubles were indeed glass bees. "Look carefully now, sir," said Marley, his voice pitched low, as though he were about to impart some secret knowledge. "Normally, a piece like this would have to be cast in a mold, leaving an unsightly ridge running the length of the body. These can be filed down, of course, but you end up scraping the glass, ruining its luster and risking further damage to the piece. Go on, sir, take it in hand. Run your fingers over the surface. Hold it up to the light. If you find a single scrape or scratch or tool mark or any other such imperfection, it's yours, free of charge. Consider it my way of thanking you for ridding me of a failure of craftsmanship."

Robert inspected the bee closely, turning it this way and that. It was no bigger than his thumb and impossibly detailed, right down to the texturing of its compound eyes and the fur on its head and legs. Its body was striped black and yellow, its gossamer wings remarkably thin and fragile. "Not a mark on it," he said. He handed it to Erinella, whose face lit up as she admired it. "It's wonderful!" she exclaimed. "Perfect in every way."

"Why thank you, miss, thank you very much. Now, I want you to think about this for a moment. If I'm willing to let you see such masterworks of vitreology for free, imagine the wonders that lie in wait behind that velvet curtain. T'would be a real shame to deprive yourselves of such a once-in-a-lifetime opportunity over adult-ish pride and a few coppers, wouldn't you say?"

Erinella giggled. "We aren't the ones you have to convince, Mr. Marley."

"Oh, posh! Plain old Marley will do just fine." The showman's radiant smile returned as Robert dropped his coins into the hat. Then the Farriers went up the ramp one after the other and through the curtain and into Marley's Marvelous Traveling Glass Menagerie.

The family found themselves in the middle of a lush grassland. Verdant hills rose and fell on either side of them, while above fluffy white clouds floated across a calm blue sky, all rendered in paint by an expert hand. The landscape was lit by actual sunlight, collected and reflected by cleverly placed mirrors in the caravan's roof. Marley's miniature treasures awaited them in shallow alcoves set into the walls. Each alcove was fronted with a pane of glass so translucent it was nearly invisible. The animals were arranged in whimsical nature *scenes. A majestic stag stood proudly athwart a hill, muzzle raised toward the sky in the act of bugling, while below groundhogs peeped from their faux burrows. Foxes prowled in the grass, eyes fixed on a brace of dashing hares. Above, birds soared on gossamer wires. True to Marley's boastful claims, they were all exquisite, lifelike in every detail. "Wow," Damon breathed, his mouth hanging open as he turned in a slow circle.*

"This is . . . really well done," said Robert, admiring a family of whitetail deer. Little Sophie, who still rode his hip, reached out for them and succeeded only in smudging the glass with her tiny fingers. "I'm sure it must have taken an incredible amount of patience and skill to create each one, but the way he talked it up I assumed there would be more. Explains why he charges so little."

"I think there's another room, dear," said Erinella, pointing toward another black curtain at the far end. They stepped through and were whisked away into a nocturnal forest. There were deer and elk here, too, but now they were accompanied by predators, bears, wolves, and more. Great horned owls looked down greedily on the scurrying mice below. Damon recoiled in surprise as he caught sight of a great spotted cat hiding amongst the trees, glaring at him with its brilliant yellow-green eyes. The cat held its body low to the ground, ready to pounce. "A strider," his mother whispered in his ear. "So beautiful, and so fierce."

"Sounds like someone I know," Robert said, giving her a playful nudge with his elbow.

"Better than being a stodgy old toad," she teased.

The forest was L-shaped, and around the turn another curtain awaited them. Passing through it transported the Farriers under the sea. Shoals of tiny fish darkened the waters like living thunderclouds, while massive whales launched themselves skyward. Dead-eyed sharks patrolled the deep. Crustaceans and other crawling creatures made their home amongst the corals. Sophie took one look at an octopus and began to cry, reaching out desperately for her mother, who held her and shushed her as they quickly moved on.

The final chamber took the Farriers to a land they'd never experienced before, neither in life nor story nor song. Everything was flat and sparsely covered with tall grass. A narrow river wound through the landscape. A herd of what looked like cattle were gathered to drink, only they were charcoal colored and had ridged, sharp horns curving backward from out of their skulls. Nearby, black and white striped horses galloped across the plains. Great dun colored cats with bushy brown manes stalked the plains, watching a herd of gargantuan grey beasts that had hoses dangling from their faces. The family looked on in disbelief at all the bizarre, unimaginable beasts.

One final curtain deposited them back outside, where Marley sat chatting up his next customers. Half the village had come out to investigate, and while the children were eager to see what mysteries awaited inside, a great many of the adults were directing distrustful looks at the traveling showman. Marley's smile, his sword and his shield, had begun to falter. He caught sight of the Farriers and saw his salvation. "But don't take it from me, friends! This intrepid family of explorers has just returned from lands unknown, and can tell you of the wonders of worlds unseen." Attention shifted to the Farrier family, stunning Robert into embarrassed silence.

"It's true!" said Erinella, gesturing grandly with the hand not holding her daughter, aping Marley the Magnificent in her demeanor and delivery. "The animals on display are fantastic, and their beauty is unbelievable until you see them with your own eyes."

"You would say that." Horace Halderman, considerably younger but no less porky. "Outsiders like you always stick together, don't *you? Trying to bilk us out of our hard-earned coin. Who gave you permission to be here, sir? What gives you the right to come into our town and disrupt an otherwise unremarkable day?"*

"An otherwise unremarkable day? Surely you don't mean to make that sound like a good thing?"

"Surely, I do."

"We don't appreciate unnecessary disruptions," said Michael Spindler, to a roar of approval. Marley's smile slipped farther.

"I think we've had quite enough of your imaginative tomfoolery," said Horace. "It is time you leave our fair village. Go on. Pack up and get out. There's no place for you here."

"Now you wait just a minute," said Robert, coming to stand before Horace. His face was enflamed, hands balled into fists. "First you accuse my wife of huckstering, then you try to run this man out of town? He is a guest here and has every right to ply his trade in this public square. You've overstepped your bounds, Horace. I demand you apologize this instant."

"I will do no such thing." Horace took a step forward. "And I would guard my tongue if I were you, you outsider-loving—"

Robert's fist smashed the rest of Horace's words from his mouth, along with his bottom front teeth. The portly man fell sideways like a limp sack. Others surged forward to put an end to the violence, but it was already over. Horace was hefted and lugged from the square. The crowd quickly decided they had better places to be and dispersed. Robert turned to see his son looking up at him with the same amazed look he'd worn in the menagerie. Sophie was crying again. "You shouldn't have done that," said Erinella, though there was no anger in her reproach.

"He went too far," said Robert. "I only did what was right."

Marley descended from his carriage with his top hat held solemnly against his chest. "My word, mister, I've not seen a right hook like that since the skirmisher's pits in old Akkavir. Care to take your talents on the road? We could put on quite the pugilistic spectacle. Marley and . . . what's your name, sir?"

"Robert Farrier."

"Marley and Farrier's Mobile Fisticuffs! Step right up, folks, and witness the champion at work. If you're feeling tough and made-of-the-right stuff, step in the ring and test your guff!" He chuckled. "The barking writes itself."

"I only did what was right."

"And I thank you for it. It's a rare person indeed who will stick their neck out for a stranger. All the same, it's probably best I move on. Seems your village has lost its appetite for wonder. A shame. I had hoped to eat a proper meal and sleep in a proper bed tonight, but I doubt the innkeeper would have me now."

"I wouldn't concern yourself about the innkeeper," said Erinella. "We don't have one."

"You don't—my word, I've met cannibals more hospitable than you lot! Present company excluded, of course."

"We don't have a bed to offer," said Erinella, "but we would be honored if you'd stay for dinner. I'd love to hear about your travels, and I have so many questions about your lovely animals."

"Oh, I couldn't possibly impose . . ."

The pleasantries continued as long as etiquette demanded and ended with Marley accepting her gracious invitation. Robert and Damon helped prepare the caravan while Erinella went to the market. The giant red contraption was parked in the field beside their home when she returned, leading little Sophie by the hand. Marley sat smoking a pipe in the living room, entertaining Damon with stories of perilous adventure in faraway lands. Gradually his guard dropped and he spoke more plainly to the adults while Erinella worked in the kitchen. He expounded on the difficulties of nomadic life and how he had come to his lifestyle in the first place. Damon, being still a child, found the conversation boring and took Sophie outside to play.

Damon had no intention of going in the bright red caravan. Not at first. He was content to follow Sophie around as she toddled in the grass, making sure she didn't get into anything gross or dangerous. But the caravan had been designed to inspire curiosity, and it worked its slow magic on the boy, drawing his eye over and over again, sparking memories of the amazing mythical figurines inside. He knew it was wrong to go in without permission, especially without paying; even at seven years old, he understood it was a form of stealing. All the same, the pull was irresistible. With a quick glance toward the house, Damon picked up his sister and carried her into the menagerie.

They entered from the opposite direction this time. With the rooftop shutters closed, all was cast in a sinister monochrome. Damon took his time exploring, noticing details he'd missed before, like the herd of tiny spotted deer half hidden behind the tall grass, or the funny creatures up in the trees that ate fruit with furry, humanoid hands, or the horrific floating log with eyes hidden at the watering hole. Sophie began to whimper. "It's okay," Damon said. "They're not real. See?" He reached out and poked at a bull, his finger stopped by the display glass. "I won't let anything get you, little butterfly, never ever."

Then Damon noticed a concealed latch on the wall. Closer inspection revealed a narrow door that had been painted over. He unhooked the latch and pushed it open. Inside was a tiny, cramped space with a thin mattress lying on the bare floor. A portmanteau stood open in the corner. Multiple suits in wild colors hung within. Guilt swept over the boy. This was Marley's private space, and he was intruding.

"Damon!"

His father's voice. Though muffled and faint, there was a note of anger in it, and now fear and shame joined Damon's guilt. He had been caught. Not wanting to make things worse, he hurried from the room, back through the foreign land and out into the entryway, where its gate hung open. His father stood in the yard with his arms crossed over his chest. "I'm here."

"Get down from there." The boy did as he was told, coming to stand before his father, shoulders slumped and head down, ready to accept his punishment. "Damon, what were you thinking?"

"I just wanted to see the animals again. I didn't touch anything, I swear."

"What's all this, now?" said Marley, coming around the corner of the house. He'd been taking quick nips from a hip flask, and now his nose and cheeks were as rosy as his pocket square. The eyes above his smiling lips were shaded by annoyance.

"Mr. Marley, I found my son sneaking around in your caravan. I thought he knew better than to treat guests this way, but it seems I was mistaken. Damon, you owe this man an apology."

"And a couple of coppers," the merchant grumbled to himself.

"I'm sorry," said the boy.

"For what are you sorry?" Robert prodded.

"For going in your caravan when I wasn't supposed to."

Marley took another nip from his flask. Suspicious eyes glared at the boy. Then he seemed to remember himself, and his disarming smile returned. "Well, that's alright, lad. I can't say you're the first boy to let his curiosity get the better of him. Might be I did my own share of sneaking at your age. I'm certain a good boy like you wouldn't lower himself to thieving, but you've betrayed my confidence once, so I must ask: did you take anything from in my caravan?"

"Well?" said Robert. "Did you?"

"No, sir."

"Turn out your pockets now and let's see," said Marley.

"Now hold on," said Robert. "He's already apologized to you and he said he didn't take anything. My son's curiosity got the better of him, but he is no liar."

"Look, Robert, you seem like a decent man, but I've only just met you, and I have a business to protect. Every piece in there is precious to me. I can't be without one. Just turn out your pockets, boy, and this will be over and done."

"He will do no such thing."

"Dad, it's okay, really . . ."

"What's going on out here?" Erinella had come straight from the kitchen and wore a bright yellow apron over her green house dress, her hair tied up with a long red ribbon.

"It's nothing, dear."

"I'd hardly call the robbery of my caravan nothing."

"Robbery? How dare you make such a wild accusation against my son!"

"Why don't we all just go back inside? Dinner's almost —"
"Gah!"

They all turned as one to see tiny Sophie standing in the caravan's entryway. In her hand was a glittering glass scepter. She smiled at the attention, bobbing up and down and waving the wand with a child's reckless lack of coordination.

Marley's eyes went wide. "Get that away from her," he said, pointing, his voice tense and strained and on the edge of control. "Now, if you would."

"Gah!" said Sophie again, swinging the scepter sharply at the ground. Marley jumped back while the others looked on, confused. The ground at their feet began to crackle and groan. A patch of lush, emerald grass glittered crystalline in the evening light. Comprehension dawned on the Farriers, all except for little Sophie, who squealed with delight and clapped her hands in excitement.

The three adults converged on the girl. "Sophie, dear, give that to mommy . . ."

"Gah!" A bolt of magic flew through the space between the two men and struck the house behind. Marley, terrified, barked incoherently and ducked back behind the Farriers. Now came that same crackle and groan, only much, much louder, as a circular patch of the wall converted to glass, spreading, and to this tumult Robert and Erinella added their raised voices, imploring their daughter to put the scepter down while Marley begged them to make her stop. The two-year old sent bolts flying in every direction, emphasizing each blast with a gleeful cry.

Erinella was struck first.

"Robert!"

The blast took her in the shoulder. Her right arm shrank and began to change color. As with the house, the glass expanded, reaching outward, ever outward to envelope her whole body, climbing down her torso and up her neck. One blue eye bulged wildly outward like a frozen bubble made of ice. Her nostrils contracted into two tiny pinpricks as her face both elongated and widened, her mouth stretched to a thin line that wrapped equatorial around the hemisphere of her face. In the end, Robert was left holding a glass frog in his hands, its body a bright yellow-green with a single stripe of red down its back. Its bulbous eyes were Erinella's shade of blue.

"Erinella? Erinella?!" Robert looked up at his daughter in horrified confusion. There was nothing else he could do. In a withered, sobbing, pitiful voice that would haunt Damon for the rest of his life, he spoke his daughter's name for the last time. "Sophie?"

"Gah!"

Robert dropped the green frog as a bolt struck him in the chest. It fell to the ground and broke into three pieces. A squat, stately brown companion joined it a moment later.

"It's all ruined," Marley said, speaking dully to himself. His marvelous traveling menagerie had been struck and was slowly vitrifying. "This is your fault you little shit, all your fault, you ruined it, ruined it ruined everything. *Don't just stand there, boy! DO SOMETHING!!!"*

Damon, shocked into action, saw his opportunity. He walked calmly toward Sophie, as if nothing was wrong, as if he hadn't just watched his parents turned into glass figurines, and held his hands up to her. Flatly, he said, "Want to get down, little butterfly?"

"Yes!"

Damon lifted her down by the armpits and gently took the scepter from her hands. Then Marley ripped it from his yielding grasp. The merchant loomed over the children, his eyes frightfully alive, scepter aimed squarely at the innocent little girl. Damon stepped in front of her, defiant. Then came the sound of voices from up the lane, neighbors coming to see what the commotion was about. Marley panicked. His hands trembled madly as he unhitched his remaining live horse, mounted it, and galloped hard down the lane. "Get the fuck out of my way!" he roared, drawing a gasp from the oncoming crowd. Marley disappeared over the hill and was never seen in Seaside again.

Denouement

"We went to live with Aunt Elle after that." Damon's cheeks were wet and warm, but his voice was even, the worst parts finally uttered aloud. "They came and took everything out of the house and packed it away. The house itself was smashed to bits and thrown into the sea. So was the caravan and everything else. Everything except for them. Aunt Elle used to keep them in the house. 'That way they can watch you grow up,' she said. I couldn't handle it. Every time I saw those frogs up on that shelf, it put me right back in that moment when they . . . changed. I hid them, and she never asked where they went."

Damon hesitated. There was only one thing left to say. The horribly mute vision of his sister watched him expectantly. "I want you to know that I never blamed you for what happened. There were times I wanted to. Everyone else got their share of it. Mom and Dad. Marley. Horace, the whole village, really. Myself most of all. I can't tell you how many times I've wished I could go back and stay out of that stupid caravan. But I never could blame you. You were so little. You didn't know any better. I don't blame you, Sophie, and you shouldn't blame yourself." He wiped at his eyes. As his vision cleared, he saw that he was alone.

"If you ever find out."

FAIRPORT

At the City Gates

It was almost noon by the time Melina and Sophie emerged from the forest canopy and out into the warm light of day. The land sloped out and away like a wide, shallow bowl. Farmhouses stood at irregular intervals, their adjoining fields divided into rectangles, squares, and wedges by heavy, green hedges. A river snaked across the valley, cutting through it all and feeding the surrounding cropland on its way to the ocean. The Queen's Road intertwined with the river like a stony twin. And there, on the other side of it all—Fairport.

Sophie studied the city as they rode. From the valley's rim it looked like an odd, geometrical smudge. Its boundaries were defined by a flat stone wall, while the interior was a textured wash of orange rooftops. Descending to the valley floor, it became only a faceless grey plane on the horizon. It was so impossibly huge that Sophie scarcely believed it was real.

They rode on, past the farms and along the river and over the bridges, and in the approach Fairport began to reveal its true character. Tall spires peeked up over the wall, with blue pennants flapping lazily in the breeze. The brilliant flash of sunlight on steel announced the presence of soldiers walking along the wall's parapets. Somewhere, behind all that stone, within the endless maze of streets that separated all those rooftops from one another, walked the Navigator.

Or so she hoped. There had been more stops than she'd expected, but thanks to the kindness of those she'd met, Sophie had completed the journey much more quickly than she would have on foot. Still, there had been no sign of the Navigator. It was possible he'd found his own ride to the city, a faster one perhaps. If that was the case, he might have already set sail, and then who would teach her about the wonders of the world and the people in it? She had a sudden urge to lean over and spur the plodding draft horse with a quick smack on the rump.

Closer now, and Sophie could see a tall, arched gateway where the wall and the road intersected. It was crammed with traffic—dray animals, carts, carriages, and people on foot, all fighting to squeeze through going one way or the other. *Great, another obstacle.* Guards stood to either side, looking bored. Occasionally they shouted at those impeding the flow of traffic, but did little to actually help. They wore blue armor and carried long, sharp spears. Sophie wondered why they needed either.

Melina reined up a hundred yards or so from the contentious crush. "I'm afraid this is as far as I go," she said, helping Sophie dismount before climbing down herself. "It'll be much easier to get through that mess without this big fella, believe me. Just go slow, keep your wits about you, and you'll be through the wall in no time. Now, where is it you're heading to?"

"I don't know for sure," Sophie answered. Some part of her had never quite believed she would actually reach Fairport. Now she was faced with the task of trying to find one man in a city of thousands, a city she had never been to and knew nothing about.

She felt foolish for not having given it more thought. "I think the Na—*my mentor* lives down by the docks," she said.

"You think? You aren't certain?"

"What I mean is, he definitely lives by the docks, but I'm not sure where, exactly . . . by the docks . . ."

"Awfully irresponsible not to give you an address. *Artists.*" She huffed, blowing a stray strand of hair from her face. "Well, easy enough to find the waterfront. Follow the Queen's Road to the center of the city, where you'll find the Red Market. You'll know it when you see it. Follow your nose to find the fishmongers, and from there it's a straight shot down to the water. I'm sure you'll find it just fine."

"I hope so."

Melina's face grew serious, and she wagged a finger as she spoke, as she'd done with her little ones at home. "You mind me now. Fairport is a big, big place. You can find every sort of person living behind those walls, but one thing binds them together—they care not a whit for you or your wellbeing. Find your mentor before anything else. If he's as strange as Feeney says, he'll stand out like a flame, so I don't imagine you'll have much trouble. But if it gets late and you haven't got a place to stay, search out the Blue Yapper. It's a guesthouse near the city center. Give them Loren's name, he's a regular customer. And make sure to be in before nightfall. There's naught fair about Fairport after dark." She took Sophie by the shoulders. "Promise me you'll be careful."

"I promise," Sophie said, and meant it.

Her motherly wisdom imparted, Melina gave her a quick hug, wished her good luck, and turned back for home, leaving Sophie alone to face the challenges of the big city.

The Red Market

Sᴏᴘʜɪᴇ·ʜᴀᴅ ʀᴇᴀᴅ ᴀʙᴏᴜᴛ ᴄɪᴛɪᴇs in her books. She quickly realized that reading about a place and actually being there were two very different things.

No amount of imagining could have prepared her for the size and scale of Fairport. Orange clay tiles, identical and innumerable, sat atop the largest buildings she'd ever seen. Row after row after row of shuttered windows looked out over narrow, paved lanes. Laundry hung lazily out in the open air. Innumerable doors lined the streets, each one different from the next. It was that way with everything she saw—a thousand tiny variations on the same theme, all built by human hands and for human purposes, but for no one in particular. Sophie suddenly felt incredibly small.

Berlin had spoken of Fairport as a place of limitless possibility. As she neared the city center, Sophie began to understand. Row-homes were replaced by an endless variety of storefronts. There were butchers, bakers, and cafes, pubs and restaurants, tailors and dress-makers and cobblers, jewelers, haberdashers, guest houses and inns, banks, general stores, toy stores, and most exciting of all, book stores. Sophie stopped briefly to marvel at the volumes lining the walls. Even the people were livelier here. There were women in fanciful colors and shapely cuts, accompanied by men in sharp, serious suits. Horse-drawn carriages rumbled through the streets, their passengers looking out haughtily on those below. Gradually, Sophie realized that there was freedom in anonymity. No one knew her for an orphan here. No pity would darken their eyes and force them to choose their words with care. In Fairport, Sophie was no one; and in being no one, she was free to become anyone. With a newfound spring in her step, she hitched up her pack and pressed onward into the city.

*   *   *

Sophie heard the market well before she saw it. The noise began as a wash of featureless, echoing static, to which was added the garbled clamor of raised voices. They weren't angry, necessarily, just loud, all struggling for a place amongst the chaos. The percussive clattering of heavy things being tossed about cut through the din, and buried somewhere within were the strains of music. With each step the raucous cacophony gained in strength, drawing her closer to one of the city's greatest wonders.

You'll know it when you see it, Melina had said, and she'd been right. One hundred sheets of red canvas had been stretched out and suspended high above an expansive circular plaza. They hung at random angles and heights, casting the market below in a smoky red haze that was shot through with shafts of brilliant sunlight. Market stalls stood in uneven rows separated by narrow walkways. Shoppers carrying baskets, bags, and boxes maneuvered carefully around each other in search of the next great find, while the merchants employed their selling techniques on each potential customer. Some smiled languidly, hoping to attract with innocuous good charm. Others sold by sheer force of will; they bellowed and cajoled and made sweeping gestures to catch the eye. Still others put their voices to sweeter use, singing siren songs of unique finds and unbelievable prices to lure in their prey. The entrance to the market was haunted by those with nothing to sell but their meager talents. There was a juggler who kept dropping his balls, a guitar player with broken strings, a drummer with no rhythm. Sophie ignored them as she pressed on, intent on finding her way toward the fishmongers, and from there to the sea.

And that was when she saw it. Magic.

A man was levitating on the end of a rope.

She gasped, amazed. He was floating three feet in the air above a round, purple carpet, while the loose end of the rope lay coiled below him amongst a pile of golden pillows. A blanket of violet velvet was draped over his crossed legs, and his head was covered in a turban of tightly-wrapped golden silk. Each finger was adorned with a glittering, jeweled ring. He watched her intently as she walked around him in a circle, trying to divine the source of his power.

"Excuse me," Sophie said to the floating man, "are you a Navigator?"

He stared at her blankly.

"I only ask because I met someone recently who looks a bit like you. I mean, not a lot like you, but your clothes are the same, kind of. He has magic powers, too. Anyway, I'm trying to find him and he's supposed to be in Fairport and I was just wondering if you had seen him around." Sophie described the Navigator to the golden levitator. In response, he swept his open palm toward a small box that lay on the ground before him. It bore a message—*Generosity is repaid in kind.* A smattering of coins lay inside.

"Oh, I see." Sophie pulled a coin from her pack and tossed it in.

"I have seen the one you seek," said the magician.

"You have? When was he here? Where did he go?"

The sweeping palm gesture again. Sophie's brow wrinkled as she tossed another coin in the box. "Which answer would you have of me?"

"What?"

"You have asked me questions three: when, where, and whether I speak truly. I repeat—which answer would you have of me?"

"If I give you more money will you answer them all?"

"Indubitably."

Sophie took out a third coin, held it up meaningfully for the man to see, then tossed it in the box.

"The one you seek I did truly see. He appeared as competition to me. When I saw him last, the day that's just past, he was walking away toward the sea."

"But what about—" Sophie stopped herself. He hadn't told her anything she didn't already know, and more answers meant more money. Melina's warning came back to her mind. *They care not a whit for you or your wellbeing.* She thanked the man and walked away, feeling foolish. "May you have good fortune all this day," he called after her, rubbing salt in the wound.

As disorganized as the Red Market seemed, there was a method to the madness. Sophie entered through the garment corner, where she passed by merchants selling the latest fashions from both near and far. She had considered her mother's wardrobe to be flashy and extravagant; now she saw how reserved it really was. There were embroidered dresses, hats lined with fur, jeweled brooches and shimmering beads and fringed leather and strings of pearls and glimmering earrings. While it was all certainly curious, Sophie had no particular affinity for clothes. She ignored the beckoning shopkeepers as she moved quickly on.

From there she reached the food vendors in the market center. Some sights were familiar, like fresh fruits and vegetables stacked in colorful displays, but even here most everything was beyond her reckoning. One woman's shop consisted solely of bin after bin of colored powders. She placed a pinch of red in Sophie's palm and bid her to taste it. Fire engulfed her tongue, and the woman laughed as Sophie huffed and puffed to try and put it out. Nearby, a man was selling dried fruits. He gave her a candied fig to try, and it was so irresistibly sweet and delicious that she bought a whole handful. Then she went next door, where a family sold sandwiches topped with flat strips of charred, spiced meat, fresh vegetables, and a cool, creamy sauce. Last, she stopped and got some freshly squeezed orange juice. The merchant sprinkled flakes of fine sea salt over the top, which she hadn't asked for and found odd, until she experienced its considerably brightened flavor. There were long tables nearby for hungry patrons. Sophie sat and wolfed down her lunch, alone, her only company the mad music of the Red Market.

Satiated, she continued on to the next section of the market, which held household items, decorations, and art. It was like being surrounded by her parents' possessions once again, only this time they were proudly on display for the world to see and not hidden away like shameful secrets. Her eyes swept over the ostentatious displays as she wandered the aisles and saw an entire stall devoted to glass ornaments, including a collection of animals. Sophie stared, entranced, remembering the two frogs she'd found in the storage room. A flicker of hope ignited in her heart. *They had to have come from somewhere,* she thought. *Why not here?*

That vain hope dimmed considerably on seeing the sullen, bored-looking young man slumped behind the counter. He looked to be about her own age, a little older perhaps, his face dotted with pimples and freckles both. Something about the sheen of his eyes and the set of his mouth made him unfortunately unattractive. He perked up when he saw her and flashed a lopsided grin. "Shee shomething you like?"

Sophie didn't particularly want to talk to him, but didn't know if she would ever have an opportunity like this again, so she smiled back and said, "They're so pretty."

"Oh, thanks. My dad makes them." All of his S sounds came out as *sh.* "He's supposed to be here right now, but he put me in charge and left. He does this all the time. 'You have to learn how to run the stand, *Bernard.* How are you ever going to take over the family business if you don't learn how to sell at the market, *Bernard?*' He makes me so mad sometimes. Do you want to buy something?"

"Maybe," Sophie answered, pretending to pick through the selection. "Do you ever sell at other markets?"

"Yeah. We don't come here very often, only when the ships come in. Usually we go up north and try to sell where there isn't as much competition. But most of the time we just stay home and make new stuff to sell. I told my dad like a million times I don't like blowing glass but he never listens."

"Why don't you like it?"

"It's really hard!" said Bernard. "You can spend, like, all day working on one thing and then it just breaks. One time, I made a really cool vase with like, all these different colors and stuff. It was really really good. But then my stupid dad bumped me and it fell and broke into like a thousand little pieces. Then I cut myself cleaning it up. Those furnaces get really hot, too, and I burn myself all the time. See?" He rolled back his sleeve to reveal a patchwork of scars. Sophie grimaced. "Yeah. It's pretty bad. So, my dad will be really upset with me if I don't have any money when he comes back . . ."

Sophie suddenly understood why Bernard didn't have any other customers. She turned fully toward the display of forest creatures and leaned in for a closer look.

"Oh yeah, those ones are really nice," said Bernard. "You like squirrels? I could make you a squirrel."

Sophie ignored him, picking up one of the bushy-tailed creatures. Unlike her frogs, these were made of clear glass. She turned it in the light and noticed a slight blue-green tint around the edges. Another had a rose hue to it. They were pretty enough, but not one came anywhere close to matching the bold colors and lifelike beauty of the masterworks back home. "What I'm really looking for are frogs," she said. "Does anyone else in Fairport sell glass animals?"

"Uh, *rude*."

"Oh, I'm sorry," said Sophie, surprisingly stung by the accusation. "I didn't mean to—"

"It's fine," said the boy, waving a hand at her and sitting back down on his stool, dejected. "Ever since Maestro Marioletti came around we can't sell hardly anything. It's all my dad ever talks about. 'He's stealing all our business,' he says, or 'If I had the same fancy training as him I could make pieces like that, too', or 'You could be as good as Marioletti if you just tried, *Bernard*'. It's not true, though. He's the best. Only people like the Queen and the Duke and, like, really really rich people can buy his art. Everyone else just tries to copy him, except for my dad and me, 'cause we don't even know how."

Sophie's pulse pounded. "Where can I find Mr. Marioletti?" she asked.

"That's the thing—nobody knows. He just shows up in the big cities with a whole bunch of new art, then disappears again for months at a time, sometimes years. He's a really weird guy. Are you gonna buy something or not?"

The tiny flame of Sophie's hope guttered and went out. Even if she did somehow find the reclusive artist, her parents couldn't have afforded such masterpieces. They had to be fake. They could have been made by anyone. Well, anyone except for Bernard or his father, that was. Sophie politely excused herself and moved on, ignoring the boy's promises to make her, like, a really good deal or something.

At The Pier

Sᴎᴇ sᴏᴏɴ ᴄᴀᴜɢʜᴛ ᴛʜᴇ ʟɪɴɢᴇʀɪɴɢ, pungent scent of seafood and followed it toward the fishmongers. Beyond them lay the port for which the city was named. Sophie ambled along the steadily declining road until she reached the wide, blue expanse of the bay. Great wooden ships were moored along piers that jutted out into the water. More sat at anchor on the bay, bobbing gently on the waves, while fishing boats skirted around below the masted giants like children playing under their parents' feet.

Sophie approached the first ship with the bravado of one wholly innocent of the enterprise to which she was engaged. Several scruffy looking deckhands sat on some crates in a circle, surrounded by a cloud of tobacco smoke and passing around a bottle of amber liquid between them. One of the men noticed her. He said something and stood, while the others turned to leer at her like a pack of hungry wolves. "Well well well," the deckhand said as he approached. "Lookee what we've got 'ere, boyos. An enterprising young lady come to relieve us of the burdens of a long voyage at sea!" His gapped, brown teeth showed in a lupine smile. The other men laughed, though at what joke Sophie couldn't fathom.

She froze in place. Every instinct told her to bolt, to run as fast and as far as her legs could carry her and begin her search elsewhere. Instead, she held her ground. She had come too far to give up now, and besides, what was an adventure without a little danger? Plucking herself up, she said, "I'm looking for the Navigator."

The grinning jackal guffawed. "That withered fig? I reckon it's been many a year since 'e's had any use for the likes of you."

"Pushing naught but rope, that one," said one of his fellows.

"Maybe 'e just wants to show her his sextant!"

"I saw him eatin' oysters ashore, a whole bucket full of 'em. Best watch yourself, girl, or you'll be listing to port come high tide!"

The pack erupted in raucous laughter, all but the one standing, who stepped forward slowly, his hand outstretched as though he were trying to corral a nervous cat. His smile stretched wider than ever. "Forget about the old timer. We been out a long, long time, with naught but each other for comp'ny. S'alright, come with me, I'll treat you real nice like . . ."

"Oy! You jackals!" A walking brick of a man pounded down the gangplank, swinging a heavy cudgel belligerently in the air. "Back to work 'fore I mash your heads in and toss you in the drink. M'on now, move or I'll move ya!" The layabouts abandoned their leisure and jumped up to start moving the crates again. All except for the one already on his feet. His eyes hadn't left Sophie's; it was as if he were trying to hypnotize her with his gaze. It took a sharp jab in the ribs to convince him to change course, and even then it was done with reluctance. "And you," said the squat, solid sailor, "'chu doing distractin' my men? No women on the boat, captain's orders." He emphasized his point by shaking his cudgel at her.

"I'm just—"

"Piss off!" He took one sharp, threatening step forward and raised his stick like he was going to hit her. Sophie decided she'd had more than her fill of danger. She spun around and fled, turning once to shoot a sour look at the man who'd chased her off, but he was already back aboard the ship and busy threatening those under his command.

Versions of this scene played out several more times, until eventually she was made to understand that every ship had at least one person aboard with the title of navigator. "Are you daft?" one surly sailor had asked. "Might as well go to the market and ask if anyone's seen any fish!" She was disappointed to further learn that none of these navigators were like her Navigator, which is to say that they possessed no magic at all.

Sophie also learned that not every ship reserved space for non-crew passengers, and that she could save a lot of time simply by mentioning she wanted to book passage. Those captains that did accept passengers were significantly more friendly. Until they discovered she had no intention of putting any money in their hands, that was.

Her most bizarre interaction of the day came when she received a marriage proposal from a particularly greasy and garlic-smelling captain. With no prompting whatsoever, he professed his deep and total love for her, reciting poetry that extolled the romance of life on the high seas. When that didn't work, he turned to bragging about his personal wealth, and claimed to be the prince of someplace she'd never even heard of. Sophie politely declined and moved on.

She was nearly out of daylight, ships, and patience when her persistence paid off.

"Yeah, I saw him. Yesterday." The man to which she spoke, who was lounging on a long deck chair, was the captain of the *Brazen Whale*. It was quite possible the ship had been named after the captain himself. Long hours in the sun had turned the rotund man a deep, brassy color and left him shiny with sweat. His stringy blonde hair was pulled back into a tight ponytail over his smooth, blunt, nearly noseless face. A linen shirt dangled open over his heavy frame to reveal the hairless flesh of his chest beneath. When he spoke, his voice was high-pitched and reedy. "Spoiled rich types. Doesn't matter where they're from, they're all the same. See something they like and decide it belongs to them. 'You will take me out to sea,' your friend says, all matter-of-fact. 'Really?' I say, humoring him. 'And where is it I'm taking you?' He says he can't tell me. I ask him why I want to take my ship and my crew to wherever it is he's going. He can't tell me that either. What he *can* tell me is how important it is that we set sail right away and that lives are on the line and it's his right and blah, blah, blah." The captain rolled his massive, globular eyes. "Look, the *Brazen Whale* is the finest ship in all the world. It would be a crime to deprive anyone of the chance to sail the open ocean and see the wonders of the world from her prow. But I can't just give away that privilege. Takes a lot of money to keep a beauty like the *Whale* afloat and in tip-top shape, to say nothing of feeding the likes of myself and my crew." At this, he plucked an oily sardine from a nearby jar, popped it into his mouth, swallowed it whole. "Then there's my reputation to consider. You don't get to be captain of the finest ship in all the world by breaking contract every time some yahoo in fancy clothes says to. I says to him, 'The only way me and the crew are going on some fantastical mystery tour to no-one-knows-where is if the duke commandeers the ship and forces us to, and even then only if we're paid for our lost wages and time, arrangements are made to fulfill our existing shipping contracts, and if the *Whale's* insured against damages or loss by Duke Truculo himself.'"

"And what did he say?" Sophie asked.

"*It shall be done,*" said the captain, mocking the Navigator's grave tone. "Like it was a done deal. Then he turns around and leaves, with not a single parting word. I'm telling you, something's not right with that one. Fallen overboard a few too many times, if you catch my drift." He shook his head, exasperated.

"Did you see where he went?"

"Away from me," said the captain. "Though if he's crazy enough to try convincing the duke to commandeer my ship, there's only one place for him to go."

"The palace?"

"That's right. And he'd better be quick, because we set sail in three days' time."

Closed to the Public

On his rare visits to Seaside, the duke liked to boast that his palatial home was larger than their entire village. The villagers privately derided these claims as preposterous, impossible even. Standing in Fairport's central square in the fading, evening light and taking in the building's immensity, Sophie no longer found the duke's claims to be quite so ridiculous.

The palace was squat and wide, far wider than it was tall, making its four levels appear shorter than they were. Six towers reached up into the sky, one at each of the palace's four corners and two more flanking the main entryway. From these towers flew the duke's signature blue pennants, the ones she had noticed while approaching the city. A paved drive led from the entryway down to the square, where it met a grand, golden gate that was being watched over by a handful of guards. Their polished steel armor glimmered in the firelight thrown by a row of nearby lanterns. Hungry, exhausted, but still determined to succeed, Sophie approached the guards at the gate. "Um, excuse me?"

"Palace is closed to the public."

"Oh. Well, I don't want to go in, I'm looking for someone."

"Palace. Is. Closed."

"Okay." Her voice strained as she tried not to let her frustration show. "Could you tell me if you saw my friend? He was supposed to talk to the duke today and I'm sure you'd remember him, he has—"

"*Closed.*"

"Please," Sophie said plaintively, "I know he was here, I just need a little bit of help . . ."

The guard turned his scornful glare on her then, and when he spoke, his words came out slow, edged, a warning. "You know what, I did see your friend after all, bloody and bludgeoned down in the deepest, darkest cell of the dungeon. Care to join him?"

Sophie sniffed. "No."

"Then get *knotted.*"

She turned away quickly. Her tears caught the firelight, leaving luminous streaks of orange on her trembling cheeks. With privacy nowhere to be found, she flumped down against the fence and hid her face in her hands as she sobbed.

. . . one thing binds them together—they care not a whit for you . . .

Sophie's frustration built as the events of the day replayed in her mind. Every jostle, nudge, or bump in the street, every insult, trick, and swindle, every lascivious look, all repeated in rapid succession. Though each in itself was feather light, their sum was too much to bear any longer. She'd spent most of the day on her feet, in the sunshine. Her shoulders ached from the constant pull of her pack. She had eaten little and drank less. Simply put, Sophie had reached her limit. She was done. Her body yearned for the safety and comfort of her own bed.

(desire is like a flame)

Sophie removed the watercolors from her pack. There

was Cass and Feeney's inn, a captive ghost, a paper memory of a pyre stacked tall and set alight, a raging conflagration of desire eventually choked down to ashes by unfulfilled longing. Somewhere within the plane of that image were the pyre's creators. Sophie felt an immense pity for them, not only for their lost past or the bright future that had never come, but because they had simply watched it burn down and counted themselves lucky for the warmth. She flipped to the next image, and the next, studying the collected scenes both alien and familiar. Through them all had been woven a single thread—hope. Sophie imagined her mother as a woman aflame with passion, so much so that her own inner light had spilled over into her art. *I wish I could be like that.*

(all are responsible for the path they tread)

It was time to decide. She could either accept defeat and dwindle away to nothing, or she could stoke the fires within and see this journey through to its end. Sophie stood, readjusted her dress and her pack, and left the square behind. Not a tear marked her face.

I choose to burn.

The Blue Yapper

The Blue Yapper was a small guesthouse tucked away off the city's main thoroughfare. It was popular with Fairport's lower caste, a hideaway where the downtrodden could commiserate and speak freely about those they served without fear of repercussions. A sign hanging over the doorway depicted a blue terrier barking at an ornate white carriage as it sped past. This was a joke at Duke Truculo's expense. He had been trying to court Queen Avantia's favor for many years. His efforts were notorious for being annoyingly loud, obnoxiously persistent, and largely ineffective.

As befit its lowly status, the Yapper's common room was in a half-sunk basement. Getting in was a bit like entering a house through its chimney; as Sophie opened the door, she was met with a billowing cloud of smoke that singed her nostrils. She stepped into a confined antechamber with a steep, narrow staircase that led down to the common room floor. A warm, insistent updraft blew around her as she descended. The staircase ended on a raised landing from which she could see the entire room, and they her, as conspicuous as if she had climbed straight from the hearth. Candles hung from sconces on the wood paneled walls. Their dim light struggled through the spent tobacco fumes only to be swallowed up by the deep walnut furnishings. Everywhere were the signs of hard labor and strife. Torn, shabby clothes. Weather-beaten skin. Worry lines and tight jaws. Sophie thought, *Damon would fit right in.*

The woman behind the bar looked an awful lot like a goat.

Thin of frame and ropy, she had a long, pointed face, high cheekbones, and wide-set, circular eyes. A pair of variegated ridges ran the length of her skull, created by tightly bound braids that stuck straight out from the back of her head. She eyed Sophie suspiciously, arms crossed, jaw working up and down as if chewing her thoughts. "'At's a real pritty dress you got there," she said as Sophie sat down on one of the stools. "Jus' like a proppa li'l princess, you look."

"Oh," said Sophie, taken by surprise. "That's the nicest thing anyone's said to me all day."

"Don't get many princesses in 'ere. Not really the place for 'em." Hard eyes stared as the absent chewing continued. "If you take my meanin'."

Sophie felt herself flush. She pushed her rising frustration aside and said in a firm voice, "My friend Loren sent me. He told me to tell you so."

"Is 'at right?" The caprine woman leaned on her hands. "Never heard of 'im."

"Either way, I want a room. A private one."

A mock smile revealed crooked, overlapping teeth. "Only got one private room, princess, an 'at's my own. Ain' leavin' it for the likes of you."

Cass and Feeney had warned Sophie about this. Most every innkeeper kept private rooms but would claim otherwise, thinking to trick their patrons into paying more for it than was fair. The bartender's fuss was likely a ruse. Sophie wasn't about to be taken in. "How about for some silver?"

The smile disappeared as the goat woman chewed air, thinking. "'Ow much silva ya got?"

"Some."

"*Some.*" She snorted. "Right then. You put *some* silva on the bar, li'l princess, and I'll consider beddin' down in one of the guest rooms for the night." With an air of confidence she didn't quite feel, Sophie removed a single silver piece from her pack and set it on the bar top, pushing it forward deliberately with her index finger, all the while keeping her eyes locked on those of her counterpart. The woman glanced at the money. "Fought you said *some.*"

"One *is* some," Sophie retorted. "It's more than you'd get from anyone else in this room, and more than fair."

More empty chewing. Long seconds stretched as she waited for Sophie to buckle.

"Fine." The bartender produced a heavy key from under the bar and tossed it beside the coin. "'ave it your way. Top of the stairs, far end of the hall."

Sophie tried to hide her triumphant glee as she picked up the key. "Thank you," she said, unable to resist a little smirk. "I would also like some dinner. Please."

"'Course. We got beef pie, fish pie, or roast chickin. Whadja want?"

"Chicken," Sophie said, "and a big glass of water."

The bartender snatched up a heavy mug and filled it from a barrel. Water slopped over the edges as she set it down roughly. "Here. Now go sit somewheres else, li'l princess, I'm sicka lookin' atcha."

Sophie was happy to oblige. She rose from her seat, heart racing, feeling proud and powerful for having stood up for herself. With the mug in one hand and her pack dangling from the other, she surveyed the room, searching for a place to sit. A table near the back was empty save for a single older man. He stared morosely into his beer, face drawn and dour. It was depressingly like looking into Damon's future using a seer's crystal. Sophie made her way over and set down her things. "Can I join you?"

"You will not be happy." He spoke without looking up.

"Excuse me?"

"It will bring you no joy to make yourself my table mate."

Sophie sat. "It's not like this place has brought me much joy, anyway."

The miserable man looked up at her then, his eyes faded and worn. "Of course you have been received poorly," he said, "coming to this dismal place whilst wearing such bright colors, with your unblemished skin and unlined face and a look of naive hope in your eyes, presenting yourself as if the world were anything other than an enormous grindstone that slowly peels away one's humanity a layer at a time. Oh, sweet child, how I envy you! Would that I could return to your adolescent state, and become once more blissfully unaware of the devastation wreaked by plummeting from life's vertiginous heights. Flee, flee I beg you, else you too shall become ensnared by my miresome, malappropriate, misfortunate fate."

The man's gaze returned to his mug as Sophie studied him, bewildered. There was a refinement to his voice and mannerisms that was very much out of place, to say nothing of his odd manner of speech, yet he appeared as damaged and careworn as anyone else in the room. It was then that she noticed his bandages—each of his fingertips was bound with a strip of bloody cloth. "What happened to you?"

"To me." He gave a sad little chuckle. "That is very human of you. As if the events of my life sought me out for reward or punishment in some secret accordance with my actions. No, young lady, events do not happen *to* people, they simply happen, and happen to leave the unfortunate broken in their wake. But my woes are no fit tale for one as fresh and unburdened as you."

"I'm not unburdened," Sophie said defiantly.

"No?"

"No."

"Pray tell, what horrors could life have imposed upon one so radiant and young?"

"I'm an orphan." She cringed internally, regretting the admission at once. How easily the words had formed on her tongue, inviting that wretched look she so despised. Wrinkles like spiderwebs appeared around the man's eyes as he looked into her own, searching, a pale imitation of the Navigator's affecting gaze.

"My apologies," he said. "I should have taken care before speaking. There is sorrow in your soul, after all. You disguise it far better than I, but alas, I have lost the will to deny my pain a face. A toast, then, to our miseries." He lifted his mug, wincing as he did so, and the two drank together. Soon afterward the bartender delivered Sophie's supper, half a roast chicken with peas and mashed potatoes. She noticed her dispirited companion eyeing the plate. "Would you like some?"

"You are very kind. I could not accept such a gift." He said the words simply, with no false modesty, and so she offered again. This time he accepted. They ate in ravenous silence. Sophie wasn't quite full at the meal's end, but neither was she starving, and that was enough. "In years past," he said, "I would have had the servant who dared bring me such dry and flavorless fare scourged for their insolence. Now look at me. Accepting charity from a child like a dog begging for scraps and slavering for more. Truly, this is a new low."

"You used to have servants?" Sophie asked. "Who are you, and how did you end up *here*?"

"I dare not utter my own name in this place," he answered, leaning in conspiratorially, "for there are those who know me only by my reputation, and on the character of it, would do me harm should they come to know the shape of my face. As to your other questions, I was wealthy for much of my life. Quite wealthy. I had the good fortune of being born a shipping merchant's son, from a line of ambitious and capable businessmen. Our company's fleet doubled in size under the directorship of my grandfather, while my sire expanded our business into new territory through the overland transportation of goods. For my own contribution, I entered the world of politics. My intent was to befriend Duke Truculo and bend his ear to the needs of my enterprise so that I might simultaneously ease my own path and remove my competitors. It was a bold plan, and a risky one. But fortune favors the bold, or so I had been taught, and I carried on with it heedless of the dangers."

"What happened?"

"Rothschild! That conniver!" His eyes burned as he said it. "I shall spare you the sordid details, as the whole affair is wrapped up in the interpersonal politics of Fairport's elite, and it would take far too long to provide the context necessary to fully appreciate the color and depth of my tale. Suffice to say I was not the only one intent on securing the Duke's favor. I succeeded in removing most every competitor from the game, but I underestimated the cunning, the guile, the sheer manipulative genius of the man who engineered my downfall. You see, early in the contest he arranged a private audience with the duke and warned him against my machinations, did, in fact, suggest that the duke pretend to befriend me in order to earn my confidence! With each skirmish I won, the duke saw the proof of my untrustworthiness, his vision colored according to Rothschild's dark lens. My every victory brought me closer to defeat."

"Then fate arrived for me. Duke Truculo sought me out for a private audience. My opening, my opportunity, had at last presented itself. I would become the duke's sole friend and counselor, and secure my family's position at the pinnacle of Fairport's aristocracy. But it was not to be. When I presented myself at the duke's apartments, he was accompanied by Rothschild. I tell you, that slimy, self-assured smile haunts me still. The duke accused me of plotting treachery. I denied it, of course, for it was not true. It made no difference. His mind had been long poisoned against me. He threatened to lock me in the dungeons, but the little worm had other ideas. Rothschild had engineered not only my downfall, but also my punishment, a form of torture and abuse meant to afflict my very soul. 'Consider it an opportunity to regain an appreciation for the status afforded you by chance,' he said to me, without the least trace of irony, as though he himself were not the benefactor of similar good fortune but was instead like those mystical practitioners from afar who are able to lift themselves bodily by seizing hold of their own bootlaces!"

"My wealth, my property, seized. My business ventures, dismantled and distributed to those I'd conspired against. My wife and children, who were innocent of the whole affair, were provided a meager home and a monetary allowance on the provision that they neither see nor speak to me again. As for myself, I was given a job. Behold, my young friend, for your eyes now rest upon the duke's thorn plucker." He spread his damaged fingers and smiled. There was no glee in it whatsoever. "The palace rose garden is quite expansive. Even more so when you must see to every stem individually, I assure you. So ends my sorry tale. But what of your own? What path has led a young woman of some means to this dingy, overblown hovel, this sink of misery and destitution?"

Sophie hesitated, unsure of how much she wanted to share. In the end she told him everything: of Seaside, of life in the loft, of her brother who meant well but rarely lived up to his ambitions. She even shared with him her mother's paintings. "Quite good," the thorn plucker judged. Sophie wrapped it all up with her quest to be reunited with the Navigator. "Fascinating," he said when she had finished. "We are like the sun and the moon, you and I, two opposites sharing the same sky for a brief moment as our paths intersect, one shining bold and bright, the other waning and nearly out. Yet our apposition is fortuitous, for I can say, without hesitation, that your friend did not speak to Duke Truculo today."

"Really? How can you be sure?"

"A simple deduction. Duke Truculo only meets with the public on Tuesday mornings, after breakfast but before his mid-morning snack, or on Friday afternoons between cream tea and pre-dinner pudding. No exceptions. Today, I am happy to report, is Thursday. Therefore, if this Navigator fellow truly means to convince the duke to intervene on his behalf, tomorrow will be his next opportunity."

Sophie's heart sang with joy. She sprang from the table and wrapped the thorn plucker in a tight hug. "Thank you, thank you!"

"Happy to be of service," he said when she finally let go. "Consider it an act of penance on the part of one who is still learning what it means to be downtrodden. And now I must excuse myself. I have an arrangement with one of the palace guards, and if I do not return before shift change, I risk being caught out of bounds and punished. It was a pleasure to share your light this evening, young lady."

"Thank you," she said again. He'd walked a few paces away when something occurred to her. "The moon always waxes again, you know." He turned back, and for just a moment the corners of his mouth lifted in a smile. Then, with a brief nod, he bid her goodnight and climbed up the stairs and was gone.

An Audience With the Duke

THE PALACE GATE STOOD OPEN when Sophie arrived the following day. A thin trickle of foot traffic streamed through the portal and up the wide stone drive. She joined them, flashing a sour look at the guards as she passed. In the daylight, she saw the palace's true character, with its blue walls and shining, gilded window frames. That sense of being small and insignificant returned as each step revealed its true scale. Servants moved about the grounds. She recognized them by their uniforms, a rough, dun-colored shirt and matching pants. They went about their menial tasks with a complete lack of alacrity that was uncomfortably familiar. She thought of her morose new friend and wondered if these others had similar tales of woe.

One of the palace's ornate, heavy doors was propped open to allow visitors in. Sophie entered, and found herself in a hallway that was unimaginably decadent. Crystal chandeliers hung at intervals from the high, paneled ceiling. Generations of Truculos past looked down from their portraits at the commoners passing below, guarded by empty suits of armor that stood stiffly at attention. Sophie glanced down and saw her own face reflected in the stone floor's mirror shine. At the end was a spacious rotunda, with a tiled, mosaic rosette set into the floor and a pair of arching staircases that led up to a mezzanine-level balcony. The opulence was stunning, and for a moment there was nothing she could do but stare.

A woman stood in the center of the rosette. She was also dressed in uniform, but unlike that of the other servants, this one was more like a formal suit. Everything about her appearance was impeccable, from the pressed lines of her dark jacket and trousers, the gleam of her brass buttons, and the spotless brilliance of her white shirt and gloves. As the other visitors approached her, they were directed either through a set of doors behind her or up to the mezzanine. She caught sight of Sophie and motioned her over impatiently. "Petitioner or observer?" the woman asked.

"I'm not sure."

"Young miss," she said, her lips puckered tight, "do you wish to speak to the illustrious Duke Truculo yourself, or are you here simply to feed your curiosity?"

"I don't need to speak to the duke," said Sophie, "but my friend does. Maybe you've see—"

"Mezzanine level." The woman made a sharp, sweeping gesture. "Choose any open seat. By order of the duke, any person found distracting, disrupting, disturbing, agitating, mocking, impersonating, prevaricating, opining, annoying, or being obnoxious in any way, shape, or form will be summarily ejected and possibly imprisoned. Enjoy your visit to the palace." She smiled emptily at Sophie, indicating that their interaction had come to an end.

A doorway on the upper level opened onto a balcony that overlooked the Duke's audience chamber. It was furnished with cascading rows of simple, cushionless chairs. Half of the seats were filled, most of the occupants alone or in pairs. Sophie wandered up the main aisle and found a place by the railing where she would be sure to catch sight of the Navigator. Assuming, of course, he showed up at all.

Compared to the rest of the palace, the audience chamber was spartan and practical. Wood paneling covered the lower half of the walls, while frescoes decorated the spaces above, each one bordered by painted, twining vines of gold. Hard benches lined the walls, all unoccupied. Sunlight filtered in through stained glass. There was a dais near the rear wall, and on it sat a large, sturdy-looking chair with pretensions of thronery. Its frame was made of the same dark wood as the walls, and its plush cushions were, unsurprisingly, blue with gold buttons. There was no sign of the Duke.

Impatient murmurs bubbled up from below. Sophie took hold of the banister and leaned over the edge to peek at the waiting petitioners, but saw only a few surly guards lounging against a dividing rail.

Then the air solidified as a door at the far end of the room swung open. Every guard came swiftly to attention, their armor rattling as they shot upright. Silence swept over the observers and petitioners both. Then two young pages entered. "All rise for the arrival of Duke Alfred Truculo and his court!" cried one, her voice squeaky and breaking. Everyone rose. The other page stuck a brass horn to his lips and blew a hasty flourish that sputtered out like a wet fart.

Next came a trio of armed guards. Two were the same blocky, nondescript brutes she'd seen around the palace. The third was the apotheosis of every brave knight archetype

Sophie had ever read about, a fictional character brought stunningly to life. She stared, transfixed. With no helmet on, his high cheekbones, granite jaw, and flowing blonde locks were on display for the world to admire. His personalized armor was ornamented and fitted to accentuate his muscular body. He strode with a swarthy swagger and had a habit of sweeping his hair back from his cocksure face. They took up positions around the dais, their leader coming to stand beside the big chair. He winked at someone in the audience. *No doubt she swooned,* thought Sophie.

A wizened greybeard entered next, stringy wisps of frail white hair hanging long from his piebald pate. He shuffled on unsteady feet, back bent at a right angle, one gnarled claw gripping the head of a cane. His black uniform hung loose from his bony frame. A younger man walked beside him, wearing a matching uniform and carrying several heavy tomes. These he set carefully on the bench, then helped his counterpart sit before taking a seat himself. Within moments the old man had nodded off, as older men are wont to do.

Finally, Duke Truculo himself entered the audience chamber. Far from being the svelte, lithe warrior depicted in Seaside's square, he was a short man of indeterminate shape and considerable heft. His face was childlike and round, with shiny, plump cheeks and a nearly spherical nose. Ringlets of oiled black hair dangled to his shoulders. Lacy frills adorned his cuffs and collar, and jewels flashed from the rings on his stubby fingers. This was the man the common folk were meant to rally to, their hero in times of crisis. Sophie thought, *The only thing he's ever conquered is a mountain of mashed potatoes.*

Beside the duke walked a tall, middle-aged dandy that

Sophie disliked on sight. *Rothschild.* He was very finely dressed in a red doublet of slashed velvet and matching pantaloons, with white stockings beneath, and a wide brimmed hat festooned with a swan's feather. There seemed to be no meat between his flesh and skeleton. A pencil mustache ornamented his snide upper lip, though it was barely noticeable beneath the man's obscenely protruding nose. *I tell you, that slimy, self-assured smile haunts me still.* Sophie shuddered. He stood beside the duke, who took his seat on the *faux* throne.

Nothing happened.

The book-bearer gently nudged the old man, who woke with a start. With an effort he stood, cleared his throat, and said with a weary, failing voice, "On behalf of your illustrious lord and master Duke Alfred Truculo, I hereby call this session to order. Petitioners will approach the dais in the order arrived. All judgements are final and binding. First petitioner, you may proceed."

Sophie looked on expectantly, waiting for the Navigator to come into view. But he was not the first petitioner that day. Neither was he the second, third, nor fourth. Sophie's foot tapped anxiously, her mania a reflection of the duke's obvious boredom. His face remained impassive throughout the entire proceeding. He only ever gave one of two responses, both of which were delivered flatly and by rote: "I shall look into this matter further," or "Petition denied." It soon became clear that both answers meant the same thing.

Then the duke sat up in his chair, his attention finally engaged. The smug smile disappeared from Rothschild's face as suspicion filled his eyes. The handsome guard flipped his hair back, the pages nudged each other and pointed, and even the old man leaned forward, blinking. Sophie's pulse surged, knowing that only one man could inspire such interest by appearance alone, and sure enough the Navigator came at last into view. His vest and frills made him look more a part of the proceedings rather than less. "At last," said Duke Truculo, "a petitioner with the decency to dress appropriately for the occasion. Speak, friend, tell me how I, your gracious lord and master, can be of service on this fine day."

The Navigator bowed deeply, then spoke. His clear tenor came from everywhere at once, a voice both sourceless and omnipresent, words spoken by the very air itself. The attendant crowd looked about and murmured uncomfortably. "It is not I who seek your service, Duke Truculo, but the countless lives depending upon my successful return to the sea." Though his words were grave, his tone was reserved and calm. "As a Navigator, I hereby invoke the Right of Ministration, a privilege which all nations afford to those of my ancient order. I request that you remand a sea-faring ship, the *Brazen Whale*, to my custody so that I may reach my destination and prevent the coming calamity."

There was a collective gasp from the assembly, followed by shocked silence. Over and over again the duke had put off or refused the most mundane appeals for assistance, appeals that were well within his power to fix. No one quite knew how to respond to the Navigator's ridiculous and grandiose request.

Duke Truculo burst into laughter.

Rothschild followed suit. Soon the whole room was laughing at the Navigator, all except for Sophie, who hid her head in her hands, and the old man, who was busy rifling through one of his dusty tomes with the aid of his assistant. And of course the Navigator himself, who bore their ridicule stoically. "Well done!" said the duke once the ruckus had died down. "Oh, I do so love a good jest. Well done, indeed! For a moment I thought you were serious. Can you imagine? Clearly one of my admirers is putting me on. How delightful! Tell me, my aspiring thespian friend, who was it who put you up to this? Was it Cunningham? Fassbender? Certainly this isn't your work, Rothschild?"

"Certainly not, my lord," said the snide man at his side. "You know, I cannot help but wonder if this is the work of *Beringford*."

"Beringford? That slimy snake in the grass? Or perhaps I should say, snake in the *rosebushes*." A light, bouncy, babyish giggle escaped him. "But why would he do this, and how?"

"The man is quite resourceful. Perhaps he believes he can slither back into your good graces with a bit of whimsy."

"Ha! A fool's errand, particularly after his clumsy efforts to manipulate me like some moldable buffoon. Come now, seafarer, give us the name of the one who sent you, and quickly. I have many other petitioners to see to this day."

"I do not speak in jest, duke."

The title was spoken not as a polite recognition of Truculo's position, but as a forceful command. It wiped the smile from the lord's lips. His eyes narrowed. His cheeks puckered. "Clearly you are a stranger to the ways of courtly manner, so I will forgive your momentary insolence. For the nonce. Tell me, who are you?"

"A Navigator."

"And you are invoking your right of . . ."

"Ministration."

"Right, right. Chamberlain!" The old man looked up

suddenly, then stood. "This man invokes a right with which I am unfamiliar. Enlighten me."

"My lord," said the chamberlain, "we are referencing the Royal Code of Laws now. I am so far unable to find the appropriate listing, but if I could have a few more moments . . ."

"It's not in the book?"

"I have not found it, but that does not mean—"

"I've heard enough. You, seafarer. You cannot invoke your right here, because you have no such right, because there *is* no such right. *I*, on the other hand, have the right to imprison you in a dark dungeon cell for as long as I deem fit, long enough to make you forget what sunlight is, and then to remind you by having you flogged through the streets. However," the duke said sharply, "you say there are countless lives depending upon your success. Were I to imprison you, I would be complicit in their calamity, a fate I would sooner avoid. Perhaps we should begin again, as friends, so that I may know the people to whom I would give aid and the details of their plight. For my part, I am Duke Alfred Truculo, son of Waldendorf, Lord of the Westerlands and loyal subject of Queen Avantia. And you are?"

"My name is my own."

Oh no. The crowd murmured once more.

"As you wish. From where do you come? What nation's fate lies upon your shoulders?"

"My business is my own, as well."

The duke threw up his hands. "Can you at least share with me your destination, then?"

"I cannot."

The clamor was positively uproarious now. Even the guards were so caught up in the drama that they failed to hush the crowd, so that the Duke had to raise his voice in order to be heard. As it happened, he felt like raising his voice. "Let me get this straight. You come to my court and spin this colorful yarn, pretending to be some sort of hero, and demand that I expend precious resources and materiel in the form of a ship and crew to take you out to sea, and yet you won't even extend me the courtesy of your own name? My patience has worn through! Captain Rectifer, *seize him!*"

The handsome knight drew his blade, as did his companions. Sophie recoiled, certain that the captain was about to be electrocuted in front of everyone. The Navigator, meanwhile, remained still. The guards hadn't taken more than two steps when the chamberlain shuffled into their path, breathing heavily. "Stop! Please, my lord, a moment of your time, just one moment." The guards halted, swords raised, awaiting the Duke's command.

No one breathed.

The duke drummed his fingers on the arm of his chair. "Fine. Approach."

The chamberlain and his assistant went to the dais to confer with Duke Truculo. Their voices were hurried and far too low to be heard. After a few moments of tense discussion, the chamberlain stood aside. The duke raised a hand and said, "Stand down." The guards resumed their post, Captain Rectifer giving the Navigator a look that suggested he was very lucky, indeed.

"It has come to my attention," the duke said with practiced grandiosity, "that there is, buried in the ancient tomes of lore, a tale of one such as you claim to be, a woman who came to this island bearing the gifts of magic and the power to *navigate* to anyplace she chose. This skill could be very useful to me. People have been vanishing from Waldendorf's Woods. The source of these disappearances, be it man or beast, has so far eluded my men. Their repeated failures have tarnished my reputation. I despise tarnish. Therefore, I offer you the opportunity to earn my gratitude. Venture into the woods and return to me with this bothersome villain in hand, and your request shall be granted. But be forewarned: return empty-handed, and you will live out the rest of your days in the dank darkness of my dungeons. You have a fortnight to complete the task. Well? What say you, seafarer?"

The Navigator bowed again. "It shall be done."

"Excellent," said the Duke, clapping his hands together. "You hear, good people of the Westerlands? You shall be delivered from the evil haunting our forest, and soon, for this man, your savior, departs before sundown. Chamberlain, we're done here."

The crowd erupted in confusion as the duke stood to leave. "Our lord will hear no further petitions today!" cried the chamberlain. "Should you wish to try again you may return . . ."

"No!" Sophie shouted, leaping to her feet. "Navigator, wait! Wait for me!" But her cries were drowned out by the uproar. "Please, you have to wait, don't go!" She waved her arms frantically, hoping to catch the Navigator's attention. It did not work. She slumped back into her chair, defeated, as he crossed the audience chamber and followed Captain Rectifer through the rear door and disappeared.

Fortune Favors the Bold

Sophie sulked.

She sulked as she went down the stairs, shooting a backward glance at the disappointed petitioners streaming out of the audience chamber. She sulked past the uniformed woman who impatiently herded them all out. She sulked the entire length of the decadent hallway, feeling the judgmental gaze of the duke's lofty forebears. She sulked out through the huge palace door and into the sunlight and down the wide stone drive that would return her to the bustling, cruelly indifferent city.

It was over. Sophie had missed her chance. Her time spent at the clinic, her midnight flight from home, her days of travel in the company of strangers, her exploration of Fairport, every effort had been for nothing. Against all odds, she had finally tracked down the one person who might be able to satisfy her curiosity about the world. But he had slipped away once again, had gone where she could not follow. Sophie stopped and stared up into the sky as the traffic trickled by. *What do I do now?*

Her first thought was to return to the Blue Yapper, but with the Navigator lost again—this time for good—there was no reason to stay in the city. The cetaceous captain of the *Brazen*

Whale came to mind. Maybe she could pay for passage. It would mean tolerating Fairport a day or two longer, but then they would set sail and she'd experience a life at sea, hopping from port to port and seeing the world with her own eyes. But when the money ran out, what then? She'd be lost and alone in foreign lands with no way to get home. No, she needed a real solution.

I could go back.

There was still plenty of light left in the day. If she hurried, she could reach Loren and Melina's cabin by nightfall. Surely they would take her in again. They would all eat dinner together by the fire, and then she'd play with the little ones and whisper late into the night with Berlin. She and Berent could go down by the river with a flask of elm brandy and listen to the water's endless babble and rush. Maybe they would fall in love. He would build a cabin for them both, one much nicer than the one that belonged to his parents, and they would—

"Ah! Blast it!"

The voice, which shook Sophie from her daydream, came from a hedge not far off the path. Bright pops of color stood out from the cloistered, dark green leaves. *Roses!* She stepped off the path and approached cautiously. Pink petals trembled and branches shook as a dun-colored blur labored on the other side of the hedge. "Curse my deciduous fate," a low voice grumbled, "once verdant and gravid, now brown and withered, desiccated, frail . . ."

"Mr. Beringford?"

There came a hasty rustle of fabric, and then the man's head popped into view, low and parallel to the ground. His eyebrows were quizzically raised. "My celestial counterpart!"

"Mr. Beringford, I—"

"*Shh!*" He held a finger to his lips and then gestured her over. Placing his fingers with care, he pulled back several branches to reveal a hollow in the hedge. He bid her enter, then followed. "I know not how you have come to learn my identity, but I beg you, do not use that name in this place or any other. It is poison, to you and I both. I see the duke has dismissed his petitioners for the day, and yet you walk alone. Were you unable to locate your friend?" She told him the story, explaining not only how she had learned his name, but also where the Navigator had gone. "Oh ho, the trials of destiny are cruel, indeed. What will you do now?"

"I don't know," she said, sounding helpless. "Go home, I guess."

"Hmm. I see." Beringford nodded thoughtfully. "Perhaps I was wrong about you."

The remark caught Sophie off guard. "What do you mean?"

"Last night, I fell asleep wearing these same foul garments, lying on what amounts to little more than a wooden plank, listening to the nocturnal rumblings of a dozen similarly out-fitted servants, happy for the first time in months. Yes, happy, impossible though it may seem. Happy, because I had met a kindred spirit, one born into different circumstances than my own, yet with the same ambition and drive that allowed me to increase my fortune. Happy, because even in my diminished state I was able to play some small role in your success. Now it seems my confidence was misplaced."

"Tell me," he continued, "for what purpose should you return to Seaside? To remain under your aunt's oppressive thumb? To live out your days dreaming of a time when you nearly succeeded and instead turned away at the first difficulty? I ask you this: do you wish to become the regret-besotted wretch you see before you now?"

"...no..."

"Then, I beseech you, rise up! Fight against fate, rage against destiny! Do not allow yourself to be as driftwood in the current. Unfurl your sail and set your own course, onward unto the horizon if need be, else the grim shade of failure darken your days forevermore."

"But what am I supposed to do? Duke Truculo said the Navigator had to leave before nightfall. Maybe I could wait for him outside the gate..."

"No no no, a scheme like this requires more courage, more cunning. I wonder, if I were still my former personage of renown, what would I do? Think!" This last injunction seemed directed more at himself than Sophie. They sat in silence for long moments. Then, a slow smile spread over Beringford's face. "I have it. It will require a performance on your part, but I believe you are up to the task. What say you? Will you persevere, or will you slink home in defeat?"

"You haven't even told me your plan!"

"It matters not. If you do not possess the confidence to leap blindly, my scheme will not succeed. Either you will take part or you will not. I ask again, what say you?"

Sophie thought it over. It didn't take long.

"I'm in."

A Guard Named Went Meets a Famous Artist

Went hated being a guard.

He hadn't meant to become a guard. He'd meant to become a knight. When he was five years old, the Queen herself had come to Fairport. The entire city had witnessed the royal procession, including young Went and his family. A detachment of infantrymen marched before her alabaster traveling coach, and there, riding at the head of the column, were her knights. They carried long, painted lances and wore impenetrable armor. Even their horses were clad in steel. That fact alone had made a considerable impression on the boy, but his desire for knighthood crystalized in a single moment when one of those mounted knights honored him with the briefest of salutary nods. That was all it took. From then on, Went was bent on a path to greatness and glory, driven by the memory of a moment's recognition from one so high to one so small.

However, wanting a thing and pursuing it are two very different matters, and Went had not been born with the constitution for pursuit. This would not have mattered had his family been rich, powerful, and respectable, for they would have simply purchased his knighthood, as most others did. There was another path to knighthood, though, one that did not depend on wealth or status. Once a year, the Royal Captain of Knights visited each of the Queen's lords and held a tournament. Those who performed admirably were invited to High Vandermeer to compete again, this time before Queen Avantia herself. Any victors could be inducted to the Royal Brotherhood of Knights at her pleasure. Therefore, Went's path to success was clear—become a palace guard, train in combat, and win the tournament.

Becoming a guard had been relatively easy. Went was tall enough to be intimidating, able-bodied, and surprisingly comfortable with being ordered around. But the job was more difficult than he'd anticipated, and far less glorious. The first time he'd strapped on his armor, he'd felt mighty and invincible. Now he only ever felt hot and sweaty. Most of his time was spent battling a particularly nasty, pernicious, and persistent nemesis—boredom.

His off hours provided an opportunity for combat training, though this, too, had become a source of frustration and disappointment. Far from being the best fighter in the troop, he was, in fact, the worst. Horses frightened him, lances were heavy and unwieldy, and getting hit with a blunted sword hurt, even through padding. Make no mistake, he could have become a capable fighter, if he'd only developed the necessary discipline. But the most difficult business of all is that of self-improvement, and Went, faced with this arduous path, chose to believe that some people, *other* people, were just born lucky.

Due to his lowly status, he'd been assigned to watch a little known and seldom-used gate at the far end of the grounds. As if it weren't torturous enough to stand for hours on end before a gate that was never opened, dripping in the solar-powered sweat lodge of his armor, he was forced to do so within sight of the cool shade of Duke Truculo's private wood. Day after day he watched the shadows creep across the grass with tantalizing sloth, never quite reaching the place where he stood. It was enough to drive a person mad.

And so it was that Went had developed an awful habit for a palace guard. Knowing that he was unlikely to be disturbed at his lonely post, he often set aside his halberd and sat with his back against the fence, daydreaming. Went liked to imagine himself in battle, usually facing whoever had bested him most recently and rewriting the ending so that he emerged victorious. It was easier than facing the truth, and much less threatening to his identity.

Went was in the midst of mentally smiting his latest rival when a moving yellow flash caught his eye. Horror gripped him. A young woman in a stunning sundress was approaching. She walked with the assuming air of the well-to-do and was followed by a servant with a knapsack in hand. Went recognized her companion on sight. Beringford had been one of the duke's closest friends for many years, until he'd tried to stab him in the back, according to the rumors. The other guards delighted in taunting, beating, or otherwise abusing him since his fall from grace. Not Went. He was still terrified of the man, particularly now that he'd been caught lazing. One word to Captain Rectifer could see him in the dungeons. Went grabbed hastily for his halberd and scrambled to his feet, his dripping face a mask of shock and embarrassment. "Halt!" he said. "Who—who are you?

What do you want?" His words carried no real authority. They were mostly for him, anyway, a feeble attempt at self-deception. He had already failed at becoming a knight; being a terrible palace guard would be unbearable.

The young woman gasped and put a hand to her chest. "Well, I never!"

"Do you address all of your lord's guests in this manner?" Beringford asked. A long life of privilege had left him with a keenly honed tone of command. Went's armor was useless against it. "You are speaking to Clara Solis, the most accomplished, most talked about, most rapidly rising young *artiste* in the Westerlands."

"The duke is an admirer and asked me here personally," said Clara. There was something odd about the way she spoke, her words stilted, unnatural. Rehearsed. "He has commissioned several custom pieces as gifts for Queen Avantia. I'm performing a survey of the grounds to find the right subjects, and wish to do so before the light slips away. If you would . . ." She indicated the gate with a flighty flick of her finger.

"You want to come through here?" Went asked doubtfully. "Not much to see. Just a couple of old sheds falling apart in the woods. Rose garden would be much nicer for painting, I think."

"The sheds are precisely what Miss Solis would like to see," said Beringford. "Perhaps you should leave the decisions to your betters, hm?"

A funny light came into Clara's eyes then. She looked at him as no woman had looked at him before, as if seeing him at his core, clearly, completely. "Although," she said, "you might make a fascinating subject yourself."

"Really?" Went perked up suddenly.

"Yes." Clara tilted her head and squinted, then held out a thumb and sighted along her arm. "I'll call it 'Slouching Guard'. It will capture the plight of the commoner at work, or rather, *not* at work. The duke will be so—"

"No no no," said Went, fumbling for his keyring. "I don't want to be no plight." Balancing his halberd in the crook of his arm, he searched frantically for the right key. *Why's there got to be so many?!* He finally grasped the one he wanted and jabbed it hastily at the keyhole. Sadly, Went was no better with a key than he was with a sword. He scored a glancing blow and scraped the tip across the lock's iron faceplate. He glanced up and met two excoriating, expectant glares. Went dropped his weapon and went at it with both hands, finally managing to seat the key and turn it. The tumblers rattled and clicked. Went sighed with relief, then stood to attention, saluting as they came through the gate. "Don't bother locking that," said Beringford, "for I will return shortly."

"Sir!" It was an automatic response, one conditioned into him by both his upbringing and profession. The artist and the servant walked up the footpath and into the forbidden shade. The urge to speak overwhelmed him. He needed to ensure that he would remain in their good graces. It took some time, but Went finally landed on something he considered simple yet meaningful. "Enjoy your plight!"

Miss Solis's laughter floated back to him on the breeze.

The Duke's Private Wood

"Capital performance!" cried Beringford once they were out of earshot. He had coached Sophie on how to behave and speak during their long walk across the palace grounds, feeding her a few lines and showing her how to appear lofty and entitled. "Your portrayal was magnificent. And that improvised twist of the knife at the end—inspired! I daresay the poor fool was frightened near to tears."

"Thank you," she said, embarrassed at the praise. The moments leading up to the interaction had been terrifying, but once she'd seen the guard's frantic fumbling and fright, she knew they were in little danger. After that it had been a simple matter of pretending to be Aunt Elle. She'd felt a strange, unexpected power in being Clara Solis. It was both thrilling and unsettling. Her stomach turned as she thought back to the night when Aunt Elle had squeezed her for details about the Navigator, sickened at the thought that she might have actually derived pleasure from it. The intensity of Sophie's disgust convinced her of its truth.

At the end of the path they found a collection of abandoned sheds in various states of decay, insect ridden and covered with lichen and vine. "And so we reach the end of our short journey together," said Beringford. "Today's events have been most invigorating. I must confess, until this very moment I have considered the remaining days of my life to be spent as one of these sheds, a lonely monument to the steady, destructive power of time. Yet now I feel this kinship wane. Your words were powerfully correct, my celestial companion. The moon always waxes again." Smiling, he handed over her knapsack. "I thank you for showing me the way. Allow me to do the same for you."

Beringford took her gently by the arm and pointed through the trees to where a dirt path was just visible at the edge of her vision. The Navigator would take that path into Waldendorf's Wood, he explained. He knew this because he knew the duke. "He will not miss the opportunity to flaunt his private sanctuary. It is a tour I have myself endured on several occasions. I do not envy your friend." He also told her of a bridge where she could safely hide, advising her to come out only after the duke had turned for home. "It will be some effort to catch up to your friend, but I have the utmost confidence that you will succeed. And now, my friend, I must bid you farewell."

Sophie thanked Beringford for his help and assured him she would be careful, then set off along the line he had set for her, hurrying to reach the bridge. She only hoped she wasn't too late.

Sterling Departs

Aᴛ ᴛʜᴀᴛ sᴀᴍᴇ ᴍᴏᴍᴇɴᴛ, Sophie's aunt and cousin were seated in the parlor of Halderman Manor. In truth, Horace's house was as much a manor as the duke's chair was a throne. Sterling sat beside Petunia, as close as was acceptable for a young man and woman on the verge of being betrothed—their knees were nearly almost touching. They were allowed to hold hands, however, and Petunia stroked Sterling's with such obsessive abandon that his skin was visibly abraded. Aunt Elle and Horace looked on with carefully controlled approval, sipping their tea and saying little. What was there to say? Both were very close to getting exactly what they wanted.

A carriage pulled up before the house.

"About bloody time," Horace complained. They all stood, rubbing their legs and shaking out their feet. They had only been sitting for about fifteen minutes, but Horace, mindful of his reputation as the most practical man in Seaside, had furniture that was only comfortable for seven minutes at a stretch. Aunt Elle quietly admired the pins and needles pricking her calves as she followed Horace out onto the front lawn.

From his perch on the driver's seat, Albert watched them

come outside. He wore a light duster and a vicious scowl. Doctor Murphy had volunteered his services to Horace, a circumstance which had, for the first time in his tenure at the village clinic, made Albert abandon his desire to leave Seaside. Horace was lugging a trunk behind him. He dropped it on the grass, then looked up at Albert expectantly. Albert muttered as he assumed the role of porter. "Ridiculous. Me, a graduate of the Royal College of Sophisticated Learnings . . ."

"Must you go?" Petunia pleaded, clutching the arm of Sterling's traveling jacket. "Surely someone else in the village could do this job just as well."

"Me. I could do this," said Albert, wrestling with the heavy trunk. "Alone."

"Pish tosh," said Horace, flapping a hand at him. "You would as soon abscond with the doctor's carriage and leave us to our fate. It is only for your *worldliness* that you have any part in this at all, and even then only because your mentor made quite the compelling case for you as a guide."

"Babysitter, you mean."

"But you will bring him back, won't you?" asked Petunia. "Oh please say you'll bring him back safe and sound."

Aunt Elle tutted loudly. "Do try to retain some decorum, dear, it is unbecoming to beg."

"I promise you," Albert said, regaining his seat, "this will be done with the utmost haste."

"See that it is," said Horace. He produced a coin purse from his jacket. "Here, for your traveling expenses."

Albert raised a skeptical eyebrow. The purse was quite small. And light. "Thank you for your generosity."

It was time to leave. Throwing impropriety to the wind,

Petunia stood on tiptoe and gave Sterling a quick peck on the cheek. He was still climbing in the carriage when Albert cracked the reins, tossing him backward onto the carriage's cushioned seats. The three others watched from the lawn until they had disappeared down the hill and out of sight. "That's one thing settled," said Horace. "Elle, dear, shall we discuss my other proposition?"

Aunt Elle's upper lip twitched. Without looking at her daughter, she said, "Petunia darling, run on home and light the fire for supper. I'll be home shortly." Petunia, who thought they meant to discuss wedding arrangements, gladly left them to their conspiring, her mind filled with blissful marital fantasies.

Reunion

"Now!"

Rax and Mondor leapt into action and tossed the Net of Nullification over the unsuspecting Emperoro. He fell to the floor, writhing, spasming, screaming, and for a moment no one moved, for this was not what they had expected to happen. Alec looked to Fairveena, who had for so long been the princess's handmaiden and looked up to Emperoro as a father. Sorrow was in her eyes, and satisfaction also, for his end meant vengeance and a return to peace in the realm. "Go on, Alec. Do it. End this before his racket brings the guards."

Alec raised his Mandrel blade and prepared to thrust its point into the twisting figure on the floor. Through his torment the old man pierced him with his gaze. His eyes were red.

Something was not right.

A low rumble shook the stone floor beneath their feet. Emperoro's body spasmed and his limbs became rigid, his spine bowed backward at an unnatural angle, head wrenched in agony. The candles blew out of their own accord and thrust the room into darkness. "Do it, Alec!" implored Fairveena. "Do it now!"

The rumbling ceased. Emperoro's writhing faded. No one in the party moved.

An unfamiliar voice spoke.

"Congratulations," it hissed. Unseen fingers snapped, and the candles flared suddenly to life with an eerie green flame. Beneath the Net of Nullification were two captives. Emperoro lay curled, fetal, unconscious. A monstrous figure sat on crossed legs beside the evil ruler. It bore the shape of a woman, nude, with long hair cascading down over her powerful muscles and oily red skin. Two pointed horns grew from either side of its skull. Blazing red irises regarded Alec coolly. "You have succeeded in casting me out, though I can assure you, your victory is very, very temporary. I do hope you have other accomplishments to make you proud of your short, pitiful lives, for they are at an end." Another snap of the fingers and the Net of Nullification dissolved into the aether. "And with you interlopers gone, I will possess this wrinkled sack of flesh once again."

"Not if we have anything to say about it!" Alec raised his blade and—

Sophie was rudely yanked back into the real world by the hollow clop of hoofbeats. She raised her head and blinked rapidly as awareness returned. Fallen leaves littered the ground beneath the bridge, and the air was cool and moist. Rough stone scratched at her back and shoulders. The light had shifted noticeably since she'd started reading. There weren't many pages left. Marking her place, she closed the book and stashed it in her bag. The thrilling conclusion to *Alec Ventureforth and the Dastardly Devil of Demonia* would simply have to wait.

Clip-clop-clip-clop. The oncoming hoofbeats grew fractionally louder and were soon accompanied by voices. Duke Truculo's haughty tones inspired laughter that sounded fake even at this distance. Conspicuously absent was the voice of the Navigator.

Sophie stayed calm. Even if she couldn't hear him, he was up there. He had to be. She was sure of it.

"And so then I said, 'Perhaps your reaching grasp would be put to better use in the rose garden, *my friend.*'" This was followed by one of the duke's puerile giggles.

"An excellent jibe," said some unknown sycophant.

"Right you are, Captain," said Rothschild. His voice was that of a peacock: high pitched, nasal, and whiny. It made Sophie's skin crawl. "Your deft wit never ceases to astound me, my lord."

Each human finger contains three bones. The first and largest is called the proximal phalanx, and it connects the finger to the rest of the hand at the knuckle. Sophie bit down nervously on the proximal phalanx of her index finger as a buzz of nervous excitement filled her. The hoofbeats had drawn so close she could feel them. Earth and stone reverberated, trembled, and she along with them, sympathetic resonance feeding her anticipation and driving her teeth incrementally deeper into her flesh. There was discomfort, but it was useful, a focus, for within moments they would pass over her head and she had to be still, so incredibly still, else she would be caught. Sophie concentrated on the pain, dove into it like an ocean wave that would obscure her from the world and make her disappear from it entirely.

The clopping stopped overhead.

"Now this is one of my favorite features of the wood," said the duke. "My father built this bridge as a gift to my younger self. This area used to be a mill yard of sorts when it was annexed, and pits just like this one pockmarked the land. Why, you ask? Because the sawyers used them for sawing lengths of timber. Look carefully, my friend, and you will see how one end is gradually sloped while the other drops sharply off. They would tip the tree in here, keeping it elevated on one side in order to saw it into lengths from underneath, then carry the timber up the slope. I find it simply fascinating how adaptive the peasantry can be when they lack resources, don't you agree?"

There was a moment of silence. Rothschild's noxious voice filled it hastily. "Yes, my lord, quite fascinating."

(they're bored can't you see they're bored move on)

"My father ordered the pits to be filled in," the duke continued. "Officially, he did it to dissuade commoners from harvesting trees illegally, but in truth they were simply dreadful to look at. He left this one, however, because as a child I had a certain fondness for bridges. My architectural tastes have broadened since then, but I still appreciate his gift. It reminds me of him, may he rest peacefully."

"May he rest peacefully," echoed his lackeys.

"From time to time I come here to muse over his memory. It was whilst standing on this very spot that I decided to rename the forest Waldendorf's Wood. He was an able ruler, beloved by the people, and I felt it wasn't fair for I alone to have a lasting monument to his greatness. Besides, the name given it by the common folk came from a story filled with anti-aristocratic fervor, and was terribly difficult to say. Truthfully, the renaming was a favor for the entire nation."

(no one cares please you have to keep going)

"Sometimes it occurs to me to go down into the pit."

(no)

"Why should you want to do such a dreadful thing, my lord?" asked Rothschild.

(you can't)

"I feel there must be a certain undignified romance in the life of a peasant. How simple the world must be when it is directed by one's betters. Think of it, Rothschild, to be liberated from the chains of reputation and comportment, to have the courage to be unwashed and ignorant. It must be splendid to live so easy and free."

"Perhaps that is why they choose to remain impoverished."

"Perhaps so," agreed the duke. "What say you, my saturnine acquaintance? Shall we indulge fancy and venture into the pit?"

(no no no no)

"I must decline," said the Navigator.

"Are you certain? It will only take a moment. A soupçon of the simple life must have its benefits."

(NO NO NO NO)

"I have no doubt," said the Navigator, "but I am anxious to complete the task you have given me. I thank you for accompanying me this far, Duke Truculo."

"But there is so much more to see," the duke whined, "another hour's ride, at least."

"Lives are at stake."

"You have a singularly focused mind, Navigator," said Captain Rectifer. "Perhaps disrespectfully so."

"Quite," sneered Rothschild.

Silence as Duke Truculo and his companions waited for the Navigator to relent. Clearly, they did not know to whom they spoke.

(just go please)

"Very well," said the duke. "Far be it from me to impede the duties *I* have laid upon you. Come, friends, let us leave him to his work. But remember this: I expect your return within a fortnight. Do so empty-handed, and you shall never see your precious ocean ever again. Are we understood?"

"We are."

"Then I bid you farewell."

The duke's arrival replayed itself in reverse. Little by little Sophie's bite relaxed as the rumble and quake overhead faded away. Sharp, stinging pain seeped into the deep crenellations molded by her teeth. Still, she stayed put, not daring to move except to gently shake out her aching, damaged digit.

"Reveal yourself."

Sophie jumped, then smiled in spite of her surprise. Taking care to avoid the pit's mushy muck, she crept out from under the bridge and climbed the slope. Halfway up, she looked back and there he was, the Navigator, mounted on a dappled grey mare. She waved and continued her ascent.

Her wave was not returned.

Standing on the stone bridge, Sophie looked up at the Navigator, bashful. "I bet you weren't expecting to see me again."

"Rid yourself of expectations and you will never be surprised." His words were spoken simply, as a piece of self-contained knowledge rather than a lecture or even mere advice. "Do you mean to accompany me?"

Sophie shuffled her feet. "Is that okay with you?"

The Navigator's eyes narrowed. Doubt wrenched her guts, a sudden queasy tightness that made her question every step she'd taken thus far. He was going to send her home. It was the right thing to do. She had no useful skills, she couldn't fight, and she was as much a stranger here as he was, only without his powers of magic. All she had to offer were a few books, some old paintings, and the last morsels of a bread loaf. It had been foolish to come. Worse than foolish. It had been CHILDISH NONSENSE.

(i didnt mean to make you fly away

desire like a flame

for what purpose should you return

desire needs hope

driftwood in the current do not allow yourself

burn down to embers

all are responsible for choosing their own path)

Sophie adopted the posture that Beringford had taught her. "Yes, I mean to come with you."

The Navigator's serene calm returned. Wordless, he offered his hand and pulled her up onto the mare. He clucked at the horse, and the two of them rode off into the forest together, reunited at last.

Sparks

Sᴏᴘʜɪᴇ sᴀᴛ ʙᴇғᴏʀᴇ ᴀ ʟᴏᴡ ᴄᴀᴍᴘғɪʀᴇ. It had begun as a bundle of scavenged leaves, needles, and twigs set alight by a word from the Navigator's arcane vocabulary. Fed with consecutively larger sticks and limbs, it now crackled away contentedly and filled the campsite with its dancing, lively light. Sparks carved serpentine paths toward the sky, their fiery brilliance briefly eclipsing the stars before winking out of existence. Sophie wondered where the sparks went, if any trace remained after their disappearance, if there was any evidence of their existence beyond the fading afterimages in her memory.

She also studied the Navigator. He sat across from her, legs crossed and hands clasped loosely in his lap, eyes closed. His ebon hair drank the firelight so that his face stood out in sharp relief. The shifting shadows made his tattoos flicker and leap, yet the man himself was static and silent, monolithic, elemental. She had followed his stoic example as they rode, rather than give in to her nervous effulgence as she had before. But like the campfire with its sparks, her curiosity had been kindled. Unanswered questions traced bright lines across her consciousness, bursting into sudden life before fading into the aether.

She could stand it no longer.

"How did you know I was hiding under the bridge?"

The Navigator's eyes slid open, two pits of glimmering obsidian set in granite. "She told me," he said, gesturing toward the mare.

"You can talk to horses?"

"Anyone can speak to an animal. Listening is a different matter."

"It's easy to listen to a horse when you have magic."

A faint smile brushed his lips. "A fair point, though there was no need for it. The language of animals is simpler than our own, more honest, and universal. Humans, on the other hand, are far more complicated."

"And that's why you wear that thing around your neck, right?"

The Navigator touched the choker and said, "Nearly correct. This charm allows *you* to understand *me*. I am still speaking according to my natural language, yet it alters the sounds I produce and renders them intelligible to the listener. To understand you, I must enlist the aid of the noble earworm."

Sophie's eyes widened at the memory of the wriggling, pink worm sniffing and slithering its way into his ear. "Gross!"

He shrugged. "It is mildly unpleasant, but it must be borne, for accurate communication is of vital importance to a Navigator."

"More important than your necklace?"

"Necklace?"

"That," Sophie said, pointing to the medallion. "Doc Murphy said it must be very important to you because you wouldn't let go of it even in your sleep."

"Ah," he said, nodding in comprehension. "This is no mere decoration. This is a Navigator's greatest asset, an item of incalculable value and utility, the very thing that makes me what I am. This is a compass."

"Oh. *Oh!*" Sophie grew suddenly excited. "That's how you know where to go all the time!"

"Not exactly." He gestured for her to sit beside him. Once she had, he held the compass in his palm and spoke another mystical word of power. A storm of golden sparks swirled up out of the pearl seated in its center, more numerous and chaotic than those rising from the fire. Gradually they slowed and came to rest above the compass's surface. He rotated the disk back and forth; the sparks remained fixed in place. "The purpose of a compass is to remain on a constant bearing. It does not itself provide guidance, but allows the person using it to set their own course. Do you understand?"

"I think so," said Sophie. "But then why is this one so important? You could just get another one if you lost it."

The Navigator chuckled, a sound so surprising that Sophie couldn't help but smile. "Every Navigator is soul-bound to their own compass. Such a bond is unbreakable. If I removed it from my neck and tried to drop it on the ground, I would be unable to release the chain. And woe be to those who would try to take it by force."

Sophie giggled. "I remember."

"What sets this compass apart," the Navigator continued, "is what it points toward—my purpose, my reason for being."

"And what is your purpose?"

"That remains to be seen. I know only that I will learn my purpose once I cross the sea."

"Which is why you need to get back on a boat so badly."

"Indeed."

"So, if the compass isn't telling you where to go, how will we find what we're looking for?"

"Have no fear. This compass is but one of the many tools at my disposal. And this detour is not uncommon for those of my order. Navigators are often called to serve. Now, we should get some rest. The journey will be arduous and fraught with danger." With that, he closed his eyes again and said no more, temporarily extinguishing the fire of Sophie's curiosity.

Unfinished Business

Damon should have seen it coming.

Night had fallen, and he was sitting alone by the rear window of Walden's Pub, staring at the sea. Isolated clouds drifted across an otherwise clear sky. Waves crested and fell, casting brief shadows by the light of the quarter moon which hung low on the horizon. Damon sipped his beer. It was his fourth of the evening, already half gone. He set down the glass and wrapped both hands around it as though it were the neck of an enemy.

Sophie still had not returned, and somehow the blame for her disappearance had fallen squarely on his shoulders. In some versions of the story, the Navigator had returned under the cover of darkness and kidnapped her. Others held that Damon had driven her away. What it was he was supposed to have done varied as much as the storytellers themselves, but it was always ugly, and nowhere near to the truth. Those rumors had finished the work that Horace had begun—he hadn't earned a penny in a week and a half.

A fugue of anxiety and resentment had befallen Seaside, one that grew worse with each day that passed and did not see the Navigator's return. The Queen's Road was watched day and night in case he should turn up, and everyone had become obsessed with the phases of the moon, marking the infinitesimal progress of the terminator with dread. Damon had been blamed for all this, as well. That Walden still allowed him in his pub was the only kindness left to him in Seaside.

A moving reflection caught his attention. Gregory Tacklesmith, coming toward him. He watched the approach of his teetotaling former mentor through the glass with weary surprise. Tacklesmith stood stiffly beside the table, looking afraid to touch anything for fear of contamination. "Damon."

"Mr. Tacklesmith." Damon turned from the window, his expression neither smirk nor smile, but somewhere between. "Have a seat. Has lunacy driven you to finally tarnish that sterling reputation of yours?"

Tacklesmith shook his head gravely. "Your snapping at an outstretched hand, son. Elle asked me to speak to you. I told her it wouldn't do any good, but that I'd at least give you the chance to prove me wrong. Come on, let's step outside. The fresh air will clear your head a little."

"My head's fine."

"I am trying to help you, Damon."

"Help me? You offering me a job?" When he received no answer, he grunted and said, "More lectures. As I thought. Well, you can save your breath. If you really want to help, buy me another round and then walk away."

Tacklesmith wrinkled his nose in disgust. Then he turned, gestured to Walden to bring another, and sat.

Damon stared hard, blinking, trying to judge the older man's intent. It was difficult with Tacklesmith swaying and spinning as he was. Walden came over and set a beer on the table. He was swaying, too, as if the pub had set sail. Dizzy, defeated, Damon lowered his head and planted his hands on the table. "Go on, then. Help me."

"Look at you. Saddled down by your sorrow and pride, with alcohol holding the reins. You could've been something, Damon, a master farrier. You've got the knack. I wouldn't have taken you on as an apprentice if you didn't. But when I tried to show you how to be a man you just wouldn't listen."

"I didn't need your words. I needed money. A job, so I could get Sophie away from that manipulative, abusive shrew."

"Hey," Tacklesmith said sharply. "Take care how you speak of Elle. She's done more for you than you know."

"Oh please. I know all about her *generosity*. False as Horace Halderman's smile." Damon drank, swallowing heavily. "If you really cared you would have kept me on at the shop."

"How could I? No one trusted your work. If not for my reassurances and close supervision, I would have lost all my business. Why do you think I watched over your shoulder so closely? I had to let you go to protect my own name. Believe me, I was sorry to do it, but I had no other choice."

"Bullshit. No one else in Seaside can do your job and you know it."

"Lower your voice," hissed Tacklesmith, looking around sharply. "You're getting belligerent. Let's go for a walk."

"No one else but me," Damon pressed. "You wanted me to fail so you wouldn't have any competition."

"Don't flatter yourself, boy. You don't have half my skill, not in the workshop, and certainly not with clientele."

"You are just like Horace." Damon leveled a finger at his

former mentor. "He had the whole village turned against me even before those things came up out of the sea. And for what? He wanted to kill a man! Does no one remember? Does no one see?"

"We remember," Tacklesmith said quietly. "We remember very plainly." He stood and put a hand on Damon's shoulder, gently, but firmly. "This has gone far enough. Let's get you sobered up, son."

"I'm not your son," Damon said, pulling away roughly. Too roughly. He tumbled backward off the bench and spilled onto the floor. The room quieted as heads turned to watch the commotion.

"I'm sorry, I didn't mean it like that. Let me help y—"

"*NO!* Get your hands off me!" Damon scrambled furiously to his feet. He shoved Tacklesmith aside, stumbling for the door. "That's right, stare!" he yelled at the watchers. "Judge me! It's all you're good for, anyway. Go on, get a good look!"

Walden came out from behind the bar. "Damon Farrier, you will never step foot in my pub again. Get out!"

"Gladly!" Damon turned to wag an angry finger at the barkeep, tripped, fell to his knees. "I can't get out fast enough." He crawled the rest of the way to the door. His hands and knees were sticky and coated with dirt and debris by the time he reached it. Grasping the handle, he hoisted himself to an unsteady vertical, worked the latch, and bumbled outside.

Where Horace Halderman was waiting for him.

He was not alone. A posse of Seaside's most upstanding citizens had volunteered to assist him that evening. Eagerly. They stood in a rough semicircle, seven pairs of eyes watching Damon coldly as he careened out into the street.

An eighth pair watched from behind the wall of angry men. Those eyes Damon knew all too well.

"Damon Farrier," said Horace, "we are placing you under arrest."

"What? What is this? Aunt Elle, what's going on here?"

"The Merling King has demanded a soul. We're going to give him one. You should be happy, boy. You will finally be of some use to the people of Seaside. Now, are you going to come quietly or not?"

"No. Definitely not. I'm gonna finish the job my father started and put out the rest of your teeth." Damon swayed forward and swung his fist as hard as he could. He missed completely. A moment later he was flat on his back and staring up at the stars, both those in the sky and those in his eyes. They swirled and spun and streaked wildly against the black.

Faded.

Dimmed.

Went out.

The Strange House in the Woods

Uninvited and Unannounced

Sniveling little snit.

This thought belonged to Albert. It was directed at his traveling companion, Sterling Halderman. The words had become a constant refrain in his mind, repeated with an unhealthy, almost obsessive regularity. Here he was, in a proper city once again, finally given a reprieve from his internment in that dull den of dismal dreariness that was Seaside, yet he couldn't even enjoy his return to civilization because he'd been forced to play chaperone to a privileged, pusillanimous piglet. It was no fit job for an esteemed graduate of the Royal College of Sophisticated Learnings.

His mental anguish, however, was nothing compared to Sterling's. He was Out There, and it was every bit as awful as he'd heard. A scowl was frozen onto his jowly face. Each step was forced, deliberate, his eyes focused downward so that he could only peripherally sense the enormity surrounding him on all sides. Sterling's body was so rigid that only the shortest, shallowest breaths were possible, which suited him fine, for the air was so odorous, so heavy, so *foreign* that he would have preferred not to breathe at all. Luckily, he hadn't mentioned this preference to Albert, who would have happily helped him achieve this goal.

"Look," said Albert, "we're nearly there."

"There" in this case was Duke Truculo's palace, where they would present themselves for an audience with the duke. Sterling's eyes waxed full as he looked up. That a single building could be so big was simply unimaginable. "It's . . . it's . . ."

"Garish, I know," said Albert, sneering. "This pitiful thing isn't even a quarter the size of the royal castle in High Vandermeer. Now that is a sight to see. So regal, so majestic. This, well, this is just an embarrassment!" He chortled. "Ah, Duke Truculo. I swear, I've never seen a man with such an inflated sense of his own importance."

Albert, apparently, did not own a mirror.

Sterling set his feet in motion again, approaching the gate with his short, halting steps, gaze protectively downcast, all the while being prodded and wheedled by his sneering companion. He tried to block out Albert's words by repeating a new mantra under his breath:

". . . nearly there, nearly there, nearly there . . ."

Sniveling little snit.

A hand touched Sterling's arm, causing him to jerk so suddenly and sharply that he nearly vacated his skin.

"Spare some change for a widow?" The stodgy, stocky pig-man looked down into the kindly, gnarled face of an old woman. Wispy, grey hair hung down over wispy, grey skin. Holding onto his arm for balance, she smiled, revealing what few teeth remained to her.

Sterling began to stammer. "I . . . she . . . there's a—"

"Only a few coins. Please."

"I don't know you!" Sterling shouted into the widow's face, yanking away as though he'd been stung by a wasp. Albert leapt forward and caught her as she stumbled. He apologized and sent her off, then hurried to catch up with the huffing, puffing, stutter-stepping human locomotive that was Sterling Halderman. ". . . nearly there, nearly there, nearly there . . ."

"Get a grip on yourself, man. Where is your self-respect? I swear, if we were at the Royal College . . ."

"*. . . nearly there, nearly there, nearly there . . .*"

Only now they were there. Albert took Sterling by the arms and shook him. "Quiet down, you sniveling little snit! I will do the talking. You just stand here and try not to make a spectacle of yourself." Sterling quieted. Mostly. A low grumble lived in his throat. His lips moved wordlessly, the precursor to all the loud and angry objections he had about the world Out There and the people in it. Albert left him idling and approached a pair of guards. "Excuse me, good sirs, we would like to arrange for an—"

"Palace is closed to the public."

"You're a bit rude, aren't you? Does Duke Truculo approve of this habit of interrupting your betters?"

"Palace is closed. Move along."

"See here, my good man," said Albert, aggressively straightening his collar, "I am a graduate of the Royal College of Sophisticated Learnings and a member in good standing of the medical community—"

"Palace. Is. Closed. Or is that not clear enough for such a learned man?"

"I demand to see your captain this instant, you insufferable . . ."

Sterling's throat grumble grew and grew as Albert berated

the guard. He blinked rapidly, bouncing up and down on his toes, fists clenching and unclenching, until finally he could hold back no longer. He threw himself to the ground, took hold of the guard's ankles, and cried, "There's a strange man who washed up on the shore in Seaside he ran off with one of our girls and now the Merling King is going to destroy the village if we don't give him back *and you have to help me so I can go home!*"

Albert and the guards looked back and forth at one other in shocked silence as Sterling burst into shuddering sobs.

"Please."

The guard sighed heavily, thoroughly inconvenienced by this introduction of actual work into his day. He turned to his partner and said, "Went, go and get the captain while I scrape off this blubbering idiot."

"Captain's not here."

"Fine, get somebody else, then."

"Who?"

"Anybody, you useless tit!"

And so it was that, through a combination of overinflated self-importance and sheer hysterical panic, Albert and Sterling were able to gain access to Duke Truculo at an hour that was neither on Tuesday morning (after breakfast but before his mid-morning snack) nor on Friday afternoon (between cream tea and pre-dinner pudding).

Following The Path

Noon had already come and gone when the Navigator led the mare off the road and directly into the woods. He gave no warning or explanation. There was simply a light tug on the reins, and then they were crashing through underbrush while descending into the thick of the forest. Sophie had come to dislike these shortcuts. The trees were pretty to look at, but it was hard to ride while constantly ducking under or pushing aside branches. Dry, withy scrub brush snagged on her dress, or else scratched her exposed skin. Gnats, mosquitoes, and all manner of buzzy, bitey bugs swarmed around them, attracted by the musty smell of the horse. She much preferred the easy travel of the forgotten roads they had discovered. Some of these were more-or-less intact, wide and flat and clear of debris. Others had been almost completely reclaimed by nature, recognizable only by the absence of mature trees or the occasional twin strips of bare earth running parallel through the grass. Yet even these were easier to traverse than going through the woods directly. Thankfully, these difficult detours never lasted long, and always ended with them reemerging onto a new path.

The character of the woods had changed considerably

after they'd left the duke's private sanctuary. Oak and elm had given way to aspen, fir, and pine, leaving the forest floor littered with dusty brown needles and cones. The terrain rose and fell sharply, sometimes impassably so, forcing them to go well out of their way to continue onwards. Wildlife had grown more plentiful, as well. Clouds of tiny birds flitted above, seeming to follow them as they sang their twittering, tremulous songs, while low, unseen creatures prowled the underbrush, scattering leaves and snapping twigs with their hidden, scurrilous movements. Every morning, the sun was welcomed by the rapid fire *chit-chit-chit* of squirrels; every night, choirs of wolves filled the chilly night air with their paeans to the ever-waning moon. Their songs set Sophie's heart galloping and banished sleep for hours at a time.

Arduous and fraught with danger, the Navigator had said. They had already encountered difficulty. Danger had yet to be revealed.

They came to a wide, shallow pond. Reeds and cattails grew along its banks, while water lilies covered its surface, fluffy blooms of pink, yellow, and white supported by broad green pads. Insects hummed busily in the moist air above the murky water. The Navigator suggested they take a rest. Sophie wholeheartedly agreed. They dismounted and led the mare along the pond's edge toward the higher, drier ground on the other side. A fallen log awaited them, sun-bleached and worn smooth by the weather, the perfect picnic bench for two weary travelers. They sat and ate in contented silence beneath the warming rays of the sun.

"How much farther do we have to go?" Sophie asked.

"I cannot say."

"What?" She had come to accept his silence on certain

subjects, but this seemed an awfully strange secret to keep. "Why not?"

"I know not where our destination lies."

"I thought you knew where we were going!"

"I do."

"But you just said you didn't."

Calmly, patiently, he said, "There is a difference between knowing the destination and knowing its location."

"That doesn't make any sense."

"Does it not? Consider this clearing. I had no knowledge of its location, or even its existence, until we arrived. Yet had you shown me a picture of this place and asked me to take you here, it would have become our destination. You have experienced this yourself, have you not?"

"No."

The Navigator's brows drew together. "You are not taking this seriously. When have you tried to go somewhere but did not know the location?"

Sophie thought it over. "When I came to find you."

"Indeed. Your destination was by my side, but you knew not where I was."

"I suppose. But I still had to find your location before I knew where to go."

"Therein lies the heart of a Navigator's power—the ability to choose a path that leads to any destination, even when ignorant of its location."

"How is that possible?"

"Tell me," he said, "when we arrived, from which direction were we traveling?"

"That way," she said, pointing.

"Correct. But we could have come a different way. In fact, there are an infinite number of paths that lead to this place, or any other. My powers show me which paths lead to the chosen destination and which do not."

"Hmmm." An idea formed in Sophie's mind. She retrieved the watercolors from her knapsack. Keeping them hidden, she leafed through them until she found one that would suit her purposes. Then she showed him her mother's painting of the busy marketplace. "Do you know where this is?"

"It does not look familiar."

"But you could tell me how to get there?"

"No."

"Why not?"

"Because of the nature of my abilities," he replied. "Perhaps you imagine I see something that you do not, such as lines on the ground as one would draw on a map, or else a mystical arrow that floats before me and points the way forward. That is not the case. It is a feeling, more unconscious than felt, a vibration of sorts that tells me I am on the right path. Where precisely it leads I do not know, only that it is the way. I cannot direct you to the place in this painting, but I could lead you there if we went together. Do you understand now?"

"I think so." Sophie tucked the watercolors away, slightly disappointed. "If you don't know where our destination is, how will you know when we get there?"

"It will not be difficult. This path leads to conflict. And resolution." With that, he stood, signaling that their rest was at an end. He helped her mount and then led the mare on foot. Sophie looked blankly out across the clearing, wondering what form that conflict would take and how it would be resolved.

They were nearly at the tree line when she spotted the snowdrops. Her heart caught in her throat at the sight of them, a patch of white flowers that rippled and moved in the breeze like a puddle of nymph's tears.

The Eyes of a Predator

THE NAVIGATOR'S SHORTCUT proved to be anything but short. As the canopy grew thicker, drooping boughs weighed down by old man's beard and lichen forced Sophie to dismount, reducing their pace to a careful walk. She waved her hand protectively to ward off the thirsty mosquitoes, or worse, the silken traps laid by hungry, devious spiders. More than once she had clawed their invisible webbing from her face and hair. Networks of knobby, gnarled roots covered the bare earth, making every step treacherous; Sophie had already turned her ankle twice. Hours passed with agonizing slowness as they wound through the legions of sentinel trees.

Evening came early as the overcrowded evergreens blocked out the sun, ushering in an eerie calm. Colors faded to muted shades of violet, and the shapes of things became fuzzy, blurred, indistinct. The flittering, twittering birds returned to their nests, the chittering squirrels to their boles. The only remaining sounds were those of the travelers as they negotiated the treacherous terrain.

Granelith's Weald. The name, the true name of the forest, ran through her mind over and over again, as did other snatches of phrase from Feeney's tale. Queen of the Wood Nymphs. Invisible, jealous creatures. Don't much like sharing their dominion with humanity. Living memories of the slain majestic wonder. *Snowdrops.* Loren had assured her that the jovial innkeeper's story was nonsense, and in the warm glow of the cabin, she had believed him. Now she wasn't so sure. *The nymphs speak to us in subtle ways,* Feeney had said, but there was nothing subtle about this. They were intruding. The spirits wanted them out.

crrrACK

Sophie looked up sharply and stopped, turning her head toward the sound, but as quickly as it had come it had dissipated, muffled by the heavy, fissured bark of the surrounding trees, and she found nothing. The Navigator didn't miss a step. She tried to draw strength from his stoic persistence, to reaffirm her trust in him to see them both safely through. It was hard. Her trust had been abused before. Once again her fate was in someone else's hands, this time a stranger's, and he was leading her into the black heart of the forest to do battle with an unknown, deadly force. She wished he would say something to put her mind at ease. But the Navigator was not that sort of man. A low moan of uncertainty escaped her lips as he disappeared with frightening speed, walking away as he already had twice before. The message was clear—he would keep going, with or without her. *This was a mistake,* she thought, gazing off into the distance.

Glowing eyes gazed back.

Adrenaline is a hormone produced by a pair of glands that sit atop the kidneys, one on each side of the body. It causes the heart to race, the body to tense, and the pupils to dilate in response to danger. When Sophie's eyes locked onto those of the shadowy predator, a series of ganglia in her brain fired signals to her adrenal glands, which promptly flooded her veins with adrenaline. The fuzzy, evening world was thrown into sharp relief. Her muscles grew taut. Her pulse quickened. Dull pain bloomed in her abdomen from what can only be described as non-consensual terror.

<stand>   <flee>

The beast's feline head materialized as it prowled out from the gloom. A thick mane of fur, dusky grey and tipped with black, ringed those glowing eyes like an inverse halo. Its ears lay flat against its skull, two sharp, red points like needles dripping blood. Its massive paws padded silently. Sophie watched, helpless, its glacial crawl daring her to run, run, *run*, to run while there was still time, but there was no time, a horrible truth known to both predator and prey. Its maw slid open and juddered rapidly up and down, producing a series of deep, hollow clicks in its throat that sounded vaguely like a woodpecker at work. Sophie was paralyzed by the beast's iridescent eyes, those twin windows through which the predator's burning soul shone, she was lost, trapped in that fiery pit, she saw herself consumed, by the beast, by the flames, by—

A cloud of sparkling, rainbow sprites flew from the darkness and struck the beast. It reacted not at all. No yowl of pain or surprise or anger. Only a rippling, crackling sound that ricocheted off of the trees as the beast grew still.

"Incredible!"

Sophie, freed from the beast's petrifying gaze, looked around as the voice's owner revealed himself. He was an older man, stocky, wearing a shabby hunting jacket and heavy black boots. Frizzy grey hair stuck out from beneath his flat, tweed cap. One hand was busy tucking something into his jacket pocket. He sprang across the forest floor on surprisingly nimble feet, not toward Sophie, but toward the solidified cat. "Incredible," he said again, mumbling as he carried out his inspection, running his hands over its glassy fur and brushing at it as though it were covered in dust. He tested one of the ear points with his finger, yanking it back suddenly in pain. "In-*cred*ible," he whispered.

When one person's life is saved by another, the polite thing to say is, "Thank you." And had the man acknowledged Sophie or shown any concern for her safety, that's exactly what she would have said. But he hadn't. He was held rapt by his curiosity, was captivated by it, so much so that it reached out and ensnared Sophie, too. "What is it?" she asked him.

"A strider," he answered. "And a big one, at that. Look at those ears. You see 'em? Red as the blood of his unfortunate prey. Means he's the dominant male in this neck of the woods. Oh ho, there's gonna be a lot of yowling and scratching and pissing on trees to figure out who takes his place." The old man finally glanced at Sophie. "You must pardon an old man's vulgarity. I sometimes forget myself in my excitement." He stood, straightening his jacket and dusting himself off. His pitted, ruddy complexion and comically wild hair matched the worn appearance of his clothing. Deep set laugh lines scored his loose jowls, and the hint of a grin played about his lips. Gin blossoms had found fertile ground on his nose and cheeks. Sophie thought he would be a perfect fit for the inn, throwing back pints with Feeney and Cass. He rocked on his heels as he spoke. "Now what the blazes are you doing traipsing around out here all by your lonesome, young miss? There are predators in these woods, or didn't you know?"

"I'm not traipsing," said Sophie, "and I'm not alone. "I'm exploring with my friend."

"Is that so?" Suspicion narrowed his eyes. "And, uh, where is your friend now?"

"We got separated," she admitted. "I heard something and stopped. I guess he didn't notice."

"Some friend, eh? That's just shameful, isn't it, a real shame indeed. Didn't even notice. I guess it's good for both of us I came along when I did."

"What are you doing out here?"

"Me? Hunting, in a manner of speaking. I'm a collector, you see, a lover of animals, though the more dangerous ones are easier to appreciate in this form. Isn't that right, Mr. Kitty Cat?" He stroked the strider's fur and turned a huge, beaming smile on Sophie. There was so much warmth in it that she couldn't help but smile in return. "Go on, give him a pet. He won't bite."

Reluctantly, Sophie approached the feline monster that had, only moments before, been preparing to make her his latest meal. She tried to run her fingers through its fluffy mane, but succeeded only in brushing her hand over its smooth, solid surface. "It's glass! How did you do it?"

"Oh, this?" He waved a hand dismissively. "Nothing to it. Easiest thing in the world. Even a child could do it." Something about his tone hit Sophie's ears funny, but he continued on, leaving her with no time to think. "Been after one of these fellas for quite some time. Got the perfect place for him in my garden at home, which, as it happens, isn't far from here. Tell you what, why don't you help me haul him back? I'll treat you to some supper, and I've even got a spare bed for you. Sounds like a fair trade if you ask me."

"But what about my friend?"

"I know every inch of these woods. If you like, we can search for him first thing in the morning. Shall we go?" The bright spotlight smile returned.

"I don't know . . ."

The mare's nickering announced the Navigator's reappearance. His eyes quickly assessed the scene, grew stern, suspicious. Sophie wanted to run to him, to be swept up in a big bear hug, the kind Damon would have given her before calling her "li'l butterfly" and rumpling her hair and telling her everything would be alright. But before anything of the sort could happen, the old man clapped his hands together and cried, "Hold my hat!" A child's eyes looked out from an old man's face. "Look at you! This is a night to remember, rarity piled upon rarity. A Navigator, here, practically in my own backyard!"

The Navigator inclined his head in response.

"*Exploring,* is it?" The man chuckled, shaking his head and wagging a finger at Sophie. "Gonna need a better story than that, young miss, especially walking around in *his* wake. Exploring, feh! If I hadn't come along when I did, you'd be exploring the inside of that cat's stomach!"

"It seems we owe you a debt of gratitude," said the Navigator.

"Thank you," Sophie mumbled, now that it seemed appropriate.

"Think nothing of it! But, if you were so inclined, perhaps you could give me a hand with this terrible beauty. It'll be a real burden to get it back to the cabin all by myself. Afterward, I'll fix us up a spot of dinner, you can tell me why you're *exploring*, and after a good night's sleep you can see this fella and the rest of my collection right up close and personal in the bright light of day. Whad'ya say? Would you like to come and see?"

Sophie looked to the Navigator, allowing him to speak for them both. "It is a most gracious offer," he said, "one we will accept. What shall we call you?"

"I've been called many things in my life," the old man said with a wink, "but I'd prefer if you called me Marioletti."

The Weird and Wonderful
House of Marioletti

It took them a little over an hour to haul the glass strider back to Marioletti's home. The two men carried it between them while Sophie led the mare on foot, stopping frequently so the older man could catch his breath and fuss over his back. Sophie offered to trade with him, but he wouldn't hear of it. He led them on a winding, seemingly aimless path to a vast clearing in the woods. It was obviously man-made, bordered as it was by the stumps of felled trees. Above, the first stars were twinkling in a violet sky tinged with the last traces of sunset orange. "Nearly there," he said, puffing as he set down the cat once more. "Cabin's just up ahead."

Marioletti's home was a cabin in the way that the duke's palace was a house—each word was an absurd understatement of the building's full character. There was indeed a squat, square building with log walls, a cabin in the traditional sense, and it had been more competently constructed than Loren and Melina's. It was also twenty or thirty feet up in the air on a platform built onto the roof of a barn. It was as if someone had planted a seed in the ground, a barn seed, and then built a cabin over top of it, so that as the barn sprouted and grew, it incorporated the cabin as part of its roof and vaulted it high into the air. Connecting these incongruous, interconnected buildings was a pair of castle-like stone turrets. Each had a single, heavy door that opened onto the roof terrace above. Even Sophie, with her love of the outrageous and weird, thought it was a bit much. *Aunt Elle would drop dead if she ever saw this*, she thought as they approached.

The main entrance to the house was on the side opposite the turrets, a pair of double doors set high up on the wall that was reached by way of a switchback staircase. It was here that the old man led them. "Careful, now, careful," he said as they set the strider down at the bottom of the stairs. "Glass is a lot more fragile than most people believe. Brittle. Easy, easy . . ." With that done, he showed Sophie where to stable the mare, then preceded them up the stairs, huffing and puffing the whole way. He was waiting outside with the Navigator when she returned.

The interior of Marioletti's home was every bit as eclectic and strange. There were no rooms, no dividing walls at all, just a single expansive space divided into different areas by a series of cascading floors. It was like standing atop a long, shallow waterfall, with gravity drawing the occupant down toward the creature comforts waiting at the bottom. The uppermost tier, where they had entered, served as a mudroom of sorts, with benches for shoe removal and coat hooks. Next came the airy, well-appointed kitchen, with its hanging pots and pans, doorless cabinets, and multiple wine racks. An attached dining area was furnished with a broad table fashioned from a single, irregularly shaped slab of wood, lacquered and polished to a mirror shine. A reading nook followed, with bookcases against either wall and inviting, comfy chairs. The bottom tier was the largest and served as the main living space, with a wide hearth, thick carpets, and plenty of seating. The rear wall was flanked by the two sandstone turrets, and between them were floor to ceiling windows, seamlessly bringing the outdoors in. And, of course, there was art everywhere, not only masterworks of glass, but paintings, sculptures, and carvings, as well.

With a grand, sweeping gesture, their host said, "Welcome, my new friends, enter, make this place your own, come in, come in, and explore Marioletti's misfit, mischievous mansion!"

The World In Miniature

Evening turned to night as their host labored in the kitchen. The Navigator, totally unaffected by the strange environment, sat cross-legged on the floor in the center of the living space, eyes closed, face serene. Sophie, on the other hand, had gleefully accepted the invitation to explore.

Her first stop was the reading nook. In Seaside, books were a possession to be ashamed of and kept hidden away. Marioletti, meanwhile, had his proudly and prominently displayed. She lingered long at the shelves, reading the titles and running her finger along their spines, as though afraid they were only illusions.

It quickly became clear that there were multiple readers in the house. One section held thin, colorful kids books, many of which starred cartoon animals. Sophie skipped over these and moved to the novels. She saw many of the entries on her list, but for every one there were three more that were unknown. Then came a section on philosophy, history, and biographies of people she had never heard of. An entire bookcase was devoted to glassmaking, which was a shock to Sophie because she had no idea there was that much to be known on the subject. She thought briefly of Bernard, the glassblower's son from the Red Market, and his insistence that no one could match Marioletti's skill. *Why does he need so many books when he can just use magic?* she wondered. That made her wonder if he'd built his reputation by selling real animals turned to glass. That wasn't very fair if true. It felt a lot like cheating.

"Feel free to have a look through any title that strikes your fancy," their host called from the kitchen, "though do take care with them, if you please."

Sophie thanked him and, being polite, decided to open a few covers, though there were other things she wanted to see more. She started with *A Comprehensive and Illustrated Guide to the Natural World*. Plants and animals leapt off the page, each accompanied by a lengthy description of its habitat and relevant features. The book's owner had penciled in notes, along with arrows and lines to highlight particular details of the anatomy. Sophie was delighted and bewildered by the staggering variety of wildlife on display. There was no mention of gnomes, pixies, or wood nymphs.

Next she moved to an enormous volume with a one word title—*Atlas*. Lifting the cover, she skimmed past the introductory pages, then stopped, puzzled. The book wasn't really a book at all, but a collection of maps. Carefully, she lifted out the first one she came to, unfolded it on a nearby table, and for the very first time saw her world in its entirety. She ran her finger over its surface in search of her own island nation. It took quite some time. Finally, she found it floating all alone some distance from the nearest continent. Sophie was floored by how small it looked, barely more than a smudge. One fingertip covered it completely. Fairport had made her feel tiny, inconsequential, yet where other major world cities had been marked and labeled on the map, it was nowhere to be found. Not even High Vandermeer was included. To anyone looking at this map, her home was a barren, uninhabited rock. She wondered how many other villages, towns, and cities had been sacrificed for the sake of expediency. Sophie refolded the map, closed the book, and hefted it back up onto the shelf.

She decided to explore the stone turrets next. From outside they had looked bizarrely out of place, but inside, they looked stately, powerful, the sandy stone matching the shade of the barn's wooden walls almost exactly. The way the towers framed the tall picture windows imitated a castle's gate that was open to the wilderness beyond. Sophie looked to see if there was a portcullis dangling from the rafters. There wasn't.

Each turret had a heavy door at its base, with iron hinges and a weighty ring for a handle. Sophie tugged one open and found herself in an unlit antechamber. Inside was a staircase that spiraled up into darkness. Where the rest of the house was colorful and warm, the stone felt sterile, cold, uninviting. It pressed in on all sides. A ghostly, low moan echoed from above, and though Sophie was pretty sure it was only the wind, she'd had enough wandering alone in the dark for one day. She went back into the living room and pulled the door firmly closed behind her.

There was one other thing that had caught her eye, and that was the dollhouse. It sat on a semi-circular table beneath the picture window and was a replica of Marioletti's home. Sophie undid the latch and opened it up. Everything had been recreated in miniature, each tier furnished and decorated to look just like the real thing, including a tiny dollhouse. A doll in the shape of a little girl sat before it, her black hair done up in pigtails and secured with pink ribbons. Another doll was in the reading nook, this one a grown woman, presumably the child's mother. She sat in a studious pose with a book in her lap. Beneath the terraces was a hidden glassblowing workshop, with multiple kilns, pipes, and a tool-strewn workbench. There was a third doll inside, a man with the same jet black hair as his daughter, busily stoking one of the kilns.

Sophie marveled at the exacting detail of the dollhouse's construction. It wasn't merely a toy; it was a work of art. Her eyes bounced back and forth between the dollhouse and the room, spotting each object's real life counterpart. She found herself growing jealous. Sophie had never had a dollhouse of her own, and even if she had, it wouldn't have been anywhere near as nice as this one. It was simply another reminder of the life she should have had. *You're being silly*, she told herself, preparing to close the dollhouse.

That was when she saw it. Above the real hearth, there was nothing but bare wall. But above the hearth in the dollhouse was a tiny family portrait showing a man with his wife and daughter. She leaned in close to get a better look at the miniature painting. The man in the picture was tall, thin, and handsome, with short black hair and a trim mustache. His wife had long, curly hair and shadows beneath her eyes. The smiling little girl was the perfect blend of them both, wearing a pink dress with white lace trim. *Must be an old picture*, Sophie thought. Time had evidently not been kind to Mr. Marioletti.

"My guests! Dinner is served."

Sophie closed the dollhouse, securing the latch with a loud, final snap.

The Glassblower's Tale

THE THREE OF THEM SAT DOWN to a dinner of grilled sausages topped with caramelized onions and a creamy leek sauce, mashed potatoes, steamed vegetables, a nice crusty bread, and a glass of white wine. The old man lifted his and said, "To new friends."

"To kind hosts," the Navigator returned.

"And warm beds," said Sophie. They drank as one, then set to work on the meal before them.

"It is kind of you to open your door to strangers," said the Navigator. "Not all are as welcoming. I trust we aren't putting anyone out of their beds this evening."

"Oh not at all, not at all." He sipped at his wine, which was sweet and crisp like a green apple. "My wife and daughter are away at the moment. Her mother's health has taken a turn for the worse. Bit of a surprise, if I'm honest. I assumed she'd be around to badger me right into my grave! Oh, I suppose I shouldn't joke. Truth be told, my better half was nervous about building so far out for just this reason. But solitude is necessary for my creativity, and without that we wouldn't have a home in the first place, so here we are. I do hope my darling wife arrives in time to say goodbye. She'll never forgive me otherwise."

"That would be a terrible shame," the Navigator said gravely. "You have our gratitude."

"Thanks for letting us stay the night," Sophie put in. "Your house is very interesting."

"Interesting? I've heard many different words used to describe this place, but few so mild as *interesting.* Not to your liking, I take it?"

"No no, it's not that. I've just never seen anything like it, that's all."

He chuckled. "Few have. No need to be embarrassed, my dear. It's not for everyone. To be perfectly honest, I'm not even sure it's for me. Would have made a few changes if I'd had a hand in designing it, I can tell you that. But I don't make the decisions around here, no, no, never have. I leave those things to my better half and stick to my art."

"What exactly is it you do?" asked the Navigator.

"He's Marioletti!" said Sophie. "The famous glassblower."

"I suppose I am," he said, winking at Sophie over a mischievous grin. "Though I prefer the term 'Master of Vitreology.' Obsessed with it, I am. Been studying glasswork for as long as I can remember, or near enough as to make no difference."

"How did you come to be here?"

"That is a bit of a story. Thankfully, we have some time, don't we? I'll give you the abbreviated-but-not-quite-short version. I started out life as an urchin, a ruffian, running wild through the streets of a foreign city unknown in this part of the world. My mother did her best to look after my brothers and I, but young lads can be a terror even at their best, which we never were. My father was no help. Spent his days laboring, his nights whoring, and every waking hour with a flask lifted to his lips. We didn't see him much, and that was a blessing."

"One day, we're out getting up to our old tricks when I

hear this rhythmic jingle-jangle coming from around the way. We go and find a man in the craziest getup I ever saw turning a crank on a music box. He had bells on his shoes, and he was marching in time to the music as he went. 'Come one, come all,' he shouts, 'a thousand and one marvels, wonders, curiosities, oddities, and sights beyond reckoning at The Carney Twins' Traveling Circus.' What child could resist such a pitch? My brothers and I promptly abandoned whatever plot we were hatching and set out to find the circus."

"It was the grandest thing I'd ever seen. Still is, and I've been around the world twice! Three enormous tents pitched on the edge of town, large enough to hold two, three hundred people each, and all around were caravans and games and merchant stalls, food vendors, petting zoos, troubadours, poets, clowns, jugglers, and more. Of course, such spectacles are not enjoyed for free, and as you might have surmised, money did not flow like water in my household. Sad to say, poverty and misfortune have a way of breeding a certain disregard for the strictures of polite society, and being both impoverished and lacking in good fortune, we snuck inside unnoticed."

"'A thousand and one marvels,' the crier'd said, and it was no lie, but it only took one to change my life forever. Didn't look like much at first. Just some bored, tired looking fella sat outside a caravan and taking coppers from kids so they could go inside, and a sign up above the door. I assume it said 'Glass Menagerie' or something of that sort, though it might've said 'Slave Recruiter' for all I knew. Wouldn't figure out reading until several years on. Anyway, it made no difference. I had a few coins jingling in my pocket, so I got in line, gave one to the man, and stepped inside."

"Thinking back on it now, it's almost laughable how paltry

his display was, rows of glass statuettes on plain wooden shelves and some half-hearted attempts at scene setting. None of that mattered to me. It set my little boy's heart on fire. Ya ken, I'd barely ventured beyond the confines of my neighborhood up 'til then and never saw anything more exotic than a stray cat. The smatters of brown and green paint were just enough to let me believe I was standing in the forest, gazing upon the majesty of a bugling stag on a hill. What did I care that the poor thing was scratched and chipped and missing a couple of points from its antlers? I had journeyed to another realm, one where a poor child like myself could have incredible adventures and escape the real world, even if only for a few moments. And to think that people would pay for that experience! I was transformed. I knew right then what to do with my life."

"I went back every single day until the circus left, lost in worlds of imagination I could never hope to visit in reality. The way I loitered, the barker was well within his rights to demand more money or kick me out altogether. Instead, he was kind to me and let me stay as long as I liked. I thought then he was happy for the company, but now I don't wonder if he knew exactly what it was I was escaping from. He told me about the places he'd been with the circus, where he'd purchased his pieces, what their names were, things like that. I listened as well as any young boy can, which is to say not well at all. Then, on the last day, he surprised me with a gift: the stag that had first captured my attention so. 'Anytime you're feeling lost or down,' he said, 'you just take a gander at this beauty and all your cares will go away.' I hugged the man and thanked him, then left. I carried that thing so gingerly all the way home, cradled it to my chest like a newborn kitten. I was so proud of it that I went straight home and showed it to my parents. 'Where'd you get that?' says my old man. I told him how I'd come by it. He starts shaking his head. 'My own son, a liar and a thief. I wouldn't have believed it.' He snatched the stag from my hands and said, 'Son, next time you steal something, make sure it's actually worth a damn.' Then he smashed it on the ground. I stood there bawling my eyes out as he ground those beautiful antlers to powder with his boot heel."

"That's terrible!" Sophie cried.

"Aye, it was. I hated him for it, so much so that I decided I would make my own glass stag to spite him. The next day I tracked down a glazier and started hanging around the workshop. Told him I wanted to learn everything there was to know about glass, and instead of running me off, he fed my curiosity, bless his heart. I made my first window panes at the age of twelve. Then I started learning to blow, and moved on to vases, bowls, objects with simple shapes, you see. I learned how to infuse glass with color and how to mold and shape it, how to create texture. Along the way I started selling my pieces, and the rest is history. My only regret is that my father never got the chance to see what I've become."

"Why not?" Sophie asked.

"Hmmm." His eyes softened and lost focus. His tone, serious. "Now, I could tell you some lie to soften the blow, a sad tale of father and son yearning for reconciliation yet separated by time and space and fate. But lies are a poor foundation for a friendship. My father was murdered. Wound up with his throat slit by a broken bottleneck. It's not proper dinner conversation, I know, but that's the way it went. My success wouldn't have made a difference to him, anyway. Not the sort of man to atone for past wrongs was my father." The old man came back to himself suddenly, as if waking from a dream, and sipped from his glass. "But gone is gone, and if the past was dark, then today is bright. I have a loving wife and a child, fame and fortune, and I live in an unorthodox, eccentric house far away from the outside world where I can spend my final years doing what I love in peace and quiet. And, occasionally, I get the chance to make new friends. What more could a man ask for?" A bright, beaming smile shone on Sophie and the Navigator. "But enough about me. I want to know what brings a Navigator to these far shores."

"There is little enough to tell," he replied, "for I have little memory of my arrival. I was crossing the sea when my ship was overcome by a powerful tempest. Never before had I seen its like. We were tossed violently about on the waves, lurching sharply from side to side so that men were thrown bodily into the sea. The skies had grown so dark that all vision was reduced to afterimages imposed by the bursts of lightning. It was by this ghostly light that I saw a horrific, swirling funnel open up before our vessel. Indistinct shadows moved below the surface of those skirling waters. Then, in the darkness, I heard a final splintering snap, and knew no more. I was lost in the void for time indeterminate, aware of nothing save for the mere fact of existence. And, at times, a steady, recurring voice. What it said I did not know, for it spoke in a tongue that was not my own, but its presence reassured me that I was not alone." He looked at Sophie as he spoke this last. Neither his tone nor the shape of his face changed, but she felt the depth of his gratitude all the same.

"Incredible. And how is it that the two of you have come to be *exploring* in my neck of the woods?"

"I do not wish to be rude," said the Navigator, "but our business is our own."

"Oh." The man's smile faltered. "I see."

A sudden pang wrenched Sophie's stomach from intense and unexpected embarrassment. The man had saved her life, given them a free place to stay, fed them dinner, and told them his whole life's story. It didn't seem right not to share some piece of their tale, no matter how small. Besides, he might know something useful. "The Navigator was leading us on a path and it happened to come this way," she said, hoping her words would be explanation enough.

"You don't say?" Their host's eyebrows went up as he spoke. "A confluence of events, then, is it? Much like me coming upon you at just the right moment to save your life?"

"The universe conspires to put us in the right place at the right time," said the Navigator.

"Interesting." He toyed with his wine glass, not looking at either of them. "Some might call it simple coincidence, or blind luck. Good luck for me, certainly. That bloody-eared fiend out there is a real showstopper. Been looking for a strider for quite some time. I used to have one a long time ago, a miniature, but I lost it in a bit of misfortune and haven't been able to replace it since." He turned to Sophie. "Of course, I never expected to catch one in such a provocative pose, on the verge of striking, its eyes full of such singular dark focus, moments away from bearing tooth and claw . . ."

The Navigator broke in. "It seems your good fortune was ours as well." There was a sharpness in his tone that suggested the topic should be changed.

"We're on a quest from Duke Truculo," Sophie blurted. "People are disappearing in the woods and the duke wants us to end it."

"Is that so?" He sat back in his chair, astonished. "What a

terrible thing. I had no idea. One of the disadvantages to living such a private life, I suppose. You're always the last to know. How many have gone?"

The Navigator answered. "Twenty in the last two seasons."

"Is it so many?" His voice was quiet, almost to himself. "That's a real shame. What manner of beast is it you seek? A bear, perhaps, or a pack of prowling wolves?"

"It could be man or beast," said the Navigator. "We do not know. Possibly, you have done our job for us in capturing the strider."

"Do you think so? He is a terrible, ferocious looking thing, isn't he? The way he lusted after the young miss, I think it's fair certain he had a taste for human flesh. Perhaps you're right. I suppose the only way to know is to wait a while and see if the disappearances come to an end."

"I feel confident they will."

"So do I."

A look passed between them that made Sophie uneasy. *He doesn't like the Navigator.* She felt a sudden urge to break the tension. "So, how *did* you catch him?" she asked. "You never told me how it works. It's some kind of magic, isn't it?"

He chuckled. "We all have our secrets, young miss, and I'm afraid this is one of mine." The rest of his wine disappeared in a gulp. "Imagine that, me, a hero! Slayer of the killer strider, savior of the people."

"Well, you saved me, so you're already a hero in my book," said Sophie, glad that things had steered back into friendly territory. "Mr. Marioletti, can I ask you a question?"

"Certainly."

"Have you ever made any glass frogs?"

All light left his eyes.

The moment was brief, less than a second, so fleeting that Sophie registered it only subconsciously. But register it she did. What was revealed was a hollowness so empty that no human could exist within. Unease invaded her mind, intensified by the measuring gaze that followed, and the fact that his infectious smile had remained plastered on his lips throughout. "Now why would you ask me that?"

Her words came out in a nervous rush. "I'm trying to learn more about my parents. I'm an orphan, see, and they had these two glass frogs with all their stuff, and the other ones I've seen weren't nearly as good as the ones my parents had so I thought maybe you might have made them, and if you did, maybe you might, I don't know . . ." She trailed off, looking at him with hesitant hope.

"I understand." He picked up the wine bottle, shook it, found it empty. "Sorry to disappoint you, but I have never made anything so vulgar as a frog. Nasty, slimy creatures they are. Can't stand the sight of them. I can assure you, your parents weren't made them by me."

"Okay. Thanks anyway."

"What do you say we move on to dessert, eh?" The friendly tone had returned, erasing the bizarre tension of the preceding moments. "Then we can all get some rest, and in the morning I'll give you a tour of my glorious glass garden. It's a real wonder at sunrise, not to be missed."

"Perhaps you could capture the scene with your paintbrush," the Navigator suggested to Sophie. She shot him a glance, wondering what he was playing at.

"Paintbrush?"

"My young friend is an artist in her own right. She has a keen eye for seeing things as they truly are and capturing them in vivid detail. That is why the duke asked her to accompany me. Perhaps she could honor her savior with a portrait? To lend credibility to the tale, of course."

Why is he lying to Marioletti?

"Oh, that won't be necessary, not necessary at all! It would ruin my carefully cultivated mystique." He stood, clearing the dishes as he spoke. "A painter, then? I've always envied the painters of the world. Tried my hand at it a few times, but, sad to say, I never could get it quite right. Let's just say I won't be changing mediums any time soon." He picked up the wine bottle. "But now my curiosity is piqued. You must have quite the talent to have caught the attention of the duke. Do you have any samples of your work with you, child?"

I'm not a child.

Sophie watched him walk around the table, passing behind the Navigator. "Yes sir, it's in my backpa—"

Her words were cut off by a horrendous clattering as he dropped the dishes. Startled, the Navigator turned, and at the same moment the butt of the wine bottle crashed against the back of his skull, once, twice, sending him into oblivion. Sophie screamed. For the second time that night her eyes met those of a predator. He pounced, putting a hand over her mouth and nose, cutting off her breath. She struggled against him. The world spun and greyed around the edges, consciousness trapped in a dizzying, swirling funnel, one with shadows playing just beneath the surface, grasping at her, pulling her down into darkness, and she knew no more.

REVELATIONS

Murphy Makes A House Call

Damon woke to the muffled sounds of argument. Dim light filtered into the woodshed through its slatted walls, interrupted by the shadows of the two men outside. He lifted his head from his cot and winced as the iron shackle encircling his throat plucked at the short hairs of his neck. His muscles ached from another night spent shivering so much he'd hardly slept. The scent of pine from the surrounding firewood failed to mask the sour, musty smell of old sweat. The fatigue, the fevers, the insatiable cravings for beer, those things didn't worry him. The approaching voices did, or more specifically, what they likely meant.

"I appreciate the gravity of the situation, Horace . . ."

"I'm not sure that you do."

". . . but as the only trained medical professionals in this village, it is our duty to tend to his health."

"We have been more than generous in providing for his comfort and well-being, given the danger in which he has placed the entire village."

"I will judge for myself."

"I'm not letting him out, Murphy."

"*Doctor* Murphy. And I am not asking you to release him. I am asking you to let us in." A pause. "Please."

Horace huffed. Then came the sounds of metal on metal as a lock was unfastened and removed. Damon shielded his eyes as sunlight streamed into the shed. A shadow approached. The doctor stopped short when he saw Damon, pity plain on his face. Then he doffed his hat and sat on a round of pine before the miserable figure. Albert filed in behind, carrying the doctor's black bag. "That bastard," Murphy muttered. "Come on, sit up, son. Let me have a look at you."

Damon did as he was told, shrugging off the coarse wool blanket he'd been given. His voice was hoarse and cracked as he asked, "Is it time?"

"No. Not yet." The doctor felt his forehead, cheeks, and neck, then lifted the shackle from his collarbones so he could inspect the flesh below. "Albert, the antiseptic tincture, please." His assistant pressed a bottle and a clean cloth into his hand. Murphy wet the cloth, then dabbed it on Damon's raw, irritated skin. The bright sting cut through his exhaustion, and he hissed, eyes flaring. "Unpleasant, I know, but it will keep the wounds from mortifying."

"Why bother? They're just going to give me to those creatures anyway."

"It might surprise you to learn that not everyone agrees with this course of action. Myself included."

"Nor do I," Albert put in.

Damon, who sat with his elbows cupped in his palms, nodded his head weakly. "Sophie?"

"No word, I'm afraid."

Another nod.

"I mentioned her to the duke," Albert said. "He knew nothing of her disappearance, but said the stranger had come to him making a number of odd demands. Truculo promised to return him to us as soon as possible." A rueful smirk played across Albert's lips. They all understood the anemic strength of Duke Truculo's promises.

"Here." Doctor Murphy produced a flask from his pocket and handed it to Damon. "A sip to warm you." The acrid tang of whisky stung the young man's nostrils. He drank, wanting to upend the flask and guzzle it all, but limited himself to a single mouthful. The heat ignited his chest and radiated out to his limbs. A calming tingle washed over his skin, his muscles finally relaxed, and the shivering abated. "Thank you."

"We shall do what we can, son." Murphy squeezed Damon's shoulder, trying to infuse him with confidence. Then doctor and assistant took their leave, but not before presenting Damon with a bundle containing some bread, cheese, cured meat, and a bottle of clean water.

There were more words with Horace on the way out. Damon barely heard them. Despite her promise, Sophie still hadn't come home. Part of him was relieved. He didn't want her to see him this way. It wasn't about humiliation; she had already watched his pride dwindle and disappear over the years. No, the arrival of the Merling King had revealed the true ugliness in the hearts of the Unimaginative, a petty smallness that ran deeper than he could have imagined. If she returned and saw what Seaside had become, her home would be lost, whether the village was spared from waves or not. *Stay away, little butterfly. May the winds of fate slow your return.*

Then he was alone with Horace Halderman.

He stood near the door, leaning on his cane and needling Damon with his sharp, bully's eyes. "A few days more," he said. "Four, five at the most. Then we'll finally be rid of you once and for all. This used to be a peaceful place, you know. A simple place. There was order, and everything made sense. A few days more and the village will be as it was before that Unnecessary ever arrived."

"Why?" Damon croaked. "Why do you hate him so much?"

"Him?" Horace shook his head. "Oh no, boy, this began well before that foreigner washed ashore. He is merely the latest in a string of unwelcome visitors who have left their mark on Seaside. *She* was the one who started it all, who ruined everything."

Tired as he was, Damon found the strength to meet Horace's eyes.

"We were friends, once, your father and I. More than that. 'Brother', we called each other. We even shared a birthday, only Robert was two years my senior. As boys we were inseparable. Once we grew older and came into our own, we made a pact to look out for one another and our families. What fools we were." He bared his small, piggy teeth, revealing those that had been ejected by Robert's angry fist.

"There had been girls before, but they never came between us. Not so with your mother. She captured his attention completely. We were brothers one day, strangers the next, our bond severed by this outsider who wanted nothing more than something pretty to paint. At first she was only staying a night or two. Then it stretched to a week, a fortnight, a month . . . a lifetime."

"I wanted to be happy for him. I did. But I couldn't manage it. The loss was simply too much to bear. And before you start thinking my resentment was borne out of jealousy, know that I never had any designs on Erinella. I never did understand what Robert saw in her, with her vulgar clothing choices, sloppy housekeeping, and ridiculous flights of fancy. It would have been easier if I had loved her, I think. At least then I could have understood why he set me aside. But she was just so *different*. It was maddening."

"That's it? You hate outsiders because my father fell in love with one?"

"He was my best friend!" Horace jabbed his cane at Damon to emphasize this point. "I kept his counsel on everything—business, love, family, all of it! We were going to run this village together. Your mother took that from us. So I made new friends, ones who recognized her corrupting influence and the threat she posed to the very fabric of our village. Erinella has been dead for over a decade and still she is not gone from this place." Horace smiled. "But that will change soon enough. Your sister's done me a great favor by leaving. I hope she has the good sense to stay away."

Damon exploded to his feet, hands outstretched. The iron collar around his neck jerked him sharply backward. "I won't let you hurt her!" he coughed, one hand going to his bruised throat.

"And why should I fear you, boy? All you can do is run to the end of your chain and bark." Horace turned and opened the door to leave. "Five days at the most. Best make peace with your miserable life while you can. Before those things use your bones to pick their teeth." Damon Farrier collapsed to the floor as he was shut in with the darkness once again.

Marioletti's Workshop

SOPHIE CAME AROUND SLOWLY. Somehow she was upright, head drooping, hair hanging limp in her lap. Her mouth was dry as an old sponge, her tongue heavy and numb. A dull ache pulsed at her temples. There were sounds. Incoherent muttering. Objects in motion. She opened her eyes. Everything was dim, blurry, doubled. The pulsing ache disappeared as she lifted her head, replaced by a sharp tingling in her scalp, as if each hair were waking up one by one. Her neck protested weakly. She tried to move her arms, and could not. Same with her legs. With an effort, she focused her gaze, and saw for the first time the ropes that held her fast. Solid wood pressed into her back, her buttocks, her legs.

(chair i'm tied to a chair what's happening)

Details slowly made themselves known, and before long she recognized the space as Marioletti's basement workshop. Light seeped in through narrow, rectangular windows near the ceiling. Stout wooden tables stood against the stone walls, littered with tools and half-completed bits of glasswork. There were glass animals everywhere. A wolf stared into the center of the room, its head lowered, hackles raised, fangs bared. Every detail was exquisite, lifelike, except for its bright yellow fur.

The others were also colored unnaturally. A black and green fox gazed at her from the corner, it's posture one of escape, while nearby, a pink owl stared into space with surprised eyes.

White-orange fire blazed in a furnace at the far end of the room, obscured by a dark, hunched figure laboring maniacally.

Marioletti!

Sophie began to struggle, twisting and turning to loosen the ropes that bound her. Her fingers explored the bindings on her wrists in search of knots to work at. She had to get free, now, while her captor was occupied. Then she could find the Navigator, wake him up, and the two of them could escape. *Where is he?* Her rocking tipped the chair sideways, and for a sickening moment Sophie thought she was going to overbalance and topple headfirst onto the floor. Instead, the chair legs hammered down with a hollow *clunk*. The glassblower's head lifted sharply. He turned. Crossed the room. Leaned in close.

"Where's the Navigator?" she asked, the words struggling out from her cottony mouth.

The man did not react. He reeked of alcohol. Broken red and purple veins spidered his nose, cheeks, and sclera. Scraggly, stringy white hair stuck up from his balding pate. Hollow eyes scoured her features from the glabrous mask of his face. There was no one behind those eyes, no one at all.

"I wanna go home," she said. "Where's the Navigator? Where's my friend?"

His gloved hand took her by the chin. Sophie tried to turn away, but his grip was surprisingly strong, and she was tied to a chair and still groggy. She ceased struggling and stared right into his blank, empty eyes.

"I should've seen it sooner." His fermented breath made her

gag. "Seen hundreds of faces in my time and I've never forgotten a one. And no man would forget your mother's face. You look like her. Different through the cheeks, perhaps, and that's your father's hair, but otherwise the resemblance is uncanny."

"You knew my mother? How?"

He let go of her face and stalked over to a workbench. There he tossed down his gloves, uncorked a bottle, and took a long draught of the clear liquid within. "You asked me how I did it. You, the one who took everything from me, the one who left me destitute and broken, the one who should know how the trick is done better than anybody." The crazed old man pulled an object from his leather apron and held it up for her to see. It was a clear glass scepter, about a foot and a half long and shaped like a paintbrush. Its textured surface glittered rainbows. "My mentor's dirty little secret. Though the way he treated me I think 'master' is more fitting."

"His name was Marley, he of the marvelous menagerie. I first set eyes on him some years after the circus left. He was a liar, a cheat, and a swindler, but I wouldn't find that out until it was far, far too late. I took up with him the day my father met his untimely end. So. Maybe we were meant to find each other, after all. Who can say?" A cold, humorless smile split his lips. "To this day I'm certain Marley never put his lips to a blowpipe in his life. But he didn't need to, not with this in his possession. I followed him one day when he was 'making an acquisition', as he called it. A stag of all things. He spends a moment admiring it, and then with a quick flick of the wrist . . . *bam!*" Spectral dust fired through the air and struck one of the leather gloves. It whispered and crackled as it turned to glass. "Vitrified."

"I signed on with him to learn how to make glass. Charm,

wit, duplicity, those were the skills he taught me instead. And cruelty, that most of all. Even my old man could have learned something from Marley in that regard. Wresting the scepter away from him was messier than I would have liked. But he was unworthy to carry it. He had no idea of its true potential. It belongs in the hands of a master craftsman, not some clueless buffoon. Or those of a child."

He leveled the scepter at Sophie.

"You ruined everything," he growled. "When I inherited that caravan, it was nothing but a silly regional curiosity, not much more than a rolling charity case. I built it into a spectacle! For years I traveled the globe, capturing animals from the highest mountain peaks and the deepest oceans. I brought the world with me wherever I went, inspiring joy and wonder in men, women, and children, and all I asked in return was a few coppers each and a place to rest my head. You put an end to that. I let your beauty of a mother distract me, and then you and your insolent snot of a brother snuck into my caravan and *you destroyed my world*."

"I don't understand!" Sophie wailed. "I've never seen you before in my life!"

The scepter trembled. "I can't tell you how long I wandered after that, broken, rudderless. I'd lost my money, my livelihood, everything I'd ever worked for. But I still had this . . . and my skills . . . and a terrible new question burning in my brain. See, you did something I never quite had the courage to do, not then. You used the scepter on a *human*. The way your mother contorted and shrank and changed color . . . I was horrified. I couldn't look away. I still can't, no matter how many times I see the transformation take place."

"Wait," Sophie said, shaking her head. There was so much

coming at her that she was having trouble keeping up. "What are you saying?"

The imposter retrieved his latest piece of work and held it before her—a delicate glass frog. "Recognize her?"

Sophie did. She knew the bright yellow-green of its skin, the single red stripe along its back, the eyes of blue. The lips were wrong, however. There was no smile here, just a long, drawn out grimace. Hot tears overspilled Sophie's cheeks. "That's . . . no . . ."

"Why a frog?" he said, shaking it in her face. "That's what I kept returning to over and over again. Plants, animals, objects, they all turn into glass versions of themselves. Not her. She turned into this. Your father was the same. Frogs, both of them. I grew obsessed. I had to know why, so I began to experiment. It's more difficult to guess what someone will become than you might expect. I'm almost always surprised."

Sophie sucked in a breath. "You're the one who's been making people disappear!"

The imposter sketched a little bow. "Surely I can't take credit for them all. People disappear all the time. A lost little girl here, a drunken fool there. No one notices as long as you stay on the move and be patient. Then I learned about Marioletti and his amazing glasswork, a reclusive artist with a hidden workshop, the true master I'd always sought. I gave him the chance to take me in. I professed my love of the art form and begged him to make me his apprentice. But my charm failed." He patted the snarling yellow wolf on the head. "Tried to turn me away, didn't you? No matter. I decided to stay. And now here we are, the three of us and the truth."

The three of us . . .

He walked around behind Sophie. Then came the sound of

something sliding on wood and grunts of effort, and a moment later he reappeared, dragging a carpet across the floor. The Navigator was lying on it, hands and feet bound, a gag tied around his mouth. His eyes were calm as he looked up at her from the ground. "Let him go!" Sophie yelled at the old man. "He didn't do anything to you."

The man, neither Marley nor Marioletti, ignored her. "The universe conspires to put us in the right place at the right time. That's what he said, isn't it?" He gave a bitter laugh, then kicked the Navigator in the side. "You will be my greatest experiment yet. Marioletti, his wife, and his daughter were all different, but your parents were both frogs. Does that make you a frog as well? I cannot wait to find out. But first, I should treat you to a demonstration. You deserve to see exactly what you did. Don't worry, I'll be merciful. I won't make you live with the knowledge for long." He dragged the Navigator into the middle of the floor, right where Sophie could see him, and rolled him over so he was lying face up. She began to sob loudly as he took the Navigator's face in hand, as he had done with her. "What do you reckon he'll be? Looks a bit like a lion, I think, though he didn't put up much of a fight. In truth, he's no more than a puffed up house cat."

"No, stop it, please, just let him go, he didn't do anything, let him go!"

"Watch closely now, girl. Don't you close your eyes! *Don't you dare.*" He stood, and now his eyes were alive, gleaming with a foul, green light, the corners of his mouth contorted in a maleficent smile.

The scepter, aimed at the prostrate Navigator.

A short flick of the wrist.

"NOOOO!!!!!"

The glittering bolt of magic swept through the air, swerving off course as though blown by a powerful wind, and was absorbed by the Navigator's compass. It began to glow a blinding white. Sophie squinted against it, felt the hair of her arms stand on end. Then bolts of lighting arced violently from the compass, erupting in the confined space with a thunderous roar, their brilliance eclipsing even the raging blaze of the furnace. They raked the walls, ceiling, and floor, leaving blackened trails in their wake. Glass animals shattered as they were struck. A bolt latched on to one of the furnace's legs, writhing and jumping like a leech on flesh, only letting go once the steel had molten and given way. The lamed furnace dumped its raging contents onto the wood plank floor and set it instantly alight.

The imposter was shocked.

No, really.

Wild, brilliant bursts of godfire struck him in the face, torso, and limbs, converging on his frame and driving him stumbling backward, electricity crackling erratically over his skin. Sophie turned her head away, eyes closed, listening helplessly to the electric sizzle and spark intermingled with his anguished cries.

Then it was over.

Sophie's ears rang in the sudden silence. She opened her eyes to see the Navigator scooting across the carpet. He rolled, pressing his hands to the ground, fingers scrabbling to find a suitable shard of glass with which to cut himself free. Heavy grey smoke billowed from the other side of the room. It rose to the ceiling and roiled like an angry cloud, escaping through a broken window. The acrid fumes stung her nose. Flames licked the stone walls and left blackened tongues in their wake as they raced toward the ceiling. The Navigator's fingers worked furiously as the flames grew. "Hurry," she said plaintively.

Smoke half-filled the workshop by the time he got his wrists unbound. He sat up and pulled the gag from his mouth, then reached into his vest and removed a short length of rope. The Navigator squeezed it in his fist and said a word. All at once, the ropes binding his legs fell away, as did the ones that fixed Sophie to the chair. Then he was there, tugging her down to the ground, leading her toward the other side of the room on his hands and knees while brushing aside fragments of shattered glass. Sophie realized with alarm that he was leading them *toward* the fire. There was no time to protest or negotiate. She followed, focused entirely on not cutting herself, anything to keep from thinking about the steadily building heat and the sweat glistening on her skin and how hard it was to breathe and . . .

Sophie shrieked as she found the remains of the imposter.

He lay on the floor, back fixedly arched, limbs splayed. His flesh had been turned to glass where the lightning had touched him. One leg had been completely vitrified. It lay beside him, snapped cleanly off and ending in a flat stump, a white circle of bone centered in crimson meat. Glass fingers were fused to what remained of the scepter's shattered shaft. His face had mostly been vitrified. Mostly. One green eye rolled up to look at her, enraged and confused and wild, threatening to pin her in place with its intensity until the smoke overcame her and he cemented his vengeance once and for all.

"Sophie."

She turned. The Navigator, calm as ever, motioned her onward. A doorway stood open behind him. They scrabbled through and up the concrete stairs and out onto the lawn to safety.

Friends In The Garden

SOPHIE COLLAPSED ONTO HER BACK. Staring up at the rising column of smoke, she gasped for air, holding her chest. Each breath fanned the flames of her burning throat. The Navigator sat down beside her. A faint crackling intermingled with the morning forest sounds, punctuated by intermittent bursts from exploding knots of wood. Otherwise the clearing was peaceful as could be.

Recognize her?

The imposter's words struck her and stole her breath. Sophie threw herself against the Navigator and wept into his shoulder. He was stiff at first, surprised, but then his arms wrapped tightly around her and she wept all the harder.

It took some time to regain her composure. When she had, she pulled away, her face wet and red. The Navigator handed her a handkerchief, which she gladly accepted. "I'm sorry for crying on you," she said, wiping at her eyes and nose.

"There is no need to apologize." He took her hand in his. "You are hurt. It is only natural to seek comfort in the embrace of a friend."

A friend. The word cut through the confused chaos of

her pain like a sunbeam through the clouds. Impossibly, she smiled. "Are you alright?"

"A few minor cuts and a headache. That is all."

Silence fell between them, filled by the growing strength of the bizarre house's immolation. Sophie plucked absently at the long blades of grass, tossing them aside. "My things are still in there." She said it simply, too depleted for alarm. "My jacket. My books. My . . . *her* paintings. She's in there."

The Navigator nodded, but said nothing.

"Do you think it's true? What he said about me and him and my parents? Did I . . . is it my fault?"

"It is impossible to say with certainty, though I do not believe he was lying. As to your culpability, rest assured, you are not responsible for what happened to your parents. It was not done in malice, or even with intent, for you were too young for either."

Sophie continued her idle plucking. He was right. He always was. Her pain persisted anyway.

Does Damon know?

That her brother might have kept yet another secret threatened to reignite her anger, but only momentarily, because of course he knew. He had told her so himself. *I remember.* She understood now the true weight of those two words. He had stood by and watched as his baby sister killed their parents with magic. His silence, his listlessness, his drinking, they all made sense. His pain was deeper than she could have imagined, and she had unknowingly dug straight down to the root of it all and thrown it right in his face. Had he ever meant to tell her? If the situations were reversed, could she? Sophie suddenly realized the depth of her big brother's love for her. *I ruined everything for him, and he only ever tried to protect me. I have to make this right.*

"I want to go home."

"Then that is where you shall go."

They went first to the stable, where they found the mare standing in the middle of the stall, vitrified and small enough to fit in her palm. They left it behind and began their journey afoot.

Bright shards of sunlight flickered from all around as they entered the garden. There were trumpeting daffodils and white lilies and stalks of lavender, all made entirely of glass. Tall lilac bushes grew at intervals, their purple flowers bunched together like grapes at harvest. Puffy hydrangeas of every color lined the clearing's edge. They passed next into the orchard, and saw apples and figs and cherries dangling from vitreous boughs. Stationary animals cavorted amongst the trees. A house cat stalked a mouse, the hunt observed by a pair of squirrels, their beady black eyes expressionless and glittering. Sly foxes peeked out from a burrow. Magpies in flight hung suspended from high branches, bobbing and twirling in the morning breeze. And there, atop a distant rise, was a magnificent stag. Its head was raised skyward to sound its bugling call. Sophie felt momentarily sad for the little boy that was and the glass stag that had sparked his imagination.

If either one ever even existed.

Sophie knelt and plucked a glass clover, quickly snapping off the delicate stem. She brushed a finger over its pointed purple and white petals, so delicate and lifelike, yet hard to the touch. Orange highlights cast from the growing pyre of Marioletti's home flickered and played over its surface. Yesterday, the flower would have seemed an impossible feat of artistry. Now she saw it as an abomination, a corruption of nature, a cheap trick perpetrated by a man whose only true skills were imitation and forgery. And cruelty. That most of all.

She was so caught up in the moment that she didn't register the men on horseback emerging from the forest.

They approached in formation, an arrowhead with Captain Rectifer at its tip. His blonde hair bounced around his shoulders as his stallion cantered forward. He wore a look of smug satisfaction as he drew his sword and pointed it at the Navigator. "You led us on quite the chase," said the captain. "Using the abandoned roads, disappearing in the woods on a whim. Almost like you were trying to run from us."

The Navigator responded with a mere turning up of his palms, not even a shrug.

"You were following us?" Sophie asked.

"The captain and his men have been our constant shadows from the outset," said the Navigator. "How else to take credit for our efforts?"

Rectifer smiled. "So you are a man of the world, after all. The duke will appear a competent leader, for once, and I will be made a royal knight. Assuming, of course, you were successful." His eyes flicked briefly to the burning house.

"It is done."

"Good. Seize him."

"What?" Sophie exclaimed. "You can't do that!"

"Can't I?" The captain whistled sharply and set his men in motion. They quickly encircled their captives. The Navigator knelt and put his hands in the air. Sophie stood, defiant. "Bring her to me," the captain ordered. Two of his men dismounted and entered the circle. She struggled valiantly, but they were far larger and stronger. "Let me go!" she yelled as they hauled her before Captain Rectifer.

"Where is your gratitude? We don't always save the monster's victims, you know. Sometimes we are, sadly, too late." Rectifer paused to let the implication of his words sink in. "Now, would you like a ride back to Fairport or not?"

Sophie's shoulders slumped. She looked back at the Navigator, who was on his knees, wrists bound once again. His nod was slow and full of meaning. *Do what they say.* She stared at the ground as she mumbled, "Yes, sir."

"Good girl." His eyes narrowed as he regarded the Navigator. "Riley, get that trinket from off his neck. It'll make for a good trophy."

Sophie looked up in alarm. "No! Don't!"

A hand, clad in electrically conductive steel, reached out and grasped the compass and tugged sharply. The gold chain broke with little resistance, and with it, Sophie's heart.

The dead compass was placed into the waiting grasp of Captain Rectifer, who smiled at it greedily before stuffing it into his saddlebag. Then Sophie and the Navigator were loaded onto the back of their captors' mounts and ridden off into the forest.

A Reversal Of Fortune

THE RETURN TRIP FROM MARIOLETTI'S was much faster than the way there. Rectifer had spurred them onward with much haste, each captive riding double with one of his men. Sophie spent much of her time gazing into the forest in search of someone who might intervene and set them free. A wood nymph, perhaps. Maybe even Granelith herself. Now, having reentered the duke's private wood, she knew she had hoped in vain. They would soon reach the bridge where she'd reunited with the Navigator, and beyond that the palace grounds, where they would be separated one final time.

She studied her friend closely. He was different somehow, though she couldn't have said in what way. It escaped her conscious mind, simultaneously seen and unseen. His quiet composure remained, and he was totally compliant with the captain's orders, but sitting beside him was like being near a beehive on a summer's day. She imagined a busy, burring cloud buzzing around his head, invisible thought bees swirling in an incoherent mass. *If I close my eyes and listen, I can probably hear them zipping around.*

If I close my eyes . . .

That was it. His eyes were always open. He had taken every opportunity to close them and meditate when they'd been alone. No longer. Even now his gaze was focused, taking in the landscape as they trotted through the wood, as though he were truly seeing the world for the first time.

Sophie didn't like it one bit.

She wracked her brain for something to say, grappling with the knowledge that this could be their final conversation and the pressure such knowledge brings. There was plenty she wanted to say, important, weighty words full of meaning and significance, but doing so would underline the gravity of the situation. Instead, Sophie did what many of us do in these situations and reached for the utterly banal. "Are you alright?"

"I am," he assured her. "What makes you ask?"

"I don't know. You just seem kind of . . . lost."

He chuckled. "That's the one thing a Navigator can never be."

"Even without your compass?"

"Yes. Even then." A wan smile appeared.

"Can I ask you something?"

"Of course."

"Was it true, what you said to Marioletti? Could you really hear me reading to you?"

"Yes and no. I could not hear you as I do now, but I was aware of your presence. It was comforting." He paused. "May I ask you a question?"

"Okay."

"Why did you persist? There were many reasons to quit. You did not know me, nor I you. Others in your village clearly despised me. You did not even know if there was an audience for your words. Why continue?"

"I don't know," she said. "You needed help, so I helped you. It was the right thing to do."

He gave her a slow, respectful nod. "I never properly thanked you for your efforts. Allow me to do so now."

"You're welcome," Sophie said, blushing.

The guard riding ahead of her snorted. "For all the good it did ya. Now quiet down, we're nearly there."

Rothschild was waiting for them at the palace's rear gate. He sat astride his prized thoroughbred, wearing his slashed crimson doublet and a venomous sneer. To the captain, he said, "At last, the brave warrior returns."

"Rothschild," said the captain, his tone dripping contempt. "Come to congratulate me, have you?"

"For what, exactly? For finally eradicating the foul beast that had eluded you for so, so long? Or conceiving of a transparent plot to steal credit for another man's deeds? Really, now, you are just a simple creature. Though your choice of scapegoat is inspired. Who could doubt that one so strange is responsible for such heinous deeds? Let me guess, next comes the public denunciation and execution, correct?"

Rectifer's jaw tightened. "Justice must be served."

"Indeed. I am very sorry to disrupt your plans," said Rothschild, sounding positively delighted, "but you're not the only one concocting a story of personal triumph. After you departed we were paid a visit by two men from some village by the sea. Apparently your captive caused quite the disturbance there and the duke has taken it upon himself to . . . ." His eyes landed on Sophie. "Well now, who is this?"

"The beast's latest victim. We arrived just in the nick of time."

"Mmm. And I trust she is unmolested?" He looked meaningfully at the captain as he said this last.

"Yes," he answered through gritted teeth.

"Oh-ho-ho, this is simply too good."

"These are my captives, Rothschild, not yours. I earned my glory—"

"Save your wind, my muscle-bound friend. You have made the duke happier than you can know, even if it is quite by accident. You there," he said, pointing, "bring her to me. I must deliver the good news at once."

"*We* will deliver the news. Together."

"No, you will be busy in the stable, loading your prisoner into the special conveyance we have contrived for him, for the duke will want to leave with the utmost haste. Our taciturn friend here implored us to return him to the sea. Duke Truculo means to grant his request." Rothschild bared his teeth in a cold serpent's smile. "Justice must be served, after all, and the crowd expects payment in blood."

Full Moon

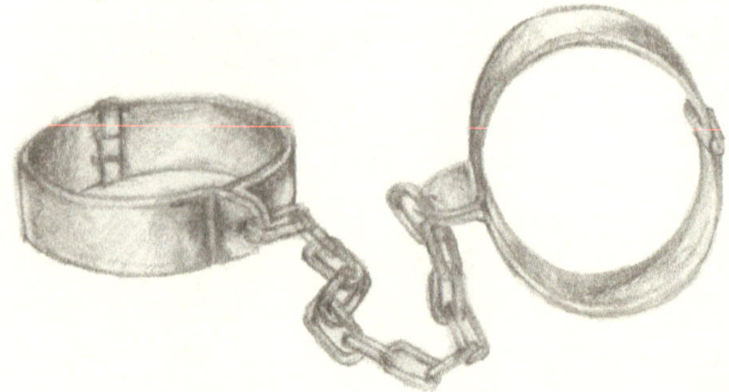

Mert's Big Idea

Mert had lost the farm.

In a manner of speaking, of course. It is impossible to lose that which was never had to begin with. What Mert had was his fantasy of the farm, or rather, he *had* had it, for now it was gone. It wasn't for lack of trying, or for opportunities to practice his imagining—Frances had been very helpful in this regard. But on this particular morning, instead of daydreaming about waking to a hot breakfast and a day spent with his sheep, he was stuck staring at the empty bowl of his spoon, which floated atop the thick, gloppy mess of his porridge. Mert turned his head this way and that, watching his imperfectly reflected features grow and shrink and warp. At certain angles, he noted, he looked an awful lot like the moon.

Today is the day.

The moon had come to dominate his thoughts. He'd been watching it closely both day and night. His obsession was so strong that the kelp harvest had suffered as a result. Instead of looking for fresh gloms, he was constantly searching for the ever-waning white orb in the sky, watching helplessly as the moon grew from a bright crescent into a nearly complete circle, with only the merest hint of shadow remaining. And yet there had been no sign of the terrifying creatures from the deep, the merlings with their giant claws and knobby, bile-colored exoskeletons and scratchy, grainy, inhuman voices. That they hadn't returned last night meant only one thing—it would happen tonight. Mert was worried about the fate of the village, but it was Damon his thoughts returned to most often, and what the return of the Merling King would mean for his friend.

"Isn't right," Mert muttered, watching his lips move in the spoon's reflection.

"What's that?" said Frances.

"I said it isn't right."

"Well then you make the porridge next time!"

Mert looked up, surprised by her outburst. "Not the porridge, mum. No problems there." To prove it, he dug his spoon in and hefted out a healthy glop. It pulled away in snotty strings, leaving a deep divot that refused to fill itself in. He stuck it in his mouth and scraped the porridge away with his teeth. In days past he might have convinced himself that it was a delicious runny egg atop a bed of crispy toast, but today it was an inescapable, tasteless paste that coated his mouth's every surface. After valiantly resisting his efforts at chewing, the glop clung tenaciously to the roof of his mouth before being forced down into Mert's empty gullet. "See?" he said, smiling. "Perfectly adequate."

Frances was appeased, but only just. "What'chu goin' on about, then?"

"S'Damon. Don't like what they're fixin' to do to him. Isn't right."

"If I've said it once, I've said it a thousand times, that boy made his own bed." As it turned out, she had said it a thousand times, to Mert and to everyone else in Seaside.

"Mm." Mert mulled it over as he battled another bite of his breakfast. He'd never found her argument particularly convincing, though he didn't quite know why. Mert had tried to work it out, really he had, but he always seemed to land in the same spot—*It isn't right.*

Perhaps losing his farm had freed up extra brainpower that morning, or maybe the urgent press of time had jogged something loose. Possibly, it had just taken that long for his mind to organize itself properly. Whatever the case may be, as he was conquering the next mouthful of snotty, gloppy porridge, the answer to the riddle finally popped into his mind with such simple clarity it surprised him into attempting to speak.

"*Wern-im-oo-innereer.*"

"What?"

Mert swallowed heavily. "I said, weren't him who interfered. Was us who found him."

"*Us?*" Frances wagged her laden spoon at her husband. "Don't you go dragging me into this, Mertrand. I told you to leave it alone. But no, you saw something shiny and had to go investigate like some empty-headed crow! Never listen to me, do you? Who am I but your loving wife? Oh, it's what I get for marrying into a line of curious thrill seekers, I s'pose."

"In any case," she went on, "Horace would have set things aright if that boy hadn't butted in. Would have been nothing for those monsters to complain about. Way I see it, that clears us from the matter. Instead, we're in this fine mess. Everyone living under threat, and you out there moonin' all day instead of focusing on what's right in front of you. Damon can rot in that shed as far as I'm concerned. 'Course, he won't. Those monsters will come and take him off our hands and that'll be that."

"All the same," said Mert. "It weren't Damon who started it."

Frances threw up her hands in exasperation. "Well wha'd'you mean to do about it, then? You gonna go up there and take his place? It would sure save me a lot of bother around here, I tell you, what with having my cooking criticized and the harvest lacking and . . ." The haranguing continued, but Mert stopped listening. His imagination kicked into action, only this time instead of being out in the fields with his flock of fluffy sheep, he was sneaking up to Halderman Manor, to the woodshed out back, where he would break in and set Damon free. Mert would be sad to see him go, but better to let him take his chances Out There than to wait around for what was sure to come.

As for Mert, he would wait patiently in the shed until dark, and when Horace and the others arrived to collect their sacrifice, they would find him instead. He would explain that it wasn't right to punish Damon for something he hadn't done. He would say it was really his fault, that he had started it, and if they wanted to sacrifice someone, it should be him. Then he'd punch ol' gap-toothed Horace Halderman right in the eye and inform him that he was nothing but a dirty, smelly, rotten old —

"Gasbag."

"*Mert!*"

A Conversation Long Overdue

Two figures approached the woodshed through the early morning mist. One was tall and broad, his movements slow and deliberate, a minute hand in motion. He loped along beside a second hand woman, footsteps choppy and prim. She wore a black gown and veil. Everything about her was neat and proper, not a thing out of place. Her hair had recently been cut to a length of exactly twenty-seven and three-quarter inches. The man unlocked the door and opened it for her. They might have been stepping into Walden's for a perfectly adequate lunch instead of visiting their incarcerated nephew. "Thank you," she murmured as she bustled inside. The man bent double as he followed her in.

Damon Farrier sat on his cot, hands folded between his knees, head bowed like a penitent. The rough wool blanket hung from his shoulders like a cape. He didn't bother to look up as his aunt and uncle entered. Their presence told him everything he needed to know.

Today was the day.

"So this is where they've been keeping you," said Aunt Elle. "Such a shame. When Horace suggested putting you away somewhere, I thought he might have a bedroom with a locked door or something. A space more dignified, at any rate."

"Like a barn loft?"

"Oh, Damon." She said it gently, with a touch of sadness. "It breaks my heart to see you this way. Truly, it does. You have to know that I never wanted this for you, neither of us did."

Damon huffed. "Okay. Sure. You didn't want it to happen like this, I can believe that. But you did want me gone. Me and Sophie both. You never wanted us under your roof. That was clear from the start. The real tragedy is that you never had a good enough excuse to do it earlier, one that wouldn't prove you to be the heartless wench you really are."

"Damon," Uncle Roger growled.

"It's alright, dear," said Aunt Elle, squeezing her husband's hand. "He's upset. He doesn't understand. What happened to your parents was terrible, but you must realize you're not the only person it happened to. Robert was my brother. We didn't always see eye to eye, true, especially when it came to your mother. I couldn't understand their love. But, strange tastes aside she was a good and decent woman. I always respected her, and I loved your father. I was there on the day he was born, just as you were for Sophie. We ran up and down these same roads together and played all the same childhood games as you two did. We lived our entire lives in this village, together. And then, just like that, he was gone. It broke my heart, Damon. You have no idea how I cried over him."

"But then I moved on," she continued. "The world did not stop spinning the day Robert and Erinella died. It kept right on going. In a single day I had lost a brother and gained two children, in addition to the one we were already struggling to raise. I could not afford to let sorrow overtake me. There was simply too much at stake. I put my pain aside, but you, you never learned how. Instead, it festered and grew and rotted you out from the inside, and for that I am truly sorry."

"Sorry? You're sorry?" Now Damon did look at her, anger projected through a filter of weariness. "Aunt Elle, if I'm rotten inside, it's because you made me that way."

"I did everything I could for you two."

"You couldn't even muster up the decency to let us live inside the house!"

"I was trying to give you space. Tell me, what is the correct way to replace a parent? How could I have possibly filled your mother's shoes? It wouldn't have been fair to try, neither to you nor to me. I thought that if I gave you some room, if I made that boundary clear, you wouldn't spend every waking moment comparing me to her."

Damon shook his head. "Listen to you. Even now you can't face the truth. No, you have to constantly bend and twist things so you can make believe that you're a good, decent person. Next you'll tell me you never gave me that loan because it was for my own good."

"You asked for a ridiculous amount! I couldn't have given you that much if I'd wanted to. Roger and I were barely making ends meet when you and Sophie were dropped into our lives. We had to scrimp and save and borrow to make it through, and the people of this village were more than generous with us because they were as shocked by the whole episode as we were. Every time one of you caused trouble I was the one who had to go and apologize and remind them of the trauma you'd suffered. Gregory Tacklesmith wanted to halt your apprenticeship more times than I can count. So yes, I thought that if you had to deal with the same financial pressures that your uncle and I did that you would rise to the occasion and take responsibility for yourself. I see now how misguided I was. But I stand by the decision. How could I trust you to repay your debts when you wouldn't even fight for yourself?"

"I never had the chance to try," Damon shot back. "You don't know what it's like to be looked at with pity and disgust everywhere you go."

"Yes I do," she said quietly. "I know all about the half-sincere pity of others. First for the loss of Robert, then for the burden of unplanned adoption, then for the troubled and exacting nature of those adopted children. For years I have suffered whispers spoken behind my back, and I've had to look into the eyes of those whisperers and hold my head high and refuse to let them diminish me with their judgments. You are not the only one who has suffered." She saw the defiance still in Damon's eyes, and sighed. "There's no sense in arguing, is there? You refuse to see anything but the monster you've made me. I merely wanted to come and say goodbye in person, and to tell you that, no matter how it may seem, I do love you."

"Then why were you there that night?" Damon's jaw clenched as he spoke, his tone plaintive. "If you didn't want this, then why did you come with them? Why did you let them take me away, Aunt Elle?"

"So that they wouldn't hurt you," she said softly. "I knew you would fight. There's too much Robert in you not to. I thought perhaps I could talk to you, try to calm you down, but when I saw how drunk and belligerent you were, I just . . . I was speechless. As for 'letting' them take you, there was nothing to be done. You've burned too many bridges, Damon. No one will stand beside you anymore, and no amount of pleading on my part will change that. Not enough to matter, anyway. I'm sorry."

A tear spilled from Damon's eye. "What happens now?"

Aunt Elle came close and dabbed his cheeks with a handkerchief. "I think you know."

"And if they won't take me?"

"Then it will be the end of us all."

Rolling Thunder

Seaside. Home. *Surrounded by uniform cubes of white, she walks. A shadow ahead. She must catch it. Imperative. There is no running. One by one the faceless blocks disappear, but the shadow grows no closer, nor does the hill in the distance. The shadow fades. She cries out, voiceless.*

Turn.

Trees now, dark and impenetrable. Her feet kick up dust. Eyes open, a single pair, dilated black rimmed with color. They follow her labored steps. Another pair, then another, then the world is filled with them, bulbous sclerae bone white in the moonglow. Flash of iridescence. Vertical slit pupils. Snapping twigs betray padded approach. She must escape. Arms lift. Flap.

Fly.

She is above, far above, and rising. The forest is a carpet of copper and bronze and gold. A clearing. Fire rages within. Billowing smoke lifts her high beyond the clouds. Stars like fireflies in the aether. Below, her home is a piebald patch on the ocean. She blots it out with her thumb. It is peaceful here, but cold. Empty.

Descend.

She floats above Seaside, but cannot land because of the storm. Gnarled fingers of lightning scour the earth. Thunder continuous.

Roiling sea. She watches, helpless, as a great wave of dense ocean water lifts and crashes over the village. Cubes reduced to their frames. Dirt roads smudged like blackboard chalk after the first pass of an eraser. "Recognize her, little butterfly?"

Turn.

She is a butterfly, flapping wings holding her bobbing aloft. There is a frog before her, enormous, world ender. Vitreous skin glints fantastic, midnight blue graven with arcane golden sigils, save for one eye that is bloodshot, crazed. Lips part to reveal pink mouth flesh. A tongue, glistening and studded with taste buds. Waiting. Hungering. A blur of motion—

Sophie woke with a start. She sat up, blinking rapidly. It took a few moments to remember where she was—the duke's private coach. The heavy rumble of its wheels echoed in the confined space. Duke Truculo himself was beside her on the plush bench seat, fast asleep. Drool dribbled from his open mouth. Rothschild was haphazardly splayed on the opposite seat. Air wheezed in and out of his nostrils. Empty wine bottles clattered on the floor between them. Outside, an impenetrable mist hung between the trees of Granelith's Weald.

Today is the day.

Her nightmare had begun well before she'd fallen asleep. Duke Truculo had insisted they leave for Seaside immediately. As they'd made for his carriage, she'd gotten a glimpse of the "special conveyance" they'd prepared for the Navigator—a wheeled cage. The Navigator himself had been sitting placidly inside. She called out to him, but was quickly bundled into the carriage without being told why or where they were going.

A crowd had been assembled before the palace gates. Sophie heard the duke's criers as they passed through. "Girl saved from known murderer!" they called. "See both killer and victim for yourself!"

"But he's not a killer," Sophie protested. "He saved me!"

"Make her be quiet," the duke said through his fake smile, waving at his subjects through the window.

"You'll keep your mouth shut if you know what's good for you," said Rothschild. He pushed her up to the glass to be seen. "Look how happy they are to see you safe."

To Sophie's surprise, they did appear happy. These people who knew nothing about her or what she'd been through, who had previously cared not one whit, seemed genuinely delighted about her supposed rescue. It was sickening. The duke was using her to make himself look better, just like Aunt Elle had. She wanted to break the window pane and scream at them, to expose the duke as a liar, to tell them they'd been tricked. But of course she could do no such thing.

More dismaying still was the sudden transformation of those happy faces upon seeing the Navigator. Smiles became grimaces of anger and disgust. They booed and hissed and shouted curses. They spat and threw things at him. If these things affected him, Sophie couldn't tell, because the coach had no rear window. She simply had to imagine his misery . . . and Sophie's imagination was a powerful thing, indeed.

She wished she could see him now. She wanted to believe he was unmoved by it all. But how could that be? *He must be cold,* Sophie thought. *Tired. Hungry.*

Scared.

The misty trees gave way to foggy fields as they left the forest behind, rolling unceasingly onward to be delivered to their respective fates.

Plans In Motion

Mᴇʀᴛ ᴘᴜsʜᴇᴅ ʜɪs ᴡʜᴇᴇʟʙᴀʀʀᴏᴡ through the square. The wet, squishy kelp inside burped and sputtered as it jounced over the cobbles. Busy as it was, he had no problem negotiating the crowd, as no one wanted to wind up covered in a sticky coating of kelp sludge. This wasn't Mert's normal route, but today wasn't a normal day. He scanned the crowd restlessly. There were few friendly faces to be found, though the face he was trying to find had never been friendly. Not to him, anyway. Regardless, Mert nodded and smiled at everyone so that they wouldn't think he was acting strange, which only made him more conspicuous. On the other side of the square, Horace's cronies were busy putting up a platform in preparation for the Merling King's return. Of Horace there was no sign.

"It is a terrible thing, isn't it?"

Mert snapped his head around and came to an abrupt stop before Doctor Murphy, the kelp settling with a wobbling belch. "Sorry?"

"What they are planning to do. I am astonished and ashamed that so many of our neighbors are going along with it."

"Terrible," Mert agreed. "Wish I could do somethin'."

"I thought you might feel that way. Do you have a moment? I should like to discuss something with you." He led Mert over toward Duke Truculo's mutilated, dishonest statue and began laying out his plan to stop Horace. Mert listened politely, nodding his head in all the right places but not really paying attention. None of it would matter once Mert had set Damon free. But, he decided, there was no point in explaining that to the doctor. The fewer people who knew, the better. Secrets were short-lived in Seaside. "What do you say, Mert? Can we count on your assistance?"

"Course you can."

"Excellent! I shall let you get on with your day. Oh, and best keep this to yourself. The fewer people who know, the better."

"Right." Mert watched him go, feeling slightly bad about being dishonest. He hadn't lied, exactly, but it was close enough. No matter. Once Murphy learned what he'd been up to, he would understand. Mert gripped the handles of his wheelbarrow, set his feet, gave it a good shove to get it going . . .

And slopped wet kelp all over Horace Halderman's shiny black shoes.

He came to an abrupt halt, mouth open in a round *O* of surprise, his shock matched only by Mert's own. "Why, what?" Horace sputtered, face reddening as he identified the gelatinous substance slobbering all over his feet. "You imbecile! What do you think you're doing?"

"I-I-I . . ."

"You you you *what?*"

"Got to dry out the kelp," Mert finished meekly.

Horace glowered at him. "Really, Mert, today of all days! These will have to be polished all over again. Expect me to call on you for the bill, kelp farmer. Now clean up this mess and see if you can find your way out of the square without slathering any other respectable members of society." Horace kicked the muck from his shoes and resumed his tromp across the square, leaving behind a trail of wet, sticky footprints.

Mert bent and scooped up the ropy, sluggish fronds from the pavement. "Gasbag," he muttered, then rushed off as fast as he could.

Few would have believed him capable of the feat, but Mert had strategically chosen his route that day. There was one particular hill where he liked to dry his kelp, and Halderman Manor, his true destination, lay between that hill and the square. This fact, combined with his generally low standing in the community, meant that his passage through Horace's neighborhood went completely unremarked.

Though the sky was overcast and the ocean breeze chilly, Mert's laboring brow was coated in droplets of sweat. They dripped into his eyes, making him temporarily blind, but still he dared not stop, not to rest or to wipe his face or for any other reason. If he did, he might lose his nerve completely. His fear would overcome him and he would simply turn around and go home and live out the rest of his days as a coward. The thought of it was unbearable. He had lived in fear for far too long already. Blinking, he looked up in search of the moon, but it was nowhere to be found. A curtain of rain blurred the horizon. Lightning flickered in the distance. Mert did not like the look of that storm, not one bit.

Today is the day.

Luck was with him. He met no one on the road, nor at the house, nor even all the way to the woodshed, which sat alone and seemingly forgotten in the back yard. Mert glanced around one last time to make sure it was safe, then plunged his trembling hands into the kelp up to the elbow. There came a sick, glurping noise as he pulled them free again, holding a chisel and hammer. Mert wedged the chisel beneath the metal plate that held the latch to the door. He was not a very smart man, but he was a strong one, and it took only a few strikes of the hammer to pry the faceplate loose from the old, soggy wood. When it was nearly free, he dropped his tools, braced one foot on the doorframe, and gripped the handle with both hands. "One . . . two . . . *three!*"

The faceplate popped off. Mert tumbled backward into the grass.

On his hands and knees, he regarded the gaping shed door in shock. He had done it. He had actually *done it.* "Damon," he said in a hoarse half-whisper. "Come out. You're free."

No one answered.

"Damon," he said again. Mert scrabbled toward the door. The shadows inside swallowed the light. "Have to go, Damon. Quick, before they come back. Damon? Damon?" Mert got to his feet. Hands held before him, he stumbled through the darkness, his eyes gradually adjusting, but not before he barked his shin on the cot lying at the end. The empty cot.

Mert was in the woodshed, alone.

Of Snakes and Their Charms

Rothschild's wretched nose wrinkled as they passed by Cass and Feeney's place. It stood skeletal in the lightening gloom, a bony frame with darkened windows like blind, empty eye sockets. Sophie followed it with her eyes longingly. Feeney and Cass would be in there, alone with each other, waiting for someone to come and stoke the smoldering flames of their lost desires. She wished it could be her. Instead, she was stuck with the duke and his obnoxious lackey. They had opened another trunk full of wine and set to work on emptying the bottles into their privileged bellies.

"I think it has rather a bit of charm," the duke said languidly. "A simple place for simple folk. Imagine it, Rothschild, spending your day toiling in the fields, feeling the fertile earth between your fingers, the cleansing sweat upon your brow, muscles aching pleasantly, and then retiring with your impoverished brethren beneath that rickety roof. No schemes, no prisoners, no overnight flights to the middle of nowhere to protect your sterling reputation. What a wonderful life it must be. Tell me, girl, is that the way of it?"

"Yes," Sophie answered, barely listening.

"Yes, *my lord*," Beringford corrected. "Begging your pardon, sire, but I would not step foot in that place even if I were one of these unfortunate bumpkins."

"It could use a bit of touching up," conceded the duke. "Perhaps a rosebush or two."

"Unfortunately, ever since Beringford started skulking around in the garden the smell of roses has put me off."

"*Beringford*. That slimy snake. A world-class schemer, that one. I must thank you again for your freeing me of his manipulative designs."

"You could say that I nipped them in the bud."

The duke brayed like an ass. "A gardening pun! Rothschild, you've done it again. Such a razor wit you have. How very delightful!" The two men tapped their goblets together, then drank. "Regardless, you simply must accompany me to the rose garden one of these days. Whatever else he may be, Beringford has proven to be quite diligent. Queen Avantia will be delighted when she sees it, not a single thorn in sight."

"Save for Beringford himself."

"Ha!"

Sophie glanced at them sideways, wondering when her torture would end. "Mr. Beringford is a nice man," she said defiantly.

"Nice?" Rothschild regarded her, bemused. "Nice, did you say? Remind me, how exactly do *you* know Beringford?"

"I—" Sophie clammed up, realizing she was about to get her friend in serious trouble.

"Whatever you think you know about him is assuredly wrong," said the duke, slurring a bit. "He is a cold-hearted, manipulative snake who devours anyone unfortunate enough to get in his way. I could tell you stories that would . . . would . . . well, you would think differently about him. He's nearly as bad as that deceiver and murderer dragging behind us."

"But he didn't murder anybody. He's my friend. He saved my life!"

"Your friend, eh?" Rothschild snorted. "You know, I don't think we need to hear anymore from someone with the foul habit of cavorting with criminals."

"No, no," said the duke, flapping a hand at his fiend, "I want to hear what she has to say. I gave him the opportunity to tell me of himself and his plight. He refused. Perhaps you could provide me with answers. Tell me, what is his name? Where does he come from? And what is his purpose here?"

"I . . . I don't know."

"Which don't you know?"

"Any of it."

"*Any?*"

"He's a Navigator. He's not allowed to tell anyone those things. And he didn't mean to come here, he was shipwrecked."

"So I heard," said the duke.

"Let me get this straight," said Rothschild, sitting up. "This stranger washes up on your shore, tells you he's some sort of legendary hero that no one's ever heard of but won't give you so much as his name, and you believed him, just like that?"

"Not 'just like that'," Sophie countered. "He has magic powers."

"Magic!" said Rothschild, clapping his hands together. "Did you hear that, my lord, we have another title for him: imposter, deceiver, kidnapper, murderer, and magician!"

"My dear girl," said Duke Truculo, "you have been taken

in. I have seen many talented illusionists in my time. In fact, there is one who performs regularly outside the Red Market. When last I saw him he was dressed in fantastic garb, much like your friend, and seeming to float on the end of a rope. The illusion is created by concealing two platforms connected by an iron bar. Interesting, yes, but it requires no magic."

"But his compass shoots lightning. I've seen it!"

"Compass?" said Rothschild, arching one pencil-thin eyebrow. "You mean that bauble taken by Captain Rectifer? Tell me, why would the prisoner allow it to be taken if it was so powerful? For that matter, why allow himself to be taken at all? Why has he not yet escaped from his cage?"

Sophie didn't know how to answer, so she didn't. Instead, she crossed her arms and set her jaw and stared out the window.

"You believe him to be your friend," said the duke, "but in truth he is a liar, a thief, and a killer. You are lucky to be here, with us, safe. He deserves what is coming to him."

"He's a good man," she said, still looking outside. "You're the one who's lying. But I won't let you get away with it. I'll tell everybody the truth."

"Go ahead," said Rothschild. "Who would believe such a foolish and gullible little girl? Only one opinion matters—that of the Queen. What she will hear is that Duke Truculo cares about justice so deeply that he risked his personal safety to save a village so small that no one would even notice if it were erased from the map."

The first drops of rain pattered on the carriage roof, punctuating Rothschild's snickering laughter.

Last Meal

D**AMON SAT AMONGST THE SACKS** of dry goods in the storeroom of Codwallader's Grocery. A double ring of dry scabs lined his neck where the shackle had hung. They hadn't bothered to chain him again. There was only one way into the storeroom, and it had been left under the watchful eye of two of Horace's cronies.

Rain pattered on the roof, light but insistent. Soon it would be torrential, big fat drops plummeting onto the poor souls below. Whether they intended it or not, being moved to the storeroom was a small mercy on the part of his captors; they had saved him from being marched across town in the downpour. Not that Damon had been concerned about it. Given what was to come, a little water was the least of his worries.

He listened for the rumble of thunder. The tolling of the town bell. The gabble of a gathering crowd. Any portent of his looming doom. What came instead was the creak of hinges accompanied by a momentary intensification of the rain. Robbie Codwallader entered the storeroom carrying a tray topped with a cloche. He carefully navigated the maze of boxes, sacks, and jars, focused on the dual tasks of keeping the tray level while avoiding the obstacles. He stopped before Damon, his eyes flicking up briefly to meet the prisoner's. "Hi," said Robbie quietly.

"What's this?"

"A hot meal, from Doctor Murphy. He sent me to Walden's with some money. I didn't know what to get, and it didn't seem like a good idea to tell him who it was for, so I hope you like it." He lifted the cloche to reveal a steaming pub pie. Gravy had leaked from the seams of the pastry, and it had fallen in the middle. To Damon, it was a thing of terrific beauty. A mug of warm, cloudy apple cider sat beside it.

"It's perfectly adequate," said Damon, accepting the meal. "You could have brought me a pint, though."

"I don't think my dad wants me buying beer."

"He wants you to be here, now?"

"He doesn't know. He's too busy getting everything ready for . . . well, for later."

"Right. Later." Damon cut into the pie. Seared chicken and vegetables floated out on a wave of gravy. Salivating, he shoveled in a forkful without taking the time to test its heat. Burned taste buds troubled him no more than the rain. Robbie stood there, shuffling his feet. "You gonna watch me eat the whole thing?"

"No."

"What is it, then?"

The boy's shoulders rose as he took a deep breath. "Is Sophie okay?" His fears finally spoken aloud, Robbie allowed himself to look Damon in the eyes. "She's been gone an awfully long time, my dad says we'll probably never see her again, that anyone who goes Out There never comes back, but that can't be true because Sterling came back, so I thought, maybe . . ."

"I didn't know you cared." Damon said it plainly, not as an accusation, but a simple statement of fact. "Thought you weren't friends anymore."

"We are. Sort of. I still like her." Robbie's face flushed. "I mean, I don't *like* her, not like that. Not that there's anything wrong with her! She's someone that I *could* like, you know, if she liked *me* like that, I'm just saying—"

"Robbie. It's okay. Does she know you feel this way?"

"Maybe."

"Maybe. You haven't told her?"

The boy squirmed. "It's hard."

"Why?"

"Well, I mean, my dad wouldn't like it, and neither would your aunt, or you for that matter."

"Or Sophie," Damon suggested.

". . . yeah . . ."

"Robbie," Damon said, "you should have told her while you had the chance. Sure, she might have turned you down. That would have hurt. But at least you'd both know how the other felt. And you have to stop worrying about what your dad or anyone else is going to think. You decide what makes *you* happy. For what it's worth, I wouldn't mind you going round with Sophie."

"Really?"

"You're a good kid, Robbie Codwallader. A bit spineless, maybe, but you care about people, and you're a hard worker. Better you than one of those brainless idiots you call friends. Or Walden."

"*Walden?*"

"Mm-hmm. Aunt Elle was working on him as a potential match."

"Sophie wouldn't really marry Walden, would she?"

"She might." Damon popped another bite of the pie into his mouth. "If she didn't know there were other options." Robbie blinked rapidly, shellshocked by the possibility of Sophie marrying a barman twice her age.

The bell began to ring in the square.

"Um, I should go."

Damon nodded. The boy clumsily made his way back toward the door. He was nearly out when Damon called to him. "Hey, Robbie."

"Yeah?"

"Sophie promised to come back. Maybe she will, maybe she won't. But if she does, I need you to tell her something. Tell her I love her, and I always have. Can you do that for me?"

"I think so."

"That's not good enough. You need to promise. Doesn't matter if it's tomorrow or thirty years from now, when you see her, you tell her that her brother loved her."

"I promise."

"Thank you." Damon went back to work on his pie. The hinges creaked again, the pounding of the rain swelled, and when it was gone, he let his tears flow.

Taking Sides

They came for him soon after.

Johnathan Codwallader took hold of him by an elbow. Michael Spindler took the other. Horace looked him up and down with naked contempt. His broken, porcine smile conveyed what words could not. Then he turned, gestured, and stepped outside under the protection of a heavy umbrella held by Sterling.

Spindler's boys went first. They ordered the crowd to make way. Damon was forced into the created space, half hoisted and half pushed, though such roughness was unnecessary. He was too numb to fight back. Water plastered Damon's hair onto his head and dribbled into his eyes, yet he fought to keep them open, for he wished to look upon them, this wet and dripping mass of the fearful who would forsake him and make of their home a place that was truly beyond redemption. Damon would see them all and know their names.

He had expected hatred. Instead, he saw shame. They stood back from him and his captors in silence, suddenly as meek as young Robbie. *No, they were always like this*, he thought. *Hate requires effort. Easier to stand aside and let someone else do the work.*

They had nearly reached the newly-assembled stage when their path was blocked.

"Make way!"

"We will not."

Doctor Murphy stood before them, arms tucked behind his back, face set and stern. Behind him was a line of men and women with their arms linked in a chain. Albert was among them, as was Allie Tacklesmith, wife of Gregory, and the widow known as Old Lady Magpie. Damon was blindsided by this show of support.

Apparently, so was Horace.

"*What is the meaning of this?*" His face had gone an unhealthy shade of purple. "Murphy! Explain yourself!"

"Doctor Murphy, if you please." He twitched his upper lip back and forth, wiggling his impressive, bushy mustache. "And it is my duty, as both a doctor and a decent human being, to see that this young man comes to no harm. We will not stand by and watch as you offer up one of our own as a sacrifice to these marauders from the deep. Damon has done nothing to deserve this treatment. We demand you release him at once."

"Done nothing?" Horace returned. "He's the one who got us into this mess to begin with! It's only fitting that he should be the one to get us out."

"It's for the good of the village," said Johnathan Codwallader. A cry of assent went up from the rest of Horace's gang.

"Don't you understand?" Horace said. "All of our lives are at stake, including your own."

"So is our dignity," Murphy shot back. "Including your own."

"Look around you, man! These people are frightened and lost. I have given them a direction. I have shown them a way out!"

"Horace, you have not thought this through to completion. If we let you offer Damon to the Merling King, there is no guarantee he will spare us. Certainly we would not deserve his mercy. Every one of us will go to our grave a murderer."

"That's what you're afraid of," Horace said, jabbing the doctor in the chest with his cane. "Complicity. You don't care about Damon's wellbeing, none of you do. You only wish to keep your hands unsullied!"

"That is not true and you know it."

"Well, have no fear, *Doctor* Murphy!" he cried, raising his arms and turning to the crowd. "I have heard your objections. If I alone must bear the weight of this boy's death, then I will do so and I will do it gladly! Don't you see? This is the only way to save the village. What choice do we have?"

"We can say no."

"And allow our homes to be washed into the waves? To be eaten alive by those *things*? Be reasonable! The Merling King asks for one soul, and that is all I mean to give him. If you wish to join Damon on that stage, be my guest." Horace made to push past. Doctor Murphy stepped in front of him. A moment of silent understanding passed between the two men, and then both sides were pushing and shoving each other, with one side fighting to get Damon to the stage and the other to prevent it.

"No!" Mert dove into the midst of the row, waving his hands for attention. Few paid him any mind. "My fault. Not his. Let me go instead."

"Shut up, kelp farmer," said Michael Spindler. "Get out of the way."

"Yeah, out of the way!"

"Move it!"

The villagers moved, some out of the way, some into it, lining up on either side of the tumult. Gregory Tacklesmith tried to dislodge his wife from the human chain by way of reason. Robbie, who had been walking behind his father, turned and linked his arms with the others. Johnathan, shocked and embarrassed, chose to deal with his son and let go of Damon. New hands took hold of him then, large, powerful hands that pulled him away from his captors, away from the stage. He turned toward his new ally and was dumbfounded to see Uncle Roger's towering figure at his side. Mert soon joined him on the other. Those onlookers who chose not to get involved recoiled from the growing melee, or else fled the scene entirely.

An eerie blast rang out over the village.

The violence came to a stop. Not all at once. Slowly, like a watch winding down. The crowd grew still, listening, waiting. Another of those alien blasts, closer this time, soon followed by the synchronous tromp of exoskeletal feet marching in time as the Merling King's infantry entered the square.

Pitiless black eyes surveyed the frightened villagers. They were menacing, with their mottled skins and oversized pincers and needle teeth. The soldiers formed a line before the stage and drove the humans back. Into this space rode the Merling King, piloting his chariot of shell and pearl and bone, propelled by his twin lobstrosities. Trident in hand, he mounted the stage with a single reaching step. Lightning struck the tines of his trident as he thrust it into the air, sending up a shockwave that parted the clouds, ending the rain and creating a godly peephole through which the full moon shone like a spotlight. Swirling winds roared and shrieked and dragged the clouds around in an enormous circle.

"Bring forth your chieftain."

Horace was steadily ejected by the crowd, the chain of

concerned citizens breaking to let him pass and then speeding him along with unkind pokes and prods. One of the invaders seized him with its scabrous hand and led him onto the stage, alone. "Kneel," it said, throwing him down before his unruly master.

"There you are," said the Merling King. Grit and gravel gurgled in his throat, making his voice clipped and broken. "I promised to return with the cycling of the moon. You see now that I am one to keep my word. I trust you have not forgotten the other promise I made, Chieftain."

"No, Your Highness, I have not."

"Good. Then there is only one thing more I require of you, and then our business will be concluded. Bring forth the Navigator."

"We do have a sacrifice for you, but I, um, well, you see . . ."

"Go on," the king growled.

". . . he's, he's right over there." Horace pointed to where Damon stood. The struggle erupted once again. The Merling King's soldiers waded into the crowd and forced the battling villagers to part. Damon made to go with them, but Uncle Roger held him fast. "It's alright," said Damon, covering his uncle's hand with his own. "Really. Thank you."

"Damon, no," said Mert.

Damon turned to the kelp farmer and took him by the shoulders. "Mert, I hereby relieve you of any further acts of heroism."

Then the creatures got their claws on him at last, separating him from the crowd and dragging him onto the stage. Damon stared up at the four-armed monarch. His lip was bleeding, his clothes were torn, his body bruised. There was no fear in him. The time for fear had passed.

The Merling King bent, bringing the bulbous black orbs of

his eyes mere inches from Damon's own. Twin flaps of white flesh pulsed and moved within the slits of each nostril. Fine bristles surrounded the monster's mouth. They twitched and tested the air. Then he drew up to his full height and pointed at Damon with his ghastly claw. "This is not the one I seek. Explain yourself, Chieftain. Now."

Horace mumbled something at the floorboards.

"*SPEAK.*"

"We don't have the Navigator!" Horace squealed. "We did everything we could to find him, honestly we did! I even sent my own son Out There," he said, pointing vaguely beyond the village, "risking his life to seek help. But the man is nowhere to be found. He has fallen off the map. Instead, we offer you one of our own in his place, a willing volunteer, to make up for the soul that you were deprived of."

The crowd voiced their disapproval:

"He's no volunteer!"

"Damon did nothing wrong!"

"Horace, you coward!"

The King slammed the butt of his trident on the stage, silencing them all. "You have failed me, Chieftain. Worse, you insult me. Did you truly believe that I would come all this way to collect one filthy, pathetic, broken boy and leave satisfied?"

"Your Highness," said Horace, "it's his fault the Navigator slipped away in the first place. He dragged him out of the waves, nursed him back to health, and allowed him to escape. I would have sent him back to you immediately if I'd had my way . . ."

"*Silence!* You have cheated me for the last time. Make peace with your iniquities, humans, for this day my kingdom comes ashore!"

The Sacrifice

The whole world had been drowned.

Or so it seemed. Great torrents of rain pelted against the duke's carriage with wavelike force and volume. Through the deluge, Sophie made out the shape of the oak atop One Tree Hill. Its branches whipped wildly in the raging winds, denuded of all but the hardiest, most tenacious leaves. Periodic gusts forced the field grass to bow over and over again like supplicants before a towering titan. A swirling wall of driven spray loomed ahead. Sophie swallowed hard. *He's out there in this. Alone.*

Steel knuckles rapped against the windowpane. "My lord!" Captain Rectifer bellowed from outside. "We must turn back!"

"Nonsense!" the duke returned. "We shall seek refuge in the village. Press on, press on!"

All outward visibility vanished as they collided with the wall of wind. Water beat against every surface. The roar drowned all thought. There came a sudden sideways jolt, and the coach tilted, wheels in the air, causing Sophie to scream and throw her hands out for balance. For one sickening moment, gravity was canceled. Then everything righted and they were through, into the calm, the eye of the storm.

I'm home.

"My word, what a tempest!" exclaimed the duke. "What a tale! Avantia will thrill to hear of it. Now, if only I had sent riders ahead to ring the bell . . . oh, Captain Rectifer has done so already. Good man." Sophie stuck her head out the window for a better view, saw that the square was indeed full of villagers, and knew that something was wrong.

Then she saw her brother.

Everything happened quickly after that. The crowd parted as the duke's retinue entered. His men, shocked and bewildered by what they were seeing, dismounted and lined up against the horrific sea creatures, who growled grittily at the armored guards and snapped their enormous claws. Sophie forced her way out of the coach before it could stop. She sprinted toward the stage, shouting her brother's name.

"Damon!"

"No," he whispered. "No, go back."

No soldier, human or otherwise, moved to stop her. She barreled up the steps and across the planks and into her brother's arms.

"Sophie, what are you doing?" he said, his voice tight and incredulous and full of fear. "You shouldn't be here."

"What is this, Damon? What's happening?"

He opened his mouth to speak, but a deafening thunderclap rent the air above their heads. There was no hope of explaining the situation in the moment, to make sense of the insanity, to tell her that she had returned to meet her doom. Instead, he squeezed her tighter and kissed her on the forehead.

Duke Truculo, meanwhile, had finally managed to extract himself from his vehicle. He waddled angrily toward the stage, waving his hands and shouting to be heard. His meager words failed to reach the Merling King's ears. However, the monstrous monarch recognized the duke's manner of dress and conveyance as signs of nobility, and judged that he was a man of considerably higher rank than Horace Halderman. Moreover, he noticed the rolling cage, and its occupant with his singular appearance. The mighty king lowered his trident. The clouds ceased churning as the winds grew still.

"Stop! Stop!" Duke Truculo shouted, out of breath. "We have him. We've brought the one you seek." He turned and made an impatient gesture toward Rothschild, who stood beside the cage. "Get him out of there, now!"

Between the shock of seeing the Merling King and the sudden responsibility thrust upon him, the duke's lackey had gone pale. Gripping the bars for support, he tried to insert the key, and succeeded only in ramming it against the lock's faceplate and knocking it from his own unsteady hand. He bent, snatched it up, then stood to find himself face to face with the Navigator. The sudden shock sent his heart into his throat. "Allow me," said the Navigator. He removed a charm from his vest and spoke. Rust bloomed like roses on the lock. A kick, and it crumbled to a fine red dust. Rothschild's jaw quaked as the Navigator climbed out and strode toward the stage.

He kept his own pace, neither hurried nor hesitant. No one dared block his path. All the same, he stopped before Captain Rectifer and held out his hand. "You have something that belongs to me."

"I captured you, therefore it's mine. If you want it—"

"*Exalac*," said the Navigator, and now it was Rectifer's sword and armor that turned to rust. Shocked murmurs went up from the crowd. Dust fell from him like red snow to pile at his feet. Defenseless, he regarded the Navigator with horror. He quickly retrieved the compass from the pouch on his belt and put it in the Navigator's waiting hand.

"You see," cried the duke, addressing the crowd and the Merling King. "I, Duke Truculo, Lord and Master of the Westerlands, have come to deliver you from this evil, and—"

The Navigator silenced him by placing a hand on his shoulder. Their eyes met. Without a word the duke was made to feel every bit the fraud that he was. Diminished, he stepped aside and said no more.

"At last," the Merling King hissed. "The final wayward soul has been returned. You escaped my grasp once, Navigator. You shall not do so again."

"It was not my intent to escape, servant of Dramora."

The king and his horrific subjects all hissed at the mention of the name. "How dare you? I am the supreme monarch of the seas, ruler of the waves, tide-maker and storm-bringer! I serve no one but myself."

"And yet you have left your realm in furtherance of her cause. Or do you deny that it was she who tempted you with tales of my order and our abilities? Your will is your own, mighty king, but your head has been turned."

"Spare me your manipulations, Navigator. I care not for the petty, reaching games you gaspers play."

The Navigator inclined his head. "You say you are pursuing your own interests. I shall take you at your word, and ask for the same courtesy in return. I did not intend to be carried here by the waves, Your Majesty, nor did the frightened folk before you request my presence. The universe conspires to place us where it will. Do not punish them, for they were only acting according to their natures, and I to mine."

"And if it is my nature to scrub this place from the land, what then?"

"Then that is the way of things."

The Merling King and the Navigator studied each other.

"You would give your life willingly for them? These frail and pitiful beings who turn on each other at the first opportunity? Not one of them is your equal, Navigator. Why do this?"

"Because I know you are wrong."

The Merling King considered the Navigator's words. No one dared even to breathe.

"You give them too much credit," he said finally. "Very well. If this is your wish, so be it. I will spare them, and in return, you will join my court beneath the waves."

"That is my wish."

"No!" cried Sophie. She slipped from her brother's grasp and jumped down off the stage. "You can't!"

"I can. And I must."

"But what about all those people who are depending on you? What about finding your purpose?"

"Look around you," he said, motioning toward the crowd. "I was meant to go back to the sea. This is my purpose."

"Why? Because that thing told you to? That's stupid! You said it yourself—all are responsible for choosing their own path. Choose something else!"

The Navigator smiled and held up the compass. "No, not because of this. It is only a tool, a guide. I choose this path because I am following my heart." He put the compass in her hands. "As you must follow yours."

Quietly, she said, "What if my heart doesn't know the way?"

"It does. You need only to listen."

"But I don't want you to go."

The Navigator held out his arms to her. They hugged fiercely, as friends saying goodbye for the final time. He whispered in her ear. She looked up at him and nodded, and then let him go.

"I thank you for your friendship," said the Navigator. Then he climbed into the Merling King's chariot, followed by the crustaceous monarch himself. With a final blast from the horns they set into motion, out of the square, down the beach, and into the stony grey waters, never to be seen in Seaside again.

Epilogue

Sᴏᴘʜɪᴇ ᴀɴᴅ Dᴀᴍᴏɴ sᴀᴛ ᴛᴏɢᴇᴛʜᴇʀ atop Two Tree Hill, as it had been renamed after it was discovered that the lonesome oak had sprouted a sapling. It was wispy, and thin, and grew in the spot where their mother had painted the village. Sophie didn't venture up as often as she used to, but the oaks didn't mind, for they had other visitors now. Visitors like Aunt Elle and Uncle Roger, or Mert with his pet sheep. Petunia had even convinced Sterling to make the climb, and though he claimed it gave him flashbacks of his traumatic journey Out There, he'd been forced to admit that the view was perfectly adequate.

On this occasion, though, the siblings were alone. Sophie held the last of her mother's watercolors, the torn and crumpled one that depicted Seaside in all its glory, like a single pearl on a bed of seagrass. It sat behind a pane of flawless crystal, framed with red cedar. Their eyes went back and forth from the painting to the village below.

"What do you think, li'l butterfly?"

"I'm nervous."

"You shouldn't be," he said. "They're gonna love it."

"You really think so?"

"What does your heart say?"

Back. Forth. Back again.

"That you're right," she answered. After a moment, she said, "You don't have to come if you don't want to."

"Of course I do," he said. "Besides, I risked my neck climbing up on that damn roof. You'd better believe I want to see what I risked it for." Damon reached over and rumpled her hair. "I'm proud of you, Sophie. *They* would be proud of you."

"Stop," she said, smiling as she pulled away. "You can't do that to me anymore. I'm a woman now, engaged to be married and everything."

"But you'll always be my little sister." He smiled and nudged her with his elbow. "Come on, they're waiting for us."

They set off down the hill together. The Navigator's compass dangled from her neck, glinting in the early evening sunlight like a lighthouse calling its rightful owner back to shore. Not a day passed that Sophie didn't think about the Navigator. She pictured him sitting calmly at court beside the Merling King, kept alive and unharmed beneath the waves by some combination of subtle magics, biding his time until he felt the pull of fate once again, when he would execute his escape. Perhaps it was only wishful thinking, a bit of CHILDISH NONSENSE she wasn't quite ready to let go of.

Perhaps.

Regardless, Sophie carried him with her always, his face and his strange ways, and his words also, those most of all. The broken compass was a constant reminder of his final injunction:

Show them the way.

Those that Sophie and Damon passed on their way through town smiled and waved. Most of them, anyway. There were still a few who scowled and sneered and spoke of the Farriers in hushed tones, but not so many as before. Damon cared little about their whispering, for he had settled somewhere Out There. Seaside was no longer his concern. As for Sophie, she'd decided that the Disdainful would either come around, or they wouldn't. All were responsible for choosing their own path.

There was a new building in Seaside. It stood on the plot where Robert and Erinella Farrier's home had once stood. It was two stories tall, rectangular, with a pitched roof. The bottom level had log siding, while the upper was done in the village's preferred style, with some fanciful additions to make it stand out. Red and blue birdhouses dangled from the rafters. Planter boxes filled with colorful flowers hung below the shutters, their carefully arranged chromaticity like painter's palettes come to life. A painted sign announced the name of the establishment— *The Glass Frog*.

A crowd of familiar faces had gathered outside, some hailing from as far away as Fairport. They milled around and chatted while waiting for Sophie. Nervous excitement erupted within her like a cloud of butterflies in flight. It was a wonder her feet stayed on the ground. Damon squeezed her hand and said, "Go on." He joined the others while Sophie slipped in through a side door.

Stepping into the kitchen, she was greeted by the smells of roasting meat and simmering stew. This was followed by a big hug and a sloppy kiss on the cheek from Cass, who shooed her out with a wave of her kitchen towel. Sophie left the kitchen and walked out onto the wide common room floor. Feeney was sat on a stool with his fiddle by his side, putting rosin on the bow. He sang when he saw her, then hopped up to give her a quick spin across the floor. He told her she looked radiant as the sun, which of course she did in her yellow-green dress. Her hair was bound with a long red ribbon. Its tail flickered out behind her as she twirled and danced.

"Not trying to steal my bride away, are you, Feeney?"

"I'd never dream of it, young Robert, I never would. Like my own daughter, she is."

Sophie took the hands of her betrothed. They kissed. It now happened so often he no longer blushed.

No, really.

"Are you ready?" he asked.

"Almost." There was one last thing to be done before Seaside's first inn opened for business. Sophie took the framed watercolor and put it on the wall above the mantel, where it was sure to be seen by every patron. It was flanked by a pair of glass frogs, one stately and dull, the other slender and bright. She stepped back and admired the tableau, pleased.

For the first time, Sophie felt complete.

"Alright, Robbie, let them in. It's time to show this wet cow flop of a town how to have a good time!"

THE END

A Message to Readers

Five years ago, I made the decision to quit my job as a research scientist, sell everything, and start living as a nomad full-time. I had no direction, no prospects, and absolutely no idea how to write, produce, or sell books.

And yet, here we are.

For me, the purpose of writing fiction is to create new experiences for you, the reader, and that is what I have worked to do in these pages. If this book made you feel in any way—if you smiled, laughed, fumed, or cried—then I've done my job. Nothing could make me happier.

However, if you feel like expressing your gratitude, there is a simple (and free) way that you can do so: *tell someone*. In person, on social media, on your blog, it doesn't matter. Or, with a single click, you can leave a rating on online retailer websites—it doesn't get much easier than that. Seriously, any positive word from you will make a huge difference. Most importantly, it will warm the heart of a self-published author who has a tendency to make reckless life decisions.

And if you got all the way to the end of this tale and felt nothing—my deepest apologies. I'll do better next time.

J. Brandon Lowry
12/28/2022

Also From The Author

A detective caught in the web of a seductive murderess. A young man discovering his roots through music. A world that is falling apart, literally. *Finding My Voice*, the debut flash fiction collection from J. Brandon Lowry, features 24 stories that explore life in all its complex and messy glory. An experiment in craft and style, this collection also features original artwork and personal reflections by the author. Each tale can be read in ten minutes or less, perfect for today's fast paced world. Love, loss, joy, sorrow, the highest highs, the lowest lows, all brought vividly to life by an emerging voice in the world of short fiction.

Available in eBook, Kindle, and paperback formats

J. Brandon Lowry was born and raised in the west-central mountains of Idaho. After high school, he left his small-town home to pursue a career in science, eventually receiving his PhD in Molecular Biology at the University of Oregon. In 2017, disillusioned with life and yearning for something more, he and his wife quit their jobs, sold their possessions, and began traveling full time. They have since explored 23 countries across six continents, living out of backpacks and house/pet-sitting along the way. The Glass Frog is his first novel. His short fiction and poetry has appeared at Reservoir Road Literary Review, Tall Tale TV, The Weekly Knob, The Junction, Lit Up, Literally Literary, and Midnight Mosaic Fiction.